Left

On

Main

Heart of Madison Series
Book 1

sands press
Brockville, Ontario

Left On Main

Crystal Jackson

sands press

sands press

A Division of 10361976 Canada Inc.
300 Central Avenue West
Brockville, Ontario
K6V 5V2

Toll Free 1-800-563-0911 or 613-345-2687
http://www.sandspress.com

ISBN 978-1-988281-75-9
Copyright © 2019 Crystal Jackson
All Rights Reserved

Edited by Laurie Carter
Publisher Sands Press

Publisher's Note

For information on bulk purchases of this book or any book published by Sands Press, please call 1-800-563-0911.

1st Printing October 2019

To book an author for your live event, please call: 1-800-563-0911

Sands Press is a literary publisher interested in new and established authors wishing to develop and market their product. For more information please visit our website at www.sandspress.com.

For Luna and Linus, with love always

For Jessica, who believed in me before I could

& for all those who survived what they once
thought they couldn't

Acknowledgements

Left on Main started as an almost-vision of a very old woman in a dress quoting Mary Oliver, who passed away this year and whose work struck a chord in me at a time I very much needed to hear it. Thank you, Mary, for your work and the inspiration.

I didn't know that I had stories in me, but there were people who knew before I did. Thank you to Jessica Holt and Jenni Hill who encouraged me from the start. To my grandparents: James and Mary Lou Beasley and Margie Peoples- Thank you for your love and support. To Dot Malone, thank you for believing.

My writing group provided invaluable support, feedback, and solidarity. Many thanks to Stephanie, David, April, Steve, Karen, Sarah, Nicole, Bob, Marilyn, and Chuck.

To the wonderful people at Sands Press for persisting, believing, & making a life-long dream come true.

Thank you to my early readers and supporters, which include (but are not limited to) Christy, Lindsay, Christina, Lisa, Michael, Parisa, Kim, Shannon, Phyllis, and David. I appreciate you all for listening, reading, and endlessly encouraging me during the process.

A heartfelt thank you goes out to Elizabeth Roses Photography, Didi Dubose (MUA), and to Paschal Orthodontics. You're a treasure! Thanks to the city of Madison, Georgia, for being an inspiration and becoming my home.

Thank you to everyone who helped make this possible!

Someone I loved once gave me
a boxful of darkness.
It took me years to understand
that this too, was a gift.

~ Mary Oliver

Chapter 1

Libby Reynolds listened to the rhythmic sound of sneakers against pavement as she ran through the historic district. As she increased her pace, she allowed her mind to revisit the day her whole life had come crashing down around her. She thought about how there had always been two lives—her real life and the life in her mind. On the day Colin moved out, she was just a woman being left by the man she still loved, standing calm and stoic outside the threshold he had once laughingly carried her over, ready to go about the business of rebuilding a shattered life. But inside? Inside, she could feel herself running through the long stone corridors of her mind, slamming heavy iron doors shut behind her as she retreated deeper into herself. She found comfort in the familiar jolt of locks and bolts slamming into place, a mental strategy she'd used even as a child to shield herself from pain.

In her real life, she was reminding Colin of his upcoming dental appointment. Did he need to reschedule, since he would still be moving into the new place across town? Should he see a new dentist, since he was already seeing new people? Or should she find someone new? A dentist, perhaps, who would remember that her teeth were a little sensitive to the cold and that she hated the laughing gas? A dentist who wouldn't ask how her husband was doing so she wouldn't have to say that she no longer had one? "And please," she reminded Colin calmly, "don't forget to leave the key. It's not as if you'll need it anymore."

She wanted to lean against the door when it closed, but she didn't allow herself that weakness. No, she had things to do and plans to make. There were dishes to wash and boxes that still needed to be

1

packed. She'd have to figure out somewhere else to go. There was nothing here for her now but memories she didn't want. Inside, Libby's world was falling apart, but on the outside, she scrubbed the pan of the remnants of dinner. She sat through two episodes of a show she liked, barely following the plot, but watching until the end anyway. Then she took a long bath before bed and poured in her scented bath oils as an added indulgence. When Libby went to bed that night, she pulled on the shirt Colin had unknowingly left behind—one she'd slipped into a drawer while he was packing—and slept on his side of the bed. She curled up with his scent, making herself as small as she could. She thought it was almost funny that his absence took up even more space than his presence ever did.

Libby hadn't expected to start over. Again. In fact, after a childhood spent learning new faces and navigating new schools every couple of years, she'd done her level best to put down roots. She'd found a sort of contentment in the familiarity of her life. She'd finished her education, gotten a decent job, and married her boyfriend. She'd thought it was a good, if somewhat unexciting, life. Perhaps her life had only grown comfortable, like an old chair she couldn't bear to throw out. She wondered sometimes how long she'd have stayed in it if Colin hadn't decided he was leaving.

As she wound up and down the small-town streets lined proudly with antebellum homes, she thought about how she had dressed so carefully for Colin's leaving, as if it mattered that she had pulled her long, thick auburn hair into its practical French twist or selected that simple plum shift dress that he had once admired her in. She'd stood on the porch with him and spoken so calmly, keeping her voice upbeat, wry even, so that he wouldn't hear the bitterness behind the words.

Even now, running as fast as the memories flitting across her consciousness, she could see his face, how it had alternated from a careful blank to a baffled hurt at her seeming lack of emotion. Even still, Libby had gone through the practical moments of disentangling their lives—her real life from Colin's. She had kept that last hug brief, packing away the emotions that might once have risen to the surface, and turned away at the brush of lips across her cheek. Her hazel eyes had stayed dry, even though she felt her heart in her throat as she watched the man she'd loved for so long leaving her. Her goodbye was perfunctory and without inflection, as she had walked back up the stairs and into the house—never looking back.

As a person who had lived two lives for as long as she could remember, it came as no surprise that when she finally moved to a new place she would pack up both of her lives and move them with her. And she would begin to unpack them as well, along with a shirt she would fold and place at the bottom of her drawer. It was how she got here, after all. From the bustle of Marietta all the way to the other side of Atlanta. To Madison, a tiny town that charmed her even at her most disenchanted. Inner Libby started opening doors again to enjoy the view, and practical real-life Libby began circling apartments for rent in the local paper.

She'd come home.

And since coming home, she'd begun rebuilding her life. She had a job that she enjoyed, and she was learning the shape of her new life. She'd begun running nearly every day. The route soothed her and gave her plenty of time to think. She read the names of the shops she passed as she ran: Brews & Blues; Lost Horizon Antiques; Found Treasures; A View with a Room; Utopia Tea, Books, & Gifts. She contented herself with a quick look at the window displays as she ran. She promised herself that she would make time to properly explore her new town. Inside her mind there were corridors and, outside of it, there were the streets of Madison, swept clean by the city workers and already in full bloom. She turned toward her apartment, gaining speed as she went into that last mile. She thought, *I can be happy here.*

Chapter 2

Seth Carver was walking through Lost Horizon Antiques, making notes on items that had been damaged by careless customers and straightening stock. He sometimes felt like a young man in an older man's world. The antique store that had once been his grandfather's and then his mother's had been the backdrop of his childhood. Now it was his. He used these quiet mornings in the shop to review inventory and plan for the week. He'd thought he was alone, so it came as a surprise when what he had taken to be part of the wallpaper spoke to him abruptly.

"'Tell me: what is it you plan to do with your one wild and precious life?'"

He turned his head toward the voice. It sounded like you would think mothballs would if they were a tone and not texture and scent. It was fuzzy around the edges, thick and indistinct. It could have been coming from under a pile of blankets or thick winter coats instead of out of the old woman herself, so paper thin and creased that she appeared to be neatly folded into the corner where she stood. Her dress was worn so fine and so pale that the tea rose pattern on blue cotton, the roses faded to a soft pink over time, could not be distinguished from the floral wallpaper that covered the wall behind her. She stood with a straight spine, her head tilted regally, although she was probably just a hair taller than five feet with long silver hair tied back at the nape of her neck.

In those first few moments, as he turned toward her, he was reminded of the libraries he loved as a child. She smelled strongly of old books—all leather and dust and whisper-thin pages. He remembered suddenly turning the pages of books so large that he could only just pull them from the shelf to the floor and the indulgent glances of the local librarian as he flipped through the pages long before he understood the words. The memory was so immediate that it took him a moment to respond to the elderly lady herself, who was waiting patiently, head still cocked in that birdlike way.

Normally, he heard the chime from the door when anyone came into the shop. He had a moment to wonder if he should feel embarrassed that she had likely been treated to his tone-deaf rendition of one of the songs playing on the vintage record player. He flushed pink, realizing that he'd yet to respond to her at all. He stood there among the antiques, a tall man with a broad build and dark hair, somehow off-kilter. His embarrassment must have seemed palpable because she spoke up soothingly.

"That's from a poem by Mary Oliver." She paused for a moment. "So, what do you plan to do with your one wild and precious life?"

"Good morning. I'm afraid I didn't hear you come in." He smiled at her warmly. She waited patiently, watching him with a curious expression on her face. "I thought that sounded familiar. I'm not sure if we have any of her volumes of poetry here, but I can recommend a great bookshop in town that's sure to carry it."

She smiled at him, a gentle half-smile, and waited still. She stepped forward, and Seth could finally separate her figure from the wallpaper behind her. She had one hand resting lightly on a jewelry box on display. He knew that if it opened it would reveal a small ballerina who would begin her clockwork twirl as the music played. He tried to recall the song.

Ah. *Love Story*. She didn't even have to open it for him to call the tune to mind. He simply remembered the last time it was opened. The owner of this particular booth had taken it down to dust, and he'd opened it up and then watched as the ballerina inside twirled around. He had watched it for longer than Seth had expected. He hadn't meant to trespass on what seemed to be a private moment, but when the man looked up at him and smiled, Seth had known he was forgiven. The man had spoken up.

"Always makes me think of my wife. Not my wife now, but my

first one. She's been gone a long time." He shook his head and sighed, replacing the box back on the shelf. "Of course, she'd have called that sentimental garbage. She didn't brook nonsense or fools, and I always was a bit of both."

The memory had come unbidden, but Seth was used to it. After all, antique shops are repositories of memories. He often would stumble upon ghosts of his younger self, playing with the tin soldiers in the little tin box or flipping through the comics, careful not to tear the pages and risk a scolding from his otherwise mild-mannered grandfather or his notably less mild-mannered mother. Seth returned his attention to the elderly lady before him and wondered if she'd yet to peek inside the jewelry box to see the ballerina spin.

"What brings you to town?" Seth asked when she only continued to watch him carefully. Tourists were an everyday part of Madison. Some came for the golf tournament each year, exploring the area on their way, but most were here for the Antebellum Trail. For a rural town, they were quite the cultural center. Other tourists came for the gardens or the music festivals, and still others had fallen in love with the town passing through and came back for a weekend getaway or vacation. They came all year long, looking for something and finding it here in Madison.

"I'm just here visiting. I like to look at the past," she remarked, nodding to the store around her. "It brings back so many memories."

"Can I help you find anything in particular?" he asked, ever-conscious of his role here.

"Not at all, young man," she said with a wide smile. "I'll simply have a look around and get out of your hair." She began to walk away, toward the back of the store.

With a smile, Seth replied, "Please let me know if I can help you with anything while you're here." He watched her nod and walk softly away, her feet making not a sound in the slippers she wore.

While he worked, reorganizing one of the displays, he watched her move through the store. She often reached out to touch the antiques softly, sometimes picking one up gently to examine it more closely. He smiled as he watched her explore. He walked quietly himself and touched the antiques with that same reverence, always conscious of how fragile they all were.

He thought back to what she had said when she first came in. "Tell me, what is it you plan to do with your one wild and precious life?" He knew the quote and the poem it came from and thought that perhaps it was just something she asked new acquaintances. He never minded eccentricities. It's best not to mind, growing up in the South where oddities were often put on display. But he thought about it while he reordered the display and she browsed. What was he doing with his life?

Seth hadn't thought his life would look like this. He'd thought by 33, he'd have a family of his own or at least the possibility of one. He knew he'd be running the shop. He'd spent most of his education learning about art and history and compiling the knowledge he would need to acquire, care for, and sell antiques. He had an eye for it, and he just plain enjoyed old things. He was afraid he was starting to become one. An old thing. An anachronism. Out of step with the times.

It's not as if he'd never had a serious relationship, of course. He'd had two significant ones, but neither had worked out. Seth had almost proposed to Marnie. He'd given it a lot of thought. They were together for almost six years, and it had seemed like the next logical step in their relationship. But then she took a job out of state and seemed to think that it was better to end things rather than to try and figure out how to bridge the distance. She didn't expect him to give up the shop or his dream. Why should she give up hers? And the fact that he was able to accept it so easily made him glad that he hadn't proposed after all. If he'd really loved her, wouldn't he have wanted to go with her? Or at least wanted her to want him there?

That was right after college when he was just starting to manage the shop. A few years later, he met Charlotte. They dated for about six months before she moved into his place. Everything seemed to be heading in a serious direction when he found the text messages. Actually, if he were honest with himself, he knew something was off long before he had proof. She'd been running late for work one day, and he'd handed her the phone when a message came up on the screen. He didn't bother to read it. After all, a picture is worth a thousand words.

After Charlotte, he just dated casually. No one he'd gone out with had made the leap from casual to serious, although he suspected one or two might have liked it if they had. But even without a committed relationship, Seth thought that his life was full, even if he wasn't where he thought he'd be at this stage. He had his business, a few good friends, and a close relationship with his family. His acquisitions were selling surprisingly well, and he didn't have to be concerned about finances. He thought he was fairly lucky, but he still thought about the poem. Was he doing what he wanted in his life or just going through the motions?

Seth looked up from his musings to see that he was alone in the shop. Shaking his head, he decided that he should really turn the record player down a little. Or else double-check the sensor on the door to make sure it was in working order. It wasn't like him not to notice his customers coming in or out during the day. He finished adjusting the last few items in the display and walked over to open the door. The door chimes sounded clearly inside the shop, so he headed to the back to cut the record player's volume down. He changed out the Beatles for Andy Williams and then wandered over to the books to see if the volume of poetry was still there.

He saw the faded hardcover nestled in between a faded hardcover copy of *Lost Horizon* and a paperback copy of *Kindred*. It was an anthology of poetry. He took it down and turned the pages quickly. He'd read the poem just the other day when he'd seen the quote online. He read the last part again now, his voice speaking softly over Andy Williams crooning Moon River.

> I don't know exactly what a prayer is.
> I do know how to pay attention, how to fall down
> into the grass, how to kneel down in the grass,
> how to be idle and blessed, how to stroll through the
> fields,
> which is what I have been doing all day.
> Tell me, what else should I have done?

Doesn't everything die at last, and too soon?

Tell me, what is it you plan to do

with your one wild and precious life?

He wondered why the old lady had quoted that poem. He wondered what it meant to her, but Seth also thought about what it meant to him. Was he paying attention? Or was he letting life pass him by even now? He heard the chime of the front door and switched his attention to the couple entering the shop. He turned to greet them, relieved he'd heard the door over the sound of the record, and thought no more about the poem for a long time.

Chapter 3

Libby walked downtown with a bounce in her steps. She was looking forward to seeing Rachel. The sisters had grown up close, a necessity when everything else in their lives was in upheaval. She rarely got to see their younger sister Faith. At twenty-nine, she was the youngest of the three and worked on a cruise ship. They appreciated that she passed along her discount, but they rarely spent time with her. Rachel was the oldest, at thirty-five, and she was a stay at home mom. The three women shared the dark hair with red tints and the same strong cheekbones, but Faith's hair was more of a fiery red to their auburn. Faith and Libby shared their mother's small and slightly upturned nose, while Rachel had the long straight nose from their father's side of the family.

She noticed Rachel sitting on a bench downtown, her suede pumps jiggling up and down with impatience. Today, she didn't look like the harried mother of three. Her kids—Oliver, Ella, and Willow (ages six, four, and one respectively)—were spending the day with their grandparents to allow for this rare sisters' lunch. She'd already called Libby that morning to wax enthusiastic about a conversation that didn't include Disney movies, the *Paw Patrol*, or anything that would require her specific refereeing skills. She admired Rachel's boy-short auburn hair, a recent change that set off her hazel eyes with those long pale lashes she slathered with increasingly darker mascara, promising added length and volume. Libby grinned as she approached her.

"Am I late? I thought I left early enough," Libby remarked, winded from her walk.

"You know I'm always early," Rachel replied, hugging her sister to her. "I love the shoes," she said, admiring the red flats that Libby had paired with a navy shift dress. Libby knew that Rachel was keenly interested in fashion and regretted how much time she had to spend in ballet flats and jeans, squiring children around from one play date and school outing to another.

"Thanks. I had trouble sleeping again so I needed the pop of color today. It cheers me. I love this dress." Libby said with a smile.

"You don't look like you had trouble sleeping," Rachel noted, peering at her sister over the top of her aviator sunglasses, examining her closely. Libby knew that she didn't look like a woman dealing with a traumatic divorce. Today, she didn't feel like one either. She'd put on her red lipstick with a real smile, but she could see Rachel's skeptical glance dart over her, searching for tell-tale signs of the bags under the eyes that accompanied sleepless nights. She knew that she wouldn't find any and credited her concealer for successfully covering up the traces.

"So, have you eaten here yet?" Rachel asked, indicating the café and taking off her sunglasses. She tossed them into the handbag that Libby knew was as much diaper bag as purse.

At a recent lunch, Libby had dumped out the contents just out of curiosity. She'd made a bet with Rachel as to what she'd find, and she'd recovered most of the scavenger hunt items including her wallet with her ID and all the insurance cards, a compact, about seven tubes of lipstick in varying shades, her cell phone, a slim paperback she hadn't yet had time to start, several diapers, a package of wipes, receipts she hadn't had time to throw away, and any number of individually wrapped snacks. Rachel had bought lunch for the two of them that day, but she'd been none too pleased with the reminder that her life was more about her kids than herself these days.

"No, not yet. Though I think I've tried every other restaurant in town. The menu looks interesting," Libby said. "How are the kids doing?"

"They're fine. I left them with their Ninny and Pops," Rachel said, referring to her husband, Alec's, parents. "They were playing with the train table when I left, and Oliver was busy with an enormous box of

Legos I'm going to be sorry they got him," she said with a laugh.

"We needed sister time anyway," Libby said. "And I'm going to save their prizes for later. I found them the cutest little coloring books at the drugstore. You just use water and a paintbrush to color them, and then when it dries, you can do it again. Mess free!" Libby grinned.

"Thank God for you! If their Ninny buys them one more toy with a thousand pieces, I swear you'll have to bail me out of jail!" Rachel said with a wry smile. "If I've asked her once, I've asked her a thousand times, but you know she doesn't really like me."

"God, she likes you more than Colin's mom liked me. She looked at me like a bug under a microscope. I was always nervous I'd forgotten deodorant or something the way she'd wrinkle her nose at me," Libby said with a roll of her eyes.

"She really was a monster. But I think she was just a little jealous. You and Colin were something, you know?" Rachel and Libby shared a moment of silence. She could tell that Rachel was considering asking about the divorce, and Libby had to admire her restraint. She knew that her sister wanted to shamelessly pry for information, but at the same time, she was trying to be circumspect about it. She'd been thrilled when she found out Libby was moving to Madison, but Libby suspected it was because she wanted the opportunity to exert a little more influence over her life. She could see the struggle on Rachel's face, as they stood in line examining the menu with more interest than it warranted.

"Nope. I'm not doing it. I'm declaring a ban on talk of Colin," Libby declared with a wave of her hand. "He's not ruining my day. New subject!"

"Well, if we aren't thinking about Colin anymore, let me tell you about the hot guy I ran into the other day. No wedding ring," Rachel said, with a wink.

"Hot guy? Now that's more like it. Tell me everything! I need all the juicy details." They stepped up to order and chose soup and half sandwiches before heading to a table. Libby leaned back in her chair as Rachel gave a detailed description of the sexy blonde firefighter she'd gotten behind in line at the Chick-fil-A while picking up breakfast for the kids, and laughed as Rachel told her how she'd almost got his number.

"God, Alec would have loved that!" Libby said, with a smirk. She and Alec didn't get along well, but that's because he avoided family events, by and large, or kept to himself when he was there. She was starting to wonder how happy Rachel's marriage truly was, but after her own spectacular failure in the marriage department, she decided to mind her own business.

"Not for me, Libby. For you. I'm going to update your profile on that dating site with the new picture you posted the other day. It's very flattering. And I think I'll spice up your description again," Rachel said. "I have so many friends who met their husbands on this site."

"Do what you want, but I don't know about online dating. And I'm not even divorced from the last husband yet. I don't think I'm ready for a new one. Let's wait and see for a bit. Who knows? I might run into your Hot Guy and start something up there." Libby hoped her smile would cover the twinge she felt any time she thought the word *divorce*. It still seemed like a word that had nothing to do with her.

"Not *my* hot guy, *yours*. Hmm. . . . Wouldn't that be something? Well, it's a small enough town, and God knows you're all the time running or walking in it. The odds are probably in your favor," Rachel said, stealing a bite of Libby's sandwich. "I think I like yours better than mine." They traded halves amicably. Rachel bit into the turkey and cranberry, which tasted just like Thanksgiving. She watched Libby take a bite of her egg salad with a good-natured shrug.

"Sorry you traded?" Rachel asked with a grin. "Look. Can we talk about what happened with you and Colin, or is there still a moratorium in effect on that subject? It just seems so sudden. I'm dying of curiosity, honestly."

"I know you are," Libby said, and then considered. It wasn't as though it was a secret, after all. "I was just as surprised as you are, honestly. I'm still not completely sure, but I'll tell you what I know. You remember the beginning?" she asked, taking a sip of water.

"You were very—intense," Rachel commented, taking a bite of her sandwich. "I was kind of jealous, if you want to know the

13

truth." She shrugged, thinking that maybe it was better not to have that sort of intensity if this was how it ended. Libby could read it in her expression, but let it go.

"We were intense. Passionate. We used to annoy people by finishing each other's sentences or communicating with just a look. I'd never experienced anything like it."

"So what happened?" Rachel asked.

"Life," Libby said with a shrug, her eyes shuttered as she withdrew for a moment into those dark memories. "I had my job change. His work hours were adjusted. There was the car accident with the uninsured driver and the bind that put us in. Things changed. I thought they would eventually right themselves, you know, like they do. But then he asked for a divorce," Libby said quietly, remembering her shock when he'd announced it was over. She had actually thought they were fine, or as fine as they could be given the disappointments over those last couple of years. She struggled to find the words to describe something that even she didn't fully understand.

"But I thought you filed?" Rachel asked, puzzled. "Didn't you say you filed?"

"You're right. I did. He said he wanted a divorce, and I gave him what he wanted. He signed every paper I put in front of him. That's how eager he was to be done with it. We started packing right away, and he was out before I was. Anyway, it moved pretty swiftly after that." Libby struggled for a matter-of-fact tone, suppressing the note of sadness that crept in beneath it.

"Do you think he was just trying to get your attention with all that talk of divorce? You know, like maybe he didn't mean it? Alec threatens to divorce me about every six months, and God knows I say the same thing after I've spent a holiday with his mother."

"It wasn't like that. He was so serious. He said he wanted a fresh start, and we weren't working out. I wasn't going to beg him to stay, Rachel. He said he was done so I let him go. Haven't you always said I need to do that more? To just let go?"

Rachel shook her head slowly. "I don't think that's what I meant, exactly," she said with a sigh. Rachel was quiet for a minute, keeping her own counsel. After all, what was done was done.

Libby could see the flash of thoughts flit across Rachel's face and wondered if she could talk her into a poker game. After all, everything she thought was broadcast as brightly as a neon sign. But maybe own face gave the same tells, she thought uncomfortably as she noticed Rachel's closer scrutiny.

"Have you heard from him since he left?" Rachel asked.

"Not a word. We don't have kids so there's nothing to stay in touch about." Libby looked away at the mention of children, trying to keep her voice light. It wasn't easy, not after all those years of trying without success to start a family. She didn't see a need to mention all of the babies they hadn't had and all the fertility tests that hadn't illuminated anything other than her own sense of failure. There was a time when she would have talked to Rachel about planning a family, but every time a pregnancy test came back negative or every time her period showed up right on schedule, Libby had grown more withdrawn.

She'd stopped talking about it, to Rachel and to Colin. It was an ache that had grown inside her and talking about it now wouldn't give her the family she wanted. In fact, she was beginning to suspect she might never have the sort of family she'd dreamed of. Still, at least she got to spoil Rachel's kids.

"So tell me about Willow's antics. Is she walking yet or still doing that goofy monkey crawl she started a couple months ago?" Libby asked to change the subject.

Rachel was always happy to talk about her kids so she began to describe how Willow had started walking, but mostly backward, a side effect of Oliver and Ella always chasing her around. One story led into another, and the subject of Colin and the divorce slipped away.

After lunch, Rachel and Libby walked over to Sugar & Spice, the chocolate and confection shop that sold homemade ice cream. Rachel chose a peanut butter scoop, and Libby tried the maple. They took their cones outside to eat at one of the benches on the sidewalk under the striped awning. Rachel started to eye Libby's cone after a minute.

"Maple, huh?" Rachel asked.

"Don't tell me you want to trade ice cream cones, too?" Libby laughed.

"No, I like the peanut butter, but next time I'm trying maple."

"You should do that. I think I've tried every new flavor. It's a good thing I've taken up running," Libby said, thinking that running had served the dual purpose of managing her weight and helping her cope with the divorce. It had kept her together in those first few weeks when she was sure every moment she would fall apart.

"I really should, too," Rachel said, looking down at her waistline with a grimace. "There's a local gym that would watch the kids while I worked out. I just hate working out. Maybe I'll do Zumba at the church up the road. Or take a yoga class."

"Zumba's good. You've got good rhythm. You'd like it. I kept falling over and making a fool of myself when I did it. Now, yoga I like. I've been cycling through the warrior poses lately," Libby said with a grin, putting her free arm around her sister and leaning her long dark hair against Rachel's short locks.

"I don't even know what that means, but it sounds cool. I could do that with you. Maybe we could try hot yoga!"

"I'm sorry, but no way in hell am I doing hot yoga," Libby said with a laugh. "Regular yoga is hot enough for me. Or if I want to sweat I'll just take a walk in the Georgia heat and soak in some of this free humidity. I don't know why it seems hotter here than just an hour north. I keep thinking I'll cut my hair off. Yours looks so good!"

"I'm surprised you haven't already. All the magazines say that the first thing you do after a breakup is chop off your hair or dye it some other color. You'd be abnormal if you didn't." Rachel looked at Libby's hair critically. "Your color is good though. All that dark brown is pretty. But you could do some highlights if you wanted a change," she suggested.

"I might do that. I'll see how I feel. I'd hate to mess up my hair just because I needed a change," Libby added with a roll of her eyes.

"Better than messing up your life because you needed a change— like that fool Colin," Rachel countered. "Just like a man to upend his world because he's bored or something."

"I'm not going to worry about Colin. I can't. I just need to move on," Libby said, her lips pressing together tightly. She couldn't think about what had been. If she did, she'd run screaming into the streets. She had to put it behind her.

"Move on, as in let me complete your dating profile?" Rachel asked.

"I don't know about that," Libby laughed. "I'll think about it. Give the kids my love, and tell them I'll be up to see them later this week. And maybe convince Oliver to keep the Legos over at Ninny and Pops' house to play with. Let them worry about the mess." She gave Rachel a hug and stood up, tossing the napkin from the ice cream cone into the nearby garbage can.

Rachel rose as well and then looked down at the stylish blouse and skirt she'd chosen for their lunch. "Damn," she muttered.

"What's up?" Libby asked.

"I got ice cream all over this outfit, and I can't even blame it on the kids." She rolled her eyes as she clicked open the door of her black Honda Odyssey with the key attached to a little keychain that pictured all three of her children's faces. She slid inside and immediately put the windows down. Libby leaned in to hear what she was saying. "So I'll update your dating profile, yes?" she asked.

"Bye, Rachel. Go pick up your kids."

"I'm just saying. You need to get back out there. You know I'm right."

"I think I'll know when I'm ready," Libby said, giving her sister some major side eye.

"Will you listen to your big sister just this one time?" Rachel wheedled, putting the aviator sunglasses back on and accidentally knocking her bag into the floor. "Damn," she swore, leaning over to snatch up the handbag and thrusting it back onto the seat. "I'll clean this up when I get home. Anyway, think about it, okay?"

Libby knew that planning everything was kind of her sister's thing. She hated to disappoint her, but she didn't think the kind of connection she'd had with Colin came around more than once in a lifetime. That had been her shot, and it was over now.

"If it'll make you feel better," she said, knowing she wouldn't give it another thought.

"It would," Rachel replied. From her smirk, Libby suspected that her sister knew that she wasn't taking her seriously. They grinned at each other with perfect understanding. Rachel would boss her, and she just wouldn't listen. If Faith were here, she'd be either off in her own head, thoroughly ignoring them both, or perhaps offering to clear their chakras or to read their cards for some insights into their next move. They all had their roles. They were long-established, and Libby was glad that Rachel at least knew when to give up.

"I'll call you," she said, as she rolled up her windows and drove away.

Libby began walking back down Main Street, stopping to admire a display here and there. She decided to take the scenic route home. Window shopping, people watching: this town had it all. She grinned as she sidestepped a redhead having a conversation with her dog by the groomer's downtown, then neatly avoided colliding with a muscular bald man who was hefting a large bureau into the back of a moving truck outside of an antique shop. He huffed out an apology, which she waved off with a smile.

At the corner, she looked both ways and reminded herself that she still needed to make an appointment for afternoon tea and to pop into the bookstore to add to her reading list while she was at it. She took a small notebook from her handbag and made a quick note, then turned on her red heels and headed toward home with a skip in her step. Maybe everything hadn't worked out according to her plan, she thought, but that didn't mean she couldn't make a new one.

Chapter 4

The next morning was busy at the antique shop. Seth finished the schedule for the following week, posted it in the breakroom in the back and left Farrah in charge while he went out to lunch. He was meeting his oldest and closest friend, Dean Walton, and then planned to stop by the tea room to check on his mom. She'd been sick a week or so back, and he wanted to make time to see that she was okay. As he stepped outside, he spotted Dean walking toward him down the street. Dean was a firefighter for the city and often had lunch in town with Seth when they could both manage it. Seth waved.

"Seventeen texts," Dean began without preamble as Seth approached, and in a voice of someone sorely put-upon. "Seventeen. Before noon. Hell, most of those came in before I punched the clock, and I've got the early shift."

"Which one is this? Mandy? Holly? Something else ending in "y" that I can't remember?" Seth asked.

"You know Molly and I broke up a couple weeks back. No, I'm talking about Emma."

"Ah," Seth remembered Emma now. She was one of Dean's newest interests, a short, curvy blonde with bad girl tendencies. "So what happened there?"

"She's just so jealous. She checks up on me about a hundred times a day, and I swear she's cyber-stalking me, too. I get texts all day long at work and half the night, and she goes crazy if I don't answer one immediately. She's just so suspicious." Dean ran a hand through his short blonde hair in frustration.

"But you are still seeing other women, right? I mean, she's not wrong about that." Seth noted out with a grin. They lined up to order their lunch.

"That's not the point. I never told Emma we were exclusive. For all I know, she's dating other people, too."

"It doesn't sound like she has time, what with stalking you all day." Seth countered.

"We're not in a relationship or anything. We're just having fun," Dean said.

"Don't tell me. Maybe you should tell her." Seth tried to hide a grin at Dean's exasperation. They'd been through this before. "I'm sure she'll be very reasonable once you explain how you don't like to be tied down and all."

"They're never reasonable," Dean lamented. "We're not exclusive. I can date whoever I want, and she can't say anything about it."

"So who else are you dating now? I know the thing with Molly went south. Anyone new on your roster?" Seth was curious. Keeping up with Dean's social life could be a full-time job.

"You know I still see Andrea sometimes. And Kristin on and off again. I've been out on a few dates with Shelby, the one whose cousin used to date Jamie? I like her. I think that's it."

"And Emma." Seth reminded him.

"Shit. I don't think Emma's going to stay in the picture much longer. She's bat crap crazy, man." Dean sighed. "Now if Lindy would just give me a chance . . ." He grinned at Seth.

"Hey, leave my sister alone. We've had this talk. You stay away from all my female relatives so I don't have to worry about all of them having broken hearts when you're done with them." It was an old argument, one they had actually begun when Dean developed a teenage crush on his sister some years ago.

"I'm just saying. Lindy's gotten pretty hot since she moved back," Dean teased. They ordered their sandwiches and grabbed a table to wait. Seth took a long drink of his sweet tea. It was one of those autumn days where the temperature rose and fell, and Seth was a little warm in his long sleeve shirt. He rolled his eyes and changed the subject.

"So what will you do about Emma and the seventeen text

messages?" Seth asked.

"I think it's time to let her down gently. She's a looker for sure, and she's smart and fun, but I don't do relationships."

"Hey, you don't need to tell me. I know all about you," Seth said with a laugh. They grabbed their orders to-go. Dean had to cover the phones at the fire station, and Seth wanted to stop by and say hello to his mother before heading back to the shop. They walked half way to Utopia Tea, Books, & Gifts before they parted ways with a promise to catch up on the Emma situation later. Seth entered the bookstore, but didn't see his mother. He decided to pester his cousin Beth before catching up with her.

*****

Libby wrapped up her morning run, happily checking her time and pace as she walked back home. It was an improvement of nearly five minutes over her best time. After a long shower and change into clean clothes, Libby headed back downtown to Utopia Tea, Books, & Gifts. She had a reservation for afternoon tea, but she wanted to browse a bit first. Although she ran by Utopia several times a week, this was her first time stepping inside the door since the day she'd made the reservation. It really was a lovely old building, and Libby admired the exposed brick and all the windows.

She walked along the bookshelves, running her fingers lightly over the spines. Libby loved to read. She didn't actually expect a small-town bookstore to be quite up to snuff on the type of books she enjoyed, so it was a pleasant surprise to see the range of fiction and nonfiction. She'd really expected only a few of the *New York Times* bestsellers and a hodgepodge of mystery and romance novels. Instead, classics nestled against biographies, and thrillers cozied up to cookbooks. It was certainly eclectic, but also interesting and unusual.

She moved on to the gift section and Libby made a mental note to pick up something for her sister's upcoming birthday. Truly, for such a small part of the store, it was well-stocked. Nothing kitschy here. Everything was lovely and different. She even noticed a rack of scenic postcards of the area, which utilized the talents of a local photographer, and there was handmade stationery made by another local artist. Libby was so involved in her perusal that it took her a minute to realize she was being closely observed. It wasn't exactly subtle, but Libby was so absorbed that it caught her off-guard.

She looked up and made eye contact with a young woman whose appearance was startling for more reasons than the big grin she was aiming in Libby's direction. Her hair was a fiery red and twisted into a messy bun. Her blue eyes were framed with horn-rim glasses, but it was her outfit that caught Libby's immediate attention—a vintage house dress, lovely and unusual at the same time. It might have looked like a costume on anyone else, but somehow it worked for her.

"You were so caught up in your thoughts that you didn't even notice I've been staring at you for about ten minutes," the girl said with a smile. "I almost hate to interrupt you, but I think I've seen you in town, and I wanted to say hello. I'm Beth."

Libby reached out a hand, returning her easy smile. "Sorry about that. I get caught up sometimes. I'm Libby."

"Are you just visiting or do you live in the area?" Beth asked.

"I moved here about four months back," Libby said, with an admiring glance around the room. "This is a lovely place."

"My Aunt Keely owns it. She used to run an antique store with my cousin, but this was what she wanted to do with her retirement. Some retirement! We're run off our feet every day. I'm the local bibliophile. I run this part and leave the tea business and gifts to her. Did you move here with family?"

"No, it's just me. But my sister lives nearby. I wanted to be close to her." It was only half the truth, but Libby didn't want to bore Beth with the heartbreak that had sent her careening into a new life.

"Do you work in town?" Beth asked. She was sure there was more to the story there, but she kept her own counsel. For now, anyway.

"I'm a travel writer actually. I freelance for a few magazines and online journals. It gives me the freedom to live anywhere I want, and I actually fell in love with this town when I first drove through it." Libby admitted with a smile. "I do a little work for the newspaper, too, but only part-time."

"That happens a lot. People come to visit and find they've come

22

home. Welcome to Madison, Libby. You're going to love it here."

Libby smiled at Beth and walked to the nearest bookshelf, again running her fingers across the spines. She pulled out a book and read the back cover, determined to find something new she could escape into at the end of the day. She actually found a couple that looked interesting and took them to the counter to pay. Beth rang up her purchases, talking nonstop about her morning adventure with her dog, which had a habit of getting off leash and wreaking havoc in her neighborhood by chasing squirrels. Libby let herself be entertained and thought that it would be nice to be friends with someone like Beth who clearly saw the humor in everything.

When the story was wrapped up along with her purchases, she turned to find herself looking into the eyes of one of the most attractive older women she'd ever seen. Her hair was silver and swept up in an elegant chignon, and she had the bluest eyes in a face that was subtly made up to show off those large eyes and high cheekbones— like an aging Hollywood film star in Technicolor. She was tall, made even taller with three-inch heels, and wore gray slacks with a bold blue blouse that brought out her eyes. She reached out a hand to shake Libby's and introduced herself.

"You must be Libby Reynolds. My two o'clock?" Her grasp was warm and firm, and she smiled sweetly. "I'm Keely Carver. I run this show. Except for the books. The books are all Beth. Just don't let her talk your ear off."

She turned to the book lady and added, "Beth, I do wish you'd remember to look into those invisible fences for Mr. Darcy. He's driving Gloria crazy. He's dug up her garden twice this month already."

"Wait," Libby said, looking at Beth. "You named your dog Mr. Darcy?"

"Sexiest man in literature? You bet I did!" Beth grinned. "He's just the cutest bull terrier you'll ever see. I decided the day I found him that I'm done looking for my perfect man. It's just me and Mr. Darcy. I've decided to settle happily into spinsterhood."

"Hmm. That's what you say, but I think twenty-six is a little young to declare yourself a spinster," Keely said. "I agree that Mr. Darcy is as cute as a button. Though considerably less cute when he's barking outside your window at 6:00 a.m. trying to get to a squirrel on the roof."

"I know. Invisible fences. I'm writing it down right now." Beth scrawled *invisible fences* in the air in front of her with a big smile, which caused Libby and Keely both to laugh and shake their heads as they walked away.

"That girl. She's sweet as they come, but of course, I'm her aunt so I'm completely biased. Still, she's the best bookseller around. I'm surprised she didn't talk you into half a dozen more," Keely said, nodding at Libby's bag of books.

"Oh, she wanted to, but I'm new in town, and this was my first day in the shop. I think she's already decided what I'll buy the next time I come in. I noticed a kind of manic glint in her eye while I was browsing."

"That's Beth for you. She has an uncanny memory for every book every customer has ever so much as touched. Now you'll be seated right here. It'll give you a good view of the park downtown. I'll have Abby come by in a minute and go over the specials with you, but I'd be happy to go over the tea menu and get a pot started while you wait. We only serve full-leaf teas here. We do a tea class at least once a month with tea tastings, a history of the different types of tea, and the most glorious chilled cherry soup you'll ever taste. It was my mother's recipe. Take a few minutes to look it over, and I can answer any questions you might have or make a recommendation if you can't decide."

Libby studied the two-page tea menu, admiring the names and descriptions. She chose a white tea infused with berries and settled herself in to review the lunch menu for future reference. Today she was looking forward to the high tea she'd reserved, a tiered tray filled with scones, fresh fruit, tiny sandwiches and a sampling of desserts. The tea was brought promptly to her table, and she admired the delicate china cup with a floral motif that was placed in front of her.

She let her gaze drift around the street. Libby liked to people watch sometimes. She could spot the tourists easily enough. Most of them carried cameras and consulted local tourist brochures from the visitor's center in town. She noticed the horse and carriage tour going by and admired the beautiful golden colored horse with the blonde mane. She searched around in her mind for the breed. She wasn't exactly a horse person, but she did like to watch the derby each spring. Palomino. That's what it was. She made a mental note to book a carriage tour some afternoon.

She also reminded herself again to take time to pop into a few of the antique shops she could see along the street. She might find a decent record or two to add to her growing collection. Libby let her gaze leave the antique shops and she turned her attention to the sidewalk in front of the tea room. There were two men around her own age walking in her direction, and she couldn't help but admire them. They were both tall, though most men were taller than her own meager height. One had blonde spiky hair and a short beard, and the other had thick, dark hair and a clean-shaven face. The dark-haired one was a little stockier, one of those men who seemed large, but still had that tapered waist. The blonde one was a little slimmer. Both were attractive.

As much as she missed Colin, Libby reminded herself that she was single now, practically divorced already, and allowed to openly admire men again. It wasn't cheating, she told herself. She rubbed the white place on her finger where her wedding and engagement rings had rested for the last five years. She'd taken them off the day she filed for divorce, but her hand still felt bare without them.

She turned her attention back to the men and noticed that they had parted ways. The blonde was heading back across the street, while the dark-haired one was approaching the tea room. She watched with interest as he entered and exchanged a few words with Beth, who grinned up at him. Libby recalled Mr. Darcy and knew this couldn't be a boyfriend. She continued to watch as Keely crossed the room and wrapped her arms around the man. Younger lover, perhaps? With her looks, Libby wouldn't be at all surprised if she had one. But then Keely pulled back to speak, and Libby noticed the similarity in their features. Mother and son, most definitely. She felt relieved and then embarrassed that she was relieved. After all, it wasn't as though she was ready to date yet. But it was nice to know there were men her age in this town, even if she hadn't met any.

Libby picked up a scone and added a dollop of fresh whipped cream and lemon curd to it. It was still warm in her hand, and she turned her attention away from Keely and her attractive son to properly enjoy her tea time. She'd asked Abby, her server, to bring one of the green teas and in the meantime, she allowed herself to enjoy the delicious food and the view. Not of the blonde man walking further up the street, she reminded herself. And certainly not the owner's son.

Instead, she took in the wild profusion of flowers in the barrels around town and the bright blue sky above. It was certainly turning into a hot day, but it was beautiful nonetheless, and the humidity was lower than was customary for this time of year. She watched the day outside the window and lost herself there in her thoughts.

Chapter 5

Keely had always had excellent hearing. She'd been back in the kitchen talking with her chef, Amie, and her newest server when she heard her son come in. She knew Beth would chatter away at him for a few minutes, so she finished her conversation and made a note for a couple of supplies that needed to be ordered before she stepped out of the kitchen and admired her big, handsome son. Keely knew she couldn't be impartial, but she'd seen enough admiring glances shoot Seth's way that she knew others would agree. He had his grandfather's thick head of hair and his daddy's wide smile. The eyes and cheekbones were pure Sanderson though, her family.

She wondered sometimes why she hadn't returned to the family name following her early divorce from Seth's father. No one would have blamed her. She just couldn't imagine having a different name from her children. So, when Zeke Carver had left to marry his secretary and move halfway across the country, she'd stayed Keely Carver to keep the name of Seth and his sister Lindy. She'd never remarried, and she hadn't really thought of Zeke since he'd left her with two toddlers and no way to support them.

Her father had stepped in and talked her through the loss and what she would do next. He'd said he needed a little help around the antique store he'd inherited from his own father. She'd taken over managing the store, often corralling her children in the back office to play until she could find an affordable sitter to help out on those initial long work days. She'd been able to cut back on her hours once those support checks from Zeke had started to come in—every month, faithfully—but she only heard from him at holidays those first couple of years and then not at all. Still, she'd raised a handsome, responsible, and kind boy. Man, she corrected herself. She'd raised a good man. She was proud of herself for accomplishing that on her own.

Seth's sister Lindy was also kind, but she'd had her problems. Keely's dad had passed away when the girl was eleven, and she'd been grief-stricken. She'd floundered for a bit in her teen years and had worked out her daddy issues with a number of unsuitable older boyfriends all the way through high school and into her early twenties. Keely regretted not being able to give her another father figure, but somewhere in college, Lindy righted herself. She continued to wear all black as her preferred ensemble, often with matching black nail polish and smoky eyes, but she quit smoking and started dating men a little closer to her own age. Then she'd taken a double major in art and education and gone in a surprising direction. Instead of working as a teacher at a local school as she'd always planned, she decided to take a few business courses in her spare time and establish a painting studio in town. While Lindy was opening The Tipsy Canvas, Seth had been slowly taking over Lost Horizon Antiques with his mother's help.

Keely waited patiently to see if Beth had finished talking to Seth. It looked like she had turned to greet a customer. Keely chose her time well. She crossed the room, calling Seth's name as she did, and wrapped him in a big hug. He'd gotten his height from her family, too, but he'd long since surpassed her own 5'8". He hugged her hard, practically lifting her off her feet, and whispered, "I love you, Mama." He'd been saying that since he was no more than a little toddler, a stout little boy always on the move. She leaned back and smiled up at him, "I love you, too, my baby," she said, and then stepped back.

"I see Dean's heading back to the station. Did the two of you meet for some lunch?"

"That was the plan, but he's going to eat back at the fire station. One of the new guys called out again so he's manning the phones. He just ran over to pick up his lunch to go. He's having some girl trouble."

"That boy is always having girl troubles. You tell him from me that if he'd just date one at a time he'd see an end to the drama," Keely said.

"Oh, I think he thrives on the drama," Seth laughed.

"Doesn't he just? He always was a charmer, that one. And far too handsome for his own good. I had thought about introducing him to the new girl in town, but I think I'll have a word and tell her to steer clear instead," Keely said. "She doesn't seem the type to put up with a man who has eyes for every girl."

"What new girl?" Seth asked curiously. He looked around the room, and his gaze landed on the brunette by the window. If he hadn't been talking with Beth and then his mom, he'd definitely have noticed her sooner. She had thick, dark hair and long bangs tucked to the side. She was sipping from a cup of tea and gazing dreamily out the window. Her mouth was pink and nearly a perfect cupid's bow. Combined with that upturned nose, he thought she was that rare blend of adorable and sexy. "You mean *that* new girl? Why would you introduce her to Dean and not to me?" he asked, only half-joking. "What's Dean got that I don't? Am I not your favorite son anymore?" Seth teased.

"Aha!" his mother said. "I thought you might be interested. But Lindy said you told her firmly no more blind dates, so we decided we'd send all the single ones Dean's way instead—or we will as soon as he starts to settle down. He's got that firefighter thing all the girls seem to like. But you're still my favorite son," Keely laughed, reaching up to pat his cheek.

"Well, only son, but I'll take it."

"She's definitely more your type than Dean's, come to think of it," she said, starting to lead him toward Libby's table. "She's a little reserved, but it could just be that she's new here. It can take some people a while to warm up."

"No, Mama. I don't want to bother her. She's trying to eat in peace," Seth said. He tried to stop his mother in her path toward the woman, embarrassed that she thought he needed her help to get a date. "Let's just leave it for now."

"Nope, nothing doing," she countered, her slight Southern accent thickening in her excitement. "You're here. She's here. You might as well say hello." Then, sensing his resistance, added sternly, "Now, it's just good manners to say hello to a newcomer."

Seth thought for a moment that his mother was like a warship sailing straight across the room toward Libby. He shook his head in resignation and followed in her wake. Besides, he thought, it would be a chance to meet a pretty girl, so who was he to stop her?

"Libby, dear? How's the tea?" Without pausing for an answer, Keely continued, "Since you're new in town, I thought I'd introduce you to a few young people like yourself. You've met Beth and I'll introduce you to my daughter, Lindy, if she stops by this way while you're here. In the meantime, this is my son, Seth. He owns Lost Horizon antiques. You seem like a woman who would enjoy a good antique store, and if you need a tour around the town, my son here's your man. He grew up in Madison. Excuse me for a minute. I need to check in a few guests."

Keely walked away with a satisfied smile leaving the bemused pair in her wake.

"It's nice to meet you, Seth." Libby reached out to shake his hand, a habit that came from meeting so many new people in her work. She'd been startled from her thoughts, and she tried to collect herself quickly. She was suddenly nervous at the feeling of her own hand in his large one and felt the heat creeping into her cheeks.

"I'm so sorry to interrupt your lunch, Libby. My mother was determined we should meet while I was here. What brings you to Madison?" he asked, holding her hand in his own for a moment longer than was strictly polite. He noticed her eyes were hazel and seemed to be picking up green tones from the dress she was wearing. Her lashes were a thick fringe over her peaches and cream skin.

She paused, as she always did when asked this question. "I was at loose ends and fell in love with this town. I'm lucky to be able to work from anywhere so I thought I'd make a change," she explained vaguely, preferring not to go into detail about her abrupt life change. "Would you like to sit down?" She gestured to the seat beside her.

"If you're sure you don't mind. I only have a few minutes before I head back to the shop. It's hard not to love this place. I grew up here and never left. I never really wanted to. What kind of work do you do?" he asked, interested.

"I'm a writer. I freelance for a few travel blogs, and I've started working at the newspaper here part-time."

Now that he was sitting so close to her, Libby noticed that his eyes were blue like his mother's, although possibly a shade lighter and she could see that he had the beginning of a five o'clock shadow. She admired the square line of his jaw and the charming Southern accent he'd probably deny having if it were mentioned.

"That sounds like interesting work. I've always admired creative types. My sister Lindy owns the painting studio in town. I'm afraid she got all the artistic talent in the family," Seth said with a grin.

"I can write, but I'm not creative in any other sense. I can't carry a tune in a bucket, and I certainly can't paint. It doesn't seem to stop me from singing in the shower or trying my hand at a canvas though."

"Would you like to have coffee with me sometime?" Seth was surprised to hear the question come out of his own mouth. When she hesitated, he mentally berated himself. It was probably too soon. Or she had a boyfriend. Could she have a boyfriend? He'd already checked her finger and noticed the distinct absence of a ring. It was unusual for him to move so quickly, but there was just something about her. He thought he'd like to know her better.

"I'd love to." Libby was surprised to hear the words leave her mouth. I'm not ready, she told herself. I'm not ready yet. "When is a good time?" Lord, now they were discussing an actual time. What if he meant it to be friendly and largely hypothetical? Dear God, this was embarrassing!

"I'm off work Saturday morning. Would you like to meet me at Brews & Blues? We could grab coffee and then maybe I could show you around," he said, relieved she'd said yes. He was guessing this meant she didn't have a boyfriend, though he'd be sure to verify that over coffee.

"Saturday is perfect." They smiled at each other warmly, feeling a spark of connection.

"Why don't we swap numbers? I can give you a call later this week just to confirm, if that's okay," Seth said, already wishing he'd asked for an earlier date. Like tomorrow.

"That's fine. I have a bit of a non-traditional schedule with my work so I'm flexible." She paused, looking at him closely, "You're not one of those really annoying early morning people, are you? You know, the kind who want to meet around 6:00 or 7:00 a.m. for coffee—when normal people are sleeping?"

Seth laughed out loud, a rich warm laugh that Libby enjoyed. She grinned at him and said, "I really had to ask."

"No, not at all. I'm not up earlier than 8:00 most days. Can we say 9:00 or 10:00? Is that too early?" Seth asked, amusement written all over his face.

"I can do 9:00 a.m. That's a perfectly normal time to be awake." She smiled and handed him her phone and accepted his in trade.

*****

Across the room, Keely smiled in satisfaction. She watched Seth trade phones with Libby. "Look at that, Beth. Someone's exchanging numbers."

Beth grinned and gave Seth the two thumbs up gesture behind Libby's back, which caused him to shake his head even from across the room. Subtlety was never one of Beth's strong points. With a chuckle, Beth turned to Keely, "I'll be honest. I wish I'd thought of it first. She seems sweet. But not annoying-sweet. Just sincere-sweet."

"I think so, too. And he hasn't really dated anyone since Charlotte. Well, not seriously anyway."

"This should be interesting. If nothing else, maybe they'll be friends. I strongly suspect there's a story with that girl. There's something about her," Beth said.

"Oh, Beth, you think there's a story with everyone!" Keely grinned at her.

"And there usually is. I think I'll see if she wants to go to one of Lindy's paint nights with me. I'll get her to bring the wine," Beth grinned. "You could come with us. We could even rope Vera into it. It's tough being in a new town when you don't know many people."

"I'll talk to Vera and see. If we can't make it, you be sure to ask her to go with you. You know Lindy will give you a good deal on the class, and I'll send some wine over myself. If she's going to be going out with Seth, I'd like to know the girl."

"We don't know that they're going to date. We just know that they exchanged numbers. For all we know, she's got him in mind for a friend of hers. Or maybe she's being polite. He should check that it's a real number," Beth observed.

"Do people still do that? Give out fake numbers, I mean?" Keely asked. Her knowledge of the dating world had grown murky. She still went out every once in a while. In fact, it wasn't unusual for her to receive requests from passing tourists. She just hadn't felt that spark in a while, and she didn't really do texting and online dating these days. Though she'd honestly given it a try a few years back.

"Of course," Beth replied. "It's the only way to be polite when someone is persistent, and we don't want to hurt their feelings. I don't do that though. I just say no and give them what for if they keep pushing, but most of my friends have fake numbers they give out. It'd be easier if everyone would just be honest."

"Look at her leaning toward him. I'd bet dollars to donuts that it's her real number she's giving him."

Beth looked across the room, watching the two of them closely. "I'm not taking that bet. I'm no sucker," she said. "Leave it to me. I'll get the skinny from one of them before they leave."

"Well, don't scare the girl. Ask Seth if you want, but you know he can be close-mouthed about this sort of thing. We'll just have to wait and see."

*****

Across the room, Seth and Libby were conscientiously saving the numbers they were trading. Libby offered him a cup of her tea, which he declined with a smile.

"I really do need to be getting back, and you're going to want to try all these desserts," Seth said, nodding at the heavily laden tea tray. "My mother bakes some, but her chef Amie is a wonder. She'll have made most of them. And if you haven't tried their chicken salad croissant, you need to add that to your list. It's incredible."

"How do you know I have a list?" Libby asked.

"You're a travel writer, right?" She nodded. "So, of course you have a list. And anyway, you seem the type to have a list."

"Well, you're not wrong. I have lists for my lists, and I'm not remotely offended by that. Though I wish it weren't quite so obvious." Libby laughed, a little self-consciously.

"Well, we'll see if I can help out with that list," Seth said, offering an encouraging smile. "Coffee on Saturday at 9:00 a.m. then." Their eyes met and held for a moment before he hurried on. "I really do need to get back to the shop. Stop in if you get time before Saturday and say hello. It's been a pleasure," he reached out his hand, taking hers one more time.

"I'll be sure to do that," Libby replied softly, her throat going dry as her eyes stayed on his. As he walked away, she took a long sip of her tea, which had cooled down. Before she could even think to ask, Keely swept by with a fresh pot and a smile.

"I hope we haven't bothered you," the older woman said. "I brought you my very favorite tea to try, and then I'm going to let you get back to your lunch. Don't forget you get a ten percent discount with your tea since you purchased a book. You let me know if I can bring you anything else while you're here." She swept away, leaving Libby with the thought that she wanted to be just like Keely when she grew up. Beautiful, dignified, and kind. She tried the new tea, a delicious dessert variety, and shamelessly checked out Seth as he walked back down the street toward his shop.

Chapter 6

Libby wrapped up the five miles she'd intended to run and drained the bottle of water she'd brought. She was hot and sweaty—her long sleeve shirt discarded before she'd even hit the first mile—and she decided to take a different route home today, admitting to herself that she didn't want to pass Lost Horizon Antiques looking like this when Seth might be working.

She made a mental note to call Rachel and ask how a first date was supposed to work. Should she get there first? Was she expected to pay for her own coffee? She was a little surprised that she'd accepted his invitation at all, but then she remembered his light blue eyes and the feel of his hand in hers, how it had warmed more than just her own hand. She thought uncomfortably that she'd run by his store earlier. It was entirely possible that he'd already seen the sweaty, workout-clothes-version of her. She grimaced as she tossed the empty water bottle into one of the downtown recycling bins.

Libby needed to shower and head into the office. She had a few ideas to toss out to her boss on articles for the next few editions. After that, she needed to take some time submitting a couple of outlines to one of the travel websites she worked for. She thought she'd send a write up of the art gallery downtown, and she needed to turn in an older story she'd written on agritourism in the area. That should keep her busy until around four, and then the plan was to swing by her sister's house to watch the kids for a couple of hours so Rachel could make it to a doctor's appointment.

Turning toward home, Libby walked slowly the last few blocks and enjoyed the brisk coolness in the morning air. She passed the fire station and noticed the blonde man she'd seen with Seth standing outside scowling at his phone. He looked up as she passed and grinned at her. He said, "Good morning," with a slow smile, and then his phone rang. He immediately scowled at it and turned off the ringer.

"Good morning," Libby replied. "Must be your boss."

"I'm sorry?" he asked, confused.

"The call you're screening. Must be a boss," she said. "I can't say I blame you. It's too beautiful a morning to work. Though I'm heading into work myself soon."

"Well, I work here, and my boss works just down the street when he's not at the station, so I wouldn't get away with screening his calls. He'd have Candace at Brews come outside and shout at me before he'd let me lay out a day." He smiled. "It was just a telemarketer. I surely need to get a new number."

The way he smiled at her made Libby dearly hope he wasn't about to ruin this whole Southern firefighter charm thing by asking for *her* new number. That sort of lame pick-up line was always an immediate turn-off. Of course, it would be kind of nice to have two good-looking men ask for her number in as many days. Still, as attractive as he was, she didn't feel the spark she had felt with Seth. She hadn't felt a spark like that in a long time. Not since Colin, she thought uncomfortably—then shook off the thought.

"I've got to get ready for work. It was nice talking to you," Libby told him.

The firefighter's phone buzzed again, and he waved at her as he headed inside the station. "The pleasure's all mine. I hope I see you around again soon."

After a quick shower, Libby got ready for the day and made a few notes on new topics and ones she'd like to revisit. She also had a quick look at her budget and decided she would probably take on that extra freelance assignment in the next couple of months. That would keep the wolf from her door a while longer, and she'd even be able to put a little back into savings. Libby was renting a small apartment downtown in what used to be a sprawling historic home. She had her own entrance and rarely saw her neighbors except in passing.

Libby had her eye on eventually buying one of the historic homes she passed every day, just a small one. After all, she wasn't sure that children would be a part of her future, although she was open to adoption. She just wanted a home in this town for herself. She'd spent a little more than she'd expected from her nest egg when she paid for the divorce and relocation. She was slowly trying to replace that money and add enough for a decent down payment. She hoped to have her own home soon, but there hadn't been much left to split when she and Colin sold their townhouse. Most of the sale went to pay off the mortgage and a few outstanding credit cards.

Libby took a deep breath and reminded herself not to go there. She didn't want to think about the divorce or the little townhouse she and Colin had once bought together. She didn't want to remember the little book nook and the picture window that had sold her on the house before they'd even taken a look at the bedrooms. She didn't want to think of her little yard with its privacy fence and lush garden that always made her imagine she was inside *The Secret Garden*. There was no point. She'd much rather indulge in the fantasy of Seth—or plan out a few travel destinations for her column.

She knew that one day soon she would receive the notice that the divorce was final. That would be another memory to add to her time with Colin. She could pack those memories up in her mind the way she did with all the moving boxes. She could feel the weight of them, heavier each day, and wondered how long she would have to carry them. She wished them away, but she knew in her heart that a part of the process would be unpacking them all in her head and dealing with them once and for all. Just not quite yet. She wasn't ready to put it all behind her yet. How do you sort through all that history—all the love and intensity she was so sure had once been there—and then just leave it behind?

She remembered walking down the aisle toward Colin in a Christmas wedding of red and silver. She remembered distractedly handing her bouquet of red and white roses with a mix of greenery and pine cones to her bridesmaid, Rose, never taking her eyes from Colin's. If she closed her eyes now, she could take herself back to that moment. She could remember her own certainty, her eagerness looking toward their future, and that pull toward Colin. She could even remember the smell of pine and cinnamon and the soft feel of petals against her cheek later that night when she woke up in the honeymoon cottage with the moon shining through the gauzy curtains of the bed. She thought of the weight of Colin's arm around her waist and how she turned toward him to find his eyes on hers in the dark. She thought of the smile he gave her and how she could see his eyes crinkle in the dark. She remembered the feel of his hands on her waist, pulling her to him.

She thought about the way that she and Colin just gravitated toward each other from the start. Their chemistry had always been a force of nature. From that first date, there was an element of something *other* to the encounter. She would never have said kismet or fate. She wasn't the type to believe in that. Well, not for ages. Not since she'd put away her dolls and princess dresses. But there was something about him, and she'd leaned toward him on the couch in the coffee shop. He'd leaned back, as if the world had tilted them toward each other, and touched her inner wrist, asking about the small tattoo she had there. She'd nearly shivered when he'd touched her, and he had gone so still. His eyes had met hers suddenly, and she was overcome with shyness for a moment. She'd looked down at her wrist, the tattoo, his finger still lightly touching her. She could imagine him tracing the outline softly or bringing her wrist gently to his mouth and tracing it with his tongue. Her cheeks flushed at the unexpected image and the accompanying arousal. She'd had to clear her throat to explain the significance of the small arrow inked into her skin. Of course, she thought it had been a smooth, almost practiced, move on his part, but she wasn't able to deny its power.

She left the coffee shop that day feeling dizzy with it. Colin had hugged her briefly and then leaned in to kiss the side of her mouth. It was a quick brush of his lips so close to her own. With any other man, she might have thought it was a failed attempt at a kiss, but something about it let her know that it was intentional. She had felt his breath mingle ever so briefly with her own, and the feel of his lips on the corner of her mouth stayed with her even as he didn't. The near-kiss had left her longing for more. When he'd sent a text soon after, and then followed that with a call later that night, she knew that she would see him again.

In those early months of their relationship, Libby was never in a room with Colin when he wasn't touching her. A hand reaching for hers or brushing over her hair or pulling her in at the waist, his mouth fusing with her own. They slept entangled, waking up in the morning light and making love before disentangling their limbs to get out of bed. They fell asleep wrapped around each other, and all day she could feel the scorching heat of his eyes meeting hers across a room. Libby wondered now if it was all just lust. Or chemistry. Or a kind of madness. They'd gone from sleeping together nearly every night to living together, a transition that had made her incredibly happy. She would smile just looking at his books nestled up to hers on the shelves or his toothbrush leaning against her own. Their lives, joined. When he asked her to marry him, she didn't hesitate. It seemed less a question and more a foregone conclusion. Of course, she would marry this man.

She thought about the box she'd packed away and placed on a shelf in her closet. It had all the wedding pictures inside. There were candles lining the aisles of the small chapel, and each guest held a candle, too, during the ceremony. In all the pictures, she was smiling and leaning toward Colin. They were always touching, a hand stretched out here or simply leaning in there. She couldn't bear to look at the pictures anymore. All the happiness then simply served to hurt her now. It was a beautiful, romantic wedding, but now just one more memory to add to the weight of all the others she carried.

There were too few of those memories to counter all the others. The other memories came to her now. When had it gone wrong? Libby replayed memories of nights spent alone, wondering why he was working later these days and if he was working at all. She remembered days with conversations that never really went deeper than the surface. Did he even listen to what she was saying? Could he see her? Their eyes never really seemed to meet anymore, and the kisses grew less frequent. If he brushed his lips across her mouth, it was an absent kiss, a thinking-of-something-else kiss. She wondered if there was someone else whose kisses he welcomed in place of her own. She couldn't help wondering. She woke up in the mornings completely unencumbered by his body touching hers, which never failed to make her heart ache. She remembered vividly the days when he could not stand to be in a room with her without touching her somehow. Then came the days when he could not stand to be in a room with her at all. He walked out when she walked in. Then a day came when he stood on her doorstep, leaving her more finally than when he'd asked for the divorce, even more finally than when she'd filed for it.

She wondered how it would feel to have that final divorce decree in her hands. Would there be a sense of closure or even relief to have it all settled? Would she finally feel able to distance herself and move on? It was complicated and made more complicated still by this new attraction.

She could still remember that flicker of heat with Seth. She hadn't been anticipating it. She hadn't even wanted it, but now it was on her mind. Perhaps she should have declined the invitation to coffee, particularly since it evoked that first date with Colin. But she'd been tempted just enough to say, yes. There was no harm in getting to know someone new. Besides, it was nice to feel that flicker of attraction again, that hint of connection. She hadn't played with fire in a long time. She wondered if it would be a slow burn or a raging wildfire. Of course, she thought with a sardonic grin, it could just be the flicker of a flame quick to blow out when they had an actual conversation.

Libby pulled on the soft pink ballet flats to pair with a simple gray dress that tucked in at the waist and flared out in the manner reminiscent of 1950s house dresses. The dress had pockets, which was Libby's favorite feature. She emptied the small backpack and threw her keys and wallet back into her purse. She headed outside to walk to work, tucking her hands into the pockets and imagining Saturday's date. She'd be at work in ten minutes so there wasn't much time to daydream, but there was always time enough.

Chapter 7

Libby walked to work thinking about coffee. She should have made some at home, but she was hoping against hope that Jenna would have made it into the office before Josie. Jenna Armstrong had become a fast friend and an ally in the office coffee wars, Libby thought with a smile. Josie was the office dinosaur—and she made the worst coffee. She'd been on staff since most of the staff were in diapers; she was practically an institution. She was also the sweetest woman most of them had ever met and so the last thing any of them wanted to do was to hurt her feelings.

Libby sighed with relief when she passed Josie out on her "morning constitutional," which the entire office knew meant one or two Pall Malls and then a heavy spritzing of perfume to keep up the illusion that she was a non-smoker. If Josie was walking, Libby guessed Jenna was at the coffee machine, working her magic. She would grind the organic fair-trade beans their boss Gloria bought from Brews & Blues and then brew a truly decent pot of coffee to the everlasting appreciation of her colleagues. Gloria also kept a variety of creamers stocked. The office loved coming in and grabbing a cup—unless Josie had arrived first and made a pot from the instant coffee can she kept at her desk.

Libby walked in and did a short but enthusiastic happy dance when Jenna looked up from the machine to signal that coffee would be ready in five. They exchanged a conspiratorial grin from across the room as Libby dropped her handbag at her desk and stuck her head into Gloria's office to give her the same signal.

"I saw Josie on the way in. She was finishing her first cigarette, although she did try to hide it," Libby said to Jenna as she walked over to the machine. "Gloria sent me out with her cup for something that doesn't resemble sludge. Her words." Libby smiled. "How was your weekend?"

"Oh, you know, the usual. Never long enough. I took the kids skating Friday night. My ears might still be ringing from the music, but they enjoyed it. Then I went out on date night with Finn. It was much needed, let me tell you." Jenna sighed. "How about yours? Other than putting me to shame running, what did you do this weekend?"

"Ran. Caught up on my reading. Got asked out on a date," Libby blurted out. She looked down at her coffee cup, embarrassed. She really shouldn't have said anything. She knew by Jenna's expression that this was a tactical error.

"You got asked out? Okay, seriously stop the presses. Tell me everything! Did you meet this guy online? Did you let your sister launch your profile?" Jenna was curious. Libby had insisted over the last few months that she wasn't ready to date. "I feel like I've been married for centuries and not just decades so I'm going to need all the juicy details. Spill!"

"I haven't gone out on the date yet. I was just asked," Libby hedged.

"Asked and you said, yes?" At Libby's nod, Jenna pressed on, "So who is this guy?"

"It's nothing. He's probably just being friendly. I mean, it's probably not even an actual date," she said taking a sip of her coffee and wishing she'd kept her big mouth shut.

"Okay, so who is this guy you're not actually going on a date with? And why, exactly, is it not a date?" Jenna asked, growing increasingly amused.

"He owns an antique store in town. I met him at the tea room. His mom runs it and introduced us," Libby said, with a casual shrug.

"You're going out with Seth Carver?" Jenna asked, wide-eyed.

"I'm going to *have coffee* with Seth Carver," Libby corrected. "It's probably not a date. His mama introduced us, and he was probably just being nice. You know, that whole Southern gentleman thing."

"Mmmm, do I know it! Of course, I married a damn Yankee,

but I remember those Southern boys and their charm. Girl, Seth Carver is hot," Jenna said. "I might be a little jealous, but I plan to live vicariously through you, so all the details, please. Start with the wild attraction between the two of you and the part where he begged you to go on a date with him. Continue." She waved her hand toward Libby to motion her to go on, a mock serious look on her face.

"It's nothing," Libby said, trying to hide her embarrassment. "It's not that interesting. It's just two adults meeting for coffee. It's probably not even a date. I'm making too big a thing of this."

"Not at all. You haven't even shared as much as a cup of coffee with a man since Colin. This is a good thing. And I don't know Seth well, but his mother is a saint. I love that woman. And I do know his sister Lindy? She made quite the impression when she moved back to town. Seth seems nice though, so it's definitely worth a cup of coffee to find out if it's a date or not."

They poured their coffee, and Libby added the creamer Gloria preferred to hers. The heavy scent of perfume announced Josie's arrival, and the two women slowly moved away from the coffee pot, Jenna sliding the covert can of coffee beans into the back of the fridge where they kept them.

"Hey, thanks for making the coffee this morning, Josie," Jenna told her as she walked by. "How was your walk?"

"Oh, just fine. I saw the mayor downtown and stopped by to ask him a question or two about that land dispute I keep hearing about," Josie said. "Might make for a couple good articles. Of course, he jabbered away like I don't have work to do."

Jenna and Libby exchanged smiles behind their coffee cups. They knew Josie had a terrible crush on the mayor, an old school friend of hers. Her morning constitutional just happened to go by his office, and she had made it her habit to stop by to make sure the city was running smoothly. Or so she said.

"I'm going to get this coffee to Gloria and run some ideas by her. Taco Tuesday tomorrow?" she asked Jenna. "Margaritas on me."

"Finn's got the kids. He knows that Taco Tuesdays are sacrosanct, so I'll be there. Is Rachel coming?" Jenna asked.

"She might stop by for a little while, but I bet she'll be the first to leave," Libby added. "If Alec could get through two hours without her, I'd be shocked."

"Won't happen," Jenna said, then switched to business. "Tell Gloria I'll have the calendar of events to her in about fifteen minutes."

"Will do. And don't forget—me, you, margaritas—tomorrow." Libby carried the two cups of coffee carefully across the office.

"You ready for some real coffee?" she asked as she entered Gloria's office.

The boss returned from watering the plants near the window and sat behind her desk wearing a tailored button-up shirt in red, dark gray slacks, and stilettos in candy apple red. Libby noticed she'd painted her lips to match. The red suited her dark coloring, a vivid reminder of the Mediterranean side of her family. She knew how much Gloria loved fashion, a copy of *Vogue* or *In Style* was never far out of reach in her office. Libby made a mental note to take Gloria shopping with her sometime. Of course, she thought regretfully, she could never pull off such a bold statement.

"Lord, I love Josie with all my heart," Gloria was saying," but I'm about to hide that can of instant crap she makes for us. Is there any chance we can get the cleaning service to 'accidentally' toss it?"

"We already tried that, remember? She kicked up a fuss and then went to Costco or somewhere and bought enough for an army."

"That's right. I forgot about that. Okay, now hit me with what articles you've got for the next couple issues." Gloria listened and made notes as Libby went through a few pitches for the month. "My sources say we have a pretty big event coming up this weekend."

"I don't have anything here on that," Libby flipped through her notes. "Did I miss something? I've got the town festival set for about three weeks out. Is the date wrong?"

"My sources tell me you've got a hot date," Gloria said, nearly hooting when she saw Libby's face flush pink. "If I'm hearing correctly, you're meeting Seth Carver for coffee over at Brews & Blues on Saturday." She leaned in with interest.

"How do you hear everything that happens in this town? Do you have the place bugged?" Libby asked, embarrassed and exasperated.

"I protect my sources. I can see by your blush that it's true. Do tell," Gloria lifted her coffee cup to her lips with an encouraging smile.

"It's nothing. It's probably not even a date. We're having coffee. He invited; I accepted. It's not really a big deal. I told you I'm not ready to date," Libby reminded her.

"But did you tell him?" Gloria laughed. "I can see by that blush that you did not. Telling, isn't it? He's a very attractive man. You're a single woman. There's no reason you can't go have a cup of coffee or whatnot with an attractive single man."

"I'm almost single," Libby reminded her. "The divorce isn't even finalized."

"That's paperwork, Libby. We both know that's a formality. The lawyer said it would be any day now. Is that what's hanging you up? Colin?" She said his name like it was bitter on her tongue.

"No. Nothing's hanging me up." She paused. "Not exactly. It's just too soon, and this probably isn't a date," Libby added, anxious to change the subject. She could feel those corridors stretching out in front of her in her mind's eye, her feet itching to run. "I think he just felt a little pressured by his mama. It's nothing."

"But do you want it to be a date?" Gloria looked at her closely. "No, don't even answer. Your face answers for you. I've got to get you into our monthly poker game," she said with a smile.

Libby wondered how her entire work day so far had revolved around her date with Seth. Not a date, she reminded herself. She didn't want to admit that she sort of hoped it was. She kept replaying his hand on hers and that spark of attraction. She turned her attention back to work and made a few notes on meeting dates coming up on the calendar and let Gloria know for which of the dates she'd be out of town on assignment. If she had looked out the window of Gloria's office, she would have seen Seth walking up the street with his cousin Beth, but she was too distracted.

Libby managed to hold up her end of the conversation with Gloria, all the while sorting through her own anxiety about seeing Seth again. It did seem like a date, after all, and it also seemed like a lot of pressure. Plus, she hadn't even had a chance to mention that she was still married. It was a technicality, but one that most men would probably want to know.

Her brow furrowed and she worked to smooth it out. Presenting that calm front was nearly second nature by now. She tried not to feel that jab of discomfort at the similarities between her upcoming date and the first one with Colin. It was easier just to push it aside and think about it some other time. She could nearly hear the click of the lock as she shoved those thoughts behind a door in her mind and firmly shut it. She didn't have time to think about that now. Colin was the past. That's what he'd wanted, after all. She needed him to stay there.

Chapter 8

"Well, hey, if it isn't my favorite cousin!" Seth was heading downtown to the store when he heard a voice he'd know anywhere. He stopped walking and turned around to wait for Beth to catch up to him, his hands on his hips and a grin on his face. He noticed she was walking Mr. Darcy. She had the bright pink leash held firmly in one hand and a large coffee from Brews in the other. She claimed that Mr. Darcy was confident enough in his masculinity not to mind the color of his leash. Besides, she always reminded him, it was her favorite color.

"Isn't there a business you're supposed to be running?" Beth asked with a laugh as she walked toward him.

"Chase opened this morning. You know he loves the early morning quiet. What brings you and Mr. Darcy out? I know you don't work Mondays." Seth looked at her curiously. Usually, Beth walked Mr. Darcy in the other direction toward the park.

"Oh, Mr. Darcy just wanted to stretch his legs, and I brought you coffee." Beth handed him the mug.

"Why," Seth began, taking a sip, "did you bring me coffee? What do you two want?"

"Can I not do something nice in this town without people thinking I want something?" she asked in an exasperated tone. They were approaching the front of the store where Jamie was bringing in a couple boxes.

"No," Jamie said simply, taking the boxes into the store.

"I wasn't asking you," Beth called after him.

"Well?" Seth asked, waiting. He gestured to the bench outside, with a pointed look toward the dog. There was no way he was letting

Mr. Darcy, known destroyer of fences and gardens, into his store.

"I just wanted to say hello." She laughed at the expectant look on Seth's face as he waited for the real reason. "And I wanted to know if you gave Libby a call yet."

He let out a groan and then grinned at her. "I knew you had a reason for the coffee. I should have known what you wanted the moment I saw you heading my way."

"Drink your coffee, and tell me everything," Beth replied with a satisfied smile.

"How do you know there's an everything to tell?" he asked.

"Well, you've never struck me as stupid, so I imagine if you got the pretty girl's number you asked her out on a date, or at least called her."

"You're not wrong. Look, it's no big deal though, and don't you and my mama go telling everyone either. We're just meeting for coffee later this week. You know Mama just dropped me on her during lunch, and she might have accepted to be polite."

"Right," Beth said with a dramatic eye roll. "You know nothing about women."

"That's what you're always telling me," Seth said, then tried a diversion. "Do you and Farrah share a closet? What is this you're wearing?" he asked, taking in her ensemble of white button-up shirt with a black and yellow plaid tie and matching plaid skirt. "Looks very school girl chic," he added.

"It's vintage, and you're not distracting me at all. So. Libby, details, spill. And drink your coffee while it's hot."

Seth obediently took another sip. "We're meeting for coffee at Brews on Saturday." He rolled his eyes at her delighted squeal. "It's just coffee, Beth."

"Honey, it's never just coffee," she assured him. "Anyway, I like her. She's sweet as pie. You could do worse. Hey, she could probably do better," she laughed.

"Thanks for that," Seth said with good humor. "Mama joked about setting her up with Dean."

"Pffft! She'd never have gone for Dean. She looks like a woman who knows when a man is too busy juggling. She's the kind who needs someone who pays attention and not to every skirt on the planet," Beth said, firmly.

"Don't tell me you're still mad about all that?" Seth asked. Dean had taken Beth out to the movies one time—and one time only. She'd practically had steam rolling out her ears the next day when she showed up early to the shop, sans Mr. Darcy, to tell him all about the debacle. Apparently, Dean had flirted with the ticket sales lady and clocked every beautiful woman in the lobby and then expounded on the hot women in the film afterward. Beth had complained that he'd just used her so he wouldn't have to go alone. It was a few years back, and she had been under the impression that it was a date when "the lying snake," her words, had invited her to go.

"No, I don't care what Dean does and who with, but I'm not sending anyone I like his way. He has no respect for women. But enough about him. I have to take Mr. Darcy to do his business, but you call me after coffee. And if you have any sense you'll talk her into a walk around town." Beth got up, and Mr. Darcy got lazily to his feet. He had been happily napping under the bench.

"I already suggested that as a possibility," Seth said with a grin.

"That's my boy!" Beth replied. "No, not you, Mr. Darcy," she said to the dog, which had sat at her feet with a paw up when she spoke. "God, now he expects a treat."

"Well, it's a good thing we here at Lost Horizon love our dogs," Jamie commented as he walked out of the shop with a bowl of dog biscuits and a bowl of water they left out for passing canine visitors. He sat the bowl down on the sidewalk and opened the bowl. Mr. Darcy circled a couple of times and then sat down expectantly with one paw up.

"That's a good boy," Jamie told him. He looked at Beth and then grinned at Seth. "She raid Farrah's wardrobe again?"

Seth laughed, and Beth let out an exasperated sigh. "What is with the two of you? You share a brain?" she asked. "Y'all just don't expect anyone to have an individual style. Farrah and I are making what is called a fashion statement."

"It's a statement alright," Jamie said, as he patted Mr. Darcy's head. Mr. Darcy had eaten his treat and then cozied up to Jamie. "Seth, I put the box from the estate sale in the office for you to go over. I can put it out on the floor after you check my prices."

"I have no doubt they're fine, but I'll take a look. Thanks, Jamie," he added. He turned to Beth. "Thanks for the coffee." Seth folded Beth in for a quick hug, patted Mr. Darcy's head, and headed into the store.

Beth looked up at Jamie. "Did you get a new tattoo?" she asked, nodding at his arm. He already had a sleeve, but she noticed something new.

"No, I just had it touched up a bit. I'm thinking about a new one, though. I just haven't made up my mind."

"I've been thinking about getting another," Beth confided. She'd had a literary quote inked on her skin from her beloved Jane Austen.

"Well, let me know if you want me to go with you. Still on for a movie Friday?" Jamie asked.

"Sounds good to me. It's my turn to pick, but it's your turn to get the pizza," Beth reminded him. Lately, they had been having movie nights about once every week or two. They had been friends for a few years now. It wasn't like the time she'd thought Dean had asked her out. She knew when Jamie asked that he was just being a friend.

"I'm pretty sure I bought the pizza last time," Jamie said with a grin. "But I'm game. You want breadsticks?"

"Would it be movie night without them?"

Mr. Darcy started to whine. "Okay, I've got to go, or he'll have an accident."

"I'll see you around," Jamie said. "See you later, Mr. Darcy," he added, giving the dog a quick scratch behind the ear before he headed back into the store.

Beth headed to the park at a much quicker pace, talking all the way. Jamie stood just inside the door, watching her go.

Seth walked up to join him. "Is she still talking to Mr. Darcy?"

"She sure is. It's a wonder that dog's ears haven't fallen off." They exchanged a wide smile. Beth was known all over town for having long conversations with Mr. Darcy while they walked. She didn't bother to stop when she passed someone. She simply greeted each person and seemed to expect Mr. Darcy to do the same. Jamie and Seth shook their heads at the same time and turned to go about the work day.

Chapter 9

"I wasn't sure you were going to make it tonight." Libby climbed into Rachel's van with a sigh. She shifted a baby shoe out from under her and tossed it on the floor with the pile of child detritus that seemed always to occupy space in Rachel's van.

"I may need to leave early. Can Rose or Jenna give you a ride home?" Rachel asked, backing out and heading to the restaurant.

"If not, I'll call an Uber. It's going to be at least a three-margarita night," Libby grinned. "I've been looking forward to Taco Tuesday since last Taco Tuesday."

"I told Alec he better not call me unless there's a real emergency this time. And not being able to find Willow's lovey did *not* qualify as an emergency. If he'd texted me, I would have told him it was in the dryer." Rachel rolled her eyes and then shook her head. "I'm going to have one margarita when we get there, and that's it. But I need the one."

"That's fine with me. Hey, is this Ed Sheeran?" Libby asked, fiddling with the radio. "Ow!" Libby snatched her hand back as Rachel swatted it.

"You know the rules: my van, my radio. It is Ed Sheeran, and I *love* him," Rachel declared.

"I was only going to turn it up. I wasn't thinking about your crazy radio rules."

"It's not crazy. It's the only time I get any peace. The kids have headphones now for their shows, and I get tired of the barrage of Disney movie songs. Then Alec is always trying to switch stations, and I have to have somewhere I can listen to the music I like."

"No, I get it. Hey, look, Rose is already here. Do you see Jenna?"

Libby asked.

"No, but I bet she already snagged us a table and ordered a pitcher of margaritas," Rachel replied.

"Think she got strawberry or mango this time? I didn't love the peach." Libby said with a grimace.

"Guess we're about to find out. Hey, Rose," Rachel called out. Rose was getting out of her car and came over to give Libby and Rachel a hug.

"I heard about the hair," Rose said to Rachel. "Give me a twirl so I can see it properly." Rachel executed a dramatic twirl. "I like it. Looks good on you. It would make me look like a twelve-year-old boy."

They laughed and headed into the restaurant. Libby remembered a time when Rose's own hair had been almost as short as Rachel's was now. That was back in early college when she'd had it cut off in a dramatic bob with a fringe of bangs. Back then, it had been more brown than blonde. Now Rose's hair was long, and her trademark curls were blonde with red streaks. She'd reinvented her look over the years and was in a professional button-up blouse and pencil skirt with heels. The soft green of the blouse brought out her green eyes. Libby noticed Rose had done a smoky thing with her eyeshadow, which was the only makeup she was never without.

They located Jenna at a back booth that they all preferred. She had already ordered a pitcher of margaritas and joked at how aghast the server had been when she'd placed the order without any other guests at the table.

"I swear to God she thought I was going to drink the whole thing myself. I was afraid she was going to give me directions to the nearest AA meeting," Jenna said with a laugh. "I promise this is my first glass!"

"Fill mine to the top," Rose commanded. "Did you order the cheese dip?"

"What do you take me for? Of course, I ordered it," Jenna said. "It should be out in a minute. The service is slow, but we don't come here for the service."

"Nope. It's all about the margaritas," Libby affirmed. "Rachel gets one, and then she's cut off. Who's driving me home if Alec can't handle the kids?"

"Alec will be fine," Rachel said. "He gets his night out with his buddies, and I don't call him every fifteen minutes asking where the wipes are or where to find the cookies he shouldn't even be giving them that close to bedtime."

"If you have to leave, I can take Libby home," Jenna assured Rachel. "Or Finn can, to be technical. I had him drop me off. He'll pick me up when we're done."

"That works for me," Libby said, scanning the menu. "Want to split a sampler platter again?"

"Let's get two this time. And extra queso," Rose added.

"Agreed," Rachel said. "Now let's get to the good stuff." She paused for a moment, taking a sip of her margarita. "Libby has a date."

"Oh my God. Are we going to go through this again? It might not be a date," Libby reminded them with a sigh.

"Oh, it's a date. There's no way it's not a date. I'll bet you a pitcher of margaritas that it's a date," Rachel laughed.

"I'll take that bet. I could really use a pitcher of margaritas courtesy of Libby here," Rose said, exchanging grins with Jenna and Rachel.

"I'm nervous enough as it is without you guys making a big deal out of it," Libby told them. "He's nice, and he's attractive, but I don't want to go into this thinking it's a thing when it might be nothing at all."

"You know what your problem is?" Rose asked.

"I'm sure one of you will tell me."

"That jerk, Colin. That's your problem. He's shaken your confidence," Rose said, pouring Libby another margarita. "He blindsided you, and now you're afraid to get back out there."

"I'm not afraid exactly," Libby started.

"Well, then what's the problem? Have you guys seen Seth Carver? That's one good-looking man," Jenna said.

"No, I haven't seen him yet because Libby here has forbidden me from stepping a foot into his store," Rachel declared.

"Just for now. You can go check him out afterward if you feel like it. Just don't embarrass me," Libby told her.

"Please. I'm your sister. I'm supposed to embarrass you."

"If you're not scared, what's the issue?" Jenna asked again. "And he's h-o-t hot," She told Rachel and Rose.

"It just feels like so much work. I finally like my life the way it is, and relationships take so much time. I just want to binge watch Hallmark movies in my pajamas and eat a pint of Ben & Jerry's if I feel like it," Libby admitted with a rueful grin, tucking away that corner of herself that wondered if she was ready yet.

"You know, instead of going on this date, we could just head over to the shelter so you can pick up a dozen cats," Rose suggested helpfully.

"Ha. Ha. Ha. I'm going to let him buy me a cup of coffee, and then we'll see how it goes. Hey, he's got a cute friend," Libby nodded at Rose. She filled them in on running into the guy she'd seen walking with Seth. "He's a little too studied for my taste, but he's got buckets of that Southern charm you like."

"I'm dating someone. It's not a serious thing, but I'm good with it. Honestly, it's all I have time for right now. Do you know they just assigned me five more cases on top of the seventy-three I already have? I don't know why they think I have the time. But I'm pretty sure my boss is Satan's spawn so it could have something to do with that. I noticed her caseload hasn't gotten any heavier lately." Rose worked for social services and had a love-hate relationship with her job. She loved the kids but hated the meetings and the workload.

"I don't envy you the work schedule. I'm finally getting into the rhythm of mine, and yours still makes me look like I'm on a perpetual vacation," Libby told her.

"And our boss is great, so I can't even complain there," Jenna added.

"My bosses are three tiny tyrants who keep me going around the clock," Rachel said with a laugh. "Any chance you're going to apply for a transfer or go after that promotion?" she asked Rose.

"I don't know. The pay isn't great. I've thought about going into the private sector. The pay is higher, but I don't think my hours would be as stable. It's something to think about though."

The server sat the sampler platters down in front of them, and they ordered another pitcher of margaritas, this time switching from strawberry to mango. Rachel immediately tucked into hers with gusto. Jenna and Rose refilled their glasses, and Libby loaded up her plate with one of everything.

"So this date thing is this weekend?" Rose asked her.

"Saturday," Libby agreed.

"We're going to need details," Jenna added.

"I'm sure I'll tell you all, but if nothing else we can catch up next Taco Tuesday for the highlights. So who's your mystery man these days, Rose?" Libby asked curiously. It wasn't like Rose not to tell her about a new interest.

"It's nothing. It's not a big deal. I'm just seeing someone very casually," Rose said with a shrug.

"Does this someone have an actual name?" Jenna asked.

"It's Dillon. There's nothing really to tell. It's totally casual. We meet up for dinner or to see a movie, and sometimes we hang out at my place. I don't want to make a thing of it," Rose told them. "It's fun right now, but I don't know if it's ever going to be anything serious."

"Well, invite him to Taco Tuesday sometime," Libby suggested.

"Oh no pressure there," Rose said. "And you bring Seth, why don't you?"

"Okay, you have a point," Libby replied. "Besides, I like having a ladies' night."

"Dammit! That's Alec calling," Rachel said, looking at her phone with exasperation. "I'm going to go outside and take this."

"So...think Finn will mind dropping me by my place?" Libby asked with a grin.

Chapter 10

The red Jeep Grand Cherokee pulled up to the curb. Jenna opened the front door and climbed in, and Libby got into the back. They'd ordered a third pitcher of margaritas after Rachel had gone home to deal with some household crisis or other, and she was feeling pretty good.

"Hey, Finn," Libby said.

"How were the margaritas?" he asked, grinning in a way that told them he suspected they'd enjoyed their fair share.

"So, so good," Libby told him with a laugh. "Thanks for the ride."

Jenna's husband Finn seemed like an easygoing guy. He never said much, but he was perfectly affable when they met him. He was tall and thin with skin the color of cinnamon and a baritone voice with the distinct accent that identified him as being from Chicago or thereabouts. Libby often claimed his deep voice was better than listening to James Earl Jones. He had a strong chin and dimples when he smiled. She noticed from her perch in the backseat that Jenna and Finn still held hands—and sighed. In the end, she and Colin hadn't done a lot of hand-holding. She scowled out the window briefly and then reminded herself that good margarita buzzes weren't to be wasted on men who didn't want to stay married to her.

She must have said that all out loud because Finn laughed that deep laugh of his, and Jenna's expression turned bemused. She explained to her husband that Libby might have had the lion's share of that last pitcher.

"I hope your date goes well," Jenna told her.

"It's not a date," Libby said, leaning her head back against the seat and closing her eyes.

"Who are you not going on a date with?" Finn asked.

"Seth," Libby said shortly, as if that explained everything. She'd let Jenna fill him in. They hadn't known each other long, but they'd forged a friendship over the last eight months since they started working together. Jenna knew a little about what had transpired with Colin and was tactful enough not to push for more details than she was ready to give.

"You seem pretty happy about it for someone not going on a date," Jenna pointed out with a grin in her direction.

"He is pretty," Libby admitted. "I can have coffee with a pretty man and it still not be a date."

"Most men might object to being called pretty," Finn noted wryly from the front seat.

"I wasn't going to call him pretty to his face," Libby retorted. "But he is."

"I've seen him," Jenna agreed. "He is."

"Well, maybe you should let him know you want it to be a date," Finn suggested, pulling up to Libby's apartment.

"I don't think I'm ready to date yet," she pointed out, searching the backseat for her purse and then grinning when Jenna passed it over from the front seat.

"It seems to me that if you said yes then maybe you are," Finn returned.

Libby paused, her hand on the door. "That's very insightful of you," she said, looking at him closely. "I might appreciate those insights tomorrow." She grinned at him. "Thanks for the ride."

"No problem."

Jenna walked with her to the door and made sure she got it open okay. "Are you coming by the office tomorrow?" she asked.

"No, but I should be in on Thursday and maybe Friday, depending," Libby told her. "Tomorrow, I sleep."

"You do that," Jenna told her with a chuckle. "Call me tomorrow and tell me if you hear from Seth. I want details," Jenna said with a wag of her finger. After a short pause, she added, "And don't text him tonight. No drunk texting," she called out.

Libby stepped into the house with a laugh, a thumbs up, and a short wave. She turned with the door held open in one hand and then turned to execute a dramatic bow. She couldn't see them grinning at her with the glare of the headlights acting as a spotlight, but she was sure they were. She waved and closed the door, swaying just a little. She didn't drink often. Taco Tuesday margaritas were her only vice, she often claimed, other than the occasional glass of wine. She put one hand on the door to steady herself and decided that she could call it a date in her own mind even if she didn't admit it to anyone else. She smiled and carefully made her way upstairs to her room, unsteady on her feet but a little steadier in her heart.

Chapter 11

Lindy stretched her full 5'9" frame in the hammock and sighed happily. This was the life! It was only a few minutes before 8:00 a.m. and Lindy had walked across the wide lawn this morning from the carriage house that she called home to the big house where her mother lived. At thirty-five, Lindy hadn't expected to still call this property home, but she'd started renting the carriage house when she moved back to Madison to open her business. She had assumed that after it took off she would buy her own place, but the carriage house worked for her. It was more than large enough for her needs, and she enjoyed having coffee each morning with Keely before they began their separate work days.

Teenage Lindy would have been shocked to know that the future Lindy would enjoy time with her mother. They had been adversaries when she was younger. They'd fought over everything that could be imagined: makeup, clothes, grades, her older boyfriends. Then she'd gone to college and finally stopped trying to punish her mom for her dad leaving and her grandfather dying. She realized that her mother wasn't, in fact, the devil and was instead always looking out for her. Since Lindy had moved back, she and her mother had started this early morning coffee date. Sometimes there were pancakes, which her mother made, and sometimes there were donuts or bagels, which Lindy picked up at the store.

Today, she sat in the hammock, already dressed for work in black leggings and a black tunic top screen printed with the words: Nevertheless, she persisted. The hammock was on a screened in back porch that overlooked the lawn and the side of the carriage house. Lindy thought it was fortunate that her side entrance couldn't be seen from here. It would have been a little uncomfortable to know that her mother could see her dates coming and going from that door. But happily, only the side of the cottage was visible from here, and in between stretched a small vegetable garden, a profusion of flowers, and a little bird bath that Seth had found for their mother for her birthday. The sky was already a bright blue, and Lindy heard the toll of the bells for eight o'clock just as the sprinkler system in the backyard came on. That was her cue.

Lindy rolled up to sitting and opened the back door with her key. She turned on the kitchen lights and got out the coffee beans. The bells were their signal for Lindy to make the coffee, and the coffee grinder was the signal for her mom to wake up. Lindy ground the beans, breathing the aroma in deeply. She started the coffee percolating and then raided the fridge for fresh fruit. It was her mom's day to make pancakes and so Lindy started slicing fruit for toppings. She sliced strawberries, peaches, and bananas and then found the pancake mix her mother had made under the counter. She pulled buttermilk out of the fridge and measured it. She lined up the mix, buttermilk, and toppings, and then went to the cabinet to grab their coffee mugs. Lindy had made the mugs at an artist's workshop a couple years back.

Lindy's said, "Blood of my enemies (Just kidding; it's coffee)" and the one she'd made for her mom said, "I can't decide what pants to put on today: smarty or fancy." Keely had laughed when she'd seen them and refused to drink out of any other mugs for morning coffee.

Keely headed down the stairs with a spring in her step. She'd opened the windows this morning when she woke up, and it was already shaping up to be a beautiful day. Plus, it was pancake day. Keely knew that Lindy would be downstairs assembling the ingredients and starting the coffee. She'd already been awake when she heard the grinder. She'd simply been enjoying the cool morning air and warm blankets before she got up and got ready for the day. She'd put on a sheath dress the color of pumpkins and grabbed her suede pumps before heading downstairs in her bare feet. She stood in the doorway a second and then exchanged smiles with her daughter.

"There's my baby!" she declared. Lindy walked across the room and enveloped her mom in a bear hug.

"I think it's pretty safe to say I'm not a baby anymore, Mama," Lindy said with a laugh.

"You'll always be my baby. Now let's get started on these pancakes. Is my griddle warm?" Keely asked with mock severity.

"You know it. I've primed it with butter and lined everything up for you. Coffee's done so I'll make us a cup. How do you want it today?" Lindy asked, referencing her mother's whimsy on how she took her coffee each day. Sometimes she took it black, and other times she added varying amounts of cream or sugar. She'd even drink it bulletproof, which was simply black coffee and butter.

"Ah, today is a beautiful day. Let's do lots of cream and sugar. Maybe the hazelnut creamer. I love this weather," Keely declared, mixing the buttermilk in with the pancake batter. She rustled around in the cabinets and pulled out a couple of spice containers literally labeled "Secret Ingredients." It always made Lindy laugh. She knew they contained vanilla and cinnamon, but they had gone along with the idea of secret ingredients since Lindy was five.

"I know. I love fall," Lindy continued. "And we're starting all the fall canvases. Those are almost more popular than the holiday ones. I'm training a couple of new teachers this week to handle the volume. I'm going to try to squeeze in some time to make a few things for the shop, too." Keely sold some of Lindy's artwork at the shop. Her daughter made some of the stationary they sold and occasionally contributed a painting.

"Do what you can. We're alright with what we've got, though you know we'll sell a good bit this weekend with the tourists. The tea room is fully booked for Friday afternoon and Saturday all day, and I've got a book club coming in Sunday afternoon courtesy of your cousin," Keely reminded her.

"Beth is a marvel. Is she still planning author events?" Lindy asked.

"She's being secretive about it, which isn't like her at all, so she must have someone good lined up. I know she's been on the phone nonstop trying to tap into her connections in the book world. It'll be great for the book sales and the tea room if she can manage it," Keely said, flipping a pancake on to a plate. "Did you get out the syrup, love?"

"It's out and heated. Syrup, butter, fruit," Lindy pointed out on the counter. "Do you want honey, too?"

"No, I think this is enough. You know we'll have to wrap a few of these up to take your brother. Who's working the store today?"

"I think it's Chase upfront. I'm pretty sure Farrah's in class today. And Jamie will probably be around," Lindy said thoughtfully.

"We'll make some for Chase and Jamie then, too. I'd make them for Beth, but she'll be off with Mr. Darcy this morning, and that girl doesn't sit still long enough to eat breakfast."

"How's the leash training going with Mr. Darcy anyway? Did Beth ever get that invisible fence you've been telling her about?" Lindy asked. They all loved Mr. Darcy, but he was a known flight risk.

"You know she hasn't. Think Jamie can talk some sense into her?"

"Mama, I told you. They aren't dating. They're just friends. If she won't listen to you, she's surely not going to take advice from Jamie," Lindy reminded her.

"Well, they may not be dating, but you'll never guess who is," Keely teased.

"I'd say Dean, but he's always dating," Lindy said with an eye roll. "That wouldn't be a surprise. It would be a surprise if he wasn't. So who is it?"

"Seth." Keely let his name hang in the air. "You're going to catch flies, dear," she said of Lindy's open mouth.

"Seth's dating who? And why haven't I heard about this?" Lindy demanded. Seth hadn't dated anyone since Charlotte, at least not seriously.

"You know I save the best gossip for pancake days. Here's the skinny. There's a new girl in town. She's a writer, and she was having tea the other day when Seth came by to say hello. I introduced them, and Beth tells me they have a date this weekend." Keely leaned in with her hands wrapped around her coffee mug.

"Tell me about her. I need details!" Lindy urged. She was leaned in an almost identical pose, and Keely nearly smiled at how much she favored her. Well, all but the eyes. Lindy had Zeke's eyes, but everything else was Keely made over.

"She's pretty. She's got long, dark hair with almost auburn tones. She's fairly petite. She seems really smart, maybe a little shy. But I like her, and Beth chatted her up and likes her. She was real friendly and sweet. I was going to introduce her to Dean since Seth has been so stubborn about being set up, and I told Seth that," Keely said with a grin.

"Of course, if you said you were introducing her to Dean, he'd jump in," Lindy countered. "I know they're like brothers, but even Seth doesn't like Dean's serial dating approach."

"I don't think it was that entirely. He took one look at her, and then he only pretended to resist when I took him over to meet her," Keely added.

"She have a name?" Lindy asked, cutting into her second round of pancakes with zeal.

"Oh, sorry. My mind must be going. I thought I told you. Her name is Libby. Beth is going to invite her to one of your classes and give you a chance to check her out. You have any openings for next week?"

"I'll make an opening if there isn't one. So where's he taking her? Dinner?" Lindy asked.

"Coffee." Keely intoned. They both exchanged an eye roll over the ever-disappearing stack of pancakes.

"Well, he doesn't get any points for creativity, and it's definitely the safe first date. But I swear I'll disown him if he doesn't at least offer a tour of the town," Lindy declared.

"No son of mine would be so slow-witted," Keely assured her with a laugh.

"Well, that was good gossip—and even better pancakes. If you want to help me load up some plates, I'll take this over to Seth myself and get the skinny," Lindy offered.

"Just don't be too pushy. It's a miracle he has a date at all. I was worried he was turning into a hermit or being influenced by Dean.

You know I adore Dean, but I surely don't want Seth to start dating like it's going out of style. Especially a whole gaggle of girls at a time," Keely said with a shake of her head.

"A woman who actually wants a relationship should know better than to give Dean Walton the time of day. Everyone knows what he's like," Lindy observed.

"Well, maybe one day he'll settle down with a nice girl and stop chasing skirts. He's a nice boy."

"You always say that. I'm going to get these pancakes to the guys while they're hot. Tell Beth to call me about what night she wants to come to a class. I'll make room," Lindy added, taking the still-warm plates of pancakes out the back door. "Love you, Mama," she called.

"Love you back, baby girl," Keely added with a smile.

Chapter 12

Dean walked down the street toward the station with a hot cup of coffee in a to-go mug. Shelby had made it for him this morning as a thank you for last night. They'd caught a late movie and headed back to his place after. Of course, he'd had to keep his phone off most of the evening, claiming his battery was low. Emma had taken to texting at least once every half hour, and there was no reasoning with her. He'd have to call her again to remind her that it was over. If she didn't stop calling, he'd have to block her number.

He hadn't intended to go out with Shelby last night, but he'd been sitting home alone watching Netflix when she'd texted to see how he was doing. They'd had a date the week before but hadn't talked much since then. Her text had been a reminder. Shelby was a buxom blonde with a keen sense of humor. He'd enjoyed their date, and it had ended with a pretty hot kiss. He'd considered trying to take her home then, but she had grinned at him in a way that said she knew what he was thinking. He didn't want to get predictable. She'd been more surprised that he hadn't offered to extend the evening. Seth always rolled his eyes when he did that sort of thing, but he'd had a lot of success with it. He nearly bumped into Lindy while he was preoccupied remembering the night before. She stumbled, and he caught her arm but nearly dropped his coffee.

"Dammit, Lindy! Watch where you're going." Since he and Seth had known each other forever, he often looked at Lindy like an annoying older sister. Well, except for that brief time he'd had a crush on her as a teenager.

"I'm watching where I'm going! You need to worry about yourself. If I had dropped these pancakes, you'd have to answer to my mom and not me," Lindy said with a glare.

"Pancakes, huh?" He said, his mood instantly lightening. "You got some for me?"

"No, I don't have some for you," Lindy shot back. "These are for Seth and the shop, not for you and who is it this time? Shelby?" Lindy read the message on the side of the travel tumbler. Shelby had written, Thanks, with a big heart and a smudge of lipstick on the cup. At the time, Dean had thought it was sweet and a little funny, but now he shifted in embarrassment. He moved his hand to cover the message.

"Shelby's just a friend," Dean began. Lindy cut him off with a sardonic look.

"A friend who brought you morning coffee with a lipstick stain? Riiiight," she drawled "I wasn't born yesterday, and I don't want to hear about your sordid love life this early in the morning. I might yack up my pancakes, which would be a shame," Lindy added in a falsely sweet tone.

"Nice, Lindy. Real classy."

"I hear Brews has decent breakfast. I'm sure you worked up an appetite. I've got some actual work to do, so if you'll excuse me," Lindy stepped quickly around him, casting her eyes to the heavens that she'd had the bad luck to run into Dean.

"Always nice seeing you, too!" Dean said to her retreating back.

He wondered sometimes exactly what he'd done to get under Lindy's skin. She treated him like an annoying little brother—always had and probably always would. She hadn't always been so caustic to him, but she'd been openly disparaging about his dating habits since she'd moved back to town. He knew Seth wasn't one to gossip so she must have heard about it around. He shook his head in regret. Those pancakes sure had smelled great. He knew if he'd run into Keely she'd have let him have a couple. She'd always liked him even if her daughter didn't. Still, that was Lindy's problem, not his. He rolled his shoulders, trying to shake off the discomfort of the encounter. He tried to go back to concentrating on Shelby and their pre-coffee activities, but all he could think about was the way Lindy had looked at him in dismissal and disgust.

He decided he would stop in at Brews and grab a couple pancakes to go. They weren't as good as Keely's, but they would do in a pinch. He wondered distractedly if Shelby cooked and if he could talk her into making some next time. He was pretty sure there would be a next time. Rumor had it that Andrea had started dating someone else, and there was no way he was going to see Emma again if he could help it. So maybe he'd see Shelby now and again. He ordered his pancakes and took a seat, careful to keep the coffee inscription covered with one hand as he flirted with Candace across the counter. He then turned his attention to his phone. He had several messages from one of the dating sites. Well, he might as well read them, he thought, as he waited for the pancakes.

*****

Down the street, Lindy was leaving the antique store and heading over to her studio. She was trying to shake off the bad mood that seeing Dean always put her in. She told herself that she was standing up for all women everywhere when she gave him hell. But she wondered if that was the whole truth. All she knew was that he'd always put her hackles up. Not that that was difficult, she thought ruefully. Still, he did it easier than anyone else. She sort of smiled to herself, thinking it was a real gift he had there, to piss her off with so little effort.

"Should I be worried?" Beth asked. Lindy looked up in surprise. She hadn't even noticed her cousin heading toward her on the sidewalk.

"Worried about what?" Lindy asked absently.

"You're smiling," Beth pointed out. "And not a happy one. It's a little scary," she said with a grin.

"Ah. That. Just ran into Dean," Lindy explained.

"Did he survive it?" Beth asked with an even wider grin. Watching Lindy give Dean hell was a great source of amusement for her, particularly after the notorious date-that-was-not-a-date.

"He'll live," she said shortly. "What brings you out this early?"

"Mr. Darcy is having a spa day at the groomer's. I just dropped him off," Beth said.

Lindy grinned. That was Beth for you.

"Did you hear the news?" Beth asked.

"Seth and his big date? Oh yeah! So what do you think of her?" Lindy asked curiously. She had always been the protective older sister, but after Charlotte, she'd increased her vigilance, not that he'd given her much reason to.

"I'm inclined to like her. I think you would, too. Though . . ." Beth paused uncertainly.

"What is it? Come on, spill," Lindy urged.

"She seems a little bruised. You know what I mean? Like she's recently out of a relationship? I don't know. I could be wrong. I just hope Seth isn't a rebound," Beth said with concern.

"Huh. Well, we'll keep an eye out," Lindy assured her.

"Are you dating anyone new?" Beth asked.

"No, but I've got my eye out for the next silver fox," Lindy said with a grin. She'd always dated older men. The fact that silver-haired men were in vogue was simply good fortune as far as she was concerned. Of course, she hoped that she'd find a partner and get started on a family. But it seemed like men her own age were too busy playing the field, and older men often had older kids and weren't interested in starting over.

Lindy didn't say so to Beth, but she'd recently been weighing her options. She had no intention of letting her relationship status dictate the rest of her life. She was trying to decide between science or adoption to start a family on her own. She'd already frozen some eggs, just in case, although she hadn't told anyone. Her mom had been an excellent single mother, and Lindy thought she could do the same.

Lindy thought that one day soon she'd talk about her options with her mom over pancakes. She knew Keely would be just as supportive and practical as she'd always been, but Lindy had a hard time admitting to anyone else that she was starting to give up on the idea of The One. She didn't think there was anyone out there for her, and she wanted a baby so bad she couldn't stand it. Sure, the science part seemed a little creepy for her, but she had a friend who had done in vitro with great success. It seemed normal when it was someone else. And the advantage of a sperm bank was being able to select a donor who had certain skills and traits. She could choose someone with a healthy family history and maybe some musical talent, since Lindy didn't have any of her own. She didn't care what the baby looked like; she didn't even care if she had to go the adoption route. She just wanted to be someone's mommy. Like yesterday.

"How about you?" she asked Beth, redirecting the conversation away from her search for the next Mr. Right Now.

"You know I'm happy on my own," Beth reminded her. "Mr. Darcy is enough for me."

Lindy grinned, but she wondered if that was the whole truth. After all, it's not like she was divulging her own need to start a family. She wondered what private pain Beth might be hiding under all that calm assurance that she was better off alone. "Well, keep your eyes out for me anyway," she reminded her.

"Silver fox, got it," Beth said with a bright smile. "Should be easy enough. Most of them won't go near the tea room, but we get quite a few in the bookstore." Beth reached the corner of the street where she lived and gave Lindy a quick hug.

"Text me later, and I'll squeeze you in for a painting session if you want to invite this woman," Lindy reminded her. "Then I can check her out."

"Just go easy on her," Beth warned. "Libby's sweet. Maybe a little fragile. But I think she might be good for Seth. You should have seen his face after they met. He looked flummoxed," Beth told her with amusement.

"It's good for him," Lindy agreed, giving a wave and heading toward the studio. She had a couple of canvases to prep before she taught a class that evening. She was relieved that seeing her cousin had shaken off her earlier bad mood so successfully.

Chapter 13

Beth finished laying out the movies she wanted to watch just as Jamie arrived at her house. He let himself in with his key like he did every time and carried in the extra-large meat lover's pizza he'd chosen for movie night. He'd remembered to get the sausage only on his side since Beth didn't prefer it, but he knew he'd still have to hear her dramatic groan when she saw the selection. She didn't disappoint.

"Meat lovers? Really?" She asked with the predicted groan.

"Hey, you made me eat that fancy one with chicken and cream cheese and green stuff," Jamie reminded her with a grin.

"That was pesto, and you loved it," Beth countered. "Tell me you had them hold the sausage," Beth begged, peeking in the box.

"My side only. I didn't forget," Jamie told her. "What are we watching?"

"I came up with a few options. Take a look. And where are my breadsticks?" Beth demanded.

"In the bag I sat on the table. Where's my beer?" Jamie shot back, picking up the DVDs.

"By your seat, as usual."

"Seriously? These are my choices? You've got *The Princess Bride*, *When Harry Met Sally*, and *Say Anything*," Jamie read, cocking his head in her direction.

"Yes, they're so good it's hard to pick," Beth teased him. "Hey, you made me pick from *The Sting*, *Terminator*, and *The Matrix* last time, so fair's fair."

"And you loved *The Sting* if you recall," Jamie reminded her. "We're watching *The Princess Bride*, and I'm going to need an extra beer."

"As you wish," Beth quoted from the film. "And I already gave you an extra for fortification."

"Where's Mr. Darcy?" Jamie asked, looking around.

"He's enjoying his evening constitutional," Beth told him, indicating Mr. Darcy's nightly walk around the perimeter of the fence. He was always looking for an escape route, and too often, he found one. Beth had taken precautions and done a walk around it herself earlier to make sure that he would be unable to find a way out. "I'll bring him back in after we eat."

Beth set both pizzas and the breadsticks on the coffee table with plenty of napkins and a couple of cups of marinara sauce. She grabbed a beer from the fridge and sat companionably beside Jamie. She pulled down the throw blankets she kept on the back of the couch and tossed one into his lap. They both kicked off their shoes and got comfortable on the couch with a slice of pizza. Her own blanket was a mermaid's tale so she pulled it on over her leggings and curled her "tail" under her. They bit into the pizza and both reached for extra napkins at the same time, which made them laugh.

"It's good," Jamie told her, nodding to the pizza.

"It's not bad," Beth agreed. They watched the tale of Wesley and Buttercup unfold, adding in their own commentary along the way. After the movie, Jamie got up to use the restroom, and Beth stepped out of her blanket and stretched. She took the nearly empty pizza box back into the kitchen and picked up the napkins and empty beer cans. Jamie'd had three to her two. She pulled out the plate of cookies she'd made earlier with a new recipe she got from Aimee at the tea room. She took them into the living room when she grabbed another couple of beers.

"Want another?" Beth asked.

"Sure. You want to watch another movie?" Jamie asked, taking the beer and admiring the plate of cookies. "What's this? Did Aimee make these?"

"No, Aimee didn't make these. I made them," Beth steamed. "They are her recipe though," she admitted.

"Thanks! So are you going to tell me all about Seth's date or do I need to try to pry it out of him, again?" Jamie asked.

"Couldn't get him to talk, huh?" She laughed when he shook his head sadly. "Ah, well, if it's gossip you've come for, you've come to the right place. Seth asked out a woman Aunt Keely introduced him to. Word on the street is that they're having coffee this weekend."

"Well, good for him. Unless she's anything like Charlotte." They shared a mutual eye roll. None of them had been fans of Charlotte, and they had suspected her of cheating long before Seth caught her at it. Not that he would listen, of course. His Charlie wouldn't do something like that.

"She's nothing like Charlotte," she assured him. "I chatted her up in the bookstore."

"Of course, you did.".

"She seems nice. Plus, she's well-read. You can tell a lot about a person from their selection of books."

"So you're always saying," Jamie reminded her.

"And I'm always right," Beth said with a grin. "Charlie didn't read books. She looked at pictures in the fashion magazines and occasionally cracked open a tell-all about a reality star. Seth's girl reads actual literature."

"I think it's a little early to call her his girl. Guess we'll have to see how it goes," Jamie added with a shrug.

"How about you? Are you dating anyone new?" Now that had Beth asked it, she felt awkward. They always talked about who they dated, but she had started to feel intrusive for asking. Wouldn't he tell her if he wanted her to know? And why did she feel so uncomfortable about it anyway? It was just Jamie.

"I've been talking to someone online, but we're just talking," Jamie replied, shyly.

"Do you have a picture? Can I see?" Beth was curious and feeling awkward about her curiosity. She almost felt like she was faking her enthusiasm, which was ridiculous. Of course, she'd be happy if Jamie found someone. She wouldn't lose him as a friend, and he'd be happy for her if she found someone. That is if she hadn't decided to just settle down with Mr. Darcy.

Mr. Darcy! She had left him outside through pizza and the

first movie, and the fact that he was quiet for so long struck her as suspicious. He was known to treat the surrounding fence like a prison, and he always had a jailbreak on his mind. Before Jamie could show her the picture he'd pulled up on his phone, he noticed Beth's look of panic.

"What? You haven't even seen her yet," Jamie said, puzzled.

"No, sorry. It's not that. Show me later. I need to go check on Mr. Darcy."

"You think he's broken out again?" he asked, moving to look outside the sliding patio door. "I don't see him in his house," Jamie said referring to the miniature Pemberley that Beth had had custom-made for him as a doghouse.

"I think it's a good possibility he's run off," Beth said in a panic. The streetlights had gone out again, and the visibility wasn't that great.

"Grab your shoes. I'll get the flashlights and some treats. You've got the bacon ones?" he asked, heading to the kitchen.

"You know I do. He'll always come home for bacon."

"Look. Don't worry. If he's not out back, I'm sure we'll find him. Call your aunt and make sure he hasn't crossed into her garden again."

"Oh, God. I hope not. This is so embarrassing. The real Mr. Darcy would never behave this way!" she added despairingly.

"You probably should have named him Mr. Wickham," Jamie joked.

"Ha! So you have read *Pride and Prejudice*. I knew it," Beth added, heading out with Jamie and holding a flashlight. They searched her street and a couple streets over where her Aunt Keely lived. They both took turns calling his name and whistling, and Jamie kept the bacon held out in hopes that Mr. Darcy would smell it and come running home. On their way back to the house for a second check of the backyard, they ran into Vera, the B&B owner, walking toward them in a housecoat, holding Mr. Darcy in one hand.

"Oh, thank God you found him!" Beth exclaimed.

"I saw this rascal trying to squeeze under the gate. I pried him loose where he'd managed to get himself stuck and came right over. I don't think he was out there long, but he put up a terrible fuss. He might have been there longer if I hadn't gone into the kitchen for a snack. I could hear him whining through the door." Vera handed Beth the dog, which immediately began trying to leap out of her arms into Jamie's.

"He's not supposed to prefer you. He's my dog," Beth groused.

"It's not me," her friend laughed. "It's the bacon treats. Here, Mr. Darcy. Here you go, boy." Jamie fed the dog a couple and he settled down in Beth's arms happily chewing.

"Thank you so much, ma'am," she said to the older woman. "We sure do appreciate the help."

"It's not a problem, Jamie. I'm just glad he didn't get into the garden again. Makes me glad we put in the thicker fence," Vera added.

"I'm so sorry about the trouble," Beth told her, embarrassed.

"You just look into that invisible fence thing your Aunt Keely told you about. It couldn't hurt since this trickster seems to escape the regular kind so easily. I'd hate to see Mr. Darcy get hurt running around these dark streets," Vera warned her.

"You're so right. I promise I'll look into them in the morning."

"I'm going to walk Ms. Vera home," Jamie said, "and then I'll be back for that beer you promised me."

"Now you don't have to walk me home," Vera told him with a chuckle. "I'm quite capable of making my way safely back."

"My daddy would skin me alive if I let you walk home by yourself this time of night. We'll just see Beth inside, and then I'll walk you home. It'll only take a few minutes, and I don't mind."

"You're a good boy," Vera smiled, adding, "Beth, if you ever decide to settle down with someone other than Mr. Darcy there, you could do worse than Jamie."

"We're just friends!" Jamie and Beth said simultaneously—and then laughed.

Beth waved at Jamie from the door and took Mr. Darcy inside, lecturing him about proper decorum the whole time. "I really should have named you Mr. Wickham," she muttered as she filled up his dog bowl with water.

Chapter 14

Libby woke up Saturday morning earlier than usual. She had set an alarm, just in case, but she woke up before it went off. Today was the big day. She was meeting Seth at 9:00 a.m. She needed to be heading out to Brews & Blues by 8:40 at the latest if she wanted to take her time enjoying the walk. Rose had come over the night before to pick out what she'd wear, so that was one thing she didn't have to worry about. She wasn't exactly excited about the date as much as she was nervous. This was her first time out there since Collin, and she wasn't sure that she was ready. She'd sworn to all her friends that it wasn't really a date anyway, but she had to admit—if only to herself—that it had certainly felt like one when he'd asked her. Still, she didn't want to mistake Southern manners for romantic interest. That would be humiliating in the extreme.

Libby got up slowly and began to get ready. She pulled her hair up a couple of times before choosing to leave it down. She looked at herself critically in the mirror and decided that she was ready. She thought she'd have a bowl of oatmeal before she left the house and added a little local honey to the mix along with a handful of dried cranberries and pecans. If she left a little early, she could go by the park, sit for a few minutes, and jot down some notes for her blog. Of course, if she did that, she would definitely have to set an alarm because she tended to lose track of time while she was writing. Best not to chance it, Libby thought. She decided to head straight to Brews instead.

On the walk over, she tried and failed to talk herself out of being nervous. It didn't help that her first date with Collin had been over coffee. She could still remember his finger softly rubbing the tattoo on her wrist. She traced a finger over it herself and thought it was sad that a tattoo that had always been a small symbol of perseverance was now nearly spoiled with memories of Collin. She wondered if she should get it covered up or add something to it to change it so she wouldn't continue to remember the way it felt to have him trace it with his hands. She hadn't felt he was tracing the arrow; she'd felt he was tracing her into existence. She'd felt raw and open, exposed even. It was like him saying that he knew everything about her from that one little thing.

Well, Collin was long gone, and Libby was leaving him in the past. Or trying to. It wasn't always easy. Random things would remind her of him, and then she'd have to shake it off all over again. But today wasn't about him at all. Today was about having coffee with a very attractive man. Maybe it was a date, and maybe it wasn't, but Libby decided that she was going to enjoy herself either way.

Her phone rang with Rachel's distinct ring tone. She answered it in relief. "I'm heading out now," she began.

"Good. I called just in time," Rachel said, sounding breathless.

"You okay?" Libby asked.

"I just tripped on some Legos on the way down the stairs to call you," Rachel replied. "Damn Legos!"

"Are you alright?"

"I'm fine. Just annoyed. Never mind about that. Are you ready for the big date?" Rachel asked. "Or just nervous?"

"More nervous than ready, to be honest," Libby replied ruefully. "I'm on my way now."

"Look, just enjoy it. Don't worry about where it's going. And don't you dare think about Collin today!" Rachel warned.

"I know. Got it," Libby said. "I don't want to be on the phone when he sees me. Can I call you later?"

"You better! Love you."

"Love you back," Libby replied, ending the call. She put her ringer on silent and headed for Brews. It was busy on a Saturday, but not terribly so. It was a beautiful day, and she was about to be treated to her favorite coffee by a handsome man. She took a deep breath and thought that things could be a lot worse.

*****

"Now if any customers come in—" Seth began.

"This is not my first rodeo," Beth reminded him. She was filling in at the shop for a couple of hours until Chase came in so that Seth could go on his coffee date. He'd spent the last twenty minutes giving out unnecessary instructions. Beth had filled in occasionally since long before Seth was running the place. "I've got this. Don't you have somewhere to be?" she asked him pointedly, looking at the clock.

"Yes. God. Okay, I'll be back later," Seth said distractedly, heading out the door.

"Not too soon!" Beth called out, as he left.

Jamie walked in as Seth walked out. "Where's he going in such a hurry?" Seth heard him ask.

"Big date," Seth heard Beth reply, as the door closed behind him.

Seth left, feeling like he was going to be late. Of course, Brews was only a block up the street. He wanted to check his reflection in the store windows he passed, but he felt like a fool doing it because he knew she could see him if she had already arrived. Instead, he combed a hand through his hair and hoped for the best. He wasn't usually nervous, but it had been a long time since he'd gone out on an actual date. Maybe too long. He was already wishing he'd picked a different first date location, somewhere out of town where he didn't know everyone. Or maybe he should have asked her to dinner. He wasn't exactly sure how this worked anymore. He was definitely getting rusty. But he liked Brews & Blues, and it was close to both of their homes and work. He hoped the convenience would be an added bonus, and if either of them felt uncomfortable, they could cut and run.

Seth was really hoping Libby wouldn't want to cut and run. He was attracted to her, but who wouldn't be? She had thick, dark hair and dark eyes with long lashes. Her nose was small and very nearly upturned at the end, and she had dimples when she smiled. She was short and curvy, and every time he'd met her she'd been in a dress. Except, of course, when she was running. He liked everything about her, but dating wasn't something he initially enjoyed. Especially those first few awkward dates. His last blind date had been incredibly boring, explaining in minute detail her latest horoscope and how it was eerily similar to a recent dream sequence. He should have known when she asked for his sign exactly what he was in for, but she was pretty and seemed to have a well-developed sense of humor. About everything, apparently, except astrology. Well, he'd lived and learned, but he vowed to take his coffee to go if Libby tried to do his birth chart or asked how he felt about dating a Sagittarius.

*****

Candace added the whipped cream to yet another latte and continued to mentally curse her deadbeat boyfriend to hell and back. It was bad enough that he'd managed to quit another job this year. But to do it after moving in with her? The latte wasn't the only thing steaming this morning. Candace pushed her strawberry blonde hair behind her ear and remembered that she needed to get it cut again. She liked to keep it in a pixie, which emphasized her large brown eyes with its thick fringe of lashes. It was a good look for her, but it was starting to grow out. Of course, she hadn't been able to afford to get it cut lately. She'd probably have to trim it herself until Michael found work or she managed to make a few extra bucks on tips.

She smiled at her customers and made the usual polite chatter, all the while thinking of how she could get Michael's lazy ass off the couch, out of that stupid video game, and back to work. God, maybe she should have stayed with the guy that bored her to tears, but at least always paid for dinner. Sean? John? Ron? Something like that anyway. Ray! That was it. There's something to be said for boredom when the bills are all paid, and there aren't notices coming in threatening to cut off the power. But one long slow kiss from Michael had wiped all her reason out of her head, apparently.

Candace called out a hello as the door opened, nodding to the woman who walked in as she served her other customer. The woman looked a bit familiar, but in a town this small, everyone looked like someone you might know. She stood just inside the door and seemed a little nervous. A couple of times she pushed her long brown hair over one shoulder and seemed to take in her surroundings. Candace had her pegged as a first date. In this town, there was only the coffee shop or a couple of local restaurants that made good locations for a first date that was just coffee or a drink.

"Can I get you something?" Candace called out.

"Is it okay if I look at a menu?" Libby asked hesitantly.

"Sure. Why don't you grab a table, and I'll bring one over," Candace told her with a smile. She watched Libby walk to a table by the window and nodded approvingly. It had the best view, and it was far enough away from the vents that she wouldn't get a chill over coffee.

Candace saw lots of first dates working at Brews & Blues. It wasn't just a great place to grab coffee; they also hosted live music several evenings a week. Brews offered organic, local, fair-trade, and gourmet coffee, local beer and wine, and good music. They carried a few tea tins from the local tea room to promote local business, just as the tea room carried a few bags of their coffee. Candace remembered that she had, in fact, met her own deadbeat boyfriend at Brews for their first date. She remembers paying for her own coffee that time, too, which should have been a sign.

Candace took the menu over to Libby's table and smiled at her thank you. Not every customer was so polite, she thought, as the one standing at the counter cleared his throat. Again. Candace went around to take his order and noticed Seth from down the street come in the door. She called out a greeting and saw that his own response was a bit distracted. When he looked over and located Libby, she understood why. Now that was an interesting match.

Hmm . . . Candace served up a plain coffee and a couple of espressos to the usual tourist crowd while observing Seth and his friend. They seemed easy together, but maybe not completely relaxed. First dates were tough. Candace took their orders and noticed with satisfaction that Seth didn't hesitate to pay, although the woman had reached for her pocketbook to pay for her own. Candace appreciated the gesture and again sent a few mental curses Michael's way for refusing to stay employed and expecting Candace to pick up extra shifts to cover his lazy ass.

Candace liked her job, but she couldn't handle any extra shifts this semester. Her course load was already heavy enough. She had taken a couple of additional classes without realizing that she'd be supporting both herself and Michael. She didn't mind helping out at first, but she was truly tired of paying for everything. Her credit card was already maxed out from all the dinners that he simply couldn't cover and the trips he wanted to go on but couldn't afford. She could drop a class, or she could drop Michael. As she took the next order, she was pretty sure she wasn't going to drop the class. Not with graduation only a year off.

When she finished serving the customers in line, she grabbed a pot of coffee to top off Martin's cup. Martin was one of the regulars. He was sitting in his usual spot concentrating on his crossword puzzle. There were a few other customers sitting around the room. One couple was sitting on the sofa in the corner flipping through a few of the brochures they gave out at the visitor's center down the street. She stopped by for a second to see if they needed anything and to give a suggestion on a couple of places to see that might not be listed in the guides. Local gal duty accomplished, she went back behind the counter and made sure everything was in good shape.

Elle liked everything to be shipshape. Elle Lewis-Lawson owned Brews & Blues. She'd taken a dusty and disreputable establishment and turned it into a hot spot of live music and damn good coffee. Candace loved working for her, but Elle didn't exactly suffer fools. They'd had some turnover when a couple of the staff showed a propensity for talking to friends more than working, but Elle had kept them on until she noticed that their friends weren't paying for their food or drinks. Then she let them go immediately, and Candace was able to pick up a few more hours each week to help out at home. Elle had told Candace a time or two to ditch Michael, but mostly she stayed out of her affairs.

Candace glanced into the kitchen and office areas while she waited for customers. Elle was there now. She had her glasses on and was making notes of stock. Her shoulder length hair was pushed back in a headband, and she'd added a little dusting of gold to her lids, which brought out gold glints in her brown eyes. Candace called back to remind her they were getting low on a couple of the brands they usually stocked. Elle looked up and acknowledged her with a grin and wave. Her eyes crinkled at the corners, and while Candace knew she was nearing fifty, Elle could easily pass for a decade younger. Her new diamond ring sparkled on a hand the color of light coffee. She had recently gotten engaged, and Candace could admit that she felt a little envious of her boss. Not only did she have a thriving business, she also had someone in her life who actually loved her.

*****

Martin looked up from his crossword puzzle to smile as Candace refilled his cup. Nice girl, deadbeat boyfriend. He shook his head. A cup of coffee always seemed to start the day off right, but it wasn't the same since his friend Jack died last summer. They'd always met up here on Saturdays and had a cup or two before heading out for a walk. Well, they'd take a good walk if the weather was friendly and lingered a while before going home if it wasn't. Those were good days. They'd had a lot of good days together over the years.

Martin and Jack retired around the same time. Hell, they'd grown up together, known each other since they were boys. Jack's mom taught them in Sunday School, and Martin's dad was the principal at the elementary school they both attended. It was that kind of community. They'd lived similar lives, marrying and having kids right around the same time. Of course, Jack had settled down a little later in life than Martin, but it was really all the same in the end. Martin had lost most of his hair while Jack had kept his. Both had gone gray around the same year though.

Martin looked at the newspaper in front of him, but had no interest in the crossword puzzle he'd started. That was Jack's thing. He preferred to read a good obituary just for entertainment value. Not that there was anything funny about death, but every now and then they noticed spectacular misspellings that added some comic relief. The paper should really get Josie to retire after the last couple of mistakes. She was an old school friend, and Jack and Martin had often kidded her about being so scattered these days.

Martin's attention was momentarily distracted by a couple sitting across from him. Pretty girl. You didn't often see young women wearing nice dresses. Anymore it was all short shorts and tiny shirts that showed everything. They weren't big enough to cover at the top or at the bottom, and it made Martin think of his four girls, long grown with their own children, and want to cover them all up. Of course, his girls always told him that he was old-fashioned, and he probably was. Now Jack had liked to ogle the pretty girls, but Jack only had a son and didn't understand these things. Well, back before the heart attack that killed him dead in his sleep.

Martin noticed that the young man with the young woman seemed awfully attentive to each other. He idly wondered if it was a boyfriend or the husband. Not all young women wore wedding bands either. He often thought that must make things mighty confusing. Still—he noted how the young man seemed to lean in, listening closely to what she was saying. You don't see that enough anymore. And look how she shifted toward him. Martin's wife Reena was always pointing out body language when they dined out. How that man was turned away from that woman and it meant he wasn't really interested in her. How that woman rested her hand near that man's; if only he would hold it. His Reena liked to people watch.

Martin turned his attention back to the crossword puzzle. He'd rather a good word search himself, but Jack said those were too easy. He had always been on about how old folks, like themselves, should keep their minds active, and crossword puzzles made a good challenge. Martin shook his head, remembering that the crossword puzzles kept his friend's brain sharp, but didn't do a damn thing for his heart. Still, he'd go ahead and finish it for Jack. Then he'd have another cup of coffee and go see if Reena was done with her book club yet.

Martin wondered idly if he would pass soon, seeing that he and Jack did everything around the same timeline. He'd never for a moment suspected there was anything wrong with Jack's ticker. In fact, Jack had stayed active. He'd even slimmed up some in his later years and had taken up tennis and racquetball while Martin had stuck to golf and fishing mostly. Martin had packed on a few extra pounds, thanks to Reena's cooking. Still, of the two of them, anyone would have thought he was the more likely candidate for heart disease. When the news had come to him that Jack had a heart attack, Martin thought it was a whole lot of bother for nothing. Jack's own father had lived to nearly 100, and they were only in their eighties. His friend was as healthy as a horse, always had been. He'd just do the surgery, like many of their friends had done, and he'd be fine. It had taken him a few minutes to understand that his friend was gone already.

For a while, he'd stopped coming to Brews & Blues. He hadn't seen the point. But gradually he fell back into his routine. He'd take his dog, Felix, a five-year-old Irish setter, out for a long walk around town; then after he took Felix home, he'd make his way over to Brews & Blues. He'd order plain coffee, although the menu was extensive, and sometimes he'd order a muffin or coffee cake. He'd take his regular seat by the window and unfold the newspaper he'd brought along. He'd open it to the crossword page, take a sip of coffee, and miss his friend.

Chapter 15

Seth hesitated at the door of the coffee shop and hoped that she wasn't one of those people who always run late. But, no, she was sitting at a table looking over a menu. The second their eyes met, he stopped feeling nervous. He remembered exactly why he'd been so quick to secure that first date and so happy when she'd accepted as easily. There was just something there, call it chemistry or what have you. He just knew that he liked it, liked her, and hoped to know her better.

"Hey, Libby. It's good to see you. You look beautiful," Seth began simply.

"Thank you. It's good to see you, too." Libby knew she was blushing but couldn't seem to stop.

"Have you ordered yet?"

"No, I was just trying to make up my mind," she told him with a smile.

"Everything here is good. I'm still working my way around the menu myself. They have a pretty good salted caramel espresso, and there's a mint mocha latte I like. Even the regular coffee is good though." Seth stopped himself from rambling any further and realized that some of the nerves were back.

"I want to try everything, but I think I'll just pick one at random and work from there," Libby said. "It's a nice place."

"It packs out in the evenings when they do live music. It's standing room only, and all the tables get reserved beforehand. People come from all over to play here so it's a pretty big deal. What kind of music do you like?" Seth kicked himself for asking such an inane question and hoped that his tongue would untie so he could be a little smoother for the rest of the date.

"Anything but bluegrass. Blues, sure. Rock, definitely. Country, maybe a little. Classic rock is probably my favorite," Libby admitted.

"Then I guess the real question comes down to the Beatles or the Stones," Seth said with a smile, as Candace came around to take their orders.

"How's your mama doing, Seth? I heard she was doing poorly a week or two back with the flu," Candace asked.

"She's better now and back to work already. I'll tell her you asked after her," Seth said. To Libby he added, "Candace's mom and mine are in the same book club."

"I love a good book club."

"You should join them sometime," Candace said. "They love having new people. You can get the information at the tea room or the library," she added, before heading back to get their drinks.

"So Beatles or Stones?" Seth asked. "And don't say both. Both is a cop-out."

"Agreed. Hmm . . . I know this is controversial, but I have to say The Beatles. I love the Stones. I mean, c'mon. *Paint It Black* or *Play with Fire?* Awesome songs. But I adore The Beatles. I have some of their records on vinyl. How about you?"

"I'm with you on that. Though I don't mind a little country from time to time either. Or jazz, blues, whatever. I like music," Seth could have rolled his eyes in exasperation. Never had he felt so unskilled at conversation. *I like music*. Well, hell, everyone likes music. Libby seemed sweet, and up close she was distracting. Her lips were painted a soft pink, and she'd done something sort of smoky with her eyes. It was damn distracting!

Candace gave them their coffee with a subtle wink and grin at Seth when Libby was turned away. He just smiled and prayed he'd get his conversational mojo back before this date crashed and burned.

Libby sat holding her coffee cup and looking at Seth. She didn't mind direct eye contact, and it gave her the opportunity to study his eyes close up. All that blue with a little tiny hint of gray. They were pale, and the dark lashes around them made them stand out. She thought she could easily trace her fingers around that jaw line. Or his mouth. Then she blushed and cursed herself for having such fair skin that she colored up at the drop of a hat. She prayed that he hadn't noticed and was glad he couldn't hear the direction of her thoughts.

She admired his dimples when he smiled and felt herself slowly relaxing in his company. She liked that he'd paid for the coffee and had done so as if it were natural and not in the showy way some men did. Her feminist hackles hadn't risen. It just seemed as though his mama had raised him to be courteous. She sipped her coffee and let the conversation flow. He was interesting to talk to, but she couldn't quite gauge his interest. Perhaps he was just being neighborly by offering to treat her to coffee and show her around town. He might not be interested in dating her, though she could have sworn he'd felt the spark that she did when they met. It seemed like there was attraction there, but she couldn't be sure. It had been a long time since she'd had to think about all that.

She took a deep breath and decided to go for the plunge. She didn't know exactly how to approach it so she decided to be straightforward. She waited for a natural break in the conversation. "I moved here because I really love this town. It's beautiful and historic, and I just felt like I was coming home. But I honestly needed a change. I filed for divorce a few months back. I'm expecting it to be finalized any day now."

"I'm sorry. That must be hard on you," Seth said kindly, grateful that she'd clarified her relationship status without his having to ask. Of course, a pending divorce could be considered a complication, but he didn't want to think about that.

"I'm fine now. Making the decision was tough, but actually filing was a relief. I've been happy here. I just wanted to be upfront about everything," Libby said carefully.

"About the fact that you're still married?" Seth asked evenly.

Libby grimaced, "Yes, that."

"But you've filed for divorce, right? He's not fighting it?" Seth asked, glad that he could clarify a few things without seeming nosy.

"No, not at all. He signed everything, and we agreed on the terms. The lawyers say it should be done in a month or two," Libby explained. She didn't want to admit it, but she'd be disappointed if this was a deal breaker for him. She was very attracted, and she liked talking to him.

"I'm sure that'll be a relief for you. If you're done with your coffee, do you want to walk around town? I can give you the nickel tour," Seth said with a smile.

Libby looked at him and felt her heart lift in pure relief. So the divorce wasn't going to be an obstacle. Good. "That sounds really great."

*****

Candace took a seat on a stool behind the counter and flipped through the messages on her phone. When there were no customers and everything behind the counter was caught up, Elle took a relaxed stance on what her employees did with their free time. Though she did have to tell one of the college girls that yoga was not exactly the sort of activity that could be done subtly in a spare moment. This conversation came after the girl had tried to go from downward facing dog into a headstand and had knocked over a few cups and some of the neatly stacked stock, causing chaos in the usually peaceful café. Candace usually played on her phone or read a book during her own breaks. Today she read through the increasingly whiny texts from Michael.

"When will u be home? Nothing to eat here."

"Are you still at work? Am bored."

"U have class tonight? Skip!!!"

Candace rolled her eyes at the thought that Michael still didn't know her class schedule and couldn't seem to feed himself in her absence. It was frustrating, and it added to the stress of her day. Would it hurt him to prepare a simple meal so that she could eat when she got home? After all, she was the one going to class and working all hours to support them. Michael mostly sat around talking on the phone and playing video games.

She saw Seth and his date get up and looked with surprise at the time. Only an hour had passed. Maybe it hadn't gone well, although their body language had suggested otherwise. Candace watched them leave and noticed that they were walking together. She sighed wistfully and realized he was probably giving her a tour of the town. The only tour Michael had ever offered to take her on was to his bedroom, and that was back when he'd shared a dump of an apartment with his roommate. She hadn't been impressed by the mattress on the floor or the pile of laundry, but he'd managed to successfully distract her. Now, of course, he slept on her bed, but still left his laundry in piles throughout the house. He didn't seem to think laundry was a chore that men did, so even though she worked full-time and went to school, she still did everything at home. It was like having a dog or a baby, only without the cuteness factor. He'd seemed moody and sexy when she'd met him, but now she just saw him as petulant and spoiled. She thought about online dating again and decided if Michael didn't get it together soon she was getting back out there.

*****

"It's a beautiful day," Seth began, and then kicked himself mentally for such an inane start.

"It seems like every day is a beautiful day here," Libby added agreeably. "Do you ever get used to it?"

"I guess a lot of us take it for granted, but I've never gotten tired of it. My sister Lindy did for a while. She took off for college, vowing to never come back, but she settled back here a few years ago. Seems she had a change of heart somewhere along the line and missed home," he explained.

"This is your sister that runs The Tipsy Canvas? Your mother mentioned her."

"That's the one. She's a character."

"Is it just the two of you?" Libby asked.

"It's always been my mama, Lindy, and me. My dad took off when we were just babies, and my mom started working with my grandfather in the shop. She might have wanted to have more kids, but we kept her pretty busy," Seth added ruefully. "Plus, she didn't really date much after my dad."

"You're kidding," Libby exclaimed. "Your mom is classically beautiful. I'm surprised she doesn't have every eligible bachelor beating down her door." Seth chuckled. "I'm not joking," she said. "I'm seriously considering being her when I grow up. She's lovely."

"I'll tell her you said so. She'll be flattered," Seth said with a grin. "You're not telling me anything I haven't heard a hundred times before from Dean. He's my best friend, and he's always joking about dating my mom. If he's not after flirting with my mom, it's my sister and every other woman who walks by the fire station."

"Wait. Is Dean the blonde firefighter in town?" Libby asked, curiously. "I think I met him."

"Ha! Well, if you only *think* you met him, I won't tell him. He'd be mortally wounded by any woman not specifically and in detail remembering an encounter with him. But just to be safe, maybe steer clear," he laughed.

"He seemed very nice, but he seems to have an odd love/hate relationship with his phone. He claimed it was telemarketers, but I'm guessing it wasn't." They shared a conspiratorial grin.

"Best friend code. On my honor, I can't tell," Seth added. "But I can show you some of my favorite houses. Most of them predate the Civil War. I'm sure you've heard the stories."

"I know that Madison is on the list of towns that weren't burned to the ground in the Civil War. I can't help but feel grateful for that. Do you have a favorite house here?" Libby asked.

"I'm biased. My mama owns one of them. She inherited it from her dad when he passed, but we grew up there after my dad skipped town. It's my favorite, but there are a lot that come in a close second."

Libby felt herself relaxing as they walked. She was happy that he hadn't asked about the tattoo or in any way reminded her of that first coffee date with Collin. This was different. She felt the chemistry and attraction, but she also was able to relax into the date and truly enjoy it. They had an easy rhythm to the conversation, and he seemed interested in what she had to say. She told him a little about where she lived before, sidestepping the details of her marriage, and she told him a little about her writing career and what she was doing now. He, in turn, told her about growing up around antiques—at home and in the store that had been his grandfather's and then his mother's and now his. They walked for over an hour before parting ways. Seth offered to walk her back to her car, but she explained that she had walked from home. He offered to walk her home, but she said that she was probably going to make a few stops downtown on her way. She agreed to stop into the antique store later in the week for a tour there.

Before she left, they hugged, and he asked if he could call her. She was sure that she was walking home with a smile glued to her face, but she couldn't help it. Everything seemed to have gone well, and it really did seem to be a date. She sighed happily, a spring in her step. Her phone beeped, signaling a text.

"Did you make it home okay?" It was from Seth.

"I'm turning on to my street now," she replied. She'd been told that using punctuation dated her when it came to texting, but she liked that he was equally comfortable with both full sentences and texting. She hated to say it, but she'd heard basic literacy was difficult to find these days.

"Would you like to have dinner tomorrow?" He replied. "It's okay if you're busy," he immediately added.

Libby grinned. She wasn't the only one who was nervous. "Dinner would be lovely. Time? Place?" she texted back with a wide smile, blushing again.

"Park Bistro? 7?" he asked.

"Perfect," she added a smile emoji. Admittedly, her emoji game was not strong, but she thought a smile was safe. "Looking forward to it," she added and then wondered if it was too much.

"Guess who has a date tomorrow?" she texted to Rose followed by an emoji with a girl raising her hand.

"OMG tell me everything!!!!!!" Came the immediate reply.

"Come over later?" she replied.

"On my way," Rose responded.

"I'm looking forward to it, too," Seth replied. Libby grinned and opened the door to her apartment, already evaluating her wardrobe choices for the following evening.

Chapter 16

Libby sat in Park Bistro sipping wine and listening to a story Seth was telling about the store. They were sitting outside on the terrace overlooking a garden and walking path. The weather was warm with a slight breeze. Her lips were quirked in a smile. She tried to decide what it was about him that attracted her so much. She studied his face, which was almost classically handsome, but she'd dated handsome men and hadn't had chemistry with all of them. She took in his bright blue eyes, which matched the button-up shirt he wore with gray slacks and the firm line of his jaw. He had generous lips and a wide smile that made crinkles at the corners of his eyes. He had managed a close enough shave that there was no trace of the five o'clock shadow she'd noticed before. There was something more here. She couldn't be imagining it. Maybe it was his manner, this confident cool attitude he projected. He was relaxed and friendly, and the conversation seemed to flow effortlessly. He even had the trace of a Southern drawl and the kind of Southern manners that seemed to have fallen out of fashion these days.

She noticed that he, in turn, was studying her as they talked, but she didn't feel like a bug under a microscope. It wasn't just the wine bringing a blush to her cheeks. It had been a long time since anyone had looked at her that way. Colin had stopped really seeing her months before. Libby reigned in her thoughts. She wasn't going to sit here with Seth and think of Colin. She wanted to enjoy the night. She'd never been to this restaurant, but she'd wanted to try it. It was arguably the nicest restaurant in town. It was upscale gourmet Southern cooking with a chef who, someone once told her, had been a guest on the cooking channel, although she couldn't remember which show they had referenced.

Park Bistro was certainly upscale, and the atmosphere was just as she had hoped. The interior had soft lighting with antique light fixtures overhead and fireplaces on either end of the dining room. The tables inside had candles lit and fresh flower bouquets as centerpieces. Outside, the tables had candles in hurricane lanterns to protect from the wind, and a profusion of greenery and flowers in pots and barrels around the balcony overlooking the garden. The front view of the restaurant looked out on the park downtown where the town held local festivals. Even in late September, the grass was still green, and the flowers around the community were still in bloom. They'd had a couple of unusually cool days during the month, but it was back to being balmy again.

She returned her full attention to Seth who was telling her about his grandfather who would hide a treasure chest of tin soldiers around the shop for Seth to find. He had taken his grandson aside and explained that, because antiques were fragile, he'd have to carefully look around the store with gentle hands. Apparently, Seth later figured out that it was a technique his grandfather used to get him to play quietly and carefully. Seth never let on that he knew because he always found other "treasures" while he was searching for the box. It's how he discovered the records and the old record player that they kept in the back, which still was in working order. It was also how Seth discovered a deep love for history and antiques.

"I can tell you love it," she commented when Seth finished his story. "I can hear it in your voice. Did you ever consider any other career?"

"I did once. I thought about being Indiana Jones for a minute, but my grandfather actually told me that real archaeologists don't carry a whip and probably wouldn't run roughshod through an ancient site. After that, I changed my mind. How about you? Did you always want to be a writer?"

"I didn't, at first. But I grew up watching *Where in the World is Carmen Sandiego*, and I had a subscription to *National Geographic*. My parents were a little bit avant-garde so we moved around a lot. I knew that I wanted to travel and see places, but I didn't realize that I'd want to write about them for a while. I started a blog in college and then I got an offer to write for a small travel page online. Now I blog and write for the paper, and I get an occasional local travel assignment. I enjoy it, but it really grew organically as a career."

Libby shrugged. It was a story that she told occasionally when people asked about how she'd become a writer with a wide array of more financially stable jobs available. But the real story was that she journaled a lot when she moved around, and she was a fan of letter writing. It's how she kept up with all the people she left behind. Writing had saved her sanity when her mother quit one job after another and her father became disenchanted with "the establishment" in any given town. When she realized she could make money off her hobby, she'd jumped at the chance. But she didn't typically tell that part of the story; particularly on what was only a second date. Yet she found herself telling him, without thinking about it or even meaning to. He leaned in and listened, interested in the real story behind her passion. Instead of feeling embarrassed that she'd told him, she felt relieved.

"I can understand that. The shop is, in a way, my grandfather. He went pretty far into debt opening it when he was young. He'd worked in it as a boy when it was nothing but a five and dime. When the owner retired, he bought him out and started the antique store. When my dad left, we moved in with my grandparents, and my mom learned to run the business. We were supposed to stay home with my grandmother, but she was sick a lot so we usually stayed in the store. Then I started working there when I was old enough. My grandfather died when I was a kid, and the store was his legacy. I took it over from my mom when she opened the tea room."

"It's nice that you had him as long as you did. My parents both left home as soon as they could and never looked back. My sisters and I used to have pretend grandparents," Libby explained with a half-smile.

"Pretend?"

"We traveled a lot, and when we met elderly people on the road, we would pretend that they were our grandparents. It filled a void," she said with a shrug." My parents still travel. They bought an RV."

"That must be interesting. Do your sisters travel much?" he asked.

"Faith works on a cruise ship. She's always had our parents' itchy feet. Rachel doesn't care to travel at all. She's been in Athens since college," Libby thought about how she and her sisters all responded so differently to their childhood. Libby liked to travel, but only if she had roots somewhere.

She itched to make notes for a blog on childhood attachment and resilience, but thought the second date was a little too soon to introduce Seth to that particular quirk of hers. Although she suspected, holding his steady gaze, that he wouldn't mind at all. She noticed that they were holding hands as they left the restaurant, and she couldn't quite remember how that had happened or who had initiated that contact. It just felt natural. He walked her across the street to the park where they sat on the porch swings that were hung from trellises around the edges of the green. They continued talking, each reluctant for the night to end.

The sky above was filled with stars, and Libby wasn't thinking about writing or Colin or anything else. She was wrapped up in this moment with Seth and an open sky. When he leaned forward to kiss her, she met him halfway. When he deepened the kiss, she wrapped her hands around his neck, running one hand through his thick, dark hair. She could feel his warm hand resting on the side of her face and the other pulling her in at the waist. Time stopped, slowed, and then began again.

When Seth walked her to her car, he kissed her again but just once, and softly. She promised to text him when she made it home safely, and he promised to call her tomorrow before work. She slid into her car, and he shut the door firmly. He watched her drive off before moving to his own car. He could have walked, of course. He lived close enough, but the sidewalks weren't the easiest to traverse at night. Plus, he felt intoxicated—not by the wine—but by Libby herself. He wanted to go home and sleep so that morning would come and he could talk to her again.

He liked that she had told him the real story behind her writing and that he'd been able to tell her something real about himself. His recent dates hadn't been so open. They had preferred to tell him their laundry list of skills and qualifications as a potential mate. He always felt like they were conducting job interviews across both sides of the table, but instead of a job, both people were screening for compatibility for a spouse. It had made dating seem awkward and a waste of time. He was always relieved when a date ended, but tonight he had wanted to make it last longer.

He got into his car and drove home. Before he'd pulled into the driveway, he'd had a text from Libby letting him know she was home and thanking him for a lovely night. He grinned at his phone, checking the message once he parked and got out of the car. He knew that Dean would advise him not to reply immediately and to play it cool, but he also knew that Dean's trouble with women was mostly because he pulled stunts like that to play hard to get. He didn't want to play games with Libby. He did, however, want to see her again, and soon. He thought about sending her flowers and wondered if that was a cliché. And was it a cliché because it worked, or was it the kind of cliché that would make her think less of him? Dating was becoming increasingly more difficult to navigate, although this date with Libby had seemed straight-forward.

He could ask Lindy, but then he'd have to have a conversation with her about dating, which he did not want to do. She'd use it against him and tease him mercilessly. He didn't even consider asking Dean. He wasn't looking for the kind of casual situation that Dean always had. He wanted something a little more serious than that. He'd ask Beth, but she would immediately tell his mom, and that would be too embarrassing. He decided to talk to Jamie in the morning. Jamie didn't seem like the ideal person to ask with his shaved head and brawny body and endless tattoos, but he seemed to go from one long-term relationship to the next with ease. He'd even managed to maintain friendships with many of his exes once they parted ways. A lot of people made assumptions about Jamie, but he was well spoken and highly educated. He was invaluable around the shop, and he wouldn't make Seth feel awkward about it. And even though Jamie spent a lot of time with Beth, he knew that he would be discreet.

Seth went inside the house and texted Libby again to say good night. He knew that also went against the Dean playbook, unless, of course, he was trying to get a woman to think about him before she fell asleep. Dean had no problem sending texts out at all hours of the night, and most of the women he dated liked it. Seth knew Libby was working in the morning and didn't want to keep her up all night on the phone and so he sent the one good night message and smiled when she immediately responded with one of her own. He shook his head. He didn't know why Dean thought this whole thing had to be so complicated. He'd tell him so over lunch tomorrow.

Chapter 17

Libby went into the office early on Monday. She'd woken up before her alarm went off and decided to walk to work again. She checked her phone a couple of times to see if Seth had texted yet. Okay, it was more like five or six times, but Libby reminded herself that she'd told him she usually wasn't up before nine. She gave him points for courtesy, while impatiently checking her phone again. At that point, she decided to stop behaving like a crazy person and go to work. Libby made it into the office at the same time Jenna pulled up, and they both beat Josie to the coffee machine.

"How was the date?" Jenna asked, adding whipped cream to a perfectly brewed cup of coffee.

"Which one? Saturday's coffee date or Sunday's dinner?" Libby asked with a grin.

"Wait. What? Did Seth take you out twice, or did you have two dates this weekend?" Jenna asked curiously.

"Who had two dates this weekend?" Gloria asked as she came out of her office. "I smell good coffee. Outta my way!" She poured a cup and then gestured at them to continue. "Libby, did you have two dates this weekend?"

"Yes, and they were both with Seth," Her phone dinged. "Sorry, I'll just turn that off."

"Did he just text you?" Jenna asked.

"Well, yeah. He said he would," Libby replied, a blush creeping up her face. Jenna and Gloria exchanged looks.

"He said he would, and he did. Points to him," Gloria added.

"Not the point system," Libby groaned, and then she mentally kicked herself for thinking the same thing earlier when he didn't call too early.

"So tell us all about coffee and dinner," Jenna said, pulling up a chair and making herself comfortable.

"Do we need the conference room for this?" Gloria asked, snagging a chair in the break room and sitting attentively in front of Libby who was pouring her coffee. "We can use the conference room if the details are going to take a while."

"You are both being ridiculous," Libby said with a laugh. "I think I can keep it simple. We had coffee and a tour of the town. He was very sweet, and then he asked me out for dinner on Sunday. It was great. The End."

"Not *The End*," Gloria said with a wave of her hand. "I have questions. Two, to be exact."

"Okay, let's hear them. And I reserve the right not to answer any of them," Libby said with a grin, taking a seat and gesturing for her to continue.

"One: did he pay for coffee and dinner? Two: did he ask you out again?"

"I have a third!" Jenna volunteered. "Did he kiss you?"

"And did you sleep with him, either or both nights?" Gloria added.

"Okay, I think that was five questions," Libby laughed. "Yes, he paid. No, he didn't ask me out again. I'm just going to plead the fifth here, and no on either night," she sipped her coffee with a smile.

"Hmm . . . he definitely kissed her," Gloria said to Jenna.

"Agreed. But he didn't ask her out again," Jenna said.

"But he did text her this morning so that's a plus," Gloria countered.

"Do I even need to be here for this?" Libby asked.

"But you like him, right?" Jenna asked.

"And did you take a vow of celibacy I don't know about?" Gloria grinned.

"Okay, I think we've concluded the question and answer portion of our impromptu meeting. I've got a field assignment to do, so I'm just going to take this to go." Libby poured her coffee into a travel mug she kept at the office. "I'll see you guys later."

Gloria and Jenna watched their co-worker hightail it out of the office, saying a quick hello to Josie and the other staff on the way to the door. They each took a long sip of coffee. Then Jenna spoke, "She definitely likes him."

"Oh, absolutely. Did you see how fast she ran out of here?" Gloria chuckled. "Alright, well, no rest for the wicked. I'm going to make a few calls on a totally unrelated matter, and you let me know if you get details first."

"I'm on it," Jenna joked.

*****

Libby left the office quickly and headed downtown. She was supposed to stop by the Chamber of Commerce for an updated calendar of events. Her cheeks were still burning from the conversation. It had been a long time since she'd been in this situation. Her last actual crush was Colin, whom she married. It had been years since she'd even experienced butterflies for any other reason than anxiety. She definitely had them now, though, and she felt somehow too old for all this. Sure, thirty-one is far from ancient, Libby thought, but it's old enough to know better. She tried not to think about the end with Colin. That wasn't fair to Seth. But the whole thing did make her nervous.

As she walking to the Chamber, she saw Seth and his firefighter friend come out of Brews with coffee. She might have quickly crossed the street and avoided the whole awkward encounter, but he saw her and waved. She walked toward him and saw his wide smile and felt her own light up her face. So—maybe not embarrassing after all.

"Hey, Libby," he said when she approached. He gave her a quick hug. "You look amazing." She looked down at the simple A-line dress she wore with a floral print, and smiled.

"Thank you. It's good to see you." She looked up at him shyly, noticing his button-up plaid shirt, jeans, and boots. He was a little more casual than she'd seen him over the weekend, and she guessed he wasn't working in the store that day.

"I'm about to head out to some estate sales, but I had to grab coffee first." At the sound of a throat clearing, Seth started and then grinned, "Sorry. Libby, this is Dean. Dean, this is Libby."

"Ah, we've sort of met. I'm pretty sure I saw her first, Seth," Dean said with a charming smile, reaching out a hand to shake Libby's.

"It's nice to meet you, Dean. Seth has told me a lot about you," Libby said, returning his smile.

"Don't believe everything you hear now," Dean warned with a laugh.

"I told her that we grew up together and used to get in trouble around town. That's it," Seth said.

"Well, that's alright then. Where are you off to this morning?" Dean asked gallantly.

"I'm heading over to the Chamber of Commerce," Libby told him.

"And do you need an escort—"

Seth elbowed him aside. "No, she does not need an escort. Have a good day at work, Dean," Seth said, giving his friend a good-natured shove toward the fire station. "Bye now."

"I'm going," Dean conceded. "I'll see you at lunch, Seth. Nice to meet you, Libby." He strutted off with his coffee, and Libby turned to Seth.

"Maybe I did need an escort," Libby said with a grin.

"I'm happy to oblige. But that one is a charmer, and I'm not going to take any chances," Seth replied with a grin of his own.

"I could see that," Libby looked at him, amused. "You really don't have to walk me there. It's only across the street, and I know you have estate sales to get to."

"They'll keep, and I'd really like to walk with you," Seth said earnestly. "If that's okay with you," he added.

"It's great. I just didn't want to inconvenience you."

"That's very sweet, but I'm fine. How's your coffee?"

"It's good. Yours might be better though," she said, eyeing his mug. Seth offered it to her, and she took a sip. He took a sip from hers, his eyes on hers the whole time.

"Yours isn't bad," Seth offered.

"Yours is better," Libby concluded. "Thank you for walking with me—and for sharing." She said, as they approached the Chamber.

"I would kiss you, but that would probably be unprofessional," Seth said. "Could I offer you dinner tomorrow instead?"

"Oh, I'm sorry. I can't. Standing engagement," At his crestfallen expression, she added, "Taco Tuesday. It's kind of a thing with my friends. I'd invite you, but it's kind of our ladies' night," she explained.

"How about lunch on Wednesday?" he countered. "We could go on a picnic."

"You had me at lunch, but a picnic lunch? That sounds perfect! I'll see you later?"

"Definitely. Have a good day!"

"You, too." She walked into the Chamber and tried to ignore the look of interest on Fiona's face. Fiona worked the front desk when she wasn't busy handling visitors, and she had clearly seen the exchange on the sidewalk. Libby switched into business mode to avoid any awkward questions. "Hey, Fiona. I hear you have an updated schedule for me—and tell me the rumors are true about the concert series."

Chapter 18

As Libby neared the restaurant, she noticed Rose waiting in her car looking lost in thought. Jenna was just walking in when she saw Rose sit up and take notice, grab her handbag, and slide out of the car. She walked up behind her friend, just in time to hear her heavy sigh.

"Bad day?"

"You could say that," Rose said with a laugh, giving Libby a hug. "Is Rachel coming?"

"No. Alec couldn't manage two weeks in a row. I'm sure Rachel's giving him hell about missing it, so I'm sure we'll see her next week," Libby added with a grimace. "It's ridiculous that he's incapable of handling his own kids for a couple hours. He even called it *babysitting*."

"That's a new low," Rose shook her head. Lately, Alec had been rating pretty high up on their disapproval list. They all discussed it, Rachel included, and tried to think of ways to get him to pull his weight more often at home. So far, none of their ideas had worked, but Rachel insisted that she wasn't giving up on him yet.

"Was that Jenna who just went in?" Libby asked.

"I think so. Let's go see what kind of margaritas we're having tonight," Rose said in anticipation.

Libby laughed. "Please be mango. Please be mango."

"And mango it is," Jenna said, overhearing their conversation. "I'm glad you guys could make it. Hey, Rose. How was the meeting? How's Dillon?"

"The meeting was canceled. Dillon's good. Still casual. No further news to report," Rose said, carefully shifting the conversation away from her own relationship. Libby could tell she wasn't yet ready to disclose more, which made her wonder if it was more serious than

Rose let on. "The real question is, how is Seth?" She turned a sly look to Libby who wished she could orchestrate a similar distraction to take the pressure off. Still, she had to admit it was nice to have something to talk about other than Colin, the divorce, and work.

"Seth is good. Great actually," Libby launched into the story of the coffee date and walk, the dinner date, and running into him over coffee the prior morning. Texts and phone calls had been exchanged, and they had a picnic lunch scheduled for the next day. Jenna and Rose provided the appropriate reactions throughout the story and then sat back, both sighing wistfully.

"Now that's a good story," Jenna said, taking a drink of her margarita. "I'm going to reserve full judgment, but I'm willing to give a temporary seal of approval. I'd like to meet him though."

"It's too soon, but if this thing keeps going, I'm sure that will happen eventually," Libby said, thoughtfully. "I mean, I don't know if it will keep going. We haven't really talked about if it's a long-term thing or what he's even looking for."

"I told you that you have to ask that on the first date!" Rose exclaimed. "Any time after that, and it just comes across as pressure."

"Hey, that's good advice," Jenna confirmed.

"I just forgot. It felt so awkward to ask," Libby admitted. "I didn't bring it up, and now I don't think I can. I feel like I'm just having to wait for him to tell me, which is completely silly. I should just ask."

"It might be awkward now," Rose said.

"Well, did you have that conversation with Dillon? How did he handle it?" Libby asked.

Rose paused for a minute, thinking. "Yeah, we had that talk. I was very upfront about the fact that my workload is crazy, and I just want something casual right now. I don't think I have time for anything else, and I honestly don't know that I could handle the stress."

"Are you both seeing other people?" Jenna asked, curious as to how it worked.

"I don't have time right now, but if I met someone I liked, I might. I don't know if Dillon is or isn't. It's a good possibility because I'm busy a lot during the week. But it wouldn't be an issue because we're not exclusive." Libby noted Rose's casual, confident tone, but she wasn't buying it. After all, if it was as casual as she said, she'd have given a lot more details, Libby thought to herself. There was definitely something rotten in Denmark, but Libby allowed her friend the privacy she'd been granted when she was struggling through her divorce. If Rose wanted to talk about it, she would.

"Okay, we want details about this picnic tomorrow," Jenna said. "Lots of details."

"Fine," Libby replied in an exasperated tone. "I feel like the town crier."

"You know we're just living vicariously through your romance, right? With a houseful of kids, the romance with Finn isn't quite what it once was," Jenna said with a laugh. "I need to hear more about this Seth. Go on: exactly how blue were his eyes?"

"Okay, now you're making fun of me," Libby said, a tell-tale blush staining her cheeks. "I will keep you apprised of further developments. It is romantic though, isn't it? Did I tell you he sent me flowers at work?" Jenna let out a sigh because she'd been there when the delivery came in, but Rose's mouth dropped open.

"He did not! Seriously? Where and when?"

"He sent them to work this morning. It was a small bouquet of daisies from that florist in town. They had a delivery man walk them over," Libby said, a smile lighting her face.

"That wasn't a delivery man, per se. That was one of the owners. Gene, I think. I don't know them very well. Gene and Gerald, his partner, have owned The Secret Garden for something like twenty years now. It's pretty spectacular in there. They even have a little hidden garden terrace in the back where they serve tea to guests," Jenna told them.

"I bet it is beautiful," Libby said. "My daisies are wrapped in burlap with some kind of greenery mixed in the bouquet. It's really lovely."

"What did the card say? There was a card, right?" Rose asked.

"It said, 'Looking forward to our picnic—Seth.'"

"Hmm . . . short and sweet, I guess?" Rose said, skeptically.

"I think it's romantic," Jenna sighed. "And if he'd put something really flowery, you know we'd all be saying it was too smooth or too practiced or just too much. Like what's-his-face that sent you all those roses, Rose," Jenna said.

"Oh, I'd forgotten about him. What was his name? Pete!" Rose snorted out a laugh. "Who could forget that name? Rachel kept calling him Pete the Rat."

"Well, he did send you something like three dozen roses the first week," Libby said.

"Between the cliché of sending roses to someone named Rose and the fact that he only called you at certain hours of the day, there were clear red flags in play," Jenna added.

"I wonder whatever happened to Pete the Rat," Libby wondered aloud, pouring them all another round of margaritas.

"I'm sure he went home to his wife and six kids or whatever he was hiding," Rose said with a roll of her eyes.

"I don't know. I still say he was probably on America's Most Wanted. He sure did try to keep a low profile other than the profusion of roses," Jenna said with a chuckle.

"And red roses, too. Such a cliché!" Rose exclaimed. "Like no one's ever thought of that before." All the women rolled their eyes.

"Well, hopefully, Dillon's not shady like that. I know you said it's casual, but you haven't even mentioned what he does for a living. Or where you met him. Or any details at all for that matter," Libby said, looking at Rose in curiosity. "Just give us a little something."

"Well, I confirmed relationship status. I always ask that upfront," Rose paused. "Okay, I can give you a couple of details. Dillon is a lawyer, and we met at a gallery opening. At the open bar," Rose said, raising her margarita.

"Ooooh. Did you have bar banter? Like did he order a whiskey straight and you ordered yours on the rocks?" Jenna asked.

"What the actual hell is bar banter?" Rose asked. "Is that a real thing?"

"I don't know. I've been married *forever*," Jenna said with a grin. She looked at Libby.

"Don't ask me. I've only been divorced two minutes. Well, God, not even divorced yet. Any day now though," Libby added, sobered by the thought that her divorce wasn't even final.

"And when it comes through, we'll pop the champagne. Or throw you a party maybe," Rose said gently, rubbing Libby's arm.

"Sorry, sorry!" Libby said with a shake of her head. "I'm bringing down the mood."

"No, it's okay if you need to talk about it. You really should let it all out," Rose said, her face showing relief that the topic was once again shifting off her own relationship and back to Libby.

"No, I'm okay. I just hate that I'm really into Seth, and this thing with Colin isn't even over yet," Libby said with a sigh.

"Wait—you haven't been hearing from Colin, have you?" Jenna asked, confused.

"No, I don't mean like that. I just want it all finalized. I want to know that the Colin chapter is completely closed. It feels . . . strange to be dating but technically married still," Libby admitted.

"Technically married, but you are legally separated," Rose said.

"I know. It still feels weird. All of it feels weird. But it's also . . ." Libby paused, searching for the words. "Kind of magic. I don't know. It's all kind of romantic, and my butterflies have butterflies when I'm with Seth. Maybe it's not anything, but just to have the possibility again of something . . ." she trailed off. "I guess it's something I didn't really prepare for. I didn't think I could feel like this again, and it's a little scary. Wonderful. But scary."

"No, I get it," Jenna said. "Sometimes when Finn is snoring, I just look at him and wonder where we went, you know? I miss the Finn who used to sing to me going down the road or whisk me off for some kind of romantic weekend. And I know that we still love each other, but I can imagine if we didn't have that and we just had the routine—well, it would help to have the hope of possibilities." They all sighed.

After a pause, Rose spoke up. "Look, I know I've been keeping this whole thing with Dillon to myself. Maybe we can open up a significant other night one Taco Tuesday. Just as a one-time thing. I don't want to lose our nights to ourselves for good."

"Hey, that's not a bad idea. Especially if Libby can bring Seth," Jenna added. "Finn would probably enjoy a night out of the house. I don't know if we can count Alec in or not, though."

"Can we wait a couple of weeks for Seth? I'm not even sure we'll be dating that long. Plus, it would give us a little more time," Libby added.

"Hey, that works for me," Rose said easily.

Libby sipped her margarita and wondered what her friends would think of Seth. Of course, she thought to herself, there was no guarantee that this all wouldn't fizzle out by then. She just had the feeling that it was only getting started, but she had to admit her gauge had been way off since Colin.

"Okay, so who's drinking Rachel's share of the margaritas?" Libby asked, dispelling her own thoughtful mood with a lighter note. Then they all laughed as they had all raised their hands. "Okay, drink up. Then we need to order something else to eat or none of us will get home before morning."

Chapter 19

In the park at the center of town, just left of Main Street, Seth was sitting down on the blanket with Libby. He'd almost opted for a tie, but he'd chosen instead navy slacks with a button-up shirt. He'd rolled up his sleeves as the day grew warm. He admired Libby's yellow dress with the tiniest of white polka dots and her matching sunny shoes. With her hair back in a braid, she looked as carefree as he felt today. She'd laughed when she'd seen the picnic, a trill of sound that went straight to his heart.

"When you said picnic, you meant it," Libby smiled widely. "You have a picnic basket and everything!"

"Too much?" Seth asked with a grin.

"No, it's absolutely perfect," she said, taking a seat on the blanket and carefully removing her shoes. She tucked her feet under her dress and waited as Seth joined her.

"I borrowed the basket from the shop, and maybe I didn't actually make the food myself, but I selected it. Does that still count?" Seth asked, sheepishly. He pulled out a couple of healthy turkey sandwiches on ciabatta bread, a container of pasta salad, a platter of mixed fruit and cheeses, and a small box of chocolates. He also brought out a couple of sodas and sparkling water. "I wasn't sure what you'd like, so I got a selection. I know we both have to go back to work. Otherwise, I'd have brought wine."

"You've thought of everything, haven't you?" Libby asked with a grin.

She felt perfectly happy, which she hadn't felt for a long time. Not really. She'd nursed so much grief under everything else. It had been a long time since she just felt content. Of course, it was hard not to be content on a beautiful day with a picnic with a gorgeous man who also brought chocolate. She leaned forward and held her hand to his face for just a moment.

"Thank you, Seth. This is perfect." He smiled back at her, placing his hand over hers and then moving it to place a kiss in her palm. When she pulled her hand away, she curled it around the kiss, holding it. Libby wondered if it was wise to feel this much this soon. But then she didn't allow herself to continue along that line of thinking on a day so lovely. Instead, she reached for her glass and met his eyes with a smile.

Seth marveled that what had started as a casual interest had become something more. He wondered if it was too soon to talk about it. He certainly wasn't going to bring it up on this day, during a picnic that had far exceeded his expectations. He couldn't remember ever going to this trouble for a date. Well, not since Marnie back in his school days. Charlotte was more of a dining-in person than one for al fresco. And she wouldn't have been impressed by sandwiches from the local café or pasta from the tea room or even the chocolates that were handmade just down the street. He knew that Libby would appreciate this picnic for what it was: a sampling of and a welcome to Madison.

After the picnic, Seth folded up the blanket, and Libby slipped back into her shoes—the yellow ones she loved, with elaborate buttons and a peep toe. She had painted her nails especially to wear these shoes, even though her toes would barely show at all. While Seth folded the blanket, Libby picked up the picnic basket and insisted on carrying it. They walked together back toward the antique shop, hand-in-hand. When they reached the door, they both hesitated.

"Thank you for the beautiful picnic," Libby told him with a wide smile.

"Thank you for going with me," he returned with a smile of his own. Jamie walked around them carrying a large vase, and neither noticed his simultaneous grin and eye roll as he carefully navigated the door to the shop with some difficulty.

"Here's your picnic basket," Libby said, handing it to him.

"No, that's for you," Seth said quickly, giving it back. "If you want it anyway," he said with a grin. "If you don't, I can always put it in the shop," he said, reaching for it awkwardly.

"No, it's mine," she told him with a smile. "That's really sweet." She had admired it throughout their lunch. "Thank you." They both stood there a minute or two more, each reluctant to go their separate ways. "I should head home and get back to work," Libby said reluctantly.

"Of course. Do you want me to walk you home?" Seth asked, eager to draw out the time. "Or I can give you a ride if you like?" he added.

"No, thank you. You get back to work. Besides, it's a beautiful day for a walk." He stepped forward and gave her a hug, although she knew that they both would have preferred a different conclusion to their lunch. Still, he was heading to work, and she didn't want to make a spectacle of herself in town. He promised to call her later, and she began walking home. She turned once, and he was still watching her. She waved once and grinned as he nearly collided with Jamie coming out of the shop.

Libby returned home with a spring in her step. On the outside, she was walking happily along, but on the inside, she was singing, *Fly me to the moon. Let me play among the stars. Let me see what spring is like on Jupiter and Mars* . . . She wasn't sure why Frank Sinatra was the soundtrack in her head, but it seemed to suit this lovely day even if it was autumn and not spring. She knew that her feelings for Seth had turned into something other than casual interest. They talked in the morning while they were having coffee, and during the day, they checked in with each other. One of them usually followed up with a phone call after work. Libby hadn't been out of the dating game so long that she'd forgotten what a budding relationship looked like.

Of course, the final divorce decree still hadn't come in, which gave her pause. She didn't want to start a new relationship with the old one still left unfinished. In fact, she'd had no intention of starting a new relationship at all. She hadn't even dealt with her feelings about Colin. The end had been so swift and so final that she'd only been propelled forward into an uncertain future. She hadn't intended to meet someone like Seth so soon. She hadn't imagined that there was anyone else out there for her, not in the way she'd once imagined with Colin. But this thing with Seth was certainly not casual. She didn't think it was a rebound either, although she did curse the timing of it a little. She'd wanted more time to herself, and yet she couldn't deny her attraction to and interest in Seth. Couldn't deny it—and didn't want to.

Libby smiled as she found a place in her apartment for the picnic basket that Seth had given her after the date. Her phone rang, as she was settling it into place. She answered with a distracted hello, expecting telemarketers, and smiled widely when she heard Beth on the other end of the line. They'd only met once at the tea room, but she was a little hard to forget.

"Hey, this is Beth, from Utopia?" she said. "I was wondering if you'd be interested in coming with me to paint night at The Tipsy Canvas on Friday."

"I would love that," Libby exclaimed, pleased to be included. Other than Jenna and Gloria from work, she hadn't made as many friends in the area as she'd have liked. "Thank you for thinking of me," she added, a smile in her voice.

"Of course. Besides, rumor has it that you've seen Seth a few times, and you can come check out his sister. She's a character!" Beth said with a laugh.

"I guess it is a small town," Libby said ruefully. She had to admit that she was curious about this family. As she jotted down the details, she wondered what Beth considered a character. After all, one could say that she was, too.

"Well, mostly people mean well," Beth explained. "But I'd invite you even if you hadn't been out with my cousin. Oh, and I can talk to you about our book club while you're here. You're going to love next month's pick," she enthused. Libby wondered in amusement if Beth always talked in exclamations, or if she was just excited.

"Oh, I would love that," Libby told her. "And the paint night, too. Should I wear anything special? Or bring anything?"

"Just bring yourself. Do you want me to pick you up, or do you want to meet there?" Beth asked.

"Oh, I usually just walk everywhere. What time does it start?" As Libby jotted down the details, she smiled to herself at the growing number of engagements on what was once a pretty bare social calendar. After the phone call, she sat down at her desk to work, feeling like everything was finally falling into place.

Chapter 20

Friday night seemed to arrive quicker than Libby expected. She'd told Seth that she was meeting his cousin, at her invitation, at the painting studio, and laughed when he'd apologized in advance for his family and anything they might say or do to embarrass him. He seemed to take it with good humor though. When she arrived at The Tipsy Canvas, Beth was waiting outside with a canvas bag and a happy smile. She was wearing a retro polka dot house dress in light pink with a cinched and belted waist and kitten heels in white.

"I brought wine!" Beth crowed triumphantly. "Okay, if I'm honest, Aunt Keely sent it. She wanted us to welcome you properly to town. If this runs too late, you can ride home with me or Lindy. My friend Jamie's my DD if I need one."

"How much wine did you bring?" Libby asked.

"Two bottles. That should get us through class. What do you have there?" she asked, noticing that Libby was carrying one of the gift bags from Sugar & Spice.

"Oh, this. I read online that we can bring snacks to class and so I brought some chocolates to share and a few of the praline pecans in case you hate chocolate," Libby told her.

"No one hates chocolate!" Beth declared. "I see 'this is the beginning of a beautiful friendship,'" she quoted happily.

"I love a good Casablanca quote," Libby said in delight.

"You know Casablanca?" Beth asked. "Oh, we are so having a movie night," Beth declared happily. "It's one of my favorites! I mean, just the quotes alone are enough for me."

"'Of all the gin joints in all the towns in all the world . . .'" Libby began with a grin.

"'She walks into mine,'" Beth finished. "'We'll always have Paris.'"

"'Here's lookin' at you, kid,'" Libby replied, enjoying the banter with a kindred spirit. "It's nice to know someone else still loves classic film," Beth added happily. "I'm glad you're here. If Seth will stop monopolizing your time, we'll plan that movie night."

"I'm sure we can work something out," Libby said, a blush surging to her cheeks. She and Seth had seen each other nearly every day since their coffee date, and it had not gone unnoticed by his cousin. She wondered if meeting his sister would be awkward. Then Lindy swept in, and Libby forgot about feeling awkward.

Lindy was tall, statuesque like her mother, and yet somehow completely different. She wore a pleated black skirt with a black Beatles T-shirt and tasseled black earrings. She wore ballet flats in a steely gray. She had hair as thick as her brother's, and Libby could see a faint resemblance. She marveled at Lindy's ease and confidence as she led the class through a simple painting of a tree in full autumn color. It was lovely, but Libby wasn't sure that she was going to be able to do it as well as the example Lindy had painted and displayed before the class.

She sighed and then grinned when she noticed Beth opening the first bottle of wine. "I think we could use some fortification. I'm no artist, but luckily for us, Lindy's a great teacher. I'll introduce you in a minute," Beth added, waving Lindy over.

"Oh, I don't want to bother her," Libby began.

"You're not going to get out of meeting Seth's sister. Don't be nervous," Beth said with a grin as Lindy walked toward them.

"You must be the one taking all my baby brother's attention lately," Lindy began without preamble.

"Lindy, this is Libby. Libby, Lindy. Geez—that's a tongue twister," Beth said with a short laugh. "Libby kindly agreed to give Seth a night off and come out with us."

"I guess we've been seeing a lot of each other lately. It's nice to meet you, Lindy. I met your mother last week at the tea room. She's very sweet," Libby told her honestly.

"She certainly can be. It doesn't look like you had much choice about meeting us all. Beth here would have maneuvered a meeting one way or the other, and I can admit I've been curious," Lindy said, taking a seat in the empty chair beside Beth and looking critically at her canvas. "Did you use any of the colors I suggested?" she asked Beth incredulously. "Have you ever seen a purple tree in autumn?"

"You said we could get creative with it. I'm getting creative," Beth added with a grin.

"You're getting something, I guess. Look, Libby used normal fall colors. A little russet, a little gold—"

"Does that make me boring, do you think?" Libby asked, eyeing her work critically.

"Not boring, no. Traditional. And maybe more normal than this one here," Lindy said with a laugh, nudging Beth playfully. "I've yet to teach a class where Beth paid the slightest attention to my suggestion, and yet whatever she comes up with isn't actually garbage."

"That's high praise from this one," Beth laughed.

"I'm just saying that you would think her work would be unrecognizable from the rest of the class, but it always works," Lindy said with a shake of her head. "Now tell me all the pertinent details about you. Well, not all. I do have to lead this class. Maybe start with five. Go."

"Um . . ." Libby began, casting a confused look at Beth who grinned and shrugged as if to say, what can you do? "I'm a writer. I have two sisters. I moved to Madison eight months ago. I like to run," she paused, thinking. "I have a collection of radio shows on vinyl. Is that too random?"

"No, it's a good start. Have you ever been married?" Lindy asked.

"Yes," Libby said, holding the eye contact.

"Divorced?" Lindy asked directly.

"Any day now. Just waiting for the final decree," Libby said evenly.

"Seth know?" Lindy asked sharply.

"Yes," Libby answered evenly. "I was upfront about it."

"Hmm. Kids?" Lindy asked.

"No," Libby said quietly, trying to quell the disappointment she always felt when she thought of their efforts to have a child. "It's just me."

Lindy paused, recognizing some of her own sadness about kids in Libby's soft reply. She let it go and moved on. "Ever cheat?"

"No," Libby answered, trying to contain her exasperation. She nearly rolled her eyes but held herself in check. "Anything else you need to know?"

"Right now? Nope, I think we're good," Lindy said, striding away to give the class a few tips on the next stage of the painting.

"She really likes you," Beth added helpfully.

"How can you tell?" Libby asked skeptically.

"I just can. Don't worry if she seems abrupt. That's just her way," Beth added. "She's a real sweetheart, but she's got strong opinions."

"Well, I can't hold that against her. I've heard the same about myself," Libby said, remembering how Colin would call her stubborn and bullheaded. She was happy that she hadn't thought of Colin today, at least not until Lindy had asked about her marital status. She knew that one was tricky, but Lindy seemed to be reserving judgment for now.

Libby followed directions carefully during the class. She and Beth shared the wine and chocolates, and even Lindy darted by to snag a praline pecan with a grin of thanks. Lindy reviewed her work a few times with a suggestion here and there, but no more mention of Seth. Libby wondered if she'd passed whatever test this was, but she couldn't tell. At the end of the class though, Lindy approached her with a smile, "Why don't I give you a ride home? I noticed you and Beth polished off most of the two bottles, and I wouldn't feel right about you walking home by yourself in the dark."

"Oh, that's nice of you, but I'll be fine," Libby began.

"Nonsense. I hear you're just up the street, and if I don't see you safely home, I have a baby brother to answer to. He may be younger than me, but he's also bigger," she said with a grin.

"In that case, thank you for the kind offer. I appreciate it," Libby said. She climbed into Lindy's car, a beat-up Jeep that looked like it had seen better days.

"This is Francis," Lindy said, patting the Jeep lovingly as she got in. "I've had her since college."

"Francis?" Libby asked curiously.

"I named her for Baby in *Dirty Dancing*," Lindy said with a grin. "I always liked that movie, and this Jeep is my baby."

"Hello, Francis," Libby said, patting the door of the Jeep with a slow grin. "You're not what I thought you'd be," she said, then immediately regretted the third—or was it fourth—glass of wine that had loosened up her tongue.

"No? What did you think I'd be like?" Lindy asked curiously.

"I don't know. Maybe elegant and reserved like your mother or confident and quick-witted like your brother. You're something else entirely. Like quirky and moody and probably brilliant," Libby said, cursing again her own loose lips. She should be quiet, she told herself. At least get through this one short ride without saying anything embarrassing.

Lindy laughed, "I love how you see us. I get it with my mom. She's lovely. But my brother as quick-witted? That's a stretch," she snorted. "You must really like him."

"We have this banter thing going. By text, when we talk. I can drop a topic, and he'll pick it up. It's fun and kind of adorable," Libby said, grinning.

"I think you're probably fun and kind of adorable," Lindy said with a grin, wondering just how many times Beth refilled Libby's wine glass when she wasn't looking.

"Hmm . . . Colin used to say I'm too serious," Libby added, forgetting her promise to herself to be silent the rest of the drive. They pulled up at her house.

"Well, Colin sounds like a real ass," Lindy told her, making a mental note to find out all about this Colin. He was probably the husband she was divorcing. Or who was divorcing her. That sort of detail mattered, and she'd find out. "Seth thinks you're great, obviously," Lindy added.

"Hmm," Libby smiled. "Is Lindy short for anything? Like Lindsay?" Libby asked.

"No. It's just Lindy. My mom had a good friend named Lindy, and

I'm named after her. Is Libby short for something? Elisabeth maybe?" she asked.

"It's short for Liberty," Libby said with a grin. "We all have names like that. There's me and Rachel and Faith."

"Rachel? How does that fit in?" Lindy asked, curious now. She'd have to tell Seth that apparently, two bottles of wine would work to get Libby talking.

"Oh, her first name isn't Rachel. It's Destiny Rachel, but she switched to Rachel in college," Libby explained. "Thank you for the ride home." She climbed out of the Jeep slowly and added a "Good night, Francis" that made Lindy nearly snort with laughter.

She noticed that Libby wasn't exactly drunk. She was just a little on this side of tipsy.

"Stop by tomorrow, and your painting will be dry," Lindy reminded her.

"I'll do that. It was nice to meet you, Lindy," Libby said with a smile as she opened up the door and went inside.

*****

Lindy sat in the driveway for a minute. Interesting, she thought. She'd been prepared not to like Libby or to at least have some pretty strong reservations. She didn't much like that her divorce wasn't yet finalized. She didn't want her using Seth as some sort of rebound when he might be forming actual feelings for her. She also didn't like the way Colin's name had tripped off her tongue, even if it had been a negative thing she mentioned. It might be too soon for a new relationship, but she couldn't be the judge of that.

Still, even with all of that, Lindy actually liked her. Libby seemed sweet, and she was smart, too. Lindy had overheard most of the conversation with Beth. Eavesdropping was easy on the guise of dropping by to check the students' progress. Smart, sweet, and undeniably pretty were Lindy's assessment. She liked her for Seth, even if it was early days of their relationship. She hoped that they could make a go of it. Lindy thought she could spend time with Libby.

She couldn't say that of all of Seth's ex-girlfriends, she thought, as she headed home. Of course, Lindy and Marnie had been like sisters.

Lindy had been devastated when they'd broken up. In fact, she and Marnie kept in touch even now. But she hadn't like Charlotte. She thought that the whole relationship would run its course, but then Charlotte had moved in with Seth. She wanted to say something then, but it felt like too little, too late. There was just something about her that rubbed Lindy the wrong way. And she'd suspected that Charlotte's late nights at work were something else entirely, although she couldn't tell Seth without proof. When they'd broken up, she'd been properly disappointed on the outside, but inside she was cheering. They'd been very upfront, after the fact, that none of them had been crazy about her, which had come as a shock to Seth who thought that they had liked her even if they hadn't been wildly enthusiastic.

After that, Seth didn't really date much, or at least not seriously. Lindy had worried about him some, but now she worried in a different way. She hadn't seen him this interested in anyone since Marnie, and she didn't know if Libby was ready yet. She parked Francis by her little house and climbed out with a sigh. It was his life, not hers, she reminded herself. He'd have to figure it out. They both would.

Chapter 21

Libby pulled the cookies out of the oven only a minute before she heard Rose's car pull up. They were meeting tomorrow for their usual Taco Tuesday festivities, but Rose had asked to come by. Libby was curious if she would finally tell her what was up with Dillon. There had to be a story there, she thought. She walked toward the door as she heard Rose ring the doorbell.

"I made cookies," Libby said with a grin when she opened the door.

"Oh, good. I brought wine," Rose held up the wine bottle with a grin of her own. "What are we listening to anyway?" She walked into the living room to see what record was playing this time. Libby had lit candles around the house, but Rose didn't even remark on it. Libby always kept candles lit and a record playing when she was relaxing at home. She used to talk about reclaiming her space when she left Colin, but now it was just what she liked.

"It's an old radio show. A big band concert," Libby called from the kitchen. She came out carrying a tray of cookies. "Snickerdoodle and chocolate chunk. I couldn't make up my mind and I just made both. And the record is Benny Goodman."

"Nice mood music. So—did Seth get any of these cookies while he was here?" Rose asked with a smile.

"How did you know he'd been here?" Libby demanded, blushing to her roots.

"Ha! I was guessing," Rose laughed.

"He took a few to go. He stopped by after work for a minute, but I told him I'd see him tomorrow morning. We're having coffee before work," Libby smiled happily. "So what's up with you? What'd you want

121

to talk about?"

"Okay," Rose began and then took a deep breath.

"Wait. Are you sick? Is that what this is all about?" Libby began, sitting down slowly.

"Oh my God, you are such a drama queen! No, I'm not sick," Rose laughed, but she felt more comfortable somehow. "So you know that Dillon is coming tomorrow, right?"

"Yeah. Wait—is he actually married? And he can't come because his wife might find out?" Now Libby was just joking, throwing in a little dramatic flair to the story.

Rose rolled her eyes. "Will you listen?"

"I'm sorry. Seriously. What's going on? Isn't he coming after all?" Libby asked.

"Okay, that's the thing. He's not coming," Rose paused, and Libby wondered if it was for dramatic effect or just from pure nerves. "She is."

"She is, what?" Libby asked. "Wait—his wife is coming?" she asked perplexed, trying to grasp what was so important that it necessitated a private conversation.

"No. There's no wife. I meant Dillon. She's coming tomorrow," Rose waited, expectantly.

"Oh," Libby's face slowly cleared. Then she began to laugh. "Oh my God. You said Dillon, and we all assumed Dillon was a man." She wiped tears from her eyes and looked at Rose. "I'll admit that I did not see that coming. I mean, I know you experimented in college, but I seriously did not even guess Dillon was a she and not a he. That's totally our fault; we just assumed. This just got a whole lot more interesting. Do tell."

"I don't even know where to start," Rose said, sitting down with a sigh. Libby leaned forward, curious. This was not the plot twist she'd been expecting, and she was looking forward to hearing more.

"Well, you said she's a lawyer, and you met at a gallery opening, right? Please fill in the blanks," Libby encouraged.

"I did meet her at a gallery opening, and she is a lawyer," Rose began. "Okay, so I wore that little black dress. You know the one?"

"The one that gets shorter every time you move?" Libby asked with a grin. She'd warned Rose that it would likely be uncomfortable. Rose was petite but curvy, and the black dress had fit like a glove. It was sexy, but it made sitting down—or even walking—complicated. Forget picking anything up if you dropped it! Plus, the front of the dress also dipped generously down. Libby had cautioned her that it was the kind of dress that wasn't meant to be worn for long.

"Yeah, that one," Rose said ruefully. "The slut dress."

"I never said that!"

"Well, you're not wrong. I don't know what I was thinking of wearing it," Rose said. "Alice invited me to that Women in Art exhibition, but I couldn't find her at first so I went straight to the cash bar. I ordered a Long Island and wondered how early I could sneak out since I had a full caseload the next morning. It was crowded and loud. The band was playing jazz, and it was great, but I was just tired. I didn't really want to see people, but I wanted to at least tell Alice I stopped by before I left," Rose explained. Libby nodded. "Then I realized that I was being watched."

"I knew this was about to get good," Libby declared, leaning over to take another cookie.

Rose explained that she hadn't realized she was drawing a number of looks in her little black dress. In addition to her generous curves, she'd pulled her long hair up and to the side in a style that was half up and braided with a tumble of blonde and red curls over her shoulder. She'd chosen teardrop diamond earrings with her little black dress and heels that were a blood red. Her nails were long and plain, but she'd painted her lips a red that matched her shoes. She finally turned to see who was watching her and noticed a woman about her own age sitting at the bar. She looked vaguely familiar. Rose painted a vivid picture for Libby who was reaching for another cookie without even thinking.

"There was this brunette at the other end of the bar who looked really familiar so I went up and said the dumbest thing ever. I did the whole, hey, have we met thing, but I really meant it," Rose said with a laugh.

"Now, you remember that when you're smiting the next guy who uses that line," Libby said with a smile. "So, set it up for me. What was she wearing? What did she say? I need details!"

"How about a picture?" Rose asked. She passed over her phone, and Libby looked at Dillon. She had straight dark hair that fell past her shoulders and dark eyes with thick lashes. She was beautiful with a wide smile and full lips. Rose continued, "So it turns out that I had actually seen her before, but hadn't recognized her out of context. She practices family law so she's around the courthouse a lot."

"Hey, at least she realized it wasn't just a bad pick up line."

"So she bought me a drink, and then we ended up staying almost until the gallery closed. We exchanged numbers, and I thought we'd go our separate ways. But we started walking and ended up at her loft downtown, and I just stayed the night," Rose said with a shrug. "I wasn't looking for anything. I assumed she wasn't either. But the next morning, she didn't seem to want me to go. She even let me borrow some of her clothes for work, so I didn't have to leave so early."

"Well, that's one benefit to dating women I hadn't considered," Libby said with a grin. "Assuming you're around the same size with a similar taste in clothes."

"It was kind of sexy," Rachel admitted with a shrug.

"Okay, so you've had this whole steamy romance going, and you've been letting me go on and on about Seth? Why didn't you tell us all about this?" Libby asked curiously. "Didn't you think we'd want to know?"

"It's not a romance exactly. This is casual," She ignored Libby's sarcastic uh-huh. "I guess I wasn't sure how you'd react to me dating a woman. I mean, I wasn't sure how I was going to react to it. It wasn't exactly planned. I was just attracted, and she's actually a fascinating person. I guess I didn't want to make things weird."

"I mean, I guess I get it. I just hope you know me better than to think I care who you date—man, woman, whatever. I'm just happy if you're happy. And she sounds great. So she's definitely coming to Taco Tuesday tomorrow?" Libby asked.

"That's what she said. She's really excited, but she doesn't know that I haven't told all of you, so I wanted to get that out of the way,"

Rose said, sheepishly. "I'm not ashamed of her or anything. She's pretty fantastic. I just didn't know if this was a relationship thing or a casual thing, but now we're talking about making it exclusive. I thought it was time you all met."

"Look, I can let Jenna and Rachel know, but I don't think you're giving us enough credit. Love is love and all that. I think she sounds amazing, and you just lit up talking about her. God, I hope you guys like Seth, too. Just know that the pressure isn't all going to be on you. We're going to be feeling it, too. And Alec is the one we'll have to worry about saying something tasteless. I know he doesn't mean to, but I'm sure he'll manage to embarrass us both before the night is over. Mark my words!"

"I'm glad I told you. Actually, I've been having a hard time not talking about Dillon, and now I can fill you in. I'm sorry I wasn't honest earlier," Rose admitted. "It's just different. Not everyone is so positive about it."

"Which is ridiculous when you think about it," Libby told her with a roll of her eyes.

"Well, not everyone has your heart, Libby," Rose said with a smile.

"I'm sending extra cookies home with you for Dillon. Don't let me forget to give you the box," Libby told her and then grinned. "The real question about the two of you is this, though," she said with a dramatic pause and quirk of her brow. "Are you the same shoe size? Can you borrow her fabulous shoes?"

"God, no, but I wish!" Rose said with a laugh. "Her feet are more your size," Rose said nodding to Libby's small feet.

"Really?" She drawled out with a sly grin. "I like her already."

*****

Taco Tuesday finally arrived, and Seth showed up at Libby's house half an hour before they were set to leave. He'd brought a bouquet of sunflowers this time, which made Libby smile when she opened the door to see their big, happy faces. Before she could put them in water, he was kissing her.

"I just needed to get that out of the way before your friends meet me. I didn't want to be thinking about it all through dinner and not be able to concentrate," Seth said with a grin.

"God, you're a charmer!" Libby declared. "Thank you for the flowers. I love them." She pulled him back down for another slow kiss. And then another.

"You're quite welcome," Seth murmured. "I guess I should bring you flowers more often," he said with a quiet chuckle. "Want to just stay in tonight?"

"Oh, no. You're not getting out of it that easy. You'll love them, and there will be margaritas to take the sting off. Plus, Rose is bringing her girlfriend so you're not the only new one in the group," Libby said, arranging the sunflowers in a vase.

"Her girlfriend, huh? So is this an official thing, too? Did you tell them you were bringing a boyfriend?" Seth asked, curiously.

"I told them I'm bringing you. I didn't define the relationship," Libby said, shyly, looking away.

"Can we define it?" he asked. She paused, her back to him, and thought about what he was asking her, if she was ready for this. "I'm not seeing anyone else. I don't want to."

Libby took a deep breath and turned to look him in the eyes. She replied softly, "I'm not seeing anyone else either, and I don't want to."

"So it's an official thing?" Libby nodded. He pulled her in to kiss her and then pulled back. "Are you sure you don't want to wait until after your friends have met me? What if they hate me?"

"They won't hate you, and I'm sure. I mean, what if your friends hate me?" Libby countered.

"That would never happen. As it is, I'm keeping Dean far away from you. He's charmed every woman in this town," Seth said ruefully.

"Not this woman. I find you quite charming though," Libby said with a grin.

"Okay, let's go meet these friends of yours." He reached for her hand, and they headed to his car parked on the street.

*****

At the restaurant, Jenna and Finn were already sitting at the table with Rachel and Alec. There had been an awkward silence until Libby arrived with Seth. She introduced everyone and sat down.

"Where are Rose and Dillon? Are they still coming?" Libby asked.

"They texted a few minutes ago and said they were just down the street," Jenna told her. She exchanged a look with Libby that said she'd tell her all about what she'd missed at work tomorrow.

"How are the kids doing?" Libby asked Rachel and Alec. Then turning to Seth, she explained, "Oliver is six now." She looked at Rachel for confirmation. "Ella is four, and Willow is about to turn one in a couple weeks."

"They're good," Alec said briefly, pouring another margarita.

"Oliver really likes his teacher this year, but Ella mostly likes school for lunch and recess. Willow's gone from walking to running lately, so I'm having to shore up the baby-proofing measures," Rachel added. "How's your business doing, Seth? Libby tells us you own one of the antique stores in town."

"Business is good. We get steady traffic in the store, and I've got my eye on a couple of new pieces some of our collectors will like," Seth said with a smile. "It's got to be a breeze compared to taking care of kids though. Libby tells me you're a regular superwoman. She showed me the pictures of the Halloween costumes you've made for the kids. It's pretty impressive," he added.

"Oh, it's just something to do. I used to make our costumes when we were kids, too," Rachel added, pleased with the compliment. Alec looked annoyed, but lately, she wondered if his face had just gotten stuck that way over the years.

"Hey, there's Rose. And that must be Dillon with her," Jenna added. "She's really pretty." They turned to watch the couple come in. They weren't holding hands, but they stopped at the door to talk and leaned close together to exchange a few words. Rose touched Dillon's shoulder reassuringly, and they came in wreathed in smiles. Libby had to admit she was checking out Dillon's shoes, but she figured there had to be best friend benefits that included shoe borrowing. Rose caught her looking and winked.

After all the introductions, they settled into the evening. The conversation seemed to flow without awkwardness, skipping around the table to encompass the group. Dillon and Seth took turns getting grilled by the rest of the group. Finn stayed fairly quiet, but occasionally interjected a question or two. Alec sat sullenly over his salsa and chips, adding the only discordant note to the evening. Rachel drank extra margaritas to drown out her annoyance with Alec, or at least that's what everyone assumed.

All-in-all, Libby counted it as a successful first meeting with her friends, although she knew she'd have to talk with them all without Seth present to get their real opinions. She was also going to have to tell Rose her opinion of Dillon, which is that she seemed absolutely lovely. They had all liked her, and she hoped that they liked Seth, too. Libby reached under the table and squeezed Seth's hand. He smiled at her in return, and she knew everything was going to be fine.

Seth opted to quit after the first margarita to be the designated driver. He drove Libby home and walked her to the door. She was so relieved that the night had gone well. Alec had been the only awkward note, but that was not unusual. The others had more than made up for his morose attitude. When Seth leaned in to kiss her at the door, she looked up at him and wondered why she hadn't yet invited him inside. After all, her divorce would be final any day now, and she'd been legally separated for the better part of a year. She pulled him toward her for a kiss that went deeper than the last. She opened the door with one hand and pulled him through the door, leaning against it with her mouth still fused to his.

"You've been drinking," he pointed out, leaning his forehead against hers. "We should do this another time. When you're a little more clear-headed."

"I'm clear-headed enough now," she told him.

"How many margaritas did you have?" he asked her. When she thought about it, he laughed softly. "You don't even know. I want you, Libby, but I want you to be ready. I don't want to rush this."

"Seth," she breathed, leaning back just enough to meet his eyes. He was still holding her against the door, and her arms had wrapped around his neck. "I trust you. I want this."

"You're sure?" he asked. When she pulled his mouth back down to hers, he lifted her up, and she wrapped her legs around him. He held her there against the door, exploring her mouth.

"I have a bed upstairs," she told him softly.

"In a minute," he said. "I want to take my time." Libby felt his words send a shiver down her spine. She had a feeling they were going to need more than a minute. "No regrets?" he asked her, making sure she was comfortable with her decision. He searched her eyes in the dimly lit hallway.

"Maybe regretting that we didn't do this before. I don't know what I've been waiting for," she admitted.

"It doesn't matter," he told her. "You're worth the wait."

"So are you," she told him, running a hand through his hair and then pulling his mouth back to hers softly. She let go of the sense of urgency and just enjoyed the moment. He sensed the change and brought his hands to her face, stroking one cheek with a thumb while the other hand moved to cup the back of her head gently. She sighed into the kiss and felt him move her weight away from the door and reach down to hold her. She moved to put her feet back on the ground and then took his hand. She could feel his eyes on her as she led him up the stairs. When they came to the top, she turned to say something, but couldn't remember what when her eyes met his, and he moved forward to kiss her again. All her thoughts floated away, and she let him sweep her up this time and move her into the bedroom behind her.

Chapter 22

September gradually gave way to October, which helped bring down the temperature by a few degrees. Seth and Libby were falling into a relationship as easily as the seasons were changing. Already, their friends and family were expecting the two of them to be together, and invitations to events were extended to them as a couple. Taco Tuesday went back to being Ladies' Night, but most of the other days, Libby was at Seth's place, or he was at hers. They'd decided he had the advantage of the massive television that was ideal for watching movies, but she had the ideal kitchen and dining room set up for dinners. Seth had a king-sized bed, but Libby's queen size was more comfortable. They lived just down the road from each other, and it was easy for them to go wherever was most convenient for the hours they spent together after the work day.

Libby marveled that the relationship with Seth came so easily. They talked about everything, and they'd not yet had an argument. She didn't really trust easy. Easy was Colin coming into her life, sweeping her away with his intensity and attention, and then checking out when things got harder. Easy was for relationships where you were disposable, where someone could leave you just as easily as they'd walked in. Libby stopped for a minute to catch her breath. She'd been running and thinking, but she needed a moment to reign in her thoughts. Easy isn't necessarily a bad thing, Libby thought. Seth was worlds away from Colin. She tried to stop the knee-jerk reaction to distrust what reminded her of the beginning with her soon-to-be ex-husband. She reminded herself that she and Seth had common interests and enjoyed each other's company. She took a drink from her water bottle and stretched. She decided she'd walk the rest of the way home.

She had to admit that she was falling in love with Seth. She hadn't admitted it out loud. Rose strongly suspected it. Libby could tell. But she knew Rose wasn't judging the speed or intensity of her feelings because she was just as deeply caught up with Dillon. She hadn't expected to fall in love again. Honestly, it was too soon. She'd thought a few times of pulling away from Seth and establishing a healthy distance. Surely they didn't need to spend so much time together, she'd think. But then she'd see him and all her arguments for putting distance between them just faded away. He'd reach over and run his hand down her hair when they were watching a movie, or he'd roll over in the morning and wrap an arm around her and kiss the top of her head, and she'd be sunk again.

Well, I just won't tell him, she thought. After all, my feelings are my own problem, Libby rationalized to herself. And it's not like it would do any good to tell him anyway, because it's just too soon and probably too much. She hadn't meant to start any relationship. She'd gone out on the date with Seth out of attraction and curiosity, and then it became something more. Saying that she loved him would just add pressure to the situation, and she didn't need any of that right now.

She made it to her street and walked over to the mailbox. Magazine, magazine, water bill, junk mail, postcard, and an official-looking envelope from the superior court where she'd filed for divorce. Libby made it to the porch before she sat down. She turned the envelope over in her hands and just looked at it. She noticed the group of senior citizens coming down the street on their daily walk. She waved to them and decided to open it up inside.

She set it down on the counter and went to pour herself a glass of water. Instead, she leaned heavily on the counter in front of the sink, her back turned to the envelope and whatever news it would bring. She knew that when she turned around and opened it, everything would change. She tried to hold that sense of joy she'd had when she'd thought of Seth and what they had, but all she could think about was herself, just a handful of years ago, meeting Colin's eyes over a cup of coffee. She could still see herself in a pretty white dress walking down an aisle toward what she assumed was her forever. And she could still feel that gut punch of him saying, "I don't want to be married anymore." She could see him walking away from her; she could see it as clearly as if he were doing it now.

She turned and reached for the envelope and ripped it open before she could change her mind. It was one page. One. And so simple really. The divorce was final. She was officially returned to Libby Reynolds, her maiden name. She wasn't Libby Gardner anymore and never would be again. She'd thought it would feel like freedom or closure, but it just felt like loss. Libby Gardner was gone, as if she had never existed at all.

She picked up her phone and called Rose, counting the rings. One, two, three, four, thank God. "Hey, Rose. I know you're at work. Can you meet me for lunch? The papers came in." Rose didn't hesitate. Sure, she could make it. They agreed on a time and place, and when Libby disconnected the call, she sat down on the floor in the middle of her kitchen and cried.

*****

Rose made it to the restaurant just on time. She'd had to reschedule an afternoon meeting and cancel lunch with Dillon. As soon as she told Dillon that Libby's divorce had been finalized, Dillon understood. She'd been married for a few years in her twenties, a relationship that had been deeply unhealthy and was followed by an acrimonious divorce. It was part of the reason she'd chosen to practice family law, hoping to ease other couples more carefully through the transition. She understood that this was an emergency.

Rose went inside the restaurant and saw Libby sitting far in the back corner at the booth they preferred. Her eyes were red from crying, and she'd clearly showered quickly and put on minimal makeup. Her hair was still a little damp and curling at the ends. She stood up when Rose got there, and Rose gave her a brief, hard hug, knowing intuitively that anything more would start the waterworks back up.

"Thank you for coming. I really didn't want to be alone right now, and I can't really talk to Seth about this," Libby said quietly. "I honestly thought I'd want to break out the champagne, but I really don't want to celebrate this." She pushed the paper with the torn envelope across the table to Rose.

"So it's done now," Rose said, looking at the brevity of the final divorce decree. "How do you feel about it?"

"Honestly, after everything he put me through, I'm so glad it's over. It's like he's a stranger now. But I don't feel relieved. I just feel— grief, maybe?" Libby took a sip of water. "I just keep thinking of who I was when I loved him, all those different versions of me who never would have guessed this outcome," she explained, tapping the divorce decree with her finger. "I'm grieving *her*."

"That makes sense. Tell me what you need," Rose asked quietly. "Do you want to talk about it all? I could come over tonight after work, or we could take tomorrow off and talk it through."

Libby smiled through the tears that welled up in her eyes. This was why Rose was her best friend. She always knew the right thing to say, and she always made things better. "No, I think I'll be okay, but I'll let you know if I change my mind. I just needed to say it out loud to someone who won't expect me to be excited or devastated or whatever it is people usually feel. It's too complicated for that. This is perfect though. I'm glad you suggested it."

Libby and Rose both turned their attention to the menus in front of them. This new pizza place had popped up in town over the last couple of months in one of the previously empty historic buildings. The menu was filled with options for artisan pizzas, authentic Italian pizzas, an antipasto platter, and a soup of the day. The desserts were always tiramisu or cannoli. Even though it was one page only, they always had a hard time deciding and usually ended up each choosing a different item and then sharing.

"Are you going to talk to Seth about this?" Rose asked, curiously.

"I will when I've sorted it out myself. I'm not hung up on Colin anymore. I'm really not. I just didn't expect this part of it to hurt. I seriously thought I would be relieved when it was over," Libby explained softly. "I don't know what this is, but it's not relief."

"Does it change how you feel about Seth?" Rose asked her.

"Not at all!" Libby replied quickly. "No, Seth is wonderful, actually. We've been really happy. I will tell him the divorce came through, of course. It feels awkward to even have that conversation when we've been dating a month already," Libby said.

"Well, you've been honest with him the whole time," Rose reminded her. "I'm sure he'll be relieved that it's behind you."

"True. In a way, I'm relieved. It is done now, and I don't have to wait and wonder about when it will happen. I guess I can really put it behind me. I just saw the envelope and felt a little sick about it all."

"I think that's understandable."

"Look, everything isn't about me. How are things going with you and Dillon?" Libby asked, taking a healthy bite of the pizza the server had sat in front of her. She knew it would probably be too hot, but she was hungry now that it was there. She'd ordered a single slice of pizza with prosciutto, mozzarella, and arugula. She nearly moaned in pleasure, but then she eyed Rose's Margherita slice. She wanted that, too. They amicably divided portions, keeping the pasta in the center of the table for now.

"Great. Different. I don't know. I really like her. I didn't think this was going to be a serious thing, but now I can't imagine being with anyone else. She's just really sweet and incredibly smart. We went to trivia the other night, and she knew almost every single answer. I mean, I slayed on music trivia, and there were some pop culture questions that I did okay on, but she really knew all of them," Rose said with a shake of her head.

"Smart really is sexy," Libby agreed. "Seth has an encyclopedic knowledge of antiques and history in general. It's kind of crazy. But definitely a turn-on."

"You speak the truth," Rose said with a laugh, scooping up a forkful of pasta and putting it on the plate beside her half-eaten pizza slice. "I'm saving room for cannoli, just so you know."

"You and me both," Libby said with a grin. "So, did Dillon decide if she's going to do Taco Tuesday with us or not?"

"She says not. She wants that to stay friend time for me, and I think she's going to spend some time with her other friends those nights. That gives us a little space. We don't want to smother each other."

"I've been afraid that Seth and I are spending too much time together, but it just sort of happens. We meet for coffee or lunch some days and dinner or a movie most nights. And he either stays the night at my place or I stay at his," Libby said.

"Speaking of which . . ." Rose began with a sly smile.

"What's that?" Libby responded, sensing where this was going.

"How's that going? I mean, you don't have to rate the sex, but a little detail would be nice." Rose said with a grin.

"I don't kiss and tell," Libby said primly.

"Since when?" Rose snorted out a laugh. "Okay, on a scale of one to ten?"

"He'd have broken the scale," Libby said with a smile. "I mean, the man deserves a medal. Or a trophy or something," She laughed. "No, seriously, it's great. I don't know, we just work. It's not just the sex. It's really intimate. I had all that intensity with Colin, but I think maybe we skipped the intimacy. I didn't realize it was missing until Seth. But it really was. God!" Libby groaned. "I'm really not trying to compare them."

"Hey, sometimes the comparison helps to rate it. Remember Drive-By Dan?" Rose asked with a laugh.

"Who could forget?"

"God, I didn't know a drive-by kiss was possible until you described it," Rose told her with a wide smile. Rose knew that Libby would never forget the disaster of a blind date she'd gone on with an online match shortly before she'd met Seth. Dan, the date, had gone in for a quick kiss while Libby was talking and had nearly missed the mark.

"If I could have avoided it, I would have. I wasn't even sure what happened, just that I never wanted it to happen again. God, he set the bar so low," Libby said. "And then there was Ten Minute Tony." She rolled her eyes.

"When I said ten minutes, I was being generous. It was awful. I swear he'd fall asleep right after or hop up to grab another beer. I'll never understand how you can get all the way into your thirties and not have any idea what you're doing," Rose remarked with exasperation.

"Hmm . . . you haven't commented on Dillon. Spill!" Libby

demanded.

"Oh, that's a whole other category. I mean, she understands what women want without me having to tell her, but I sort of expected that. And she's a great kisser so that's leaps and bounds better than Tony. God, he was a disaster," Rose said. "And that's all the detail you're getting."

"Seriously, Rose, I appreciate this. Your coming at the drop of a hat. I know you probably rescheduled half your day," Libby added.

"Nope, I had a clean slate," Rose said evenly.

"Liar!" Libby laughed. "You're always overloaded at the office. But thanks."

"Can I just ask one little question?"

Libby looked at her skeptically, suspecting the question she was going to ask would be a big one. She nodded.

"You're in love with him, aren't you?"

"I'm not trying to be," Libby said, looking down at the table with a shrug.

"But you are," Rose confirmed. "Have you told him?"

"Of course not! Look, it's too soon, first of all. Secondly, my divorce just came through. It's going to feel like pressure if I say anything now," Libby said, anxiety tight in her voice.

"I'm not saying you should tell him. I just wanted to be sure. Love looks good on you," Rose said.

"Well, it doesn't always look good after," Libby said, reflecting on the nightmare that had been her divorce. She could feel those corridors stretching out inside her. A part of her still wanted to run away, shut it all out. She wasn't ready for everything to change so fast.

"You can't compare Seth to Colin. It's not fair to him," Rose cautioned her.

"I know, I'm not," Libby said. "It's just scary to feel so much again. What if he leaves?" she asked seriously.

"What if he stays?" Rose countered. She reached for her friend's hand. "You don't have to decide anything now. Just try to enjoy it."

Libby nodded, wondering how to enjoy something that felt so uncertain. She let her face clear, locking those emotions away. She executed a subject change with ease and wondered why she never expected to fall in love again and what she was supposed to do about it now.

*****

Libby was working on her blog when she heard the doorbell. She looked up at the clock and sighed—7:30. It would be Seth getting off work. He said he'd drop by after, but the hours since lunch had gotten away from her. She hadn't even stopped yet to eat.

"Hey, you," she said with a smile, opening the door. He stepped inside, giving her a soft kiss that spun out slowly.

"Hey," he replied with a smile. "I can tell already from that glazed look that you're still writing. Mind if I grab a drink while you finish up?"

"Thank God for you, Seth. Do that. Let me just get this idea out. It might be ten minutes, tops," Libby said, already heading back to the living room to grab her laptop.

Seth wandered into the kitchen to grab a drink. He grinned when he saw that Libby had stocked both his preferred soda and his preferred beer, although she preferred cocktails and wine. He could almost guarantee that if he opened the pantry, he'd find some of his favorite snacks nestled beside her own. He knew that when she said ten minutes that she really meant thirty. He'd figured that out the last couple of times she got caught up in an idea. His sister was an artist, and he was familiar with the eccentricities of the creative types. He grabbed the soda, in case Libby wanted to go out for dinner after she finished what she was doing. He idly leaned against the granite counter for a minute, popping the top of the can. He heard her typing away in the other room and decided to join her when he noticed the envelope lying beside him, clearly in his view on the counter. He'd read Superior Court without meaning to and then immediately felt guilty. He wondered if she would tell him what it said. He wondered what it meant for her divorce and why it bothered him that she hadn't yet mentioned it.

He went into the living room, and sure enough, Libby was click-clacking away at the keyboard, her brow furrowed in concentration.

He took a seat on the opposite end of the sofa and knew better than to turn on the television or talk to her. Instead, he chose a book from the stack she had on the end table. She kept about half a dozen there at all times. It was her reading list for when she had leisure time. He found a title that looked interesting and settled into it. After about thirty-five minutes, Libby resurfaced with a stretch.

"What time is it?" she asked, reaching out to pat Seth's hand.

He looked up from his book. "Just after 8:00, I think. I just heard the bells chime at the courthouse. Have you eaten?"

"Not since lunch. I'm starving actually," Libby said ruefully.

"Do you feel like going out and getting something?" Seth asked her.

"What's quick and not fast food?" she asked. "And open around here after 8:00?"

"Hmm. That does limit our options. There's pizza, of course, but I thought you said that you were having that with Rose at lunch today," Seth began.

"I did. It was divine," Libby sighed in pleasure, leaning her head back against the couch and thinking of the pizza. "I'm too tired to think."

"How about I make us a couple of sandwiches and we eat here? Will that work, or do you want something else?" Seth asked.

"You're going to cook for me?" Libby asked, sitting up straight. She couldn't remember the last time Colin or anyone else had bothered to as much as heat up a can of soup for her.

"I'm going to make a sandwich for you. Does that count?" Seth asked with a grin. "I can, for the record, cook, but you might starve before I could make anything."

"I will eat anything as long as I don't have to prepare it," Libby said sincerely. "I can't believe I skipped dinner."

"I believe it," Seth said with a laugh. "When you're working, you don't think of much else. What were you working on anyway?" he asked, heading to the kitchen. "How about a BLT? Will that work?"

"Do I have everything for that?" she asked, thinking of her groceries.

"You've got one tomato left, but that'll work," Seth said. "Did you finish what you were working on?" He put the griddle on the stove and turned on the eyes. He took out each ingredient and lined them neatly up on the counter. Libby perched on a stool and watched him.

"Hmm . . . it's done enough, I guess. I had a lot on my mind," Libby said meditatively.

"I take it you were working on a blog and not an assignment then?" Seth asked distractedly, getting out the wheat bread Libby preferred and laying out the pieces.

"Yeah. I already turned in my other assignments, and I'm really overdue on my blog post anyway. So here's the thing. I don't really know how to talk about this exactly," Libby began awkwardly.

"Is there news on the divorce?" Seth asked quietly, not looking up from where he was slicing the tomato into thick even slices.

"How did you—?" Libby began and then saw him nod to the envelope she'd left in plain sight on the counter beside the fridge. She sighed. She couldn't even fault him for snooping. It was right there for all to see. "The final decree came through. It's done," she said softly.

Seth looked up swiftly, examining her face. "You don't look happy about it," he said evenly, taking out the strips of thick center-cut bacon.

"I thought I'd be happy about it or even relieved, but all day I kept seeing images of myself over the years. I'm haunted by it," Libby said quietly.

"Haunted by what exactly?" Seth looked up from frying the bacon on the griddle, confused.

"I don't know. Everyone I used to be, I guess." She leaned forward. "Like the day I met him and the me who believed in the relationship. Then there was the day we got married, and the me who never for a minute imagined we would ever get divorced. And the me who got lost inside that marriage and suffered. The me who watched it fall apart. I look back, and I feel bad for myself. For never seeing what was coming. For becoming someone else entirely. Can you look at me?" she asked Seth. He looked up and held her eyes. "I'm not missing him. I wasn't missing him when I saw the decree. I'm missing her. Who I used to be and all that blind faith I had. I didn't expect that to hit me, and I've been struggling all day with it. I guess I'm just sad, but I'm not sad because I'm divorced from him. Does that make sense?"

Seth leaned forward and kissed her softly and then pulled her close for a hug.

"I love you, but I swear I'll never forgive you if you burn the last of the bacon. I'm so hungry right now," Libby said with a laugh, pushing him back toward the stove.

Seth expertly turned the bacon over and then slowly turned around. He looked closely at Libby's face, so closely in fact that she worried that she had something on it. "What? Why in the world are you looking at me like that?" she asked.

She reviewed her last few sentences in her head and then blushed to her roots and looked away. She slid off the stool and went to the fridge ostensibly to get a drink. She stood there under the cover of the open door of the stainless-steel fridge in the only modern room of the historic apartment she was renting and was grateful for the blast of cold air on her hot cheeks. She'd had too hard a day, and now she'd said the thing she wasn't going to say. At least not any time soon.

She wondered if he would say anything. She didn't want him to do that thing where he brushed it off by telling her how much he cared about her. But she also wasn't sure if she wanted him to say anything at all. If he didn't, she would think he didn't feel the same. If he did, it would be awkward, and maybe he still wouldn't feel the same. Or if he did, would things start getting really serious so soon? She stalled, wondering how long she could pretend to be looking for a drink when Seth reached around her and pulled out a soda and handed it to her. Then he shut the fridge door gently and turned her toward him.

"I love you, too, and the BLTs are almost done if you want to find some chips or something to go with this." He pushed her playfully toward the pantry with a small smile, and she knew that it wasn't going to be awkward at all.

Chapter 23

Lindy dragged herself out of bed and looked at the clock in disgust. Sunday was supposed to be for sleeping in half the day. Sure, they did an occasional family brunch, but those didn't even get started until 11:00 am. It was never fancy. The dress code was pajamas or whatever they threw on after waking up late, and they would make brunch together. Lindy would put out the ingredients and mix mimosas or bloody Marys, and Seth would take his place at the stove. Their mom would set the table and probably bring in a bouquet of flowers from the garden to put on the little patio table where they would sit outside and eat by the garden.

Sundays weren't supposed to be for early rising to prepare for a fancy brunch with Seth and his girlfriend. Never mind that Lindy and her mom both liked Libby—so far anyway. Lindy valued sleep second only to her art, and she muttered curses as she picked out actual clothes to wear. I mean, *actual clothes* to Sunday brunch! Lindy thought in disgust. She pulled out a pair of blue jean leggings that she liked and found a black tunic top that said in gold print: "I shot the sheriff." She pulled out a pair of gold earrings and stacked on a few bracelets, but then took them off when she thought about having to cook with them. Besides, they'd already met Libby. It wasn't like she had to make a good impression or anything. She was just coming over to eat. No big deal.

Lindy chewed on her lower lip as she slathered moisturizer on her face and lined up her makeup on the sink. But it was a big deal, she thought. The last woman he'd brought home had been Charlotte. Their mom had been warm and welcoming, but hadn't made any overtures beyond what was strictly polite, so Lindy suspected that she felt the same. It wasn't until after Charlotte had cheated and left town that they admitted to each other their suspicions. Lindy hadn't liked the way that Charlie had always kept her phone face down and the screen turned away when messages came in. It had seemed wrong somehow. Then she hadn't liked how often she used the excuse of work to stay late in Athens, but then she would appear in Facebook photos with groups of friends at what appeared to be social events and not work functions as she'd claimed. Her mom had admitted that she hadn't thought that Charlie and Seth were well-suited for a number of reasons, but hadn't wanted to get involved. Although she'd been worried when they moved in together, she'd kept her own counsel.

Of course, Libby isn't Charlie, Lindy thought. Already, Lindy was inclined to like Libby. She was smart and sweet and maybe a little quirky, but as a fellow artist, Lindy was willing to give her a pass on that. She'd noticed her taking a couple of notes even in the painting class. It was probably an occupational hazard, the way it was for Lindy when she scrawled artwork on napkins at restaurants. That had led to many an awkward conversation on a date when she got caught up doing that and not paying attention to her date. But whatever her quirks, Lindy and her mom hadn't seen Seth this happy since Marnie. And maybe not even then. They were both happy for him, but also a little concerned. He had a good heart, maybe too good, and Charlie's betrayal had cut deeply. Lindy still remembered that bruised look in Seth's eyes when he'd told them what happened. Charlotte had moved out of his place and in with someone else, a co-worker who had clearly been more than a friend for some time.

Lindy finished the last touches of her makeup and headed over to the house. She didn't see Seth's truck in the driveway, but she figured he walked over from his place just down the street. She opened the door and there he was, his broad back with that tapered waist standing at the stove already. He'd lined up the ingredients already, so Lindy gave him a quick hug from behind and headed to the fridge for the juice to make mimosas.

"Well, aren't you the early bird. Where's Libby?" Lindy asked.

"I told her to sleep in and come over in about an hour. She'll get here when everything's ready," Seth said.

"Is mom up yet?" Lindy asked.

"I heard the shower go on when I first got here, so I imagine she'll be down in a few minutes," Seth paused, turning to look at Lindy who was leaning on the counter pouring a healthy amount of champagne into a tiny bit of orange juice in her glass. "I've got the coffee going if you want to start on that first," he said dryly. "Look, can we talk before Mom comes down?"

"Shit, Seth. Is Libby pregnant?" Lindy asked, growing pale and sitting her mimosa down on the counter with a sharp clink.

"No. I mean, I don't think so. God, why would you think that? That's not what this is about," Seth said, exasperated.

"Okay, sorry," Lindy felt oddly disappointed. She loved when people around her had babies she could play with, and she was hoping to be an aunt someday even if she never got to be a mother. She shook off that thought firmly. It was too early for that line of thinking, and she still had options left. "So what's up?"

"I know you guys hated Charlotte." Seth held up a hand. "No, I know you did. I always knew you didn't really like her, and then after everything happened, there was all this animosity toward her, and I don't blame you. I mean, God help the man who would cheat on my baby sister," Seth said with a wry grin. "But I knew you guys didn't like her, and we never talked about it. I want you to tell me if you don't like Libby. Whatever it is, whatever you suspect or think or fear. I don't want you to keep things from me again and feel like you're protecting me."

"I can manage that," Lindy said dryly. "I dig brutal honesty."

"Yeah, I know you do," Seth said with a roll of his eyes. He turned to her then, more serious than he'd been before. "But I also want you to know that I love Libby," Seth said, looking Lindy in the eyes. "I love her already, but if there's something I need to know, I want to know before everyone else does. Okay?"

Lindy studied Seth, her head cocked to one side. After a minute, she nodded. "Okay," she said simply and then looked at him curiously. "So—the two of you are using the big L word these days? That's fast."

"Well, it was unexpected. We know it's too soon. But this isn't like any other relationship. I don't even know how to explain it. I was with Marnie for years, and I was never certain like this. But I want you guys to love her, too, and if you don't, I want you to know you can tell me. And I definitely don't ever want to be the last to know."

"Look, I know that it hurt you that we didn't say anything, but we didn't think she'd move in so fast. And if I'd known for sure she was cheating, you know I would have said something. I'd have brought proof and everything. It was just a feeling. But I get it. I'll be one hundred percent honest about how I feel about Libby. Cross my heart," she told him earnestly. "After all that, I really need the mimosa, but I'll start with coffee until Libby gets here. I met her at the studio, and she seems nice enough. Look, it's just brunch. Don't worry so much," Lindy told her brother, reaching up to ruffle his hair, which made him laugh. It had been years since she was tall enough to ruffle his hair from above. Not since elementary school for him. She leaned against him for a minute, wrapping one arm around him.

"Well, isn't that the sweetest thing?" They turned and aimed identical grins at their mother who was standing in the door with a smile. "I smelled the coffee so I hurried down. And what are you making for us to eat, honey?"

Seth gave his mother a hug and pointed to the stove. "I've got bacon, eggs Benedict, and French toast. I thought I'd put out some fresh fruit with that, and I've got coffee going. Lindy's making mimosas, too. That sound okay with you, Mama?"

"That sounds delicious, but I think you forgot something," Keely said with a mischievous grin.

"What could I have forgotten?" Seth asked, looking around him. "I could make some cinnamon rolls or something if you want."

"Didn't you forget the guest of honor? What happened to the girl?" Keely asked with a laugh.

"She's sleeping in," Lindy said. "Seth's going to call her when we're nearly done so she can come right over to eat."

"Well, that's awfully thoughtful of you, Seth," Keely added, beaming with pride in her son.

"She stayed up pretty late writing," Seth began.

"Writing, sure," Lindy muttered, under her breath. Seth elbowed her and pulled a face behind his mother's back.

"I heard that," Keely said with a grin.

"I'm ignoring you both," Seth said, turning his attention to the food. "Will you two just play nice while she's here and try not to embarrass me?"

"Yes," Keely said at the same time as Lindy said. "No." They both laughed, and Seth rolled his eyes on a sigh.

"I don't know why I'm cooking for you ingrates. Go find someone else to bother so I can get this done," Seth said with a smile. "As soon as I start on the French toast, I'll tell Libby to head this way."

*****

Libby woke up to the empty bed at Seth's house. She rolled over to his side and wrapped an arm around his pillow. His side of the bed was cool so she guessed he'd been up for a while now. He'd promised to call when it was time for her to come over, but she decided to go ahead and grab a shower and start getting ready. She'd brought over a casual sundress with a light sweater that would be perfect for a brunch. She took a shower and smiled when she noticed that Seth had stocked the body wash she preferred. She'd noticed the night before that he'd also bought some of the wine she liked and put out a couple of candles similar to ones she kept at home. They were small things, but they meant a lot to her.

When trying on the dress, she looked critically at the bathroom mirror. It was a mustard yellow that gathered at the neckline and flared out just above the knee. It even had pockets, which always made Libby smile. She didn't know what it was about dresses with pockets that just made women so happy, but they did. She paired the dress with ballet flats in nude with a subtle lace accent. The light sweater she slipped on was a shade darker than the dress with small pearl buttons. She added tiny gold hoop earrings and a delicate gold necklace with a small heart that rested between her collarbones. She applied her makeup with a careful hand, going for a light, natural look with a little colored lip gloss. She'd met both his mother and sister before, but she wanted to make a good impression over brunch.

She thought back to meeting Colin's mother. The woman had peered at her like a bug under glass and had even wrinkled her nose as though what she'd seen was distasteful. Of course, Colin's family had been considerably more affluent than her own, but Libby remembered dressing well and trying to make a good impression. No effort on her part would have been enough to satisfy Hortencia Gardner. Of course, with a name like Hortencia, Libby was sure life had not been easy despite her regal good looks and family money. No matter how hard she'd tried, Libby just couldn't manage to like her. She insisted on being called Mrs. Gardner, even though they both knew the "Mrs." was a misnomer, as she'd never married. She'd never gotten more pleasant and had merely tolerated Libby.

Her own family, on the other hand, had made up for it in some ways. Her parents had been casually interested in their marriage, which was about all the interest they ever had to spare for the lives of their children—casual interest and no more. But they showed up at the right occasions and made small talk. Rachel and Faith, on the other hand, had warmly welcomed Colin into the family. They'd found him handsome and charming and sweet, and both had been shocked when the news of the divorce had come out. Of course, Hortencia had been delighted. She'd adopted a shocked air, but under that thin veneer was a satisfaction that said she felt she'd been right all along.

Thank God Seth's family seemed normal, Libby thought. Both Keely and Lindy seemed friendly and approachable. She knew this brunch would be nothing like the ones she'd experienced with Colin's family with the spiteful matriarch ruling over them all. Still, she was nervous. Already, Seth had met Rachel and her friends. This was starting to get serious, and the ink had barely dried on her divorce papers. She worried about that, and then she worried about worrying about it. She sighed. She was making this more than it was. Seth regularly had brunch with his mother and sister and simply wanted her to come along. No big deal!

The phone rang, and Libby nearly jumped. She started to answer when she realized it wasn't Seth's ringtone. Instead, it was the generic one she used for unknown numbers. She answered it hesitantly wondering who would be calling her now. Probably telemarketers, she thought as she answered.

"Hello?" Libby answered, slowly putting her makeup back into its bag and cleaning off the counter. She'd hate for Seth to come home to her makeup and hair accessories dotting the counter like she'd taken over. They weren't living together, after all.

"Libby?" Libby dropped the tube of mascara and watched it roll from the smooth counter top to the floor. She bent to quickly snatch it back up, holding it tighter than was necessary. Colin's voice was on the other line, and she pulled the phone back to stare at the unfamiliar number, wondering where he was calling from and why he'd bother to call at all.

"Hey, Libby?" he repeated. "Are you there?"

"Yes, I'm here," she said quietly. "Why are you calling?"

She could hear him breathing on the other side of the line, and just that easily, she could feel his heart beating. She could remember his presence in the room with hers. He spoke her name and evoked that memory. She would stand at the double sink putting on mascara while he brushed his teeth. They would move around each other as if it had been choreographed. At the beginning of their relationship, their eyes would meet in the mirror, smiles were exchanged. At other times, those glances would smolder, and the clothes they were putting on for work would start to come back off, and the mirrors' steam would obscure the reflection of bodies tangled together. Later still, their eyes stopped meeting, but the dance around each other continued. She would be conscious of his presence, of the way his eyes skittered away from her own, and know that he wouldn't start taking off his tie after he'd put it on, not for any reason. And she knew that her hand wouldn't reach for his. Scant inches would separate them, but it could have been oceans. It could have been galaxies. He took a deep breath in.

"So I have some news, and I don't know how to tell you," he began. Libby felt her heart squeeze tightly in her chest. She didn't know what words he'd say next, only that they would be the kind that hurt.

"I'm listening," she said neutrally, keeping her tone calm and polite.

"I know that you probably heard that I was seeing someone, and the thing is she's, well we're, um. We're going to have a baby, and I thought you should hear it from me before you hear it from anyone else." The words came for Libby, and she heard them. Of course, she did. The reception on the line was clear, and there were no background sounds beyond the birds in the trees outside. She leaned forward, gripping the basin of the sink and trying to remember how to breathe.

"Libby? Hey, Libby, are you still there?" Colin asked, concern in his voice. "Look, I just wanted to be the one to tell you. I never expected this to happen, but it has. I didn't plan this." He babbled out the explanation, no longer his charming, perfectly assured self.

But Libby was racing down those corridors in her mind, gathering speed, slamming heavy doors on the words, "We're pregnant. We're pregnant. We're pregnant." Repeating in her head.

"So it was me all the time," Libby said quietly. She'd said it under Colin's babbling explanation.

"What did you say?" he asked, straining to hear.

"I said congratulations. When is the happy day?" Libby asked, outwardly calm and inwardly still making her way through those cold corridors in her mind.

"She's not due until March. Libby, are you okay?" Colin asked softly.

"Perfectly. Why wouldn't I be? I'm so sorry, but I can't talk. I'm running late for a brunch engagement," Libby said calmly. She disengaged the call, not even waiting to hear his response and sat the phone down on the sink. She backed up and found herself sitting on the edge of the bathtub.

She looked up into the mirror and saw her own reflection, drained of color and looking as though she'd seen a ghost. So Colin was going to have a baby. All those years of trying, and it wasn't him after all. She'd been tested, and the doctor had said she had every chance of conceiving. Colin refused to go for the tests, insisting that nothing was wrong with him. It would happen when it happened. Well, it happened alright. With Maisie. His twenty-three-year-old research assistant at the university. Friends had made sure she knew when they made their relationship public. She'd thought for a moment that he was calling to tell her he was engaged. This was so much worse. The baby she wanted, Colin's baby, was going to happen, and it wouldn't be hers.

Her phone rang, and she looked at it curiously. She almost didn't answer it, but then she remembered that she was in Seth's house waiting for him to call about brunch. She leaped up and grabbed the phone like it was a lifeline. She heard his voice online saying the French toast was cooking, and it was time to come over. Did she remember how to get there? She asked him to give her a few minutes to get dressed, and she'd be over. She pulled out her makeup bag and decided to add a little more color. She didn't want to go to his mother's looking like death warmed over. She calmly added another layer of blush, brighter eyeshadow, and coral lipstick. She was careful not to think. She repeated Seth's name like a mantra in her head and tried to think of anything but babies and Colin and the growing pain squeezing her heart. She took a few deep breaths and locked those doors firmly in her mind.

As she walked to Keely's home, only a few streets down from Seth's, Libby paid careful attention to her surroundings. She noticed a tree whose leaves had made the change from bright green to a lovely russet. She listened to her own feet crunching the leaves along the path. She felt the slight chill in the air and was grateful for the comfort and warmth of her sweater on her arms. She noticed the squirrels running along her path, and that unique autumn scent of dried leaves in the air. She remembered her old coping skills, training of focusing on her senses to manage panic attacks.

She knew that if there was any good reason for a panic attack, this was it. Her only recently ex-husband having a baby with someone else when she was never able to get pregnant. She stopped those thoughts with a loud NO in her head and went back to cataloging which trees had turned color and which had lost all their leaves so early in the season. She noticed that several residents had put out pumpkins, gourds, and elaborate fall wreaths. A few football enthusiasts had even placed their fall pumpkins around the small statues of the Georgia Bulldogs mascot that held positions of honor on porches and in gardens along her walk. Go Dawgs, she thought, with a smile.

See? She could smile. She wasn't going to have a panic attack. She was going to go have a lovely brunch with Seth's family, and she wasn't going to think of Colin at all. She saw Seth walking out in front of his mother's home from the side path. She wanted to smile and cry at the same time. This was the man she loved now. Seth, not Colin. Seth with his beautiful eyes and his way of always seeing her for who she was. Seth, who never made her feel like she wasn't enough. She picked up her pace, and before he could even speak, she'd launched herself into his arms, burrowing her head into his chest. She heard the steady beat of his heart under his shirt, and the tightness in her own chest eased enough so that she could breathe again. She looked up at him with a genuine smile.

"Hey, what was that for? I haven't been gone that long," Seth said with a laugh.

"Long enough, I guess," Libby said, wryly. "What are we having for brunch? I'm starved!"

"You'll see. We're set up in the garden since it's warming up. There's an outdoor fireplace that will keep the chill away. You look beautiful." He said it simply, as if it were true. Libby marveled at that. It seemed like every other man who had called her beautiful did it because he wanted something. Wanted her to like him. Wanted her to sleep with him. They all said it like flattery because they needed something from her. Seth spoke the words like truth as if he were stating a well-known fact that simply couldn't be denied. He put an arm around her and rubbed her arm as he led her to the side entrance. "I'll show you the house after breakfast. It dates back to 1881 and has a carriage house in the back of the garden. That's where Lindy lives."

"It's beautiful." She marveled, putting thoughts of the morning's disastrous call to the back of her mind. They turned the corner and approached the house where Keely and Lindy were just setting out covered plates. "Good morning," Libby said shyly.

"It's so good to see you, Libby. Don't you look pretty," Keely remarked, coming around the table to give Libby a hug. Libby hugged her back, remembering how Colin's mother never hugged her at all, and her own mother's hugs were more sporadic than most. Libby wondered what it would have been like to grow up around such warm people.

"Hey, Libby," Lindy said simply. This is the one who will be the tough sell, Libby thought. She sensed that Lindy was the protective older sister, but she wasn't worried about that. The last thing I ever want to do, Libby thought, is hurt Seth.

"Hey, Lindy. Love the shirt," She said with a grin. She loved Lindy's style, even if it was so different from her own. "What can I do to help?"

"Not a thing," Keely assured her.

"You can help me drink these mimosas," Lindy offered with a slight smile.

"I'm happy to help with that," Libby said with a grin, accepting a drink and admiring the bright orange in the delicate flute. They started uncovering plates of French toast, bacon, and eggs Benedict. "Thank you so much for inviting me. This looks delicious," Libby remarked sincerely. She admired the beautiful flowers on the table, placed around the seasonal gourds and tiny pumpkins. She had been expecting store-bought pastries in the dining room rather than this elaborate spread and was happy to be proved wrong.

"Seth cooked," Lindy said simply. "The kitchen has always been his domain," she said with a shrug.

"I'm impressed," Libby said with a smile. She'd seen his kitchen with the state of the art appliances and had eaten a meal or two he'd prepared by this point. She knew he was a gifted cook, but she smiled with gratitude. "I'm just going to show my appreciation by eating a pile of French toast so you know how much I like it," she said with a wink. She wasn't shy about having an appetite. She didn't run all the time so she could eat rabbit food. She enjoyed eating, and she loved that Seth liked that about her.

"I will also show my appreciation thusly," Lindy said, tucking into a pile of bacon. "Glad you're not vegan. I love bacon," she said with a sigh.

"My baby sister is a vegan. Or was the last time I talked to her. She works on a cruise ship so I don't get to see her often. But she'd gone vegan then and was happy with the decision. I couldn't do it," she admitted, eyeing the plate of bacon. Lindy grinned and passed it to her.

"I admire and respect people who choose not to eat meat," Keely said with a smile. "They're just following their own convictions. I used to try to have meatless Mondays with these kids growing up. It was more for budget reasons than anything else, but I had to stop when these two acted like they were dying if they didn't get a pile of bacon with breakfast and chicken strips with dinner," she said. "Now, Seth has told us you're a writer, but I'd love to hear more about it. What are you working on?"

Libby explained a few of the pieces she had in progress and talked a little about the local newspaper and what she was working on for them. She gave them a peek into her process, but then turned the tables. She asked Keely questions about the tea room; quizzed Lindy on running her own paint studio and even asked her about her work outside the studio; and threw a few questions about antiques to Seth. She kept them all talking and was glad that it seemed natural. She needed them not to ask about her past or her failed marriage, not today. Instead, she kept the conversation going, a juggling act that seemed effortless, but was far from it.

On the walk home, Seth held Libby's hand and smiled down at her. "I think we can say that went well."

"I like your family," Libby said simply. "Thank you for inviting me."

"You're welcome," Seth replied. He squeezed her hand until she looked up at him. "Are you going to tell me what's wrong now, or were you going to wait until later?"

Her footsteps faltered, but then she kept walking, looking carefully ahead. "What do you mean?" she asked evenly.

"Something's wrong. You asked a lot of questions, but managed to say very little about yourself. Was it too soon? Were you just nervous?"

Seth asked with concern.

"No. It was fine. I just got some tough news this morning and hadn't really processed it. I didn't want to say anything before brunch," Libby told him honestly. She hadn't lied to him before and wasn't going to start now.

"What's going on?" Seth asked her, leading her around to the back door of his house and into the garden. They sat down on the porch swing. Libby kicked off her shoes and folded her legs under her.

"Colin called this morning. You know how he has this new girlfriend? Well, they're having a baby. He didn't want me to hear from someone else," she said it flatly, with little intonation.

"I wish you'd told me," he said, stroking her hand with his thumb. "That must have been upsetting for you," he said carefully. He still wasn't sure how to handle the whole ex-husband thing. It wasn't like a regular ex. She'd married the guy. They'd been married for years. He sure as hell didn't like him just calling her up like that.

"It was a shock," Libby said simply. "I don't think I can get pregnant." There. She'd said it. It was out there now. Seth turned to look at her, and she met his eyes calmly. "We tried for a few years. I had some tests done, and they said I was fine, but it looks like they were wrong. It must have been me the whole time."

"Not necessarily. It could have been a timing thing." He wasn't sure what else to say. He'd had a friend who'd been told he was incapable of getting anyone pregnant. He was told wrong and now had four kids. "I'm sorry. That call—it must have been incredibly hurtful for you."

Libby nodded, swallowing back tears. "It was. I honestly had no idea why he was calling. He called from a different number. Maybe a new one. Maybe hers. I was so surprised he called at all that I didn't even fully take in what he was saying. But at least that's done now. We shouldn't have anything else to talk about."

Seth couldn't imagine it. He didn't know how you could marry someone and then one day be strangers. He looked at Libby and thought that she was far too calm for the news she'd received. He was starting to wonder how much effort she had to put in to maintain the calm on the surface and when she'd realize she didn't have to with him. "Tell me what you need."

She looked up at him in surprise.

"What would make this day better for you? That was tough news, and I can't imagine how painful it must have been to hear. Tell me what you need, and that's what we'll do today. Even if you want to be alone."

Libby marveled at that. Whatever she needed. "I could use a distraction," she admitted. "Can we go do something, maybe see a movie?"

Seth smiled at her. "Sure, we can do that." He pulled her in and kissed the top of her head. "Let's see what's playing and decide from there."

*****

Back at Keely's house, Keely and Lindy were cleaning up from breakfast. They'd told Libby that they always cleaned since they made Seth come over early to cook. They'd waved away her offers to help and had given her a quick tour of the house before sending them on their way. They watched the couple go and then walked together into the house to clean up.

"Well?" Keely asked, passing Lindy a plate to dry.

"She was upset about something," Lindy said shortly. "But I like her. She was working hard not to show it. Hard not to respect that."

"She has good manners, and she looks at Seth like he hung the moon. It's hard not to like her for that alone," Keely admitted. "I noticed she was upset. She didn't do a bad job covering it up though. Maybe she's just reserved," Keely wondered aloud.

"I don't think she goes in for drama. Notice how she kept deflecting the attention from herself? At least that's a change from Charlie. That girl could talk about herself until the cows came home."

"The only girl you ever thought was good enough for Seth was Marnie," Keely said dryly.

"And so far, I've been right. Marnie's a peach," Lindy said with a grin.

"How's she doing these days?" Keely asked, aware that Lindy and

Marnie had stayed close all these years.

"She's good. She'll be in to visit in a few weeks, and we'll catch up then," she replied. "I do like Libby though. I think they make a nice couple," she said begrudgingly. "I wish I knew her story though. Her divorce hasn't been final long, and that worries me."

"Seth's been pretty close-mouthed about the divorce. Think he knows anything about it?" Keely asked, curiously.

"If he knows, he's not saying. It might be easier to get it out of her," Lindy said frankly. "When Seth wants to keep something private, he succeeds. She seems to be a little more of an open book."

"Oh, I don't know, Lindy. A girl who tries that hard to distract everyone from the fact that she's upset? There's more going on under the surface. She must be exhausted," Keely said slowly, considering Libby.

"I guess I never thought of it that way. Well, Seth's happy with her, and he won't hurt her. Guess we'll just have to wait and see."

Keely nodded at Libby, and they both were quiet as they thought about the morning. They both watched out of the window as Seth and Libby turned the corner to his street, still walking hand-in-hand and talking the whole way.

Chapter 24

Elle Lewis-Lawson had worked in this building since she was fifteen. She'd been a waitress at the then-diner that was named simply Madison Café. They'd called her that then—a waitress. Later, the language of the industry had evolved to include servers, busboys (even when those workers were women), hosts, and managers. Elle, at fifteen, had done it all. She'd run the old cash register that was like a relic from another time. It was her second favorite part of working there. She liked the big clunky keys and the ding of the bell as she cashed out her tables. But her favorite part of working had been connecting with the customers. Now they were called patrons or clients, but back then they were just customers, and Elle had loved to hear their stories and guess about their inner lives. She'd made it a game on those boring days where the kitchen was slow to serve up the orders and the tips were poor.

Elle had taken over the lease of the Madison Café by the time she was twenty-four. She was young, and there were locals who had no problem telling her that she was incapable of running a successful business. They'd expected her to take the dusty establishment and continue working it as it had always been—same name, same patterned linoleum on the floors, same wallpaper, and the same diner-style tables and chairs that they'd always used.

Instead, she'd closed for a week, to the consternation of the regulars, and gutted the place. She'd hired her brother's firm because she knew he'd give her a fair rate, and she'd even pitched in. She'd helped tear out the linoleum and had happily peeled the wallpaper away. When they were done, she'd gazed around at what was left. They'd left some exposed brick on the walls, and the remainder had been painted a rose gold. The original pine floors gleamed with a coat of beeswax, and the brass light fixtures were were the creation of a local artist who Elle had known from school. Her brother Jake had added the stage just where she'd requested it and outfitted it simply for small performances. Elle had stood proudly on the street when Jake had hung up the new sign: Brews & Blues.

At first, the locals had been hesitant to support the establishment. They'd like it just fine the way it was. But eventually curiosity won the day, and as they watched the steady stream of tourists come and go, they made their way back through the doors. When they did, they were pleasantly surprised that the dusty establishment had become spotless. While some were befuddled by the addition of a stage, they appreciated the wide planked floors that gleamed with the light coming through windows that sparkled in the sun. They appreciated, even more, the long clean counter and displays of the day's pastries and desserts. Rather than a dusty chalkboard of specials, Elle had provided a full dining menu as well as a large sign that posted the prices of the locally sourced menu options, craft brews, and designer coffee. Even the most skeptical patron had to admit that Elle had turned the Madison Café into something special. She'd even offered weekly music, poetry readings, and other events, which added a little something to the meager Madison nightlife.

Elle looked around the room and sighed. It was going to be a busy day. She would soon need to swap out the dramatic Halloween display in the window for a Thanksgiving one. She had a few ideas for that. It went up the day after Halloween and stayed up through the Saturday after Thanksgiving. Then the Christmas display went up and stayed until the new year. It was work, but it was worth it. She noticed that Candace was handling the register easily enough. Naomi was late, again. She'd have to talk to her about it. One more late day and she'd be gone. Elle sighed again and walked back into the kitchen. Marissa waved with a flour-dusted hand. She was preparing the dough for the loaves of bread that they sliced for lunch with a drizzle of honey butter on top. They used local honey and butter, and Marissa's added ingredients were also locally sourced. A lavender loaf here. A rosemary loaf there. One with garlic fresh from a garden. Another with a light mix of herbs. They varied depending on what was available.

"Did Naomi make it in?" Marissa asked as Elle walked back to check her progress.

"Not yet, and she hasn't called either," Elle said, worry lines wrinkling her forehead. Elle was forty-six now, and while she had her fair share of wrinkles, she took good care of her skin. Each morning and night she smoothed on a thick moisturizer, and it showed in her even, clear complexion that always made her seem younger than those years.

"I know she's my cousin, but you need to let her go," Marissa said with a grimace. "She's probably hanging around the fire station hoping Dean will come by. I told her to stop stalking that boy. She shouldn't have gone out with him in the first place."

"Dean's a decent man, but he's not the one-woman type," Elle said with a shrug. She could see the attraction, and Naomi was hardly the first server who'd been in his thrall. "That girl's got to realize that work comes first. She can flirt on her own time. If she's late again, I really will have to let her go, Marissa. We can't leave it all to Candace. She does a wonderful job, but it's too much for one person to handle alone."

"You know I won't fault you if you have to let her go. That's just business, and she's not been reliable. If I'd known she was so flaky, I wouldn't have recommended her, Elle," Marissa said. She began to mix the honey butter in the pan where it was melting on low heat. "Her parents are as reliable as anything, but in this case, the apple surely fell far from the tree."

"She's still young—twenty-one in a week. We'll give her another chance and see if she chooses to take it. That's her now," Elle remarked, looking out the small window in the back of the kitchen. "She's coming from the fire station looking none too happy."

Elle and Marissa exchanged an eye roll.

"Dean wasn't there, or he was there with a girl," Marissa predicted.

"I am so sorry I'm late!" Naomi said, coming into the kitchen in a flurry of scarves. The weather had only started to have the slightest chill, but Naomi liked the long layers of scarves that flew dramatically behind her as she rushed from place to place. She began to peel them off as she grabbed the simple Brews & Blues apron she'd wear over her button-up shirt and black slacks.

"We'll talk after the rush," Elle said simply, motioning Naomi to look at Candace handling the long line of patrons. "I think Candace could use a hand."

Elle watched Naomi rush off and then took a look around the café. She could spot the tourists easily enough. She waved to a few locals who noticed her standing in the doorway. She spotted Seth Carver's girlfriend in the corner with her sister. She knew Seth's mama Keely. They'd grown up together, although Keely was a few grades ahead of Elle. She'd watched Seth grow up around this town, following in his grandfather's footsteps with the store. She tried to think of his girlfriend's name. They'd been introduced once, but it had been during a lunch rush.

"Marissa," she called behind her. "What's Seth Carver's girlfriend's name?"

"It's Libby," Marissa answered back promptly. "I met her the other day when I went to drop off our ad at the paper. "She seems nice enough. She here with Seth?"

"No, with her sister," Elle replied, noticing the shared resemblances between the two women.

"That would be Rachel. My daughter had a class with her son, Oliver," Marissa explained. If there was someone in this town that Marissa didn't know, Elle would be surprised. Marissa was average in height with chestnut hair and blue eyes. She was heavyset and liked to joke that she'd never once met a skinny cook she could trust. She had a constellation of freckles across her pale skin and small even features. She could have been twenty-eight or thirty-eight, but the truth was somewhere in the middle.

Elle saw the sisters switch coffees and smiled. Candace had told her that they always ordered something different and then switched. She liked to see it. She and her brother Jake had always been close. Not drinking out of each other's coffee close, but close enough. He was the person who'd told her unequivocally that she could buy the old café and turn it into a place known for gourmet coffee, craft beer, and good music. And she'd supported his business from the start. She kept his advertisements in pride of place on the bulletin board out front, and Elle sent plenty of customers his way.

Elle had been married once when she was no older than Naomi. That relationship had ended before she'd made the transition from waitress to owner. She'd married a friend of her brother's whom she'd known since she was in braces as a child of thirteen. They'd married shortly after high school and divorced only a year later when Neal Lawson ran off with the local preacher's daughter. The girl had been nearly seven months gone with her pregnancy by then, and Neal had decided the decent thing was to divorce Elle and marry the girl. When Elle found out about his cheating, she signed the papers and rarely looked back. She'd heard some years before that Neal had married the girl, but managed to get in the same situation some years later and had left her and their three children for someone else. Elle hadn't had the chance for children of her own, but she was the aunt to four beautiful babies, although they were hardly babies now. One was practically engaged.

She watched the sisters talk and thought about calling her brother. She looked at the clock. He'd be on a job right now. Well, no matter. She'd just pack him a sandwich and some of that pasta salad and take it out to him on lunch. She turned away from the door to go back to check on the inventory one more time. She knew that they were running low on the decaf coffee they kept on hand, and she was pretty sure that they needed another order of the Brews & Blues merchandise out front. The tumblers and large mugs always sold quickly. She began to make a mental list of her supply order, as Candace and Naomi alternated taking patron orders out front.

Chapter 25

Libby was just walking around the corner as Rachel rushed up to Brews & Blues, looking harried. "I'd have been here sooner, but Ella spilled her milk down my shirt first thing this morning," Rachel told her, exasperated. "I had to go back and change, which nearly made them late for school. Then Willow started fussing, and I almost never got her dropped off at the sitter's."

"I don't know how you do it some days," Libby admitted. "I have a hard-enough time getting myself ready."

"It's a special skill that comes with being a mom, I guess," Rachel grimaced and reached out to grab Libby's hand. "Sorry. That was insensitive. Have you heard anything more from the jackass?"

"Colin? No. I guess the message has been delivered so there's no need for us to speak again," Libby said with a shrug. "I mean, did he expect congratulations?"

"Didn't you congratulate him though?" Rachel asked, giving her a significant look.

"Not on purpose," Libby said with a sigh. "I wanted to tell him to take his good news and shove it, but I was just in shock." They approached the counter and placed their orders, making small talk while they waited. When they got their drinks, they moved to a table in the back near the window. "Anyway, it's done. Yay for them," she said flatly, taking a sip of her coffee.

"Are you okay?" Rachel asked, hesitantly.

Libby paused, wondering why it was so hard to open up those doors inside herself once she slammed them shut. When she was little, she didn't often talk about her feelings when she was deeply affected. When their parents had flaked on yet another school play or track meet, she had sat quietly, making herself invisible, while Rachel and Faith held her hands and tried to make it okay. When they'd done the same to Rachel, her sister had flown at them in a rage, telling them they were awful parents. Faith had always shrugged and acted like she didn't care that they were never where they'd promised to be. But Libby took every hurt and hid it inside herself. She knew that Rachel worried about her. Sometimes she worried about herself.

She could feel all of those feelings stuck somewhere inside her, behind another door. Years of disappointment banging up against this terrible grief that maybe what she'd imagined she'd had with Colin was just that: her imagination. He hadn't been her forever love or soul mate, whatever she might have once imagined. He was starting a family with someone else when he hadn't cared to even make a different kind of family with her. She looked at her sister and tried to find the words.

"I will be okay," Libby said simply. "Look, I've fallen in love with Seth. He's wonderful. I don't even miss Colin now, and it feels oddly disloyal to still even think about him. But this isn't really about Colin anyway," she said with a dismissive wave of her hand. "It's just that we tried for years to have a—" she left off, trying and failing to get the word past the lump in her throat. Rachel reached across and took her hand.

"We couldn't. Or I guess I should say that I couldn't," she finished.

"I wish you'd have talked to me about it. I know how much you've always wanted a family," Rachel told her softly.

"It could have been enough. Me and Colin. I could have made that a family. Or we could have tried fertility treatments or adopted. Hell, I'd even brought up being a foster family. He didn't want to talk about it, and I couldn't let it go. It was okay if we couldn't, but I just wanted to know. I got tested, and he wouldn't. And then he just changed. Changed and left me alone," she spoke quietly, glad that the hum of conversations around them gave them the necessary privacy for this conversation.

"So that's what happened?" Rachel asked. "That's the whole story?"

"That's mostly it. I could tell you about all the little hurts, the things that we said to each other that just made it worse, but it doesn't really matter. I don't think he loved me anymore, and he wasn't willing to work things out," Libby shrugged and could practically see her defenses rebuilding themselves, hear the chink of stones sliding together in the fortress of her mind.

"Did you tell Seth?" Rachel asked, curiously, and Libby could see she was wondering if he was meeting the same defenses or if he'd managed to get around them.

"I gave him the basic outline. It is what it is," she said philosophically, taking a sip of her coffee. Rachel took a sip of her own and then eyed Libby's.

"What kind did you get again?" she asked speculatively.

"This one's mocha caramel," Libby said. "It's good." She took another sip, suspecting it was her last.

"I'll trade you for my vanilla maple," Rachel offered. They swapped mugs easily, a practiced slide from many such trades over the years. Both sipped tentatively and sighed. Then grinned. "Thanks for playing," Rachel joked. Faith had always laughed at how the two of them swapped food and drink, each trying the other's. Faith didn't like to share hers. She wanted what she wanted and was uninterested in anything outside of that choice. Now that Libby thought about it, she thought that it was a good description of Faith herself.

"How did the brunch go?" Rachel asked. Libby had mentioned it briefly, but with the news of Colin's baby, brunch news had flown out the window.

"It was great. I really like his family," Libby said calmly. "And Seth's a great cook."

"I'm glad it went well. I'm glad they're not as horrible as Colin's family. His mom was a real dragon lady. I thought she was going to walk out of the wedding," Rachel said with a roll of her eyes.

"She would have if it wouldn't have made her look bad," Libby said with a grin. "It almost made it worth all the stress of having her there just to see her suffer through the vows."

"You're so mean," Rachel said with a laugh. "That was almost the best part." Then she added, "Seth's family seems nice. I mean, his sister seems a little snarky, but you like that kind of thing."

"She's funny and different so, yes, I like that," Libby said with a smile. "It went really well. I just wish I'd let Colin's call go to voicemail before I went over there. I felt like I was off the whole time. I don't think it showed though," Libby said reflectively.

"No, I'm sure it didn't," Rachel said soothingly. Libby knew she was lying through her teeth just to be nice. When she was upset, it was written all over her face. She could fool most people, even Colin had been oblivious, but Libby knew that Rachel knew her better than that. She let the conversation flow away from Colin and was thankful for a reprieve from talking about something that could only hurt her.

Chapter 26

Candace made another latte and glanced over at Naomi who was doing more socializing than order taking. She liked the girl. I mean, she was nice. But she wasn't exactly efficient. Or ever on time. Candace wondered if she'd realized the hard line Elle drew with her employees. It didn't matter that Naomi's cousin worked in the kitchen. If she couldn't do the work, she'd be shown the door. She wondered how she could get her attention to signal that she needed to take the next order without being obvious to the patrons impatiently waiting in line. She didn't have to though. Naomi looked up at the line and wrapped up her conversation. She took the next order with a big smile on her face that the irritated customer couldn't help but return.

Candace nearly shook her head at how easily that was resolved. Of course, Naomi's looks didn't hurt when it came to soothing an irate client. She had long chestnut hair and big pretty brown eyes. She had a light smattering of freckles across her nose and cheeks, but nothing like the heavy ones that dotted Marissa's open, friendly face. She had a thin waist and was a bit top-heavy, and Elle had to remind her to keep her work shirt buttoned nearly to the top. She had long, tan legs and a wide smile, and she could see how Naomi had first caught Dean's attention when she'd started working here. They'd had a short fling, which had been much more serious for Naomi than Dean. Elle had tried to warn her to keep her distance from that heartbreaker, but like every other twenty-one-year-old on earth, she hadn't listened.

She turned her attention to the café and looked to see if any patrons needed a refill. She smiled when she noticed Libby and Rachel swap mugs. She'd been waiting for that. It was a quirk, but it was a nice one. She noticed Naomi had the counter under control so she went over to refill Martin's cup of coffee. She liked to stop and exchange a word with him when she could. She was glad when he started coming back. After Jack had died, he hadn't come around for a while. She'd still saved the crossword for him from the newspaper she got at home. When he'd finally come in, she'd made his order before he'd even gotten to the counter and had his newspaper sitting out marked. He'd smiled at that, a sort of sad smile, and taken his coffee to his usual seat.

Candace refilled Martin's cup and took a couple of guesses at the crossword puzzle he was working on today. She managed to help him with one, but threw up her hands in despair at the other. Then she got a bright idea and asked over at Libby and Rachel's table to see if they knew the answer. When she walked back to the counter, she noticed that Martin had joined the ladies, and they were happily completing the crossword together.

"Very smooth," Elle whispered approvingly as she passed.

Candace turned around with a grin, meeting Elle's eyes. "It freed up an extra table, and they're having fun. Why not?" she said with a mischievous grin.

"I honestly don't know what I'd do without you," Elle said with a sigh. "When you finally see through Michael, I keep telling you I have a nephew you need to meet," she said with a smile. She'd said it before, and Candace usually rolled her eyes and launched into a defense of Michael. Today, she responded a little differently.

"Actually, I think it is time I broke up with Michael. For good, I mean," she said, referencing their on-again, off-again relationship. "After that, I think I really just want to focus on work and getting through school. But after that? If your nephew's still available, send him my way." She patted Elle's shoulder and headed over to the register to take the next order.

Elle admired the register. It was the only relic she'd kept from the old café. She still loved the happy sound it made when coins dropped inside or when the bell dinged to announce a sale. She was surprised Candace was so open about dropping Michael. Surprised, and honestly delighted for her. If she'd had a daughter, she hoped she would have been as smart and as enterprising as Candace. She really did have a nephew who might be interested. It wouldn't hurt to make a little introduction.

Chapter 27

While Libby and Rachel were busy having coffee downtown, Lindy was cleaning out space in her guest room. The carriage house was only two bedrooms, and Lindy kept the second bedroom as a combination guest room and artist studio for when she worked at home, which wasn't often now. She moved art supplies and wrangled boxes deep into the closet where they wouldn't be seen. She'd known Marnie too long to think she'd care about a little mess, but she wanted to make an effort. Marnie could have stayed with her parents, in the comfortable bedroom where she'd grown up. She'd told Lindy she would probably stay one night there. But the rest of the time she'd stay with Lindy so they could get caught up.

When Marnie and Seth had first broken up, Lindy had been devastated. She'd looked at Marnie like a little sister, and they'd come to be close friends. She hadn't handled the breakup well. She'd tried to change their minds. Why couldn't they just be together long distance? Why couldn't Marnie stay here for Seth? Why couldn't Seth move for Marnie? She'd eventually come to terms with it, and she'd even managed to stay friends with Marnie when she had moved away. Now they were as close as ever, and Seth didn't have a problem with it. He and Marnie were friendly now, and their relationship was just one more part of their shared history.

Lindy had harbored hopes that one day they'd get back together, but that seemed increasingly unlikely. Seth had found Libby, which looked like it was shaping up to be a permanent thing, and Marnie had Patrick. She'd met Patrick a time or two, and he seemed like a much better fit for her than Seth ever was. She realized then that the two of them were never going to be anything more than friends. These days, Marnie visited a few times a year—sometimes with Patrick and sometimes without. Lindy smoothed down the lavender comforter on the bed and straightened the pillows with their trim of lace one last time. It would have to be enough because Marnie was due to arrive any minute now.

In fact, she heard a car door slam and knew Marnie had made it. She moved back the vintage lace curtains at the window and saw her step out of the yellow VW Bug she'd driven forever. She knew if she could see the back it would be plastered with bumper stickers that were pure Marnie. Some were faded and dated back to high school. Others were recent additions like the arrows that said: "Not all who wander are lost." She and Seth had both loved that vintage vibe and had spent hours driving around the Bug, blasting the Beatles or singing along to the Stones. Of course, they'd also alternated with Nirvana, Matchbox Twenty, and even Eminem. They would have said it wasn't about the music. It was about the drive; the music was just the soundtrack to it.

Marnie looked up at the house, her blue eyes covered by large shades. Her full lips were painted red, and they matched the red streaks in her short, straight brown hair that she wore now in an inverted bob that brushed her shoulders. She was wearing a burgundy leather jacket over a gray tunic top over black leggings with black boots. She carried a messenger bag that Lindy was sure acted as purse and camera bag these days. She seemed to take in the house in curiosity and then smiled widely as she caught sight of Lindy in the upstairs window. Lindy waved and headed down.

"Well, that didn't take you long," Lindy said, opening the door and wrapping Marnie in a bear hug. Marnie's head barely came to Lindy's shoulder even in heeled boots. Marnie hugged her hard and then stepped back.

"I had an early flight, and then I stopped by my parents to pick up Lucy," she said, nodding to the car in the driveway. "I know I'm going to have to break down and sell her eventually, but I just can't. Plus, my dad still likes to baby her." Marnie and her dad had spent weekends keeping the Bug on the road for this long. They'd bought her new in high school and kept her going all these years. When Marnie had left for Colorado, her dad had agreed to care for Lucy until Marnie decided to move her out to Denver or to sell her.

"I'm just glad you're here. So tell me everything! How's Patrick?" Lindy asked, pulling her inside and closing the door to the chill in the morning air. She moved behind the counter in the small kitchen and started pouring two cups of coffee. She added cream and sugar to each cup, remembering Marnie's preference.

"Patrick is good. He couldn't get the time off work right now, but he'll come next time," Marnie said with a shrug, accepting the cup of coffee. "I need this. Are we still having breakfast with your mom?"

"It's still a little early to go over, but we can head that way in about half an hour. She's cooking today so we can focus on the mimosas. Or do you want a Bloody Mary?" Lindy asked, taking a seat on the couch in the living room with Marnie.

"Mimosas sound great, actually. I've missed your mom," Marnie said on a sigh.

"She misses you, too," Lindy said simply. "It's good to see you."

"So how's Seth doing?" Marnie asked curiously.

"He's good. He actually has a new girlfriend," Lindy said, watching Marnie for a reaction.

"Have you met her?" she asked evenly.

"Yeah, she lives in town. Her name's Libby. She's sweet actually. You'd like her," Lindy said with a grin.

"If she makes Seth happy, I like her already," Marnie said. "So tell me: is Dean still breaking hearts left and right?"

"You know it. He has some poor girl down at Brews who stalks the firehouse. He's taken to calling for an all-clear before he heads in for his shifts. Serves him right though. His philosophy still seems to be use 'em and lose 'em."

"Some things never change. I had to tell all my friends to steer clear. Of course, I couldn't make them listen," Marnie said with a laugh. "I'll go by the store and say hi to Seth while I'm here. It's been a long time."

"Are you and Patrick still okay?" Lindy wouldn't have asked, but it was so rare for Marnie to go out of her way to see Seth. She usually ran into him at some point, but she didn't make it a point to see him. She didn't know if that signaled a breakup or an engagement, but it seemed significant.

"We've had a few problems lately. We're kind of on a break," Marnie admitted. "I got a job offer in Charleston, and I've been thinking about taking it. It's a lot closer to my family, and the money is good. Patrick doesn't know if he wants to move so he's taking some time to figure out what he wants."

"Wait—does that mean you're seeing other people, or does it just mean you're figuring out the relocation?" Lindy asked, confused.

"From my understanding of it, we can see other people, but neither of us is actively looking. I have to give an answer on this job next week, and then it wouldn't start for another thirty days after that, so he's got time to decide if he's in or out," Marnie explained, taking another sip of her coffee. She was thinking about going for another cup when Lindy hopped up to grab it for a refill. "Thanks. I'm still groggy from the 4:00 a.m. flight."

"I bet. I guess the real question is what you want, right? Do you want Patrick to move with you?" Lindy asked. She knew Marnie too well to think that she was letting some guy call the shots for her future. If the job offer was this good and this close to home, she knew Marnie would take it.

"I really do want him to come with me. That's how I know it's serious. With Seth, as much as I loved him and always will, I knew it was time for him to do his thing and me to do mine. I didn't think for a minute about Seth coming with me to Colorado any more than he really thought I would stay here. But when I got this offer, my first thought—well, after the little happy dance I did for my career— was Patrick. Would this be it for us or did he see a future with me anywhere? Maybe I was for him what Seth was for me—wonderful at the time but not permanent. It was a real moment for me," Marnie said, touching a hand to her heart briefly. "I was so excited that I never really considered he'd say no, outright. But he did. Then he said he wanted time to think about it. Like real time. Time where we weren't together and he could decide. So, I decided I'd put about 1,400 miles between us for a few days," Marnie said, gratefully accepting her second cup of coffee and leaning back on the couch with a sigh. Lindy reached over and held the hand that wasn't holding the mug.

"I'm sorry. I hope he realizes he'd be a damn fool to lose you," Lindy said fiercely.

"I'm hoping for the same thing," Marnie said. "I'm giving him the time and space to figure it out. So tell me about you. Have you talked to your mom about your options yet?" Marnie was one of the few people Lindy had told about her family planning. She'd discussed in vitro and adoption options with her late into the night when she'd decided that having a family the old-fashioned way might not work out.

"Not yet. I will soon though," Lindy promised.

"I can be here when that happens if you want," Marnie said sincerely. "But right now, I'm starving, and if I don't have some of your mom's pancakes, I will die," she said dramatically.

"I think it's French toast day," Lindy said with a grin.

"Even better," Marnie said, sitting up.

They put their mugs in the sink and headed out through the garden. There were still a few flowers in bloom, but most had faded. The trees above still held vibrant shades of yellow, orange, and russet, and a couple of the smaller trees had dropped most of their leaves in the yard. The big house was still dark, and they followed the fairy lights that led from the carriage house to the back door easily in the morning light. Marnie thought of all the times she'd been in this garden. In truth, she and Seth used to sneak out to the carriage house to make out as teenagers. She was sure that Keely knew, especially since she'd had the extremely embarrassing conversation with both Seth and Marnie about methods of protection and safe sex.

Seth's house had been a second home to her in the six years that they dated. They'd started dating when they were sixteen and didn't stop until she moved away after college. She'd known that she couldn't stay in Madison as much as she'd known that Seth had been born to stay. He fit, and she just wanted something else. It was easy not to worry about that at sixteen, but then by twenty and twenty-one and twenty-two, she knew it was only a matter of time. Still, they'd ignored the obvious and stayed together. When it had ended, they'd both been hurt, but it had been something they could survive. It wasn't enough of a heartache to change either of their minds. But with Patrick—things were complicated.

Marnie had met Patrick through friends at work. They'd all gone out for beer and trivia at a bar they liked and had invited Marnie along. She'd ended up sliding in next to Patrick in the large booth as they crowded in at the table. Introductions were made quickly as they ordered and signed up for the trivia competition. Marnie and Patrick had bonded over their knowledge of vintage cars and classic rock and their mutual lack of interest in sports history or current pop culture. They'd exchanged numbers by the end of the night, and it wasn't long before they were out again, this time just the two of them.

Marnie had dated a few guys before she'd met Seth; none of them were serious. After Seth, she'd had a string of casual lovers, but nothing that left an impact. With Patrick, they'd bonded quickly, sharing late night drinks and early breakfasts and eventually an apartment in the city. She'd been happily settling into this life when she'd gotten the call about the job. The pay was fantastic, the benefits were good, but the career challenges it offered were even better. She had been an assistant curator at a gallery in Denver all these years, but she wouldn't have to be an assistant with the new job offer in Charleston. She would see a considerable pay increase and more flexibility in managing the collections. It was an ideal job for her, and it would even leave her a little time on the side to concentrate on photography, which was a passion that she was satisfied keeping as a hobby rather than a career. It was a great opportunity for her, but she was facing facts that it might involve a life without Patrick. She was trying to imagine what that might be like and how she would cope with it.

She walked into the big house, automatically reaching for the light switch and turning it on. She knew Keely would be down shortly. Marnie was looking forward to seeing her and catching up, but she was also making time to catch up with Seth on this trip. The situation with Patrick had uncomfortable parallels that she wanted to address while she was here. She decided to focus on herself and her friends and family and to stop obsessing about this thing with Patrick. She headed to the fridge to help Lindy set up for breakfast and was glad that she'd come home.

*****

The doorbell above the shop dinged, and Seth looked up automatically and then grinned. In the doorway was Marnie, in her burgundy leather jacket and boots, with a wide smile on her face.

"Hey, stranger," she said, coming over to give him a hug and quick kiss on the cheek. "You look handsome."

Seth rolled his eyes and smiled. "You look great. I heard you were coming into town, but I didn't expect you this early."

"I took an early morning flight. I thought I'd come by and see if I can steal you for lunch," Marnie said with a smile.

"Sure, I can manage that," Seth said, looking at her curiously. It had been years since they'd gone out for lunch together alone. He wondered why now. "Did Patrick not come with you this trip?"

"No, we're on a little break right now, truth be told," Marnie said flatly. "But I've got all kinds of news to catch you up on. I filled Lindy and your mom in earlier, and I'm having dinner with my parents tonight."

"Can you give me about half an hour?" Seth asked. "I have a few things I need to do here first, and then we can meet. Where did you want to go?"

"Is Big Carl's BBQ still open?" Marnie asked.

"It is. Give me half an hour, and I'll meet you there," Seth told her. He watched as she stopped on the sidewalk outside to hug Jamie and exchange a few words with him. He wondered what was up. Then he wondered how he was going to tell Libby he was meeting his ex for lunch. It would be an awkward conversation, and he didn't know how to explain that the relationship was so far in the past that they were just friends and had been for years now. He sent a quick text to let her know that he was meeting an old friend for lunch and then would be over for their dinner date tonight. He cursed himself for a coward when he hit send but reminded himself that it would be much easier to explain in person.

*****

Libby looked at the text quizzically. She didn't care if he was having lunch with a friend. They weren't the kind of couple who texted each other about every detail of their days. They usually just caught up with each other in the evening to talk about it or talked on the phone during the day. She set down her phone slowly. She'd seen Lindy a few days ago, who ever-so-casually mentioned that Marnie was coming to town. But surely he wouldn't be having lunch with his long-time ex-girlfriend? Then she read the text again and correctly guessed that he was, in fact, having lunch with Marnie. She wondered if she should be worried and then realized that the feeling she was having was jealousy. She was a little worried, but she was mostly just jealous of this woman with years of history with Seth and his family.

"When you're done scowling at your phone, we can grab some ice cream," Rachel commented dryly. "What's with the face you're making?"

"Read this," Libby said, passing Rachel the phone.

"So what? He's having lunch with a friend. What's the big deal?" Rachel asked quizzically.

"He's having lunch with his ex-girlfriend. At least, that's my guess," Libby explained why she thought that.

"Well, I didn't see that coming. How are we handling this?" Rachel asked.

"I'm not going to make a big deal of it, but I'm going to ask him about it when he comes to pick me up for our date tonight," Libby shrugged. "They've known each other forever. I hate everything about him having lunch with her right now, but I kind of get it."

"Right. Would you just go out for lunch with Colin if he showed up?" Rachel snorted out an incredulous laugh.

"I can't even imagine that scenario," Libby said with a shake of her head. "He has no reason to come back so I wouldn't even have to consider making that call. But Marnie comes into town a lot."

"Well, I guess you should meet her. You know you have Seth in common for a start," Rachel said with a grin.

"Ha. Ha. Thanks for that," Libby said. "I thought you mentioned ice cream."

"I did. We better grab a cone before I have to go. Maple?" Rachel asked.

"No, I'm going to get the hazelnut. You?" Libby asked, wondering which ice cream she'd end up eating.

"Peach, I think," Rachel answered, wondering how the hazelnut would taste. They walked into Sugar & Spice and headed to the ice cream counter. "So you're okay with Seth having lunch with her? Is that what we decided?"

Libby shrugged, a frown line forming between her eyes. "It's not a problem until it's a problem," she shrugged again, trying not to worry. "I'll talk to him tonight. I'm sure it's fine."

Chapter 28

Seth sat at Big Carl's and tried not to feel guilty that he was having lunch with Marnie and not Libby. Added to that was the weight of the guilt that he hadn't taken the time to explain to Libby beforehand why he was having lunch with his ex at all. He wasn't used to having to explain himself, and the situation had developed quickly. He sat with his BBQ sandwich and salt and vinegar chips and looked at Marnie across the table. They'd ordered the same thing here; they always had. A lot of things change over time, but Big Carl's BBQ wasn't one of them. It was a staple of the town now and had been for the last forty years. An old garage had been converted into a small hole-in-the-wall restaurant ages ago, and it still served up the best BBQ for miles around. Seth ate his sandwich and listened to Marnie talk about Patrick.

"I guess the reason I wanted to talk to you about this is that it feels like us back in the day. But not us. Do you know what I mean?" she asked, taking a bite of the ranch chips that she preferred to Seth's salt and vinegar.

Seth nodded. "You want Patrick to come with you, right?" When Marnie nodded, he continued. "Did you tell him that?"

"Because I never told you?" Marnie sighed. "I never expected you to come with me, and I never dreamed of staying. I thought we both knew that."

"We did," Seth said simply. "I guess I just always hoped it would work out anyway. That's why I'm wondering if you asked him to go with you. If you didn't, he may think this is the end anyway," Seth explained.

"I guess I sort of assumed he would," Marnie admitted. "I started

177

describing all the places he could work, and he just kind of cut me off and asked why I would assume he'd go with me. Until that moment, I never really understood how you must have felt when I left. I just feel like I moved all these miles away, and I'm at the exact same fork in the road, but with someone else now. It's exhausting."

"Let me ask you this, Marnie," Seth said, taking a long drink of his sweet tea. "If you could do it all again, would you make a different choice? Would you really have wanted to stay here with me or for me to go with you?"

"Honestly, no. It was the right move for me, and I hope it was right for you, too. Plus, I met Patrick, and it's different," she shrugged, helpless to explain to the man she once loved how much Patrick meant to her now. Patrick was her forever, and yet maybe he didn't want to be.

"It was the right thing for both of us then, and this is the right thing for you now. If Patrick's the right man for you, it's going to work out even if you have to manage it long-distance," Seth assured her.

"I'm glad we stayed friends," Marnie said honestly.

"I am, too," Seth said, returning her smile. "And as my friend, I really want you to meet Libby. Would you have time to walk over with me when we leave?"

"I'd make the time even if I didn't. Lindy and your mother seem to really like her," Marnie added.

"I hope you do, too. I didn't know exactly how to explain this to her, but I think it's best if you just meet her yourself. Do you mind?" Seth asked her.

"No, I completely get it. I'd hate it if Patrick was meeting up with his ex for any reason," Marnie said wryly. "Although, he could be right now for all I know. And I'm here with you, so it's not like I can say anything."

"We're practically family," Seth began and then stopped. They both shuddered and then laughed. "Okay, so we're nothing like family, but we're friends now. I hope Patrick can understand that since I've hung out with him nearly every time he's visited."

As they left Big Carl's, Seth gave Libby a quick call and found out that she was still downtown. Her sister had left, and she'd run into Lindy. She agreed to wait a few minutes before she headed back to work. Seth walked with Marnie down Main Street and thought about all the times he'd walked with her in the six years they dated. Even before that, he'd probably walked with her a time or two because they'd shared a class. He couldn't separate Madison from Marnie and had long ago stopped trying. Now he kept the good memories and was glad they'd managed to stay friends through it all. But as he approached his sister and Libby, he realized that his feelings for Marnie paled in comparison to how he felt about Libby. He couldn't see a future in Madison that didn't include the life they'd created together. The long walks and shared meals and lazy morning breakfasts in bed. Her writing companionably while he researched antiques and balanced the books. When he made the introductions, Seth nearly beamed with pride.

"Marnie, this is my girlfriend Libby," Lindy stayed back and took in the scene, curious as to how Seth would handle this introduction.

"It's so nice to meet you, Libby," Marnie said genuinely. "Seth's told me so much about you when I haven't been talking him to death about Patrick." She grinned at Seth and then turned to Libby. "I'd have asked you to join us, but I really had to bend his ear about this thing with my boyfriend. Can I make it up to you and maybe we can all have dinner soon before I head back to Denver?" she asked.

Libby wanted to stay jealous of Marnie. She was beautiful, after all, and her shared history with Seth was, frankly, intimidating. But she was also warm and sincere, and Libby found herself liking her. "I would love that. We're having dinner out tonight if you'd like to join us. You, too, Lindy," Libby added, looking to Seth for his nod of confirmation at the plan.

*****

"I hope this dinner invitation will include me," Dean sauntered up to the group with a slow smile. "Marnie, no one told me you were back in town." He gave her a bear hug, lifting her feet off the ground. "You're looking good."

"Will you put her down?" Lindy asked in irritation.

"In a minute," Dean said with a grin. "You smell good, too."

Marnie giggled, a reaction Dean was used to. "Always good to see you, Dean." Her feet slowly touched the ground again. "I hear you've been charming the ladies."

"Now don't believe everything this one tells you," he said, pointing to Lindy. "She's just jealous." At her scoff and eye roll, he grinned. "It just so happens I have dinner plans, but call me later Marnie, and maybe we can go out for a drink." He sauntered off, grinning at Seth as he did.

Dean and Seth had long ago made a pact not to date each other's exes after a near-brawl in middle school over the adorable Aubrey Lynn Walker. Dean wasn't serious about dating Marnie, but it sure did aggravate Lindy when he flirted with her. She wasn't privy to the pact, and he just flat out enjoyed yanking her chain. She was far too uptight for her own good, which was surprising for an artist.

Dean headed back to the station, leaving them to their dinner plans. He really did wish he could join them, but he hadn't lied about having other plans. He let them assume he had a date, and the truth is that normally he would have. It just so happened he was moonlighting tonight for a little extra cash at another fire station. He'd agreed on a temporary spot until they found more permanent help, but the truth was that he needed the money. He'd bought a cabin up on the lake a couple years back and had been slowly making it livable. It had become a money pit, and he was still paying rent on his apartment in the meantime. He was coming to the point where he'd have to either sell it and barely break even on what he'd put into it, or he'd have to give up his apartment and live like a squatter until he had the time to make all the repairs. Seth had been helping him when they both had time, which wasn't often lately.

He heard footsteps on the pavement outside and he'd sat up and prepared a charming smile for the station's visitor when he saw it was just Lindy. The charming smile turned to a grin, and he slouched back in his chair.

"Miss me already, sugar?" he asked lazily.

He was hoping to get a rise out of her and wasn't disappointed. Her shirt today declared, "Girls Just Want to Have Fun-damental

Human Rights." She wore it over tight jeans and riding boots with her hair piled on top of her head in one of those messy buns that women like Lindy had perfected. He was really loving the look, particularly when paired with the scowl on her face. Whatever lipstick she'd put on earlier had long since come off, and her mouth was the natural pink he'd once studied avidly during his infamous crush. That mouth was about to start moving, he thought, and he folded his hands in his lap and waited for the show.

"Miss you? Look, you stay away from Marnie, you hear me? She's had a hard enough time with Patrick lately, and do I even need to remind you that this is Seth's ex?" She was gesturing wildly around the room, and Dean was nearly disappointed that he was the only one to witness her temper. But then she continued, "If you want to sleep with every single woman in this town, that's your business. But Marnie is like a sister to me, and you need to leave her alone."

At the accusation, Dean sat up in his seat, no longer relaxed. "First off, Marnie is a grown woman who is more than capable of deciding who she spends her time with in this town. Secondly, who I sleep with is none of your damn business, Lindy. As I haven't slept with you, I think your claim that I've slept with every single woman in town might be a bit of an exaggeration. But, clearly, you've been paying attention to me even if I haven't given a damn about what you do on your time. But maybe that's because I have a life to live and you don't do a damn thing but work."

Somewhere after the second damn, Lindy flushed pink in embarrassment and then pale again as she realized what he was implying. "Are you saying I don't have a life because I'm not sleeping with everything that moves?" she retorted sharply.

"I'm saying you should get laid, Lindy. Maybe then you'd mind your own damn business." Dean stood up and gave a humorless smile as Lindy took a quick step back. In her heeled boots, they were nearly eye-to-eye. If he wasn't seeing red, he could have seen the flicker of hurt in her dark eyes.

She turned on her heel and started to leave the station. At the door, she turned back to give him a brief suggestion on what he could do to himself, before she marched off, eating up the sidewalk in long strides. Dean stood at the window and watched her go and then could have kicked himself. It was his own fault for picking at that particular hornet's nest. He'd just wanted to get a rise out of her, but he got tired of her constant insinuations and judgments about his love life. He felt uncomfortably guilty about that parting shot, as her brother was his best friend, and he'd grown up eating pancakes made by her mother. Still, she'd deserved it. Dean scowled down the street. He wasn't sure if he felt more angry or guilty, but it was just enough to make him wonder if he could convince Marnie to go out for drinks with him after all. Maybe after his shift later tonight.

*****

Lindy made it to the office in her studio and managed to shut the door quietly behind her so that she didn't disturb the class, although she wanted to slam it as hard as she could manage. So that's what Dean thought of her. Maybe he wasn't the only one. Lindy shrugged and then dropped into the seat at her desk. She put her head in her hands, hoping to ward off the headache she knew was brewing there. She always got headaches when she was stressed. As a teenager, she'd had migraines that had been so debilitating she'd missed school days, which was fine with her since she'd hated school. She remembered sitting in the dark with cold compresses on her head and the fan moving slowly above. She uncomfortably remembered one day when Dean had dropped by with Seth and left what she could only call a care package, a term teenage Dean only scoffed at, by her door during one of her particularly bad headaches. There had been an eye mask to shut out the light, a compress that could be heated or chilled, and a juice that he'd read might help with migraines. She'd been absurdly touched, but also embarrassed that anyone outside the family knew of her struggle, which she always viewed as a weakness.

She took a pill bottle out of the drawer and promptly took a handful of Ibuprofen. She had learned the signs of an oncoming headache and tried to prevent where she could. Luckily, she hadn't had a migraine in the last couple of years, not since she'd gotten the daith piercing she'd heard so much about. She'd been skeptical, but it had really worked for her. She still had an occasional headache, but nothing like the debilitating migraines she'd once regularly suffered. She grabbed a cold Coke from the fridge under her desk and swallowed the pills, praying that they would chase away the headache before it really got started. She put her head down on the desk for just a minute and took a few deep breaths. Maybe it would pass in a moment.

Lindy had expected a confrontation with Dean, but she hadn't expected that. It was her own fault for storming in there and trying to protect Marnie. She'd been so angry that he'd hit on Seth's ex-girlfriend, and then added to that, she was genuinely worried that he'd try to mess with Marnie while she was going through this sensitive time with Patrick. That would only lead to heartache for all of them. Well, all of them but Dean, who she was convinced didn't have a heart at all. She thought uncomfortably of the care package and sat up. She probably shouldn't have gotten involved. But she'd be damned if she'd say she was sorry after what he said to her!

She got laid, she thought in annoyance. She had lots of sex. Well, maybe that wasn't entirely true right now. Her bedside table had the typical single gal's survival kit of interesting toys so she could take care of her own needs, but when she was dating, she had her fair share of sex. It was none of his business anyway, she thought angrily. Sure, it had been . . . she thought back. It couldn't have been five months already? She did the math in her head. Then sighed. Other than a one night stand a couple of months back, she hadn't had regular sex in almost six months. It wasn't planned. After she stopped seeing Tyler, she had taken a time out from the dating world. A moratorium, so to speak. That breakup had been brutal, and Lindy just didn't feel like putting herself out there.

Plus, after a few failed dating attempts, she'd decided that Mr. Right was probably not out there for her. Maybe he'd settled for someone else, or maybe he'd never existed in the first place. But she wasn't getting any younger, as people liked to tell her all the time, and she wanted to have a family. She'd stopped focusing on dating and started looking into her options. There was no reason she couldn't have a family on her own. She was healthy and had a steady income from a stable business. She had a home to live in and plenty of social support from her family and friends. It was simply a matter of filling out the necessary paperwork, paying the money, and taking the steps.

So, no, she hadn't gotten laid lately, and Lindy regretted that he'd brought that so thoroughly to her attention. She may have given up on Mr. Right, but that didn't mean she was taking a vow of celibacy. She'd thought about using one of the dating sites just for a casual hook-up, but she cringed in embarrassment at the thought of someone she knew seeing that out there. Plus, she could never entirely figure that out. Just because someone seemed attractive online didn't mean that they would be in person or that there would be any chemistry at all. She'd hate to show up and then feel rude if she simply wasn't feeling it. So instead she relied on chance encounters at bars or at networking events, which her friends sometimes dragged her to against her will. The one night stand she'd managed a couple of months back had been from a chance meeting at a bar. It hadn't been great sex, and neither of them had attempted to repeat the experience.

Lindy sighed. She wouldn't let Dean make her feel bad about her life. She didn't treat people as if they were disposable. She enjoyed sex, but she wanted intimacy with her lovers. Sure, she was selective, but that was okay. It worked for her. What she really wanted was a family, and she could let everything else slide for right now if she could figure out a way to manage that on her own. After all, these days she was managing everything else on her own, so why not this, too?

*****

Marnie stayed the rest of the week and had dinner with Seth, Libby, and Lindy. She'd even met up with Dean for a drink, but she didn't share that with Lindy. Marnie knew that her friend wouldn't approve, and she wouldn't believe her if Marnie said that Dean hadn't even hit on her. They'd talked instead about her situation with Patrick and the house he was restoring, which she was pretty sure Lindy knew nothing about. Well, it wasn't her secret to tell, and she was pretty sure it wasn't a secret at all. Still, she'd glossed over the night out and the drink, making it sound like she'd been with other friends and had only seen Dean in passing.

The visit had been worth it, and she had a sense of peace that Seth had met Libby. She'd watched the two of them together and decided that if Patrick was her forever then Libby was definitely Seth's. She could see how the two of them fit together. And she could see it with her and Patrick. As she boarded the plane to head back to Denver, she thought about what she would say to him when she landed. She'd tell him that she wanted him in Charleston building a life beside her, but that if he wasn't willing to do that, she'd wait for another job in a place where he could see a life with her. If that's what he wanted. She had to believe that he still wanted that. Even if she hadn't heard from him since she'd left town.

When Marnie's plane landed, it was still dark. Patrick hated how she'd always chosen the cheapest flights, booking them at the oddest departure and arrival times just to save a little extra money. He often reminded her that she spent more money on the leather jacket she wore than the cost of a single flight. And it was true. She saved money where she could so she could splurge on the things that made her feel good. As she grabbed her carryon bag from the overhead compartment, she wished that Patrick was beside her, complaining about the early flight time and how they'd arrived before the sun. She missed that right now. She decided that she would swallow her pride. As soon as she picked up her luggage, she would call him and tell him that she didn't want to be where he wasn't. If he didn't feel the same, then they could just call it a day on this whole relationship. But if he did? She wanted to marry him. It was that simple.

Marnie crossed the tarmac and entered the terminal, looking down at her phone and checking her messages. She walked through the airport on autopilot, remembering exactly where to go and walking among the other tired passengers without even observing her surroundings. When she grabbed the one bag she'd checked, she turned around and nearly bumped into Patrick. His long blonde hair was combed back as if it still hadn't completely dried from his shower. His beard was trimmed shorter than it had been when she'd left, and he had changed from his usual plaid shirt and jeans to a nice button-up shirt and slacks. She jumped back in surprise when she saw him, and then her mouth just fell open. She tried to make words come, but instead, she burst into tears. She tried to tell him to come with her, but before she could, he was holding her tightly and asking if there was still room in Charleston for him to come with her. She nodded yes, still crying, and thought that she was going to marry this man just as soon as she found an opportune time to ask him.

Chapter 29

Libby was looking forward to her first holiday season in Madison. She'd tried not to think about the last holiday season, how she'd spent the month of December filing for divorce and packing to move. There had been no Christmas tree, and theirs had been the only house on the block without lights. She'd saved her Christmas joy for time spent with her family and friends and then gone back to a cold, dark house that was slowly coming undone. Nails hung empty on the walls where pictures had been removed, and most of the furniture had been sold over the last couple of months. It looked as if someone had been moving in, not slowly dismantling a shared life. Her boxes had far outnumbered Colin's, who seemed eager just to go and leave all of the past behind him.

Libby took a deep breath. A year could change so much. Already, she and Seth had carved pumpkins together and gone on hayrides with the air crisp and cool. They had sat in front of bonfires huddled together with s'mores dripping hot rivulets of chocolate down their hands as they laughed. Her hands had held Seth's as they'd walked through downtown together, crunching leaves beneath their feet and the trees overhead changing colors, as she headed to the office and him to the shop. They'd even stayed up all night handing out candy to the trick-or-treaters and then watching classic horror movies. They'd sat cuddled together under thick tartan blankets at Seth's house and watched Vincent Price, Bella Lugosi, and Boris Karloff work their cinematic magic. She had curled her body into his, snuggling closer, and seen the future unfurling before her. She'd wondered then if a relationship could stay like this or if everything that was good eventually faded away.

Now as November gave way to December, Libby began anticipating the holiday season. They already had Thanksgiving behind them. Faith had been working on yet another cruise, and her parents hadn't remembered the holiday except in passing. They'd called from a Cracker Barrel somewhere up the East Coast where they'd stopped for a few nights. They'd called to wish both Libby and Rachel a Happy Thanksgiving. Libby had stopped in for Thanksgiving lunch with Rachel and then gone to dinner at Keely's where Seth's family had gathered. Libby had enjoyed spending time with Beth, who she'd gotten to know a little better over the last few months. Even Dean had stopped by to join them. Seth had explained that he didn't have much of a family during the holidays so he had always been invited to spend holidays with them.

"Is it just me or has Dean been shooting daggers at Lindy all night?" Libby asked Beth quietly as they sat talking on the couch after dinner.

"I think it's been mutual, actually," Beth said, reflecting on how Dean and Lindy had avoided each other during the night, a difficult feat as Keely had seated them beside each other. "They've always argued. As far as Dean is concerned, Lindy will always be like a bossy older sister."

"Hmm," Libby replied, noncommittally. She wondered sometimes. She'd watched Lindy direct all of her conversational powers away from Dean who was sitting immediately to her right. Fortunately, Keely had sat Beth on the other side, and she was happy to keep up her end of the conversation. Libby had watched in amusement from across the table where she'd sat with Seth. She had always enjoyed observing other families, trying to figure out what made them tick. Keely was clearly the heart of hers. Libby couldn't really say if her own family had anyone who brought them together like that.

Libby had a missed call from Colin over Thanksgiving, but she hadn't bothered returning it. What was there left to say now, after all? She certainly didn't need pregnancy updates. She wrote it off as an accident and didn't bother to check her messages. He'd never been one to leave a voicemail anyway. It had bothered her at the time, but she'd simply deleted the call and message and then gone a step further to delete his number. She'd long since removed it from her speed dial, but now she deleted it entirely. She'd only kept it there from force of habit anyway.

She was ready for the holidays and looked forward to all the festivities. There were holiday lights to see, Christmas concerts to attend, and a holiday festival that would follow the 10k she'd already signed up to run. It was for charity, after all, which is what she told herself as she pushed herself to double her usual miles. She'd taken to running the full 10k every other day now. The rest of the time she wrote her assignments, drove around and made notes for more, and slowly made her way through her Christmas shopping list.

But Sundays were for sleeping in, and Seth. Occasionally, they joined Lindy and Keely for brunch, but most Sundays were for waking slowly and making love while the sun was just starting to pour in through the windows, making shadows on the wall. Sundays were for stretching out in the hammock in Seth's yard or reading in bed with pastries they had picked up in town. It was for watching movies, snuggled together on the couch, still in pajamas. At least once a month, they got up a little early and walked into town for breakfast and then walked home the long way, talking the whole time. Now that the temperature had dropped, they would stop in at Park Bistro for brunch on those days and enjoy omelets while they sat near one of the fireplaces. Then they would go back home and slip off the layers of their clothes, scarves falling on the bedroom floor and tangling together as their bodies did the same.

Libby found herself wondering when the other shoe would drop, as it inevitably did. She wasn't pessimistic by nature, but she'd never had the stability that made trust easy. She sat on the floor by the Christmas tree with Seth, stringing popcorn and looking through old boxes of ornaments and found herself wondering how she could keep this when it felt so fragile. She found herself reaching for him, taking his hand or stroking his cheek. She didn't know how to ask him to stay, or how to make this how things would always be. She didn't know that she would trust it even if he promised that their relationship would stay the same. How could she after everything? But she wanted to believe so she let herself savor the moments as if she could keep them all.

*****

Rachel pulled the last tray of cookies from the oven. She'd spent the last couple of days making holiday treats with the kids, trying to keep them entertained through the school break and preparing for the upcoming festivities. Christmas was one of the few holidays where Rachel's family actually got together, although they usually held their celebration a week before or after Christmas, depending on Faith's schedule. This year, she was going on a New Year's cruise so they were getting together this weekend, a week before Christmas. Libby was bringing Seth, and Faith was getting a ride from a friend who lived nearby. Their parents had come to town the night before, but preferred to stay in the RV park rather than spending the night with either Libby or Rachel.

She wouldn't admit it to Libby, who adored the holidays, but Rachel always dreaded them. In her house, she put up the Christmas tree with the kids. And decorated it. And made the cookies. And helped the kids with their costumes for the school play. And cooked dinner for her own family and Alec's. Alec, on the other hand, arrived home as if the house had decorated itself. He enjoyed the season, but didn't lift a finger to help. After all these years of marriage, Rachel was tired of having to ask. He had hung up a string of lights outside and considered that adequate assistance for a holiday season that started before Thanksgiving and didn't end until January 2. Rachel wondered if something was wrong with her. She just couldn't get into the holiday season, and pretending to enjoy it was more difficult now than it had ever been.

When Libby and Seth arrived, she let out a sigh of relief. Seth always pitched in with making dinner, and Libby would entertain the kids while setting the table. They never even asked; they just jumped in and helped. Rachel felt some of the weight lift from her own shoulders. Alec, of course, was watching TV in the other room with the kids. At least it was on a holiday cartoon and not football for once.

190

Her parents had arrived within the last hour and had joined Alec in the living room. Her father was trying and failing to find a mutual topic of interest to discuss with her husband, and her mother was distractedly playing with Ella while Willow had fallen asleep on the floor beside Oliver.

She envied the ease of Seth and Libby's relationship. She watched them communicate without words and wondered when she and Alec had lost the ability to do that. Rachel sometimes felt that she and Alec didn't even speak the same language anymore. They simply managed their respective roles in the home and raised the children with the routine they'd established when it had just been them and little Oliver. She made a final check of everything and then went to stand in the doorway of the room to watch her family. Oliver and Ella were sitting wide-eyed in front of *Miracle on 34th Street*. Libby had scooped up Willow and was crooning to her as she held her. She noticed Seth watching Libby with his heart in his eyes and had to look away. Her own husband was checking his iPhone again, busily scrolling through his messages and only half responding to her mother who was asking him about the kids' school play this year. Rachel looked back at the dining room table behind her and wondered why she even made the effort at all.

*****

Alec looked up from his phone and answered another question from his mother-in-law. He was probably unnecessarily short with her, but he hated how they always feigned interest in the kids, but rarely made it a point to see them. His own parents saw the kids each week and always attended their school functions. He noticed Libby holding Willow and wondered when she'd ever settle down and have kids of her own. He hadn't ever warmed to Colin, but Seth seemed nice enough. He didn't have Colin's prep school polish, which is probably why Alec liked him a lot better. He'd grown up working class and didn't much care for the elitist attitude he'd always sensed under the surface with Libby's ex-husband.

He looked up at Rachel standing in the doorway. She was wearing a dark red sweater that suited her and had a headband with a red bow in her boy short hair. On anyone else, it might have looked childish and even ridiculous, but it just made her look young and festive. He still thought she was beautiful, but he didn't feel it in that visceral way he once had. Right now, she looked tired and annoyed, but that's mostly how she looked every day. He wondered how long it had been since she'd smiled for herself and not just for the kids or her sister. Everything he did these days seemed to annoy her so he found it was best to stay out of her way.

He checked his messages again. He'd taken to talking to friends online and meeting up with some of them for a weekly poker night just to get his mind off things. He envied Seth and Libby's relationship. But it was new, of course. In a year or two, if they made it that long, they'd probably be up to their ears in kids and debt, which left little time for romance. They wouldn't sit so close or reach out to touch each other just because they could. All of that would fade. Didn't it for everybody? Alec looked again at Rachel in the doorway and almost spoke to her, but she'd already turned her attention back to the dining room and he forgot what he was going to say. It probably wasn't important anyway.

*****

Jenson Reynolds walked to the fridge to grab a beer. He knew that Rachel would have his favorite on hand. She was that kind of stay at home mom. He guessed, correctly, that she'd become the mother she'd never had. She joined the PTA and baked cookies and sat outside soccer games for hours throughout the week. She probably cut her kids sandwiches into cute shapes or sent hand-rolled sushi in their lunches with motivational notes. As much as Rachel had loved her mother, Avery had never been cut out for any of that. She wasn't what you'd call the nurturing type, and she'd hated staying home with the kids. The problem is that she could never find exactly the career that she did like, but she tried them on, one after another, just to see. Jenson had always been attracted to her enthusiasm and never minded when she switched gears to go in a new direction. It had bothered the girls, but then they didn't know Avery like he did.

Jenson had loved Avery since they'd met at a bonfire on the beach on spring break their senior year in high school. She'd gone to the rival school, and yet they had mutual friends. They'd found themselves talking over a warm beer on an even warmer night and had probably conceived Rachel shortly thereafter. They'd not seen the need to make it all legal until a few years later when Libby was on the way. After that, they'd decided if they'd made it this long, they could make it through anything.

Of course, that was nearly thirty-six years back now. A lot had changed, but, as the saying goes, a lot stayed the same. Jenson had kept his hair, but it was a steel gray now, faded from the auburn it had once been. He had wrinkles where there'd once been smooth skin, but he'd kept his waist slim. He liked to think it was metabolism, but he knew it was the many miles he put in running each week that kept his figure. Avery, on the other hand, had gone from willow slim to plump over the years, and Jenson thought she was still as pretty as the day he'd met her when he'd caught sight of her long dark hair and dark eyes on the other side of the bonfire. He'd found a seat beside her and prayed he wouldn't talk too much or not enough; he had a bad habit of going in one direction or the other.

Jenson looked now at his family. Truth be told, he'd much rather be out on the road than here in the family circle, but he and Avery had agreed on this one day with the kids. Faith had arrived only a few minutes before and was sitting in the floor with Oliver, telling him a story. Of all his kids, she was the most like him. She wouldn't care to hear it though, so he kept it to himself. He looked at Rachel standing in the doorway and thought she was a little more like her mother than she'd care to admit. She could run circles around her mother in nurturing, but she seems stifled at home and that husband of hers was no help. He was back on his phone again, checking his messages. If he didn't know better, he'd think Alec had a woman on the side. But, no. It was probably something predictable and boring like a fantasy football league or an addiction to porn.

He looked away and let his gaze rest on Libby and Seth. Libby had passed Willow to Faith and let Ella crawl into her lap. She looked happy now, happier than he'd seen her in years. He'd been shocked when she'd told him about the divorce. Of all his children, she was the least like him and her mother. He suspected she'd been the most easily bruised by all the relocations and their absence. She stayed outwardly calm, but he could tell that she, of all his kids, was a storm. He looked at Seth and wondered if he knew that and if he could handle it if he did. He guessed that Colin never knew what he had, which was a shame. They'd really liked him. Well, he was gone now, and Seth looked like he was sticking around. For now, at least. He grabbed another beer and headed over to talk to him.

*****

Avery Reynolds noticed her husband Jenson heading for Seth and turned her attention to Faith. They talked for a few minutes, but even Avery could tell that Faith was saying all the things she'd say to anyone—say, a passenger on one of the cruises. When Avery was pregnant, she'd dreamed of the kind of relationship she'd have with her daughters. It would be different from the one she'd had with her own mother who would as soon yell at her as to speak to her. She'd been living with friends at seventeen when she'd met Jenson. At fifty-three, she may have been heavier than in her youth, but she still had the smooth skin of a woman nearly half her age. She'd kept the silver at bay with the help of her beautician, although she was sure that's not what they called them these days. She thought the term was colorist or cosmetologist. Something like that. She'd tried doing that once, before Faith was born, but she hadn't taken to it. She got bored with the straight-laced cuts and frustrated that she couldn't exercise her own creative vision on the hair. She hadn't done that work long before she'd found something else.

She'd offer to help Rachel in the kitchen, but it looked like her oldest daughter had it all under control. Plus, Libby would help if help was needed. They were always as thick as thieves with Faith lagging just a little behind. She wondered absently what had become of Colin when she reminded herself about the divorce. That's right. They had separated, and the divorce had come through so quickly. Of course, she hadn't expected Libby to take up with someone else so soon. She'd have suspected it began before the separation if she wasn't so sure that Libby would never do something like that. No, Libby wasn't that kind of rule breaker. She suspected that this Seth person wasn't either. Well, she looked happy anyway. Unlike Rachel who looked like she was about to break. She'd offer some motherly advice, but she wasn't interested in having it thrown back in her face.

It had always been that way. Rachel had taken on as much responsibility as she could manage, Libby had kept to herself—taking up as little space as possible—and Faith had been their wild child, the only one they fully understood. Of course, she was young yet and might settle down, but so far, she'd traveled extensively and seemed uninterested in any other kind of life. They might have enjoyed spending more time with her, but somehow, they'd never had that kind of relationship. They'd always assumed they would all be close when the kids were adults and old enough to understand, but instead there was distance in the relationships. They didn't seem to understand, much less forgive. Avery shrugged the thought away. Well, it was just one holiday a year, and it looked like they were all doing as well as could be expected.

*****

They'd finally done it, Libby thought. They'd survived the Christmas holiday with both families. They'd gotten through the awkward dinner with her family last week, and then they had spent Christmas Eve with Seth's family. When Christmas morning dawned, Libby woke up in her own bed with Seth's arms wrapped around her. He'd nuzzled her neck, and she settled back against him.

"Merry Christmas," he murmured against her hair.

"Merry Christmas," she said softly, snuggling against him.

"I'm going to make you breakfast. In a minute," he said sleepily.

"I'll help. In a minute," she said with a smile, turning toward him and meeting his own mouth with a long, slow kiss.

"We might need more than a minute," Seth said against her mouth.

Sometime later, they'd stumbled downstairs still half asleep and then had both sat on the stairs just looking at the tree. Libby leaned back against Seth's legs and watched the lights blink on and off. The cinnamon pine cones she'd put on the tree still gave her apartment that holiday smell, and she knew that in a minute, she'd get up and go into the kitchen with Seth and make homemade cinnamon rolls. They had decided that would be their Christmas morning tradition. They'd left it unspoken that there would be other Christmas mornings ahead of them.

Seth made the cinnamon rolls from scratch while Libby made coffee in the French press she'd been given by Rose and Dillon over the holidays. She had put on a Christmas record to play softly in the background, and they'd kept the lights dim to better show off the twinkling lights of the tree. He placed the rolls in the oven while she poured the coffee into matching mugs they'd painted and glazed themselves at a holiday art expo. They went by mutual consent and sat on the floor by the tree. Seth started stacking a pile of gifts in front of her while she grinned in delight. She started piling his gifts up in front of him, too.

"You first," he insisted with a smile. She opened up a heavy box that she suspected he hadn't wrapped himself. It was far too perfect. If she was honest, she'd had his professionally wrapped at a library event in town. Her own wrapping was far from ideal. She usually measured the wrapping paper so haphazardly that part of the gift peeked through. It had been a family joke that the most mangled looking gifts had been wrapped by Libby. It was usually true, too. She carefully removed the bow and then undid the tape, smiling as she sensed Seth's impatience. She ripped the remainder of the paper off with a grin and then softly stroked the cover of an antique record album. She flipped through the records, smiling in recognition at some of the titles and wondering about the others. She loved it.

She also opened up a pair of diamond earrings. She'd seen the small jewelry box and nearly hesitated before she picked it up. She suspected that it contained earrings, but just the sight of an engagement ring sized box brought up all the anxieties she had surrounding marriage. She wondered if she would ever be able to believe in it again. She had breathed out a sigh and picked it up, dismissing her wandering thoughts with a shake of her head. She opened the box and admired the vintage style he'd chosen.

Seth unwrapped the scarf Libby had gotten for him at the local alpaca farm and then a first edition of *Lost Horizon*.

"I know that's like carrying coals to Newcastle," she joked as he picked up the vintage copy. She'd stumbled across the hardcover first edition of Seth's favorite book at an estate sale. "I know you have a copy already," she added awkwardly.

"I don't have a first edition though," Seth told her with a smile, slowly turning the pages.

"You want to read it right now, don't you?" she asked with him a grin.

"You know I do." The timer went off for the cinnamon rolls, and they both stood up.

"You get out the cinnamon rolls, and I'm going to put on one of these records," Libby told him.

They left the wrapping paper on the floor and ate cinnamon rolls dripping with icing at the counter. Libby poured them large cups of coffee afterward, and they sat together on the couch. She flipped the record to the B side and lay down with her head in Seth's lap while he flipped through the first edition carefully. She knew he wouldn't leave it on a shelf only to be seen; she'd known when she bought it that he would want to read it and would carefully turn the pages, treasuring the words again. The cover was plain, a faded green with the title in soft gold on the binding. He was reading already about Shangri-La and stroking her hair absently, and she was drifting along to Ella Fitzgerald on vinyl, half asleep and perfectly at peace.

My funny Valentine, sweet comic Valentine
You make me smile with my heart . . .

Chapter 30

New Year's Eve had passed with the usual champagne and fireworks, and Libby started the new year determined to build up to a half marathon. She was running more often, and she alternated between running outside on the streets and taking a turn on the treadmill when the weather was either too cold or too wet to make an outdoor run reasonable. There had been a few cold wet days already in the month, but Libby hadn't minded them. While she had to suffer through an indoor run on the treadmill, the evenings were spent inside with Seth. They would curl up in front of the fireplace at his house or hers and listen to records or watch old movies. Once, they'd slow danced in circles around the room. They'd made rainy days the best kind of days, and Libby sometimes had to pinch herself—mentally at least—to make sure this was her life. She hadn't believed in romance like this and yet had found it. Slowly, she stopped wondering when the other shoe would drop.

And then it did. Well, a shoe didn't actually drop, of course. It was so much worse than that. On a bitterly cold January day, the kind that leached the color out of the day, her doorbell rang. Libby was busy writing. It was her morning at home, and she was deep into a blog about—well, it doesn't matter what it was about, really. The moment she heard the doorbell she froze. It was far too early to be a package delivery, and Seth would have called first and even let himself in with his key after a quick knock. She hoped it wasn't a solicitor of any kind. After having her work interrupted, she wasn't likely to handle that with her usual aplomb.

She walked to the door slowly, still in her stocking feet. Later, it would be one of her first realizations: she'd weathered the shock wearing socks. She'd had on no shoes and was, in fact, wearing silly socks, of all things. They had Wonder Woman on them, and they made her happy. She wore them at home for her own pleasure. When she thought about it all later, she would think of how vulnerable she'd been at the moment she'd opened the door. She wished she could go back and put on those high-heeled boots that always made her feel powerful. Somehow, she felt she would have been able to stride to the door and even shut it in his face had she but worn them. But no. It was a home writing day, and she'd been for a run already. She'd had a shower and dried her hair and applied the barest hint of makeup. She'd pulled on leggings and a favorite sweater and grabbed the Wonder Woman socks at the last minute, sure that her feet would get cold on the hardwood floors of her little home.

The bell rang, and she swore under her breath. Then, slowly, she headed toward the door, a scowl forming on her face. The peephole was blocked by the wreath she'd hung up, and she checked the window instead. There was a car parked outside, but it wasn't familiar. She opened the door carefully and then said nothing at all. She said nothing, and she didn't move. She simply stared in disbelief and leaned against the door.

"Hey, Libby," Colin said softly.

*****

In town, Seth was checking the displays, straightening items as he went. He'd played holiday records from mid-November to the new year, but now he switched to the Bill Evans Trio. He wanted something soothing for what was shaping up to be a depressing sort of day. It was bitterly cold outside, and it didn't look like it would get any warmer. The clouds were thick overhead, and the atmosphere was less than impressive. He had a feeling that he wouldn't get many visitors today so he focused instead on straightening inventory and assessing where he could make improvements. Farrah sat at the register and read volumes of poetry aloud as the mood struck her. She'd fallen in love recently with spoken word poetry and now was reciting the work of Sabrina Benaim into the empty shop. ". . . Love made me feel like I knew the answer, but when I raised my hand, I was the only one in the room."

Seth nodded along absently. He loved words read out loud, and he had the same habit of reading aloud when the shop was empty. He wondered if Farrah had picked it up from him, or if it was just something about the shop itself that made poetry resonate between the walls.

"What I mean is, have you ever felt the ache of swallowing starlight?"

Seth turned slowly toward the voice that wasn't Farrah's speaking the next lines of Benaim's poem. He'd recognized that mothball voice and turned to see the old lady he'd spoken to months ago standing patiently behind him. Today, she was leaning on a cane, and he wondered if it was due to illness, injury, or affectation. He remembered another day, months back when she'd come into the store quoting poetry. He smiled at her.

"It's so nice to see you back in town."

"It's nice to be remembered," she beamed up at him. "Do you like Ms. Benaim's work?' she asked him.

Seth had just a moment to wonder if she'd once been a school teacher. She had that sort of air about her, of one who asks and expects to receive an answer. Plus, she was incredibly well-read and had even memorized the poems. Many teachers had the knack of that. "I think it's amazing. Farrah has been championing her work, and I think we're stocking some of her volumes if you're interested."

"Isn't it funny how those of us who love antiques are often bibliophiles as well?" she commented. "Words are timeless, really."

"They are indeed. What brings you back to Madison? It's surely not the weather," Seth said with a smile.

"I have some family in the area. I like to check up on them once in a while. And I do enjoy a little walk down memory lane. I remembered your shop and wanted to stop by." She smiled softly at Seth. Today's dress was as old-fashioned and faded as the last, but somehow suited her. "It's been many months now, but I just wondered if you still had a certain music box—" she began.

"The one that played *Love Story*?" Seth asked curiously.

"You do have a good memory. And you pay attention to details.

That ought to serve you well." She beamed at him.

"I still have it. When we changed out some of our inventory, I set it aside. I don't remember exactly why now, but it hardly matters. Would you like to see it again?" Seth asked.

"Yes, please," she said firmly.

"Would you like to sit down while I get it? I could have Farrah make you a cup of tea," Seth suggested.

"I am not so old that I need—" the old lady began firmly, but then relented. "I would like to sit, thank you. And I'll take that cup of tea as well, if the girl knows how to brew a proper pot."

"Farrah considers herself a tea enthusiast so I think you'll enjoy a cup. Let me just have a quick word with her, and I'll fetch that music box for you."

Seth led the woman to a chair, and then he went and spoke to Farrah, who came back and asked her tea preferences, as if it were a matter of great seriousness. While she was in the back room making it, another young man came out and sat at the front register. This one was tall and muscular with a shaved head and a great many tattoos. The old lady watched him quizzically.

"I don't usually handle the front of the house," Jamie offered politely, in near apology to the elderly customer.

"Well, I don't see any reason why you shouldn't. You seem a smart enough young man," she replied stoutly.

"Not all of our customers would think so," Jamie said with a defiant grin. "But I manage."

"I don't doubt it," she said calmly. "I've no doubt of it. Now I don't mean to complain—" she began, and answered Jamie's grin with a slow smile of her own, "But I don't care for this music as much as others. Would you happen to have any Ella Fitzgerald you could play? It seems like the day calls for something a bit bolder."

Jamie smiled and said he'd see what he could do. He went to the back of the shop, and shortly the sound of Ella's sultry vocals filled the shop. "Much better. Thank you so much," the elderly woman said with a contented sigh. She took a cup of hot tea with thanks and watched as Farrah took her place in the front while Jamie headed back into the storeroom with a wave.

She sipped from her tea and then gave a brief nod of approval toward Farrah who was once again at the front register reading out another piece of poetry. She mouthed the words to herself while she sipped the tea, and she let her gaze wander around the store. She marveled at how things could stay the same and yet change so much. She'd hoped the music box would still be there, or at least one like it. She could remember being a young girl reaching up for a gleaming box where a dancer made slow pirouettes to the music. She could remember holding it gently in her hands and imagining herself into it. Then, of course, later she'd wanted to dance, but she knew better than to dance in that room, where every careless movement could result in something precious being damaged or lost, a careful history that once gone could not be recovered. And so she danced in her mind until there was room to dance with her arms and her legs, twirling until she'd get so dizzy she'd lie down and look at the clouds going by.

Holding a music box now felt like the world revolving. It was an open door to the past, to being both the ballerina in the box and the young girl holding it all at once. It was foolish, of course. There was no going back. She watched the customers browse and returned their polite smiles. She listened to Farrah's poetry read aloud, which hadn't ceased with the entry of customers into the store. She watched Jamie go back and forth between a storeroom and the sales floor, bringing out treasures held carefully in his large hands.

When Seth returned to the front of the shop, the old lady was calmly sipping tea and listening to Ella Fitzgerald. He brought her the music box, and she set the tea down on the counter softly. She reached for the box, her hands trembling only a little, and held it. For a moment, that's all she did. She held it in her hands and looked down at it fondly. Then she slowly opened it up and listened to the notes of the song as the ballerina twirled.

"Every little girl, at some point, dreams of being a ballerina," she said softly. "The dreams change later. But for a moment, we all have inside us that desire to be led by the music, to be elevated by it." She sighed softly. For the length of the song, she simply watched the ballerina spin. When the song wound down, she closed the box gently. "Thank you. I'll take this and be on my way." She stood up slowly, leaning on her cane, and looked around the room again. "It's just as I remembered it."

Seth took the box to the front counter and rang it up himself. He wrapped it carefully in tissue paper and placed it in one of their gift bags with an outline of the mythical Shangri La and a full moon overhead etched into the paper, silver words spelling out Lost Horizon shimmering on the blue paper. When he handed her the bag, she looked up at him quizzically.

"It seems like a day for memories, and for change. We all make our choices," she said cryptically, nodding her head.

"We certainly do," Seth agreed, politely. He liked her. He was glad she'd stopped by for another visit and wondered where she was from and why she was here, really. Most customers who started a conversation immediately told him these things without him having to ask. The fact that she hadn't made Seth more circumspect. He didn't want to pry, and yet he was curious about this woman who seemed to have great volumes of poetry memorized and could quote authors at the drop of a hat. Jamie held the door for her as she left, and Seth watched her go, wondering if she'd ever make it back this way.

*****

Libby finally found her voice. "What are you doing here, Colin?" She leaned against the door frame still, holding on to the door. She wasn't willing to open it up and let him into her home, and yet she couldn't bring herself to shut it either. She stood in indecision and waited.

"I hoped we could talk," he said simply. He stood there in a plain green sweater and blue jeans with one hand tucked casually into his pocket. Libby thought that at one point in time she would have wondered if his hands were cold. She'd have reached out to check, and if they had been chilly at all, she would have warmed them with her own or tucked them into her own pockets, pulling him inside. Now she just watched him, wondering why he was here and what she was supposed to say.

"Is there anything left to say?" She asked with a frown that drew the lines between her eyes sharply together. "I thought our attorneys handled all the details."

"Come have a cup of coffee with me. Just hear me out, and then I'll leave, okay?" Colin said quietly. "Come on, Libby. It's just coffee."

She froze then. Just coffee. Their first date. All those years ago. She wondered how anything between them could be just coffee, and yet she thought it perfectly summed up their relationship that things could be so simple for him. As simple as coffee. As simple as leaving. She nodded. "Not here though. There's a coffee shop in town."

"Can I drive you?" he offered. "We can go in my car." She'd noticed the new SUV in her driveway, the one she hadn't recognized. Of course, he'd gotten a new car. New car, new relationship, new baby, new life.

She looked down suddenly, and it was then that she realized she was standing in her socks. "No. Thanks, but no. I'll drive myself. It's Brews & Blues downtown. Just give me a few minutes, and I'll meet you there."

Before he could argue, she closed the door. She gently rested her head against it. She could hear him outside, still, just on the other side of the door. After a minute, he began to walk toward his car. She wondered if he would get into it and drive away completely or if he really would meet her for coffee. She went to find her boots and figured that she'd find out soon enough.

She grabbed her leather jacket and her purse and did a last check to make sure she had her keys. She stayed focused on the details of leaving the house—anything to keep from concentrating on the heavy rhythm of a heart beating off-key. When she'd seen him, her heart had stopped, raced, and then slowed. Now she could feel it pulsing inside of her, and she wasn't sure how she felt. She'd never expected to see him again, and the sight of him standing on her doorstep had brought with it a flood of memories. She didn't want them. She wanted Seth and the life she was living before Colin rang her doorbell. She wanted to enjoy the beauty of loving Seth without the complication of knowing that she had loved Colin once. And loved still? She wasn't sure. Because she wasn't sure, she double-checked the keys and then the lock and even waited an extra minute for her car to warm up. She backed out slowly and drove at a speed barely approaching the limit and tried to decide what she felt.

She pulled up to Brews and parked beside his car. He got out as she pulled in, and she wished that she'd picked somewhere else— somewhere that didn't have memories of Seth or where she could run into people she knew. She didn't want to have to answer questions or make introductions. She just wanted to find out what he wanted and see him go. She walked just ahead of him and made it to the door first. She opened it before he could and stepped inside. She returned greetings with Elle and Naomi as she went inside. Colin ordered their coffees while Libby waited nearby, mindlessly looking over the menu.

"Would you mind if we just walked?" Colin asked her quietly.

"Fine," Libby acquiesced with a shrug of her shoulder. As they walked out to the street, Colin handed Libby her coffee. As she turned to take it, her fingers brushed his own. Time stopped for just a moment as she met his eyes. Then the coffee was in her hands, and the moment passed. She looked deliberately away and started walking toward the park in town. It was public, and Libby wanted public. She wasn't hiding anything, and she hadn't had a chance yet to let Seth know what had happened. She just wanted to get this conversation done, but she refused to start the conversation. She let the silence hang in the air and wondered how he would break it.

"Maisie lost the baby," Colin said simply, looking straight ahead. "It was right after we'd found out and started to tell everyone."

"I'm sorry," Libby said simply, and she was sorry. She knew that it was possible to miss something, or someone, you'd never had, so she could only imagine how tough this must have been. "How's Maisie?"

"She's fine. She's okay. We decided that we weren't right for each other. It's been over for a few months now," he explained.

"Why are you here?" Libby asked. "A phone call would have been enough to tell me that. So why did you come?" They reached the park, and she climbed the stairs to find a bistro table where they could sit and talk. She sensed that he would have preferred the swings, but the swings were where she sat with Seth.

"I think I made a mistake," he began. She looked at him in confusion. "With us, I mean. I don't think we really tried to work things out, and I think we could. I'm still in love with you," he admitted calmly.

Libby drank her coffee and looked at him blankly. "We're divorced, Colin. You didn't want to work things out if you'll remember. And I have a boyfriend."

He looked pained for just a moment. "Okay, so you have a boyfriend. I had Maisie for a while. But what are a few months of history compared to six years?" he asked her in a reasonable tone.

"Five years. Our shared history didn't seem to trip you up when you asked for the divorce. I don't know why it would be an issue now," Libby said, her temper simmering under the surface. How could he do this to her? She'd finally managed to get over him and build a new life, and here he was: shaking the foundations.

"Look, I'm sorry! I know now that I should have told you how unhappy I was, and we could have worked it out. I just want another chance to try. I do love you, Libby. I never stopped," Colin said sincerely. "Can you honestly say you stopped loving me?"

She looked into his eyes. It used to be his eyes that tripped her up, how when he was happy the smile reached all the way there and lit them up. She'd loved the crinkles at the corners, and the way his mouth quirked in a smile only after his eyes lit up. And she'd loved them when he was serious, when he looked at her and told her about his hopes and dreams and fears and failures. She'd walked down an aisle toward those eyes, and then later still, she'd sat across from him when those eyes were cold and saying that he just didn't care enough anymore. He'd said divorce, and the word hadn't made a ripple in those eyes, but they'd made rivulets of grief from hers. But now? She looked into his eyes and only felt the shock of what he was saying. It was like one of those fantasies where the lover you once wanted came back filled with love and regret, except it was real and she was in love with someone else.

Seth. She held on to his name and took a deep breath. "Colin, this is crazy. The divorce has been final for months. You had every opportunity to stop it if you had wanted to, and you didn't. I'm with Seth now. That doesn't all of a sudden change because months later you had a change of heart," Libby told him sharply.

"I never had a change of heart, Libby. I loved you through it all. I thought when I talked to you about a divorce, things might change. You didn't seem like you cared about me anymore, and the second I said I was unhappy, you agreed to separate. Just like that," Colin snapped his fingers, his voice tense. "I had my pride at least. I wasn't going to try to make it work when you were so quick to get out of it. I thought you didn't care anymore. But then I remembered that you always shut down and acted like you didn't care when you were hurt, and I had a little hope that maybe you still loved me, too. You haven't said that you don't." She was quiet, looking down at her hands, so he continued. "Libby, we had five years. Can't we try again to make it work?"

"Do you think the last year just magically erases because you're sorry?" Libby asked, her voice rising. "Because it doesn't." She struggled to reign in her temper and all of the emotions spilling out. "I have a life here, and I love it. I love Seth. Whatever we had is in the past now, and we can't go back." She took a deep breath. "A part of me will always love you, but what we had is broken. This thing with Seth isn't casual," she told him softly.

Colin looked at her, never breaking the eye contact. She hated to see the sadness there, but she couldn't be swayed. "I'm sorry. Of course, you're right. I just needed to say that I'm sorry I quit on us so easily, and I hope you can forgive me, Libby. And I hope he deserves you," he told her. "Look," he continued. "I'm going to be around a few days. Can we at least talk, catch up a little?" he asked.

"I don't think that's a good idea," Libby said quietly.

"Well, if you change your mind . . ." He let that sentence hang, waiting for some kind of acknowledgment. She nodded briefly. "It really was good to see you, Libby. You look beautiful." She met his eyes and saw again the smile that traveled all the way up, the crinkles in the corner, and the quirk of his lips. She gave him a half smile and sat back with her coffee while he started to walk away. Then, he turned and came back quickly as if he was afraid that if he didn't now, he never would.

"Look, I wanted a baby, too. Not just a baby, but a baby with you. And we just couldn't do it. You got so lost in that, and I didn't feel like there was a place for me. I know that I didn't handle it well, and I'm sorry about that. But every month that you grieved, I grieved right along with you. And it just broke something in me. I know you wanted to be a mother, but I needed you to be my wife."

The words stung, and Libby recoiled as if she'd been struck. "I was your wife, Colin. You just stopped seeing that I was still there, even if a baby wasn't." They stared at each other, realizing that between them lay a gulf of misunderstanding and resentment.

"I'm sorry I stopped seeing you," Colin said simply. "I'd change it if I could."

"I know," Libby said, nodding. "But we can't change it. And my whole life is different now." She paused. "I'm different now."

"I can see that," Colin said sadly. "It suits you." He gave her a half smile and walked away, no longer striding confidently the way he always had. He looked defeated.

Libby guessed that the conversation had taken no more than half an hour. Maybe forty-five minutes at the most. When he left, she sat there for a few minutes replaying it in her head. Then she got up and walked. And walked some more. She walked all over town, just thinking. She knew that she needed to call Seth, but first, she wanted to figure out how she felt and what she wanted and why seeing Colin had shaken her so much. Of course, she'd never liked when the past revisited. She didn't even like driving through places she'd once lived. She wanted to keep the past in the past, in the neatly labeled box of memories stacked in her head where things didn't change, and they didn't suddenly show up apologizing and asking you to change everything either.

He'd seemed like the old Colin again. He'd looked at her in that way that used to make her feel like the only woman in the world. She'd later wondered if that was just a part of who he was and if every woman felt like that in his company. She'd decided that she hadn't been special, but she'd felt special, and that had made all the difference. If she hadn't felt that draw to him, maybe coffee would have just been coffee and not become something more. But she did, and it hadn't taken long to fall. And the Colin that showed up today looked at her like that. The one she'd divorced had looked at her blankly as if he wasn't sure how they'd ended up together, or why. She wasn't going to fall for it this time. Coffee was just coffee, and she needed to go see Seth.

She tried not to see the hurt in Colin's eyes and how he'd talked about their shared grief as if it had been shared and not something she'd always felt she was facing alone. She wondered how long they had each longed for the other to pay attention and how they'd managed to both miss the mark. Still, she'd seen him, and it was over now. Whatever closure she might have needed had been served up on a silver platter. So why didn't it feel over?

*****

Seth wasn't happy about the visit. Actually, that might be a massive understatement. He was nearly seething about it, but mostly he was uncomfortable. Under the surface of his irritation, questions circled like sharks in the water. Lindy had called earlier to ask who Libby was having coffee with at Brews. He hadn't known and hadn't initially thought anything about it, but then he'd decided to try to catch up with her there. If it was a work meeting, he would just grab coffee and go, but maybe the timing would be right, and he'd have a few minutes to see her between her work and his own.

The timing had been right in a way. He'd walked around the corner just in time to see Libby and a man he didn't know come out of Brews. He would have thought that they were strangers, but the man had handed her a coffee and then they stopped for a moment in the doorway. It wasn't even a long moment, but Seth knew then that there was a shared history. He froze where he was and watched them head toward the park. He wondered if that was Colin and if it was, why the hell he was here. He wanted to keep watching, to figure out this whole thing, but he made himself turn away and head back into the shop.

Jamie was confused about why he hadn't returned with coffee, but he decided not to ask about it when he saw the look on Seth's face.

Seth went into the back office and sat down. He checked his message to see if he'd simply missed a call from Libby. He hadn't. After a couple of hours, his phone rang, and he jolted away from the paperwork he'd been looking through to answer it. She'd explained simply that Colin was in town, and they'd had coffee. Colin had apologized, and that was it. Seth had a lot of questions, but he let them lie, for now. He knew they'd be having dinner tonight, and he'd ask her then.

But of course, they'd never made it as far as dinner. Seth headed over to Libby's after work. He'd kissed her, long and slow, in the doorway and then come in to find her getting ready for another run. She told him a little about the day, and he watched her nervously skip around the meeting with Colin. It made him nervous that she wouldn't just talk about it when they talked about everything. He could have gotten through it and discussed it calmly, but then her phone rang. It sat beside him on the end table, and he could see the caller ID light up clearly: Colin Gardner. Seth would have a lot of time later to regret how he reacted, but the words fell out of his mouth before he could think about them.

Chapter 31

Damn. Damn. Damn. Shit! Goddamn it to hell!

Rebecca would have sighed, but she knew she needed every breath available for the run. The first mile was always the toughest, and her normal vocabulary fell away to a litany of curses as her body labored to cover that first godawful fucking mile. If her focus weren't so much on her stride, she might have smiled a little at the thought of the library patrons hearing her inner thoughts. Mild-mannered librarians weren't supposed to curse like sailors—but hell! Training for a 5k after years of being sedentary was tough! She'd never smoked, but her breathing labored as if she'd spent sixty years smoking a pack or two a day.

She alternated between cursing, breathing, and blaming her roommate Jillian for preaching the benefits of regular exercise blah, blah, blah. How had she talked her into this? They'd both signed up for what was listed as a "fun run," but was surely the path to hell itself! Still, Rebecca noted that she had recently been doing more running (or slow jogging) than walking, so that was an improvement. And those ten pounds that were lost in the last six weeks were certainly not missed. She could use another twenty gone, but she was pleased with her progress.

She was the same height as Jill, but that's where the similarities ended. Rebecca was all curves, and Jill was all angles. Rebecca had long curly blonde hair, and Jill was experimenting with short, brightly colored styles. Right now, it was pixie pink, short, and spiky. She was an artist so she could pull it off. Rebecca's job at the library would never, ever have allowed her to experiment with her hair like that. And they definitely would have nixed the little diamond stud that Jillian proudly wore in her nose. Of course, they didn't know about Rebecca's tattoos, but she kept them well hidden. She liked her sexy secrets, like the lingerie she wore under her sedate librarian attire.

Of course, Jillian was determined that they'd be running half marathons by next year, and Rebecca couldn't imagine how she was going to run that many miles when just over three of them were liable to kill her. Mile two was completed with minimal cursing, and she hit her stride by mile three. Rebecca tried to remind herself that she was always glad that she'd run, even though she never started out feeling that way. She thought maybe she and Jillian might work up to a half marathon after all. Someday.

She walked over to the local park to stretch out, noticing that it was starting to turn a bit dark earlier today. Looked like rain. Well, she was glad she was nearly done. Checking her time, Rebecca sent a quick gloating text to Jillian and then noticed the couple on the other side of the park. Hmm . . . well, someone was pissed. Rebecca watched without trying to look like she was watching. She had a naturally nosy nature, and people watching was just her thing. It actually made the slow hours at the library a bit more interesting to imagine the secret lives of the patrons.

It seemed like an argument was really heating up, but they seemed pretty evenly matched. She wasn't close enough to hear anything, but they weren't exactly yelling either. In fact, she guessed that they were probably straining to keep their voices down since they were in such a public place. Well, at this late hour, it was pretty private actually. Just smack dab in the center of town. The woman looked familiar, but Rebecca couldn't quite place her. The man's back was to her so she couldn't see his face. It was a nice backside so at least she had the view.

She didn't think it would escalate so she tried to stop watching. Really, she did. They looked like an attractive couple. Maybe they were the type to fight like that all the time. Some people did, although Rebecca never understood why. Jill and Mark were like that, constantly at each other's throats. She often left the apartment for a run when they'd start in on each other. She tried to stay gone long enough for them to fight and then make up, the usual pattern of their relationship. Rebecca would happily stay single rather than deal with that constant drama.

In fact, some days she felt pretty sure she would stay single for the rest of her life if her dates kept turning out like the last one. God, this online dating shit was for the birds. Of course, it was funny at first when she and Jillian both signed up, but then Jill met Mark, and Rebecca was left out in the wilds of the dating scene on her own. She shot a quick glance at the arguing couple as she left the park. Well, it could be worse.

Rebecca had been surprised when Jillian brought Mark around. She'd gone out with him a few times, but she hadn't prepared her roommate for meeting him. Where Jill was artistic and quirky, Mark was buttoned up and a little geeky. He even wore glasses and old man shoes. Normally, Jillian would have steered clear of any man who casually wore penny loafers, but she and Mark just hit it off. They had the same weird sense of humor, and there was this mutual adoration thing they had going, too. When they weren't at each other's throats anyway. Rebecca was a little weirded out by the change. Now all of Jillian's plans included Mark. He should have been the third wheel, and yet it was becoming clear that the third wheel was, in fact, Rebecca. Jillian had even stopped running regularly, even though she promised she'd show up for the race. When she did run, she ran with Mark. Rebecca found the whole thing mildly unsettling.

She walked to her car slowly, allowing her breath to slow. She knew she'd feel the burn in her calf muscles in the morning. While she thought about a good soak in Epsom salts, she recalled her last relationship. She'd met Ian at work. He'd been browsing the shelves for a particular book, and she'd been stocking the shelves nearby with new titles. He'd struck up a conversation, rightly guessing that books were her weakness. Of course, she may or may not have been stocking that particular aisle after catching sight of him. He was tall and well-built with dark hair turning silver. A silver fox is what she and her friends called the type. Between the hair, the full lips, and those dark eyelashes, Rebecca was sunk. Luckily, she had plenty of sexy secrets to wield. She liked to dress almost primly in dresses that buttoned to her throat with skirts that brushed her calves, but underneath, she wore a lot of silk and black lace. She had brushed on a soft pink lip gloss before heading his way with her armload of books. So maybe it was more planning than kismet, but the chemistry had been incredible!

Of course, then it had burned out too soon, as nearly all her relationships did. She'd tried to figure out why that was, but the best she could come up with is that her bullshit tolerance was considerably lower than other women. Ian might have been seriously hot, but he was also seriously selfish. Their relationship had revolved around his convenience, and Rebecca found that she felt more annoyance than lust in the end. She'd cut her losses and headed back into the world of online dating with more fear and trepidation than confidence. If Ian could see her now, ten pounds lighter and leaner, he might have reconsidered his behavior. She thought maybe she'd get in touch sometime soon just to say hello and let him suffer a little.

She unlocked her car and grabbed the water bottle she'd left inside. She nearly dropped it when she noticed the woman from the argument earlier jogging her way. Her face was white, and it was obvious that she was trying not to cry. Rebecca glanced inside her car to give her some privacy. Hopefully, she lived that way because it would start getting dark soon, and the sidewalks on those streets were in pretty bad shape. For runners anyway. She wondered idly if the man she'd been arguing with would go after her. Clearly, he should. Isn't that what any woman would want in her shoes? Rebecca glanced into the park and saw that he was standing where the woman had left him, unmoving. Well, hell. Maybe they were a done deal. Rebecca got into her car and sent a text Jill's way to tell her that she and Mark better be decent when she got home. She was in no mood to wait outside or to walk in on them as she had that one time she'd come home unannounced. She just wanted to grab a shower and catch up on one of her shows.

As she reversed out of her parking space, she noticed that the man had finally walked out of the park and was heading to his car. Rebecca shook her head and hoped the woman wouldn't run for too long. Or maybe her guy was only heading to the nearest store to grab flowers. If he wasn't, he'd be toast for sure. She turned up her music and drove away, daydreaming about carbs and a shower.

Chapter 32

Libby was trying to keep her voice down. Ever since she'd had that year of therapy as a teenager, she'd worked hard to keep her temper in check. She didn't allow herself to yell, to rage, or to indulge in childish displays of emotion. She took her deep breaths and tried to count to ten—trying and failing to calm down. She felt like the losing side in a battle of tug of war, but maybe all she had ever been was the rope. And she was so damn tired of it.

"What did you expect me to do? Should I have just slammed the door in his face?" Libby kept her voice down and began counting. One, two, three, four . . . No, it wasn't working. Five, six, seven . . .

"What I expected was for you to tell me. You couldn't have taken five minutes to call or send a text? Just a quick, 'Hey, my ex is here and hanging out at my place now?' I don't think that's too much to ask." Seth's voice was low, dangerously low. He was staring at Libby as if he were only just seeing her, and not particularly liking what he saw.

"He didn't set a foot in my house. Do you think I invited him here? That I want him here in my town? I just listened. That's all I did. We talked some things out. It's closure. That's all it ever was," Libby insisted, frustrated that she was having to explain this again. "We went out for coffee, in separate cars I might add. We had a conversation in a public place. He left. We've been through this."

"And the calls? Are you taking his calls, too?" Seth looked at her phone, remembering when it rang earlier and Colin's number had come up on the screen like a beacon. He had just looked at the phone and then looked at Libby in shock. Maybe his temper had taken over. He could admit that now, if only to himself. Perhaps he shouldn't have asked what he'd asked in that tone. They'd had a few minor disagreements, but they hadn't argued. He'd certainly never lost his temper around her. Maybe he should have just let her explain. Now it was spiraling so much further than he'd intended. She'd gone out for a run, and he'd followed. Now they were having this argument right in the center of town.

"I talked to him earlier when he called, but just long enough to tell him that there's nothing more to say." She hadn't expected the call that afternoon. She'd taken it without checking the number. They'd ended up on the phone longer than she'd expected. He'd explained what their marriage had been like for him and why he'd brought up a divorce. They'd talked for a while, but Libby had told him that, while she appreciated the apology and explanation, it didn't really change anything. "You talk to Marnie. You've never heard me complain about that," Libby reminded him sharply, trying and failing to reign in her temper. She could still hear him with that angry tone, *Why the fuck is Colin calling you?*

"Marnie was ages ago. And I wasn't married to her. You were married to Colin. Recently married. The divorce is barely final. I just want to know one thing. It's the only thing I want to know." Seth said quietly, meeting and holding her eyes.

"No, I did not sleep with him. I didn't do anything but hear him out. There's nothing more to tell because nothing else happened." Libby said fiercely.

"That's not the question. Are you still in love with him?" Seth asked.

Libby hesitated. "We were together for a long time—"

"Are you still in love with him?" Seth asked again, never breaking eye contact.

Libby shifted. It wasn't a straight-forward question. How could it be? "You know that I'm in love with you." She said it quietly, all the anger leaving her. She just deflated, knowing her answer would never be good enough. How could it be? It was a question she'd asked herself enough, and the answer was never satisfactory. Could one still love an old flame and fall in love again? Could all of those feelings coincide? Could there ever be peace? She didn't know so how could she possibly explain it?

"Are you still in love with him?" He wouldn't ask again. It was a straight-forward question, and it deserved a straight-forward answer.

"I have a lot of feelings for Colin. I'm hurt some and still angry. But there's still love in there somewhere, too. None of that matters. I'm in love with you. I want to be with you. You're making this something that it's not. There's not any confusion here. He came over. I didn't want him staying at my place. We went out for coffee. I let him talk. I sent him away. I don't know what else you want from me. I came and told you as soon as he left." Libby explained, exhausted with the effort of going through it all again.

"You know I saw you there. Just for a minute. Lindy called and said she thought she saw you at Brews, and I thought I'd catch up with you. But when I came around the corner, I saw you leaving with him. I saw him hand you your cup of coffee and how you both paused there in the doorframe watching each other. If I didn't know you were with me, I would have sworn you were with him. And it was another two hours before you came and told me he'd been here. Do you have any idea what those two hours were like for me?" Libby stepped toward him, reaching out. "No, don't. I don't want you to touch me."

She stepped back like she'd been slapped. The tears began to fall quickly now, a force beyond her control. "I loved Colin for almost six years. And when he left me, he didn't say a word. Not one word of explanation. I grieved for that love, and I suffered not knowing what I did or why he'd left, so when he walked back in the door and wanted to explain, I needed to know. I needed answers so that I could lay it all to rest and just be with you. So, yes, we got a coffee and had a conversation." Libby took a deep breath, the tears still falling unchecked, "I was in love with you. Am in love with you," she corrected herself. "But I needed to know. And I needed to make sure that the feelings I had for him were gone now. I needed to be sure. I'm sorry that you saw that and sorry that you were hurt and worried and angry, even. But I needed to know. I haven't lied to you. I've never lied to you."

"But you still love him," Seth said quietly, his eyes still holding hers with a burning intensity. "And if you're still in love with him, what the hell have we been doing here, Libby?"

"I didn't plan any of this," she said helplessly, feeling everything spinning out of control. "Yes, I still love him, but it's not the same. I love you. I'm choosing you."

She waited for him to say something. To say anything. To save them. But he was silent, struggling with his emotions. Libby turned and started walking away, and she began to count. But this time, she was counting in hopes that he would stop her from going. One, two, three, four . . . She took a deep breath and prayed. Five, six, seven . . . It wasn't too late. Eight, nine, ten. But maybe it was. Maybe it was broken now. And if it was broken now, maybe it had never been strong enough. She could see that corridor again in her mind, the one that had never really left. She was in her mind running, slamming, and locking the doors until she could manage the pain. One, two, three, four, five . . . It's still not too late. Six, seven, eight. She was almost at the exit of the park. Nine, ten. One, two, three, four, five, six, seven . . . Libby went through the exit and turned right instead of left and broke into a run. She'd told him she loved him and was choosing him, and it still wasn't enough. She wasn't enough.

She'd come out for a run, and she'd get one now. The argument had just been a detour. She thought a run would give him time to either think about things and come after her or to get his things from her place and leave. She didn't want to know what he was deciding yet. She ran to the sound of her feet slapping against the pavement and began to pray that it wouldn't get dark quite yet. The sidewalks were uneven where the roots of the tree poked through, and the flashlight on her phone didn't give her enough light to run on these back streets.

Libby ran through the twilight and let the thoughts run through her head. She thought about the first time she'd met Seth and their first date. She remembered that first kiss and the first time she'd fallen asleep thinking of him and not Colin. She remembered falling in love with him and believing that she could be loved in return. And she remembered what Colin said when he came for the visit earlier today. She remembered sitting across from him and replaying their first date, the first kiss, and when they fell in love. She let both relationships play out in her head and wondered now if Seth was waiting for her back at the park or if he'd gone home alone.

She ran miles further than she usually did, forgetting how quickly night could fall. On the last mile, she tripped over a large root in the sidewalk and went flying to the ground. She banged up her knee, hands, and wrists and sat for a few minutes on the sidewalk just breathing. Everything hurt. Her knee, her hands, her heart. She could feel the scratches on her skin and suspected that the wrists and knees were bleeding. She got up, limping. She had almost a mile to go to get back to the park and then another mile home. She gave up and took out her phone.

"Hey, Jenna? Are you home? Can you come get me? I'm out running, and I fell down. Yes, I know it's dark already. No, I can't call Seth. We had a fight. Can I tell you about it when you get here?" Libby explained where she was and sat back down on the sidewalk to wait. She checked her messages for one from Seth. Nothing. Radio silence. But she noticed that there were three new notifications from Colin. She'd check them, but not tonight. She put her head in her hands and let the tears fall.

*****

Seth watched Libby walk away and hoped that she would turn back around. He didn't mind fighting it out if that's what they needed to do, but he didn't have it in him right now to go after her. He watched her get back to the park entrance without once turning around, and then she broke into a run. He watched her go, helpless to stop her and unwilling to follow her. Instead, he decided to go by her place while she was gone and get the few things he'd left over there. She wouldn't finish running for at least half an hour, maybe more. It wouldn't take long to take what was his and leave. Then he could go out and grab a beer with Dean.

He couldn't understand why Libby didn't understand the problem. She had been in love with Colin. She'd talked about their connection, but always in the past tense. He'd never expected the guy to show up at her door. He certainly didn't expect her to do anything but slam the door in his face. When Seth saw them together, he wondered for the first time if she was really in love with him or if he was just the convenient rebound. He'd seen the way she looked at Colin in that moment in the doorway. It hurt. It hurt a hell of a lot more than he expected, and he'd probably overreacted when she came in to talk to him. He knew he'd overreacted after dinner when he saw that phone call come in.

Still. She'd have to make up her mind. If she wanted to be with Colin, he sure as hell wasn't going to stand in her way. And he wasn't going to wait for her to choose. It shouldn't be a choice. Colin had left her. He hadn't even offered an explanation. Seth shifted uncomfortably as he remembered that he'd never let Libby finish telling him what explanation Colin had offered. It would help to know what he'd said and what she'd said back to him, but he couldn't get over how hard it was to hear her say she was still in love with Colin. He couldn't reconcile her saying that she loved them both. What did that even mean? He sure as hell wasn't going to stay with some woman still in love with some other man. Not in this lifetime.

He made it to Libby's and opened the door quietly. He flipped on the lights and took the key off his keyring. He sat it in a bowl where Libby dropped her keys when she came in. He knew she'd find it there. He walked by the kitchen and saw the vase of wildflowers. He paused for a minute. That, she had not mentioned. Of course, Colin had brought flowers! The asshole. Seth went upstairs and grabbed his toothbrush and razor from the bathroom. He went through the bedroom, which looked exactly the same as it had when he left it this morning. Well, that was a relief anyway. He collected a couple of changes of clothes he kept there and grabbed his phone charger, too. He looked around and decided that he didn't have that much to take with him after all.

As he walked back down the stairs, it hit him. If he left, if he walked out with his stuff and left his keys, it would truly be over. He'd be ending it, and she'd be out of his life. He sat down heavily on the stairs and thought, "I'll stay here for another ten minutes. If she comes home, we'll talk. If she's not home by then, I'll go." He sat and watched the clock, unmoving. Ten minutes passed. Then fifteen. When thirty minutes had passed, he stood slowly up. It was dark outside. If she hadn't come home yet, where would she have gone? Her car was in the driveway. She'd have to walk. Or, and he didn't want to think this, she could have called someone to pick her up. Someone like Colin.

That was it. He walked down the hallway, locked the bottom lock, turned on the porch light, and closed the front door behind him. She'd know that he had been there because of the light. He'd do that much for her. But that was it. He was done. He took a deep breath, trying to breathe past the hurt. He'd never loved anyone as much as he loved Libby, but if she hadn't come home, where had she gone? He had too much pride to call and ask her.

He got in his car and pulled out. He turned left onto the main road and passed Jenna's car downtown. It was dark, and he didn't notice Libby sitting in the passenger seat, catching her tears with her cupped hands. He turned toward his house and didn't see the taillights of Jenna's car turning into Libby's neighborhood. Instead, he drove home and thought he'd skip going out with Dean and instead have a drink at home. It wasn't a beer night. More like whiskey.

Seth pulled into the driveway and turned off the car. With the windows down, all the night sounds were magnified. He could hear the loud hum of cicadas and the sound of a train whistle in the distance. He sat in the dark in his hot car and leaned his head back against the headrest. And thought of Libby. He closed his eyes and thought about calling her. If he called her now, maybe it wouldn't be too late. Maybe she wouldn't have seen his keys yet. Maybe he could reach her before she realized that he had wanted to end it. But then if she wasn't home, was she with Colin? It was unanswerable. Well, not if he called her. But he didn't want to know if she was there with *him*.

*****

Libby noticed the porch light was on, but she didn't see Seth's car. Maybe he'd walked from the park? She knew that she shouldn't get her hopes up, but surely it was just a simple fight. A bad one, of course, but it was nothing they couldn't work through. She walked in and turned on the entry light. No, he'd gone. She could tell she was alone in the house. She walked through the rooms, checking to be sure. She noticed the wildflowers in the vase. She'd picked them up the night before when she went grocery shopping. She thought they would brighten up the house a bit, and maybe she'd light a few candles when she made dinner for Seth the following night. She couldn't have known that the night would end like this.

She walked up to the bedroom, noticing the absence of all the little things that had marked Seth's presence in her life. Not just his keys. It was more than that. She checked her phone, but he still hadn't called or sent a message. She sat down heavily on the bed and wondered if it was over just like that. Could it be that easy for him? What was it about her that made it so easy for men to just leave? She was tired in a way that she knew sleep wouldn't fix, but she still curled up on the side of the bed, still in her running clothes and cried herself to sleep.

Chapter 33

Colin sent one last text message, his third tonight. He hoped Libby would at least respond. He had made reservations at a local bed and breakfast in town. He sat out on the balcony in the dark and looked down at the moon reflected off the inn's saltwater pool. He hadn't expected Libby to forgive him. Not exactly. But he'd still been surprised when she'd told him she was in a relationship now, that she'd fallen in love with someone else. Even when they'd divorced, he had thought that they had a special connection, one that neither was likely to find with anyone else. He hadn't expected her to move on so soon and so finally.

But maybe it wasn't final? There had been a spark, just for a moment when he'd opened the door and handed her the mug. Their fingers had brushed, and she'd met his eyes fully for the first time since the day he'd moved out. He knew that there was something there still, no matter how much she said she loved this Seth person. Maybe this new relationship was just her rebound. He certainly couldn't judge that. He'd had a number of rebounds if he was honest. Then there'd been Maisie. He wondered if they would have stayed together if she hadn't miscarried. They'd gotten along. Their casual relationship had become something more after she'd gotten pregnant, but when they no longer had that shared future ahead of them, they found they'd run out of things to talk about.

Even if Libby was in love with this guy, it didn't mean that she didn't still have feelings for Colin. After all, she'd been with this guy for only a few months. He and Libby had been together for over five years; it was nearly six now. Even with the finalized divorce, he still thought the history might make a difference. Colin went back into the hotel room. It was spacious and decorated in a vintage hunter sort of style. There were lots of leather books on the shelves. It had a masculine feel that appealed to him. He sat down heavily on the bed and thought for the first time that Libby was actually in love with someone else. Someone she didn't seem to want to leave, no matter what explanation he'd given for why he'd left their marriage. He realized that he could have lost her completely. She might already be so far gone that she wasn't ever coming back. He still loved her, maybe more now than he'd ever loved her.

He felt jealous of this new man, but had to remind himself that he was the one who'd left. He'd gone away. He couldn't exactly be angry with Libby for trying to move on. Well, now he was back, and he was going to stick around for a while to make sure Libby was really okay. If she wanted to stay in this new relationship, he'd go. But he wanted to know that this man could take care of her and make her happy. Oh, she'd hate that, Colin thought with a grin. If she knew he was thinking that way, she'd be quick to tell him that women are capable of taking care of themselves, thank you very much. She'd give him a dressing down on misogyny before he could blink an eye. He loved that about her. She really was cute when she was riled.

But Colin really did want to make sure she'd be alright, even if she didn't want to be with him anymore. He decided to book a longer stay until he could be sure it was over, or if maybe they still had a chance. She thought he'd softened a little when he'd apologized. He needed to try to make amends. For some reason, he'd always played out this whole scenario in his head differently. He hadn't imagined that she'd be in love with someone else. He thought she'd still be waiting for him. Which was foolish. Libby was never the patient type, and he'd given her no hope that he was ever coming back.

He remembered now, standing on the doorstep with the last couple of boxes. He thought about how she laughed when she reminded him to leave his key like their separation wasn't something she could take seriously. Or as if she didn't care at all. He'd watched her turn to go inside and willed her to just turn around. To do something to save this. To show that she still cared and didn't want him to leave. He'd hoped for that, but she'd never looked back. He'd even sat in his car for a few minutes, feeling like a fool and wondering if he was doing the right thing. But she never came out or glanced outside. He drove away slowly, looking back all the time. She never did.

It had taken him a few months to remember Libby's walls. When he'd first met her, she'd been beyond reserved. She was prickly and distrusting and always thought the worst of men. She had her reasons. Most women with walls that high had a good reason for them. But they'd had such chemistry that before long she was counting on him and trusting him. And then loving him as he'd never been loved before. He'd forgotten about those walls and about how tough she'd been in the beginning. It hit him one night over Chinese takeout that she hadn't turned around when he left because she was slowly erecting those walls like the Libby of before. He'd set down the box of lo mein and felt hope for the first time. Maybe it wasn't that she didn't love him anymore. Maybe all of the distance in their relationship had made her stop trusting him. And if she couldn't trust him, how could she show him love?

That night he'd called a mutual friend and made idle conversation until he'd found out where Libby had gone. Some town east of Atlanta called Madison. Apparently, it was a big tourist destination on the antebellum trail. It didn't necessarily sound like Libby's speed, but maybe she'd changed without him. He'd listened and waited for a decent time to get off the phone, and then he'd Googled Madison, Georgia. He'd looked up local inns and then thought about what he could possibly say after all these months. After all, the divorce had just been finalized. How could he explain the timing?

He didn't care. Colin started planning the trip and planning what he would say. He checked out Libby's social media pages and read some of her recent articles on the town. Just reading her work made her voice come back to him. He could feel her presence with him, and he wondered why it had taken him so long to realize what he'd lost. And why the hell he'd thought it was so imperative that he leave her then. It might be too late, but he was damn sure going to find out!

Chapter 34

Libby woke up slowly and sat up groggily. She looked down in confusion at her exercise clothes and the athletic shoes she was still wearing. It only took a moment for the night before to hit her like a freight train. Colin was back. Seth had left without a word. It was like a bad replay of the breakup of her marriage, but more complicated. She moved slowly to the bathroom, feeling the ache of her fall on the sidewalk in her hands and knees. She peeled off her clothes, dropping them into the laundry basket, and surveyed the cuts and bruises. The ones she could see, anyway. They would heal. Would she? She stepped into a hot shower and allowed herself to hope that Seth would call or stop by. Even a text would be better than nothing. Anything but this cold, empty silence.

She let the water run over her until it grew cold. When she turned off the taps, she sat down in the bathtub and drew her knees to her chest. If it was over, it wasn't the worst thing she'd ever experienced. She'd gotten through her marriage imploding and all the months of trying and failing to get pregnant. She'd survived relocations and job losses and had her life turned upside down. She reminded herself of her own resilience and wondered why this felt like the worst thing when it couldn't possibly be. She slowly stood up and grabbed a towel. As she dried off, she wondered what Seth was doing and how he was feeling this morning. She hoped if he was leaving her, it would at least make him as miserable as she felt.

Libby took extra care with her makeup and started to decide how she would handle the day. She had work to do, of course. She couldn't miss that just because she felt broken. Life didn't work that way. She dressed carefully, making sure she chose a longer skirt that would cover the worst of the bruises. She sent Rachel a quick message to confirm their lunch plans. As she set her phone down on the bathroom counter, she noticed all the little absences. Her toothbrush stood in its holder as lonely as she felt. His razor and shaving cream were missing from their usual spot, too. She had a feeling the entire day would be seeing his absence. Could he have been so angry that it was over just like that? He'd taken all his things and left, which seemed cold and deliberate.

She looked in the mirror, feeling her grief bleed into anger. What was she supposed to have done? She didn't ask Colin to come back. She'd handled it the best she could. She leaned heavily on the counter, feeling the anger course through her. He could leave if that's what he needed to do. He could decide she wasn't worth it, as Colin had obviously done before. He could do whatever he wanted, but she wasn't going to sit around and grieve herself to death over it. She wasn't going to wait for him any more than she had for Colin. She was good at moving on, or at least she was practiced at it, which she thought amounted to the same thing. Libby took a deep breath and calmly turned away from the mirror. She wouldn't call him or go see him. She was tired of being the one they could all leave so easily.

*****

Seth hadn't slept. Not for a single moment. He'd drunk a couple of shots of whiskey straight, but they'd done nothing to mask the pain. He'd lain in bed for hours, wondering if he'd made a mistake. By the time his alarm went off, he had finally concluded that he'd overreacted. Taking all his things from her place had been petty and short-sighted. After all, it was one fight. They rarely argued at all so they were in unfamiliar territory. He told himself that he should call her, but then he remembered that she'd still be a woman in love with her ex. He didn't love Marnie any more. He'd always think of her as a friend, but he could easily and unequivocally say that he wasn't in love with her anymore. He rubbed his tired eyes and remembered that Libby's relationship with Colin had ended only in the last year. He and Marnie had been over for ages. It wasn't the same thing, but he wasn't sure he could be with someone who still had feelings for an ex.

Apparently, the guy hadn't even left town, which made Seth think that Libby had given him some hope. She said that she'd been very clear, but none of it seemed clear. Why had he come back at all, and why wasn't he leaving again? Seth sat up slowly, turning off the alarm he'd failed to shut off before. He got dressed, feeling an ache in every one of his bones. Luckily, Farrah was working most of the day so he could stay in his office and go over some paperwork. He was hoping that he wouldn't be called upon to have conversations with people today. He just didn't feel like it, and he wasn't sure if what he felt was more sad or angry. He stood at the bathroom sink where he'd dumped all his stuff the night before and wondered why the sight of his toothbrush falling out of the opening of the bag made him feel so lost.

*****

Rose sat at a coffee shop in Athens with Dillon. It was a hole in the wall place they'd found near Rose's apartment. They both liked the variety of coffee and tea and the enormous selection of pastries available. Dillon had chosen a chai tea and a bear claw, and Rose was working her way through a generous slice of coffee cake and a steaming espresso. They had a table by the window, but there wasn't much to look at outside. It was early still, and the sun had only begun to rise. They were talking through the work week when Rose got the text. Something in her manner changed, and Dillon sat at attention.

"Is everything okay?" She reached over and brushed her hand across Rose's.

"Seth and Libby broke up," she said slowly, looking up at Dillon to meet her eyes. "Last night, apparently."

"That doesn't even make sense. What happened?" Dillon asked, genuinely perplexed.

"She said Colin came back to town, and they had a conversation. Apparently, Seth found out about it and went off the deep end." They both rolled their eyes.

"But that's all that happened? Just a conversation?" Dillon's eyebrows drew together as she tried to connect the dots on a picture that wasn't becoming any clearer. "That still doesn't make sense. Is

Libby okay?"

"No, she's really not. I mean, she's saying she is, but that's how you know she's not at all. Read this." She passed Dillon the phone and let her read the extremely formal, brief explanation.

"Honestly, she sounds okay," Dillon admitted with a shrug.

"I know. That's the problem. She was like that the day Colin left, too. She thinks she doesn't break easily, but she breaks easier than anyone I know. She just doesn't like people to see the cracks." Rose sent a quick text back and reached over to squeeze Dillon's hand. "Would you mind if we went to dinner tomorrow night instead? She's going to say she doesn't want the company, but she's going to need it."

"Of course. Since you're in meetings all day, do you want me to pick up something that you can take over there? Maybe grab some dinner or something so she doesn't have to cook?" Dillon asked.

"You're an angel!" Rose exclaimed. "That would be great if you have the time. She won't think of it, and I'll honestly have to head straight there from meetings."

"I'll drop it by your office before you leave. Tell her I'm here if she needs anything," Dillon assured her. "Including you. If you need to stay the night with her, just let me know so I don't worry."

"I will," Rose assured her. They finished their pastries and got ready to leave. Both were distracted, wondering what had gone wrong and so quickly. There was always that fear in relationships: if it could happen to someone else, it could happen to you. They held hands on the walk home and prayed it wouldn't. After all, no one would have expected it of Seth and Libby.

*****

Rachel got the text after she'd dropped off the kids at school. Oliver hadn't wanted to go today, and she'd practically had to bribe him to make it happen. He was getting an extra hour of television after school. Ella had been mutinous because she'd wanted two ponytails and not pigtails, and no amount of explaining that two ponytails are actually pigtails would suffice. She'd stomped around in her little shoes all morning to express her displeasure. Rachel suspected she would forget about it at some point, or she'd take them out herself and let her hair hang wildly around her face for the rest of the day. It was always one or the other—she'd forget or rebel completely.

When the text came through, she was trying to interest Willow in a puzzle and failing completely. When she read it, she sat straight up and absently grabbed the remote control. She turned the television to *Baby Einsteins*, which Willow loved right now. It would be enough of a distraction for a quick call anyway.

"Hey, Libby, I just got your message," she began in a rush.

"Is twelve not okay for lunch?" Libby asked curiously, her voice all too calm.

"Twelve is fine. Look, what do you mean you and Seth broke up? That's not even a thing," Rachel said in confusion. "You're happy. We all know you're happy."

"Apparently, it is a thing," Libby said wryly. "I'll tell you all about it at lunch. We can start with the part where Colin is back in town and go from there."

"Wait—you're not back with Colin, are you?" Rachel tried to keep the judgment out of her voice. Surely, Libby wouldn't leave Seth for Colin after all these months.

"No, I'm not back with Colin," Libby said in exasperation. "And I have no intention of it. Look, can we talk at lunch? I have a deadline on this article, and yesterday's drama cut into my writing time. I need to get this done before lunch if I can."

"Yeah, sure, that's fine. What do you want—BBQ, pizza, Mexican, sandwiches?" Rachel asked solicitously.

"Do you want to go over to the drugstore? I wouldn't mind a burger and shake," Libby admitted, referring to the drugstore in town that still had an old-fashioned soda fountain. They were known for serving up the best burgers around and still did hand-dipped milkshakes. They used fresh ingredients, and even their fries were hand cut and not from a freezer. Rachel agreed that it did sound good, and then sat wordlessly beside Willow on the floor. How do you go from being in a great place in a relationship to having nothing at all left? Well, she was going to find out. She picked up the phone and put in a call to Alec's mother.

"Estelle, I hate to bother you, but would you mind if I dropped Willow off with you about an hour earlier? I need to run a quick errand, and I know she'd love some extra time with you," she knew she was laying it on thick, but she had a plan.

After dropping Willow off at Estelle's, Rachel marched in the opposite direction from the drugstore. She had a little under an hour to kill, but she knew where she was going. She walked into Lost Horizon Antiques and greeted Farrah at the front desk. Today, Farrah appeared as if she'd been transported out of a sixties-era love-in to the store. Still, it suited her. Rachel would have seemed like she was dressing up for Halloween, but Farrah pulled off the style like a hipster.

"Looking for something?" Farrah asked with a smile.

"Seth," Rachel said shortly.

"Well, I figured something went down with Libby. He's been a bear all morning. You'll find him in his cave back there," she said, pointing to his office in the back.

"Thanks," Rachel said briefly.

"Don't feed the bear," Farrah warned her in passing.

Rachel snorted out a brief laugh and headed to the back. She didn't get angry anymore, at least not outwardly. Instead, she was seething almost all the time. At the pick-up line at school, in line at the grocery store, in traffic, making dinner, cleaning up after her family, listening to Alec snoring through the night. But right now, all that universal anger redirected itself to one specific target, and she was sailing toward his office as if she were the storm. She didn't bother to knock, but rolled right in on her dark cloud.

"What—the—hell," she said quietly, dropping into a seat. "What is wrong with you?" she asked angrily.

"Rachel, it's really not a good time," Seth said, running a frustrated hand through his hair.

"Want to make an appointment then? Because we're going to discuss this. What did you do?" she demanded to know. She noticed that he looked miserable. His eyes were red like he'd either drunk too much or not gotten enough sleep. His clothes were a little wrinkled, and she noticed that he hadn't shaved. She didn't even feel a little sorry for him. She knew when her sister was hurting, and she could say she was fine to everyone else, but Rachel knew that Libby saying she was okay meant she wasn't actually okay at all.

"This is between me and Libby, okay?" Seth began.

"No, it's not okay. You hurt her, and you better have a damn good reason for it!" Her voice was slowly rising, and Seth got up to shut the door.

"I hurt her? She crushed me! Do you know she saw her ex yesterday?" Seth asked angrily.

"Of course, I know," Rachel said angrily. "And I know Libby. Do you think she did anything other than show him the door? What kind of man are you that all it takes is one argument, and you're done?" Rachel asked in disgust. "Did you even bother to hear her out?" When Seth was silent, Rachel shook her head. "Then you don't even deserve her."

She walked out of his office and said in passing to Farrah. "He broke up with Libby. The idiot." She kept walking. She sailed out of the shop and would have slammed the door if she could have. Instead, she heard the bell sound behind her, and she just kept walking. She didn't see Farrah's look of shock or her quick worried glance at the office where Seth's door remained closed. She didn't see Farrah send a quick text over to Jamie to come to relieve Seth in the store. She kept walking until she reached a bench in the park downtown. She sat heavily and decided she'd spend the half hour before lunch trying to calm herself. She took deep breaths and tried not to feel her sister's hurt, but she could still feel it anyway.

"You look like you could chew up nails and spit them out."

She looked up and saw Beth walking by with Mr. Darcy on a leash.

"Your idiot cousin dumped Libby," Rachel said shortly. She knew that she shouldn't tell Libby's business, but the big sister side of her was so incredibly angry that she just wanted to share the outrage.

"He did what?" Beth asked, dropping to sit down beside her. Mr. Darcy hopped up on the swing beside her and rested his head in her lap.

"You heard me. I just had it out with him," Rachel told her.

"Hmm," Beth said thoughtfully. "Did you get anything out of him?"

"Unfortunately, no," Rachel said angrily.

"Is Libby okay?" Beth asked with concern.

"No. She'll say she is, but not really. I'm meeting her for lunch," Rachel admitted. "Apparently, her ex showed up in town, and Seth flipped out. That's all I know about it."

"Well, his last girlfriend cheated so maybe he's still hung up on that," Beth said. "Give Libby my love, okay? I've got to get this one home so I can get ready for work." She stood up, and Mr. Darcy followed suit, happily sniffing around at Rachel's feet. "Sorry my cousin's an ass," she offered regretfully. "He usually isn't."

"Yeah, I'm sorry, too," Rachel agreed. She decided to head over to the drugstore. Maybe she'd go ahead and place their orders or look through the gift shop. She walked away and didn't notice that Beth detoured from the road to her house and took the road to Keely's instead.

*****

Keely opened the front door and gave Beth a firm hug. "We weren't expecting you," she said. "It's so good to see you."

"Family emergency," Beth replied firmly. "I know I need to get ready for work, but we need to talk first."

"You're not going to ask for a raise, are you?" Lindy called from the doorway. "Might as well dig into some French toast while you're at it, gold digger," she said with a laugh.

"Um, I've got Mr. Darcy with me. His feet might be a little wet from the grass," Beth answered, staying in the doorway.

"You know he can come in for some breakfast, too. A little wet won't hurt anything," Keely said calmly. "Now what's this about an emergency?" They walked into the kitchen where plates of French toast were already waiting. Lindy had stuffed her mouth with a big bite and was happily chewing when Beth broke the news.

"Seth and Libby broke up," Lindy gasped, almost choking on her breakfast. She swallowed quickly.

"When did this happen?" Keely asked in concern.

"Yesterday, I guess. Or last night? I just ran into Rachel at the park. She's really angry. She went to see Seth at the store, and she's meeting Libby for lunch," Beth told them.

"Wait—Seth broke up with Libby?" Lindy asked, confused. "He must have had a good reason."

"Rachel doesn't think so," Beth said honestly. "She said Libby was broken up about it. Or that she was fine, but fine isn't fine, you know?"

"I actually understood that," Lindy said. "So, he screwed it up, huh?"

"That's what I'm hearing," Beth said. "I know it's not my business, but I thought that maybe you should know."

"You're sweet to come here and tell us. Have some French toast, and I'll get Mr. Darcy some treats," Keely said calmly. "I hate to hear about this, but you know we can't get involved. It's for Seth and Libby to sort out." Lindy snorted derisively. "No, I mean it, Lindy. He's grown, and so is Libby. We need to let them figure it out. It hurts my heart, too, but if they're meant to be together, they'll do something about it," Keely said firmly. "There's nothing else we can do."

She decided to herself that she'd check on Seth later. She hated to think of him hurting, and if he'd done something foolish like letting Libby go, he would certainly be hurting. She shook her head. It didn't matter how old she got: when her babies hurt, she did, too. That's motherhood.

*****

Rachel and Libby sat across the retro diner table from each other. They'd both ordered burgers, fries, and shakes, and Rachel watched Libby eat hers carefully as if there was nothing in the world wrong. Rachel had grown up looking out for Libby, the one who had been most bruised by the lack of roots in their lives. She knew that a careful, unconcerned Libby was just a cover for a deeply hurting one. She'd watched her build those defenses time and again. It was worrisome when Colin left, and she'd so easily picked up the pieces. But now Seth, too.

"Do you want to talk about it?" Rachel asked.

"No, there's no point. How's your burger?" Libby asked, wondering if Rachel would want to trade her bacon mushroom burger for hers with the tomato and fried egg. She waited for their usual switch.

"The burger's fine. You're not," Rachel said bluntly. "I've known you since birth, Libby, and you don't just get to say you're fine with me. Do it with your friends or people you just met, but not me," she said evenly.

Libby sighed heavily. "I'm doing the best I can, Rachel. I didn't expect any of this, and I'm just tired." She stopped, and Rachel was about to speak when she continued. "I'm tired of being left so easily, like I don't even matter. Colin did it, and Seth is doing it, too. I think I have the right to say that enough is enough. I just want to move on from them and build my life with people who think my place in it matters. I don't want to sit here and cry over someone who could say I'm not worth it after a single argument."

"Did he say that?" Rachel interrupted, aghast.

"He didn't have to. He showed it. I have no interest in grieving myself to death over everyone that's ever picked up and walked away and left me behind. I just want to live the best life I can with what's in front of me right now. I love him so much it hurts, but I'll be damned if I chase a man who doesn't want to hold on to me." She said it quietly but fiercely, and Rachel sat back in her seat, studying her face.

"Okay," she said simply. "Want to try my burger?"

Libby let out a surprised laugh and switched plates with her. "I told you it was good."

"You were not wrong. Now let me tell you what Oliver did the other day . . ."

*****

Dean and Seth sat across from each other over pizza at the station. Dean was on a shift, and Seth didn't really want to be out in public. He'd already had Rachel storm into his office, and then he'd had to deal with Farrah's prying. Between the two of them, the whole town could know by now. Jamie had even come in and relieved him for lunch like he was the boss. It was humiliating enough when people had found out about Charlotte, but this was worse. He and Libby had been a team. They were friends as well as lovers, and he'd begun to see the rest of his life with her in it. Now he didn't know what to think.

"Bitches, right?" Dean said, flippantly over a slice loaded down with carnivore options. "I'm joking," he said, when Seth shot him an angry look. "You know what's going on, right?" he asked curiously.

"What? With her and Colin?" Seth asked in confusion.

"No, with you and Libby," Dean said simply. When Seth said nothing, he continued. "Charlie was a real piece of work, and I get that makes you not the most trusting of men. But we both know Libby's different. If she said she booted that guy's ass back to wherever he came from, she did. And I think you forgot something else."

"What's that?" Seth asked, genuinely curious.

"So the guy that kicked the shit out of her heart shows up, for whatever reason, out of the blue. Not only does she have to deal with that hurt all over again, but she goes to see you probably hoping for comfort and instead gets dumped," Dean said honestly. "I know you love her, but you just kicked the hell out of her while she was down, and if you have any sense, you'll make that right before she's gone completely."

"I hadn't thought of it that way." Seth sat back and looked at Dean speculatively. "When did you get so smart?"

"I may not have a lot of success with women, but I know them," he answered honestly.

"Ha! The way you tell it, you can get any girl if you just crook your finger," Seth said with a roll of his eyes.

"I'm not saying that's not true. I'm just saying I haven't found one I want to be with who'll stay. Might as well play the field if you can't find 'the one,' right?" Dean said with a shrug. "So what are you going to do?"

"I don't know," Seth said, struggling between his fear of being hurt again and the growing anger with himself that he'd managed to hurt Libby in the process. "She's still in love with him. She admitted it."

"You still love Marnie, right?" Dean asked with an eyebrow raised.

"That's not the same," Seth objected.

"How is it not the same? She was your girlfriend forever. Libby was married to that guy. Of course, she still loves him. Why would you even ask her that?" Dean asked. "Do you want her to be the kind of person who'd have no feelings left for someone she once married?"

"You should have seen them together," Seth told him, brooding. "It didn't look like it was over."

"And if I didn't know you and Marnie, I might have thought the same. Look at how she handled that. Then look at how you handled Colin," Dean pointed out.

"Shit," Seth sighed.

"Yeah," Dean agreed. "You should probably apologize. Maybe say it with flowers." Dean said, taking another huge slice of pizza from the box.

"Man, you've eaten half the pizza," Seth complained, trying to change the subject.

"I've been picking up all those extra shifts. Believe me when I say I'll burn it all off tonight," Dean told him.

"I've got to get back to the store. Do you want me to help out with the house this weekend?" Seth asked, happy to turn the subject to Dean's renovation issues.

"We'll see. Tell Libby hi when you see her," Dean said innocently, digging into the last slice with a wink.

"I don't know if she'll see me," Seth admitted, hesitating at the door.

"Well, you won't know unless you try."

Chapter 35

Gloria picked up the work phone and called Jenna to come to her office and to bring coffee. Jenna walked in with two full mugs carefully balanced, and Gloria shut the door quietly. She sat behind her desk and took the mug with a hearty, "Thank you." Then she looked at Jenna carefully before beginning.

"Have you talked to Libby this week? I mean, outside of work?" Gloria began.

"No. She even skipped out on Taco Tuesday. She claimed she had a deadline on one of her blogs and needed to get that out of the way," Jenna said quietly. "Has she talked to you?"

"Nothing but work. That's all she'll say," Gloria admitted. "Did you see the flowers that came in yesterday? And the ones that came in last week?"

"Yes, and they were beautiful. But you know what she did with them, right?" Jenna asked, referring to the large bouquet of sunflowers that had arrived that week and the bouquet of daisies that had come the week before. "She read the cards, threw them away, and then took the flowers to the senior center after work. I ran into Georgianne at the post office, and she told me."

"That's too bad. I wonder what the cards said. They're from Seth, right?" Gloria asked.

"I hate to admit it, but I got the cards out of her trash when she left for lunch. They were both from Seth with some version of I'm sorry, and I love you. That sort of thing," Jenna admitted.

"Did she tell you what happened?" Gloria asked, concerned. She was Libby's boss, but they'd gotten to be friends. She worried about her.

"Not really. Apparently, they had some kind of argument over her ex being back in town, and then it was just over. It doesn't make sense," Jenna said.

"Well, we both know that sometimes it's the little things that break you," Gloria said, thinking of her own decade-long relationship and some of the small arguments she'd shared with Corinne. The worst ones were over things that would have been insignificant to anyone else.

"I guess that's true enough," Jenna said, thinking of Finn. "If she talks to me, I'll let you know. I asked Rachel about it, and she said that Libby was really hurt and just wanted to move on. She wasn't comfortable being much more specific, but she said it's what Libby wants so that's what she's doing."

"She's our friend. We don't really have a choice. But I do worry," Gloria admitted.

"So do I," Jenna agreed.

*****

Josie sat at her desk and tried to talk herself out of another cigarette break. There were only so many walks you could convince other people you were taking in a day. Plus, she hadn't told anyone, but she was trying to quit. Her youngest daughter was pregnant again and had said that if Josie was going to smoke, she couldn't be around the baby. She'd tried to explain that she never, ever smoked around the children, but Lauren had reminded her that the smoke was on her clothes and in her hair. She'd been adamant that this baby wouldn't be around it; her oldest girl had been diagnosed with asthma and didn't need to be around it either.

Josie had gone home and cried. She'd been smoking since she was fourteen, back when everyone did it. She'd borrowed a pack from her cousin and had practiced all weekend long so she could do it casually in front of her friends in the parking lot behind the school. That had been ages ago, and it wasn't until she was in her forties that she'd started paying attention to the news that cigarettes were harming her health. She'd dismissed the warnings because she'd always been as healthy as a horse. Now she wondered. She was down to half a pack a day since the conversation with Lauren, but she wasn't going to tell her until she had quit completely.

She looked around the office to find something to take her mind off the cigarettes, and she noticed Libby sitting quietly at her desk with her eyes closed. If Josie hadn't looked up right at that moment, she'd have missed the closed eyes and deep breaths that Libby was taking to calm herself. She wondered if anyone else had seen it, but a quick glance around told her that no one had. Jenna was in the office with Gloria, and everyone else was heading out or busy with their work. She crossed the room quietly and sat down at the extra chair beside Libby's desk.

"Sometimes it's best just to get things out of the way," Josie said, startling Libby. "I noticed your flowers. Well, everyone noticed them. They'd be hard to miss. Either talk to him or tell him to stop, but if you don't, they'll just keep coming."

Libby looked at Josie curiously. "It's not that," she began. "Not the flowers, I mean. Well, that's part of the problem."

"And the rest of it?" Josie didn't care that she was being nosey. If the girl didn't want to answer, she certainly didn't have to.

"My ex-husband keeps sending me messages. He wants to have lunch. Or dinner. Or coffee. He wants me to call him so he can say again what he said before. Between that and the flowers, I'm just tired," Libby admitted unexpectedly.

"You want me to go tell that boy to stop sending you flowers? That would take care of one issue," Josie asked helpfully.

"No. I have to sort this out myself. Look, I'm going to be out of the office for the rest of the day. Can you cover for me? I can explain to Gloria later."

"Of course," Josie said.

"Hey, Josie, thank you. I mean it. Thanks," Libby said as she turned to leave.

Nice girl, Josie thought. She always had such good manners even if she did have highfalutin' tastes in coffee. Well, that had been a few minutes reprieve from thinking about smoking. Now she'd have to do some actual work to distract herself. She went over to the coffee pot and poured herself a cup of their fancy brew. She tasted it tentatively and decided that it was good, but she liked her own just fine.

*****

Across town, Colin sat at his laptop in his room at the B&B and finished up grading some papers. He was teaching online classes this semester, a first for him, so he could really be here for as long as he liked. He checked his messages again and wondered why Libby wouldn't just talk to him. He just wanted a conversation. Well, if he was being honest with himself, he really wanted another chance. He missed her. Sure, she could be closed off sometimes, but usually, she was only like that when he brushed up against one of those raw spots from her past. He remembered early on in their marriage. He'd have been content to stay in that first apartment. It had been convenient to work, and the price was right. They'd been happy there, but Libby had always wanted roots. She seemed to think that a baby and a house would give them to her, but Colin wondered if she'd ever feel rooted after all she'd been through.

At first, it had all been wonderful. They'd had all that chemistry and intensity, and he'd enjoyed figuring out all those things that made her tick. They'd spend hours talking or going out to explore. It seemed like things changed so gradually that he didn't really notice that what they had was leaving. They'd bought the house and started trying for a baby. Every month that went by without a pregnancy would cause Libby to withdraw still further. She was anxious and weepy, and even after she'd had tests and found out she was fine, she wasn't satisfied. She wanted him to get tested, too, and he didn't want to do it. He thought that if they got pregnant, great, but if they didn't, he wasn't bothered by it. He thought it was just one of those things that happened when it was supposed to. But then he'd taken on all those extra hours at work, and he'd let everything slide.

He wondered now if he was open to the fertility treatments if she'd want to give it another try. Of course, he really should have tried to talk to her long before the divorce went through. If he was brutally honest with himself, a conversation should have happened long before he'd cheated. He'd been seeing Maisie only casually. They'd met on

Tinder, and it was really supposed to be a one-night stand. She was sexy and smart, the polar opposite of Libby in personality, and he'd just gravitated to her. She'd also been a convenient excuse to leave the marriage and try on a different life. When she got pregnant, he thought that everything would work out, but the more time he spent with Maisie, the less he really liked her. When she'd lost the baby at the start of the second trimester, he'd been upset, but he'd also been secretly relieved. He could break ties without feeling like he was losing a girlfriend and a baby, although, of course, he'd lost them both.

Colin jolted out of his reverie when he was alerted to a new text message. "Meet me downstairs in the library," it said briefly. Libby was here, and Colin grinned to himself. He knew that if she thought about it she'd come around. They'd had so much chemistry and had been so deeply connected at one time. He still found her attractive, and God knows she was one of the most interesting people he'd ever met. Her mind didn't run along straight lines, and he liked that she was a little complicated. When their marriage went south, he'd forgotten that the things that frustrated him were things that had once been the main attraction. He knew that if they just tried they could have that close relationship again. He grabbed his phone and the key to his room and headed downstairs with a spring in his step.

Libby sat in an armchair in the spacious library of the bed and breakfast calmly waiting. She had a cup of tea in hand and another sat in front of her. Vera, the innkeeper, must have already come and gone. Colin wondered how long she'd been here. When he approached Libby, he moved to hug her, but held up a hand to stop him. "We need to talk," she began. Colin sat down heavily and realized that they weren't about to have the conversation he'd been hoping for after all.

Chapter 36

Jamie unloaded a box and carried it to the storeroom in the back of the store. He set it down with a sigh. He hated that all these estate sales packed books in one box. He thought there were a couple of first editions that would appeal to Seth. He didn't mind heading up the acquisitions, but he was tired of every single one of them packing the boxes as heavily as they could. He may have made it seem effortless, but his back was hurting from all that he'd lifted today already. They'd moved in a few pieces of furniture before the store opened, and he had another handful of boxes still waiting in his truck. He shook out a few Ibuprofen from the bottle he kept in the back and swallowed them with a cold Coke he'd gotten from the staff kitchen.

He'd once spent a couple weeks sleeping in the storeroom when he'd first started working there. He'd slept on a cot in the back and then had walked to Seth's in the morning to shower before work. Seth had offered him a room at his house, but Jamie didn't want to overstep. The storeroom cot would be good enough. He didn't like to think of himself as accepting charity and was careful to keep things tidy when he left each morning. He'd made sure to keep his stay brief, but he'd never forgotten Seth's generosity in letting him stay there. Seth had even kept the knowledge of it from the other employees to protect Jamie's privacy.

He'd been working at Seth's part-time then. He'd been trying to pay off some debt and needed a part-time job in addition to his full-time work. He'd had a regular office job. He'd answered phones and run reports, and on weekends, he'd helped Seth out at the store. Then the bottom fell out of the economy. Suddenly, he'd found himself out of work and living in an apartment he could no longer afford. He'd sold his car and most of his furniture, but he still ran through most of his savings just trying to keep the bills paid that had once seemed so manageable. He walked to work at Seth's on the weekends, and during the day, he walked around town applying for jobs. He spent the evenings applying online. Nowhere was hiring.

Seth noticed that Jamie never drove his car anymore, and he figured out what had happened. He'd offered a full-time position and a place to stay in his home if he needed it. Jamie had accepted the job, but asked if he could just stay in the storeroom until he found a place he could afford. Seth had agreed, with the stipulation that Jamie could use his shower and could always change his mind and come to stay if the storeroom grew uncomfortable for him. Jamie was former military and knew that he could manage a cot and space with a bathroom and kitchen easily. It would be more comfortable than many places he'd stayed in the four years he'd served the country. Still, Jamie had found his own place in a couple of weeks and never slept in the storeroom again.

He looked around now and made notes for which pieces Seth needed to approve to go out on the floor. He also made notes on which ones were earmarked for specific collectors that they knew. Business was good, and he could now be glad that the crash in the economy had landed him the best job he'd ever had. His schedule was flexible, and he liked the people he worked with. It beat answering the phones all day, and no one cared how he dressed or how many tattoos he acquired.

He went looking for Seth and strongly suspected he'd find him in the office. It had been a few weeks now since he'd broken up with Libby. He stayed in his office most work days, researching acquisitions and calling clients to report what he'd found. He'd changed the schedule to make sure the floor was covered by someone else most days, and he sat in his office and made little conversation. Jamie knew that the breakup had hit him hard. He knew Seth had even sent flowers a few times before he'd finally given up. He couldn't imagine what it must be like to have to keep running into the person you loved but couldn't be with. It sounded like torture. Libby still ran this way on her route around town, like she always had. Jamie wished she wouldn't. It seemed cruel somehow, as if she didn't care at all. She hadn't struck him as being unkind. But then, he didn't know the whole story either. He just knew what Beth had told him because Seth wouldn't say a word.

*****

Chase and Farrah were opening the store for the day. It was Seth's day off, and Jamie wouldn't be in until later. They'd agreed on which records they would listen to, alternating between Chase's love of the classics and old radio shows and Farrah's love of big band, swing, and jazz. They worked companionably together, getting the store in order for the day. The comic book section was the most chaotic, and Chase calmly sorted them back into a proper order. For some reason, even the adults seemed to mix them up as they looked through the collection, but yesterday a couple of younger boys had flipped through them while waiting for their mother to shop. As he restored order there, Farrah went around the store straightening the displays and making sure none of the stock was broken. Customers occasionally played with the merchandise and inadvertently broke what they so casually handled. Farrah took a couple of items off the display and made notes to see if they could be repaired or if they'd have to be tossed out.

Over coffee in the last half hour before the store was set to open, they discussed their boss. Normally, they would have talked about literature or politics. They might have been different as night and day, but they were both avid readers and enjoyed discussing their interests even when those interests varied widely. Today, they discussed Seth and his recent behavior.

"If he'd just go talk to her, they could work things out." Farrah insisted.

"He sent her flowers. Three times, I think. If she was interested, he'd know," Chase said evenly. "It's over. He's moving on."

"He's not moving on!" Farrah exclaimed. "Have you seen him show interest in anyone else? Have you noticed him going about his workday like normal? No, he holes up in his office every hour he's here," she said, proving her point.

"Well, maybe he's not moving on, but he's trying to get over her. Did you hear she had a date the other night?" Chase asked, waiting for Farrah's reaction.

She gasped loudly. "No!"

"Yes. They had a romantic dinner over at the bistro. Apparently, Lindy saw them while she was out on a date of her own," Chase said smugly, glad to impart a little information that Farrah didn't yet know. She prided herself on being the eyes and ears of the town.

"Who is Lindy dating now? Wait—never mind that. Tell me later. Who was Libby out with?" she asked breathlessly.

"Some guy," Chase said dismissively. "Lindy said he was good-looking enough, but she couldn't tell if it went well or not because she ended up pouring her own drink into her date's lap and leaving before the main course was served so she didn't get to see."

"Oh my God! That sounds just like Lindy. Does Seth know?" Farrah asked hesitantly. "About the date, I mean."

"Yeah. I was here when Lindy came by the next morning. She didn't bother to keep her voice down or shut the door so I heard it all. That's why Seth was so surly the rest of the day," Chase explained.

"I wondered why he snapped at me," Farrah commented. "He never has before. I mean, he apologized, but he usually keeps his cool."

"Well, I guess she's moving on even if he isn't," Chase replied.

"I wonder," Farrah said to herself speculatively, as Chase went to unlock the doors. She'd noticed that while Libby hadn't changed her route, she'd certainly lengthened her run. She knew a thing or two about women, and she figured that Libby was still grieving or she wouldn't be running herself to death. She wondered if anyone else noticed but then reminded herself she was surrounded by men in this store. Of course, they wouldn't notice!

*****

Seth wasn't due into the store today. He knew Chase and Farrah could cover it. They'd call if anything came up that he needed to deal with. Of course, they probably were relieved he wasn't there. He'd been difficult to be around lately. He could barely stand to be around himself. Lindy had come into the store and told him about Libby's date. It wasn't the first time that he'd heard she was dating. Candace at Brews had mentioned something in passing, her way of giving him a heads up so he didn't hear it from anyone else. He had imagined she'd met some other people for coffee there, which hurt more than he wanted to admit. That was their place as far as he was concerned, but then again there weren't a lot of options for dating in this town. Lindy was the first person to confirm that she'd had an actual dinner date, and he wished he didn't know. Knowing was somehow worse than imagining it. If he just imagined it, he could still pretend that he was wrong and that she would give him another chance after all.

Well, she wasn't back with Colin. His mom had heard from her friend Vera that Colin had stayed for a week before leaving. She'd told her that Libby had come to the B&B and asked him to go. Of course, it was cold comfort now. She hadn't gotten back with Colin as he'd feared, but she wasn't giving him another chance either. She'd started dating again, and Seth couldn't even bring himself to go out with friends. Dean came over from time to time to hang out, but that was the extent of his social life. He knew it wasn't healthy, but he'd screwed up badly. He could see exactly the kind of life he wanted now, and in every version of it, Libby was with him.

Chapter 37

"How many dates has it been now?" Rachel asked Libby. They were browsing the shops in downtown Athens. Rachel had asked Alec to take the kids for a couple of hours so she could have some time with her sister.

"Six, I think," Libby replied, counting them off in her head. She'd let Rachel launch her dating profile, and she'd gone through the motions. She'd had conversations and agreed to dates. "Two coffee dates, one for drinks, a movie, and a couple of dinners," she recounted. She'd met all of them but one outside of Madison. After all, Seth and his family were always downtown, and she had no desire to make already awkward first dates more awkward with chance encounters with her ex and his family. "I think I'm going to take a break for a while. I want to focus on myself. And my work," she added.

"That's not a bad idea," Rachel said, looking closely at Libby's face. "Have you seen Seth lately?" she asked.

"I've seen him around town. I mean, from a distance," she shrugged and then sat cross-legged on the floor of the store, flipping through a wooden crate of records.

"Are you just going to leave it like that?" Rachel asked, sliding a record up to see the title and then putting it back down.

"He's the one who left," Libby reminded her. "He took every single thing that was his and was gone." She remembered trying to find one shirt that she could sleep in, but he'd taken all of them. Everything. That had hurt more than she'd been able to talk about.

"But he did send flowers. More than once. Clearly, he's sorry," Rachel pointed out, passing Libby a record and then putting it back when she shook her head.

"Maybe he is. I'm sorry, too," she told Rachel honestly, looking up. "But I need someone who's not going to run at the first sign of conflict. If I can't have that, have someone I can depend on, I'm just fine on my own," Libby said firmly, setting one record to the side.

She had seen Seth in town, but she'd stayed out of his way. The one date she'd had in Madison had been at Park Bistro. Her date had suggested it, and she couldn't think of a reason to decline that didn't sound neurotic. Her luck hadn't changed because she'd run into Lindy on the date. They hadn't spoken, but Lindy had shot her an indecipherable look before turning back to her date.

Dinner had been fine. The food was good, and she'd kept up a smooth conversation with Owen throughout. There had been a little chemistry. He was attractive, and she liked his sense of humor. They'd been talking for a couple of weeks now, actual talking on the phone and not just texting and social media. She liked him, but she wasn't really ready for another relationship. She wanted to be ready, though. She knew that if she just kept putting herself out there, one day she would be. In the meantime, a nice dinner and a little chemistry would work just fine.

After dinner, he'd come back to her place and stayed the night. She hadn't planned it, but she knew that she needed to move on. Even Rose had said that she needed to get under someone new to get over Seth. She hadn't appreciated the sentiment, although she acknowledged its effectiveness. In the morning, after Owen had left, and she'd gotten ready for work, she realized that she wasn't in a good place. Sure, she looked like she'd moved on, particularly when she glanced across the room at the bed and its tangled sheets. But she hadn't. She was still stuck, and she needed to figure out a way to get herself unstuck without using other people. Because in the light of the morning, that's just how it felt.

She wanted to be done with Seth, to just let it all go. She just wasn't there yet. She loved him, and it hurt. But something had begun to happen to her corridors. They didn't protect her the way they once had. Lately, all those doors had been flying open and letting out the feelings she'd tried so hard to ignore.

Libby began running more. She'd extended her route by a mile each day, and then by two miles. Her time on each mile grew shorter, and she'd lost the last of the weight she'd hoped she might, with an additional five pounds beyond that. She'd lost her appetite, so she had to make herself eat each meal just to keep up her strength to run. She chose small, healthy meals, and she wondered if something was wrong with her because she didn't feel like eating. She didn't even crave chocolate, which she was pretty sure meant she was either dying or dead already, she joked to herself.

When she wasn't running, she was writing. For the first time, she started to write about herself in a way that she hadn't before. She began to open up and explain just what it had been like growing up with a family who was never happy staying in one place. She wrote about heartache and disappointment and what it was to curl up inside of yourself for fear that the outside world would break you. How you became unbreakable, not because you were so strong, but because you were so incredibly fragile. And she wrote about what it was like to love someone and still let go, how she chose herself because she wasn't ever going to be the one to make someone stay who only wanted to leave.

Her blog began to get more hits, and she was even taking more travel writing assignments outside of her work at the paper. She'd been driving around the state and exploring various destinations. She'd done a number of reviews and write-ups for an online travel journal, and they'd asked her if she would consider going out of state or even out of the country if they were able to work her expenses into the budget. She'd agreed to think about it, but she knew she would accept, even if it meant cutting back her hours at the paper.

Libby stopped dating, just like she'd told Rachel she would. She took down the profile online and took a time out for herself. She'd only missed a couple of Taco Tuesdays before she realized that what she needed was to be with her friends and not to worry about meeting someone. She had met someone. She still loved Seth. And look how that had turned out. At the first sign of a problem, he'd left. Sure, he'd sent flowers later, but all she could think about was that he'd left in the first place. If he could do it once, he could do it again. She'd taken the daisies, sunflowers, and peonies to the senior center and hoped the residents would take pleasure in them even if she couldn't.

She'd heard from Colin one last time. He'd sent her an apology note, just a brief one to say that he was sorry and understood. She filed it away where she kept her marriage license and divorce decree. She dug out her engagement and wedding ring set from a drawer in her jewelry box and sold them to a jeweler in town who was interested. She took the money and spent it on a few days at the beach. Spring had slowly settled in around the town, and the weather had warmed up enough that she'd been able to drive down to Jekyll Island and rent a cottage on the beach. She'd stocked up on a few things from the little grocery store on the island and made herself a big breakfast in the morning after she came back in from running her miles on the sand. She collected seashells and sea glass in a jar and thought that she might get a puppy so that one day she could come to visit and throw sticks to her dog the way she'd watched a woman do that morning.

Now that she'd stopped dating and started concentrating on herself, she noticed that the whole world wasn't paired up the way she'd always assumed it was when she was feeling particularly lonely. She saw plenty of men and women on the beach who traveled alone and were content to swim in the still-cold water or read their books or dine out solo. She found her confidence to do the same, and even though she missed Seth, she was determined to make a good life without him. She spent the long weekend at the beach running, writing, reading, and walking along the shore thinking. At night, she called and talked to her friends after she'd gone out for a nice dinner or made something at the cottage. When she came back, she seemed peaceful in a way that those around her immediately noticed. Most of them gave up hope that she'd go back to Seth now, but they were glad that she seemed to be opening up more.

*****

Seth put his phone down on the counter. He'd been reading Libby's blog, the way he always had. At one point in time, he'd have talked it over with her, but now he could only read it for a little peek at her life without him. He was sure that she wasn't coming back now, but he still wished she would. He read about her early life and realized that he hadn't just hurt her in the moment; he'd hurt her in all the places that had ached throughout her life. He didn't know if he could make any of it right, but he wanted to try.

He'd stopped living like a shadow in his own life. He'd started going out with friends and having brunch with his mom and sister on Sundays. He'd stopped being unbearable to be around at work, and he'd even gone out on one blind date that had been anything but comfortable. He and Sarah had sat over coffee and admitted that they were both recovering from bad breakups and didn't want to date at all. They'd laughed when they had agreed that it was total crap to try to date when you still wanted to be with someone else, even though their exes had both done so successfully. He still talked to her occasionally, but only as a friend.

Sarah was the one he talked to about how badly he'd screwed up, and she'd honestly told him that he had. She'd also told him that he could still make it right, even if Libby never took him back. He could still apologize and let her know that he could see now that what he'd done was the worst thing he could have done. She'd told him to let her know how it went, unless it went well, and then he should probably stop calling her. She told him she hoped she never heard from him again and hung up. He didn't take offense. He knew that was like Sarah wishing him good luck.

*****

It was Rose's birthday and also Taco Tuesday. They'd ordered extra margaritas and threatened to have the staff bring over the sombrero-of-shame, as they called it, to sing happy birthday to her. So far, she'd deflected their efforts by refilling their glasses liberally with the strawberry margaritas they were drinking. Dillon had joined them, and they'd all brought small presents, which made Rose laugh and point out that she wasn't a child and didn't need anything. They laughed and shoved their presents across the table to her in response.

Libby sat in the middle of her friends and was glad that she had them. If the atmosphere hadn't been so celebratory, she could have wept with gratitude at how much they meant to her. Once she'd explained her reasoning to Rachel, her sister had spread the word, and the others had been supportive. She knew that they had all liked Seth and still hoped it would somehow come out okay, but Libby knew that life rarely worked out like that. Still, she wasn't making the best of her life, and as she looked around at her friends, she knew that her best was pretty damn terrific. Rachel had even turned her phone off for this celebration and said drunkenly that if Alec had a problem, he could try to remember the number for 9-1-1. They had laughed and cheered and poured her another drink. Jenna had already lined Finn up for rides home for their group. Rose had leaned her head against Dillon's shoulder when they sang happy birthday to her and grinned happily. This was her tribe, and right now it was enough.

If there was a pang because Seth wasn't there to share it with her, she knew that she'd just have to learn to accept that it might always be there. She could keep the love, even if she couldn't keep him, she thought to herself. She could feel grateful for what she had, and the pain of what she'd loss didn't have to haunt her. She sipped her margarita and hoped Seth would be happy.

Chapter 38

Seth woke up early on Wednesday and decided that it was now or never. Well, not now-now. After all, it was barely 6:00 a.m. Still, he knew that Libby ran early. She was tough to miss since her route went near his home and by the shop. He'd decided to show up and talk to her. He'd considered writing a letter, but he thought that maybe that was the coward's way out. He'd broken her heart in person; he could sure as hell show up in person and say that he was wrong for it. After that, he needed to move on.

It had been almost five months since he'd packed his things from her house and left. He'd had five months to think about their relationship and why he'd reacted the way he had. He'd had five months to stop making excuses for himself and admit that he'd screwed it up so badly she was likely gone forever. Well, gone for him, but still in his life, since she lived just down the street. If nothing else, he could offer friendship, even though it would be painful to him. At least he'd know that he'd done the right thing—even if it had taken him too long to do it.

He gave it another hour and then headed to Brews & Blues early and ordered Libby's favorite coffee and his own. Candace looked at him speculatively, but he didn't offer an explanation. They'd chatted about the weather and the home and garden weekend that had just been held in town. She looked at him and wondered, and he chatted with her and reminded himself that he was about to do the right thing, and it was now or never. When he left, Candace watched him go and turned to exchange raised eyebrows with Elle who had been watching from the doorway. Elle shrugged and turned back to the kitchen while Candace took the next order, but they both wondered.

*****

Martin passed Seth on the way in, holding the crossword under his arm and wondering if anyone else remembered that today was Jack's birthday. Well, he remembered anyway. He was going to complete an extra crossword today in his friend's honor and drink a cup of his favorite coffee. He knew Reena would bake a cake, just like she used to when Jack was alive. She'd make the carrot cake he'd always liked best. Martin used to joke that cake in the morning was an indulgence, but carrot cake was just eating your vegetables. He ordered Jack's favorite coffee and made his way to their old table. He'd been lucky to have had such a good friend.

*****

Rebecca was stretching for her morning run. She'd taken to running mornings instead of evenings since she'd started dating again. She'd met a couple of nice guys, but she didn't know if any of them would stick around. Jill and Mark still hadn't cooled their jets on all of that mushy stuff, and they still fought just as much as ever. She didn't want that. What she did want was to make it to a half marathon by the end of the year. She'd gotten in a couple of 5k runs and had a 10k coming up in a week. She knew that if she, who had never done anything more athletic than turning the pages of a book, could do a 10k, she damn well could run a half marathon. Then she'd focus on her love life again. Or maybe a full marathon. She'd see how it went.

*****

Seth took the coffee over to a bench in the park and set the large take-out cups down on the ground in front of him. He took a deep breath and hoped that Libby wouldn't choose today of all days to write instead of run. He also hoped she wouldn't take another route. If she went right instead of left, she'd go around the park entirely. He hoped he'd made the right call. He had some things to say, and he needed to say them now before he lost the courage. He saw her coming in the distance and stood up, reaching down to get the coffee as he did. Even in workout clothes and a ponytail with her face free of makeup, she was beautiful. He tried to tell something from her expression about what she was feeling, but couldn't.

*****

Libby turned left on Main Street and headed toward the park. This route passed near Seth's home, and she often thought about finding a new route. The only reason that she didn't was that she still loved him. Yes, she was moving on, but she still liked knowing that he was close. Even if he wasn't hers, he was safe and maybe even happy. She'd heard his store had done well with the Valentine's day promotion that Farrah had spearheaded. She'd even heard that his mother and Lindy had opened their homes for the home and garden tour last weekend. She'd gone on the tour, but skipped their house out of respect for the awkwardness of the situation.

As she reached the last block heading to the park, she looked up and noticed Seth waiting with two cups of coffee in his hands. She slowed her pace and tried to figure out how she felt seeing him there. Her heart was racing, and she could only look at him standing there in a blue shirt the color of his eyes and a pair of jeans with those shoes he liked to walk in. They'd called them his old man shoes, but secretly, she thought they were cute. She headed toward him, holding his eyes and trying to figure out what he wanted and how she felt. She stopped when she was just a few feet away.

"Seth, what are you doing here?" she asked simply. She wanted to say something that wasn't a total cliché, but words failed her.

"I brought coffee." He held one out to her. "I wanted to see if you had a few minutes to talk to me," he began.

"I don't really have anything to say," Libby said uncertainly, not sure if that was even true.

"Then I'd like to ask you to listen, because I have something I need to say to you. Once I've said it, I promise I'll go," he said sincerely, holding up the coffees in a gesture of peace.

"Okay. Do you want to walk?" she asked and nearly cringed when she thought how much this conversation seemed like a repeat of the one she'd had with Colin.

"Do you mind if we sit down?" He gestured toward the park bench, and she sat down, taking the coffee and sipping from it. She knew it would be her favorite, and it was. She sipped it and looked at him curiously.

"I need to tell you that I was wrong, and I'm sorry. I didn't just overreact, although I did do that. I quit on us." He paused, setting down his coffee and turning fully to face her, even though she wouldn't meet his eyes for more than a moment. "After Charlie cheated, I had a hard time trusting other people. I knew that you and Colin had a strong connection, and the divorce was his idea. I had a hard time believing that you would want to stay with me if you could go back to him, but I didn't even give you a chance to explain. I cut you off and walked away, and it was wrong. If I could take it back, I would. I know that it hurt you, and I need to say that I'm sorry," Seth said quietly, watching Libby for a reaction.

"I accept your apology," Libby said quietly, looking down at her cup. "I don't know what else you want me to say. I've moved on."

"I haven't," Seth admitted. "I love you, and I never stopped. I'd like for you to give me another chance, but even if you can't, I wanted you to know that I'm sorry for hurting you."

Libby looked up with tears shimmering in her eyes. "It's been months. Why say this to me now?" she wondered aloud.

"I've known I was wrong almost since it happened. I even heard when Colin left, but then I was told you'd started dating. I know you've moved on, but I decided that I couldn't move on without first telling you that I don't want to. I screwed up, and you don't have to forgive me or give me another chance, but that's what I want. Give me another chance, Libby. Please."

He waited, his heart in his eyes.

Libby met them and held them.

"This isn't how things work," she told him softly. "You can't just come back and expect us to pick up where we left off before it fell apart." She looked away.

"I'm not asking for that. I'm asking to try again. We can start with coffee." He held up his cup, and she turned back to him. "And you can tell me about your life now, and I'll listen because I know it's changed. And I'll tell you about mine. Then maybe you'll let me take you to dinner one night. Maybe we can just start over."

"I don't know if it's even possible to start over," she began. Seth looked down at his coffee, his shoulders slumping in resignation. "But I wonder if we could meet somewhere in the middle."

Seth looked up and met her eyes. He could see the tears held back yet shimmering there—but he could also see the love. He reached a hand up to cup her face softly, and she leaned into it, her eyes closed. He wanted to kiss her, but he thought it was probably too soon. They stayed like that, his hand soft against her face, and her eyes closed in the moment. When he took the warmth of his hand away, she opened her eyes and looked at him, unsure.

"I'm really not sure where we go from here. I was expecting you to shoot me down," Seth admitted with a smile. "That's what I probably deserve."

"Shut up and drink your coffee," Libby said with a small smile, leaning back against the bench and wondering at this shift in their relationship. She didn't know where they were supposed to go from here, either. "Maybe we can start with a walk?" she suggested.

"That's the best idea I've heard all day," he said seriously, getting up and taking her hand.

"Actually, coffee was the best idea," she replied.

She'd run tomorrow, she thought. She'd get up early and put in a little extra time. For now, she needed to be here and to take this walk. She wanted to know what was up ahead, but contented herself knowing that sometimes life did give you second chances. If you were very lucky and very brave, she thought. Because she'd need to be brave if they were going to try again. She looked over at him, and he was looking back. For now, that was enough.

Chapter 39

Seth made a couple of changes to the display window that Farrah designed and then went to stand outside to eye it critically. They were heading into fall, and he'd given her permission to take charge of one of the front windows. He looked at it critically and decided that he liked it better the way that Farrah had had it and went back inside to undo his own changes with a shake of his head. She had a talent for design, that was for sure. Maybe she should explore marketing next semester.

As he reentered the store, he saw the elderly lady who had visited the shop months before standing near the front window, eyeing it seriously. "It looked better the way she had it," she told him frankly.

"You're right. I was just thinking that myself," Seth commented. "It's good to see you."

"Well, I was just in town checking up on my relations. You never can tell what they'll get into when I'm gone. I like to make sure they stay on track," she explained seriously.

"I'm sure they enjoy the visits," Seth said sincerely.

"Well, they certainly never expect them. I say it keeps them on their toes," she said wryly.

"I'm sure it does. Are you enjoying your music box?" Seth asked.

"I decided to pass it down to my granddaughter. Every little girl loves ballerinas, for a while anyway," she reminded him.

"I'm sure that's true," Seth said with a grin. "My sister and I always played with the tin soldiers, but we were fascinated with the ballerinas in the music boxes and the figures in the cuckoo clocks. My grandfather used to let me play right here in the store."

"That's a nice memory," the old woman said, her eyes shining.

"My father did the same. Let me play with old toys, I mean. And when I was very little, I got to look at a music box just like the one I gave to my granddaughter. Of course, I was too little to play with it then. But I loved watching her twirl."

"I'm glad I could help you find it," Seth said with a smile. "Can I help you find anything for anyone else? Or maybe something for yourself today? I noticed you were listening to Ella Fitzgerald when you were here last."

"You have such a good memory!" She exclaimed. "My parents used to listen to Ella Fitzgerald on the record player when I was a girl. My mother said that she played records for me when she was pregnant, but what I remember is my father dancing with my mother to that record when they thought I was asleep. I would creep to the edge of the stairs, and even though I couldn't see them around the corner, I could hear them dancing to the music, each foot stepping lightly on the hardwood floors and across the carpet."

"That's a nice memory," Seth responded in kind. "Were your parents married a long time?" he asked curiously. He was thinking about the ring hidden in his office. It had been the one his grandfather had given to his grandmother. It wasn't their original wedding ring. They'd been poor when they married, but years later, he'd come across the ring at an estate sale. It was old and beautiful, and even though they'd struggled with money, he chose to give it to her as a gift rather than sell it in the store. She'd still kept the other, smaller ring on a chain around her neck, but she'd worn the large ring until her hands had swollen with arthritis. His grandfather had given it to him before he died, and he had been thinking of giving it to Libby.

"Oh, they were married for ages. They grew old together," she said with a smile. "And they still danced around the room at night until they couldn't anymore."

When the old lady made her way out of the store, Seth thought about those words. He and Libby had been rebuilding the trust in their relationship. She'd been more open with him, and he'd admitted that he still had hang-ups since Charlie had left. They'd talked them over, and the relationship was better now than it had been before. It had taken months, but Rachel had finally stopped giving him the evil eye every time he saw her. They'd even had dinner with her friends and his a few times. It wasn't without its challenges, but he was more in love with her every day. He went to the back and changed the record to Ella Fitzgerald and hoped that he and Libby could have a love story just as good as that. When he put the needle onto the record, he slid the drawer open to look at the ring one more time.

Here's a sneak peek at the next book in the Hearts of Madison Series - Right on Walton. Coming soon!

Chapter 1

Keely came down the stairs to the smell of coffee and ... omelets, if she wasn't mistaken. She stopped in the doorway and smiled widely at her daughter. Lindy was at the stove, turning an omelet. She was the mirror image of Keely except for the large brown eyes she'd gotten from her father. And of course, Keely's thick dark hair had gone silver some time ago. But their faces? They could have been twins rather than mother and daughter. It still gave Keely an odd sort of thrill to see it.

Right now, Lindy was singing loudly to Springsteen's Dancing in the Dark and dancing at the stove. They both loved The Boss. Keely leaned against the door and wondered how her heart could contain all this love. She could still see little Lindy singing loudly and dancing around this kitchen as a small girl wearing a pink tutu and a superhero cape, begging her grandfather to dance with her. Watching the two of them dance had cracked her heart open, but in the good way that only mothers could fully understand.

She waited until Lindy turned around and returned her smile before heading into the kitchen. Lindy didn't stop singing or dancing until the song was done. Keely added her own voice and a couple of dance moves that made Lindy stop singing long enough to laugh. The playlist switched to I'm on Fire, and Lindy reached over to turn the volume down.

"I didn't want to interrupt." Keely said with a smile. "Looks like you've been busy, what with performing a concert and making us omelets."

"I've been up painting since four. Just couldn't sleep. I thought I'd go ahead and get started on breakfast." Lindy explained.

"Well, I'm glad you waited until now to start. I wouldn't have been happy if I'd stumbled down here before dawn." Keely picked up the mug Lindy had made her in art school. It said, "I can't decide what pants to put out today: smarty or fancy". She looked over and noticed Lindy was drinking out of the one she'd made for herself: "Blood of my enemies (Just kidding; it's coffee)". Lindy had always had plenty of sass, but Keely could admit that she came by it honest enough. Of course, her own sass and pure grit had seen her through her husband leaving without a word. It had gotten her through single parenting two toddlers and going from a stay-at-home mom to a store manager and then store owner. Sass wasn't the worst thing.

"If you don't have to be in too early today, I wondered if we could talk," Lindy began, fingering the brochures she held in her lap beneath the table. She tried to keep the nerves out of her voice, but her mother didn't seem fooled.

"Well, of course, we can. What's on your mind, baby?" Keely asked, her brow wrinkling in concern. When Lindy looked down into her lap and paused, her mildly concerned expression gave way to one of alarm. "Okay, now you're worrying me. Pass me my omelet, and then tell me what all this is about." Keely sat down carefully and offered up a prayer that nothing was wrong with her baby.

"I've been thinking a lot lately about what I want for my life. I'm going to be 36 soon, and I really haven't met anyone I want to spend my life with," Lindy began.

"Oh, honey, that will happen when it's time." Keely assured her.

"Just hear me out, Mom. I just don't want to put my whole life on hold on the off-chance that Mr. Right is just around the corner. I've decided I'm going to start a family on my own." She took out the brochures she'd picked up at the fertility clinic and sat them down on the table in front of them. When her mother simply looked puzzled, she continued. "With science. I can get a donor since I'm healthy enough, and if that doesn't work, I can look into adoption next."

Keely abruptly dropped her head to the table, and Lindy jumped up in alarm. She'd expected questions but not shock and certainly not whatever this was. She came around to the side of the table and knelt down beside her mother. It took her a full minute to realize that her mother was laughing, not crying. She sat back on her heels, perplexed. Well, that wasn't the reaction she was expecting, she thought.

"I'm sorry." Keely said, wiping tears from her eyes. "I think I've just seen one too many movies. For a minute there, all I could see was you carrying home one of those turkey basters from the hospital." Choking out a startled laugh, Lindy looked up at her mom. Relieved and a little sheepish, she stood slowly and went to sit back down.

"I'm so glad you're finding this entertaining." Lindy said wryly. "Do you know how long I've practiced telling you this?"

"I'm sorry, baby." Keely said, choking on a last laugh and clearing her throat. "I don't mean to make light of it. I think it's a wonderful idea. You'll make such a wonderful mama." She said with a grin. "My baby is going to have a baby."

"Well, not quite yet." Lindy said with a smile. "And there will be no turkey basters involved, thank you very much." She returned with a roll of her eyes.

"I think it's very brave, and I couldn't be prouder. Now, look at me." Lindy looked up. "It's going to be hard, what you're doing. So hard. But we'll be right here. Me, your brother, Libby. We'll all be here." Lindy knew that she meant it. Her brother lived just down the street, and Libby was practically living with him these days. They would all be there for her and the baby, when the time came.

"Thank you, Mama," Lindy said gratefully. "Just let me tell Seth, okay?"

"Of course you can tell him." Keely agreed. "Although I'd love to see his reaction. Do you think you could get that on video?" She asked with a grin. "Now I know all this is supposed to be expensive. Do you need any money?"

"No, it's affordable enough. Do you mind if I stay in the carriage house a while longer? I'm still saving up for a house, and with the studio expansions I have in mind I'm hoping that I won't have to be here for more than another couple of years." Lindy explained.

"You stay in the carriage house as long as you like. It's plenty big enough, and you'll be right here so I can play with the baby." Lindy leaned against her mother's shoulder, and Keely breathed in the citrus scent of her hair. She held her daughter tightly and wondered if she knew how hard her choice would be. Well, she'd done it alone and so could Lindy. She knew her baby would be a wonderful mama.

Chapter 2

Dean Walton woke up groggily and knocked his alarm clock to the floor. He'd worked a late shift at the fire department where he was subbing in part-time, and he had an early shift at his full-time job with the fire department in town. He loved his work, but he was only working the two jobs for extra money. He was restoring a cabin on the lake, and it was taking every dime he had, and then some. It was throwing good money after bad, he often thought. Still, he loved it, and when it was livable in a few months, he planned on moving in and roughing it while he fixed it up. It would save him rent, and he could use that money to fix up the place.

He picked up his phone and scrolled through the messages. Naomi from Brews & Blues in town, their local coffee shop, had already messaged him. He never should have slept with her. She was college-age, fresh-faced, and cute, but he hadn't been serious about her. Now she worked practically across the street from him and wouldn't take no for an answer. Not that he ever said no, exactly, but surely she knew that if he wasn't trying to spend time with her, it meant that he didn't want to. It was obvious to anyone with a brain. He rolled his eyes. Well, she was persistent, that's for sure. He had a couple of other messages and a few matches on one of the online dating apps he used. Not that he had much time for that these days, but he still liked to play the field.

He took a quick shower, making it as hot as it would go, and then wiped the steam from the mirror and studied his face. He had just turned 33, and he was showing a few smile lines around his eyes. His blond hair was still thick, and he could still get away with spiking it up a bit in the front. It was starting to get a little long, but he didn't mind that much. He wondered if he should shave, but the short beard he'd grown for the hell of it had seemed to suit his face. Plus, with working so much, it was easier not to have to worry about shaving every day. His green eyes stood out with long lashes that some girlfriends had referred to as "pretty". Hey, he didn't mind the pretty boy label if it kept them coming back. He was tall and in reasonably good shape from spending time at the gym- well, when he had time to spare. Of course, working on the house was at least as good a workout these days.

He left the house with a large thermos of coffee to walk to work. He lived off Walton Street, which he liked to tell the ladies was named after his family. Of course, it was a lie. His family may have shared the same name, but they wouldn't have been able to afford any of the antebellum houses that lined his street. Not even the small ones or the carriage houses. He was lucky to be able to afford the rent in the duplex he was living in right now. He'd gotten a good deal because his best friend's mom knew the owner. He took care of his own lawn and hers, and she gave him a generous discount.

No, his family wasn't from Walton Street. If there was a wrong side of the tracks in this town, that's where Dean's family had lived. They'd been blue collar people who barbecued on the weekends and saved for a vacation in Panama City ever few years. Not that there was anything wrong with that. He liked a good BBQ and beach vacation as much as the next guy. They just didn't have anything in common with the people who lived in this neighborhood with their manicured lawns and social engagements. It could have been worlds away rather than just a handful of miles. He'd always known that he didn't quite fit in here, but a little charm could go a long way to smoothing over any awkwardness so he'd developed charm in spades.

After his parents' divorce, he'd split time between living in Madison during the week and spending every other weekend with his dad out in Macon where he'd moved. Back and forth. But it was better than the fighting he'd had to put up with when his parents had been married. Not that they fought any less, but they certainly had less occasion to do it. He'd grown up to the sound of his parents screaming at each other. Walton Street didn't have people like the Waltons living on it, which is why Dean liked it. It was quiet and peaceful, and no one ever looked at him like he was on the wrong side of the tracks.

Well, home had always been Seth's house more than his own. They'd been friends since elementary school, and that was one thing that had never changed. Seth's mom still lived in that same house. It was just around the corner from his duplex. He'd had the privilege to spend most holidays with them, although he was always sure to wait for an invitation. He didn't want to intrude, but Keely treated him just like another son. Seth didn't live with her anymore, of course. He had his own house a couple streets over, and his girlfriend Libby was moving in with him in the next couple of months.

Dean was still single, but he was the kind of single that meant he could take a different woman home every night if he wanted to. He had a few friends with benefits if he ever got lonely. The last thing he wanted to do was end up like his parents, married and bitter as hell that they'd settled for less than they wanted. He didn't think the thing he wanted existed anyway. Might as well enjoy life.

Dean jolted as Lindy stepped in his path. They often walked a similar path to work, but their schedules rarely synced. It was a surprise to see her, and he wasn't sure if it was a good surprise. She'd been avoided him since they'd exchanged some heated words last year. Of course, he'd been avoiding her, too. They had both been pissed, but now Dean was just embarrassed that he'd let her get to him. He stopped to see what she would do. She stopped when she saw him and shot him a cool, appraising look.

"You're not usually up this early." She commented, coolly.

"I could say the same," he said with a shrug. "Your mama okay?"

Lindy softened. It was hard to hate the bastard when he so clearly loved her mama. "Yeah, she's good. She's perfect."

They fell into step with each other awkwardly. Dean wondered if he should apologize, but he argument was so many months back now that an apology might just be weird. If she wasn't bothered by it, why should he be?

"You alright? You look like you've been crying?" Dean asked, noticing a trace of tear tracks on her face.

Lindy sighed heavily, annoyed. He was too damn observant for his own good. There had been a few tears after the big announcement. "Onions. Omelets." She said shortly, waving her hand in dismissal.

"Omelets!" Dean sighed wistfully. He'd had a granola bar for breakfast. He didn't remember buying it so he was pretty sure one of the women who stayed the night had left it there, though he couldn't think which one. "Now I'm hungry."

"You're always hungry." Lindy said with a roll of her eyes. She'd known Dean as long as he'd known Seth, since they were little boys tagging along behind her and her friends, annoying them.

"I've got a healthy appetite." Dean said with a slow, flirtatious grin.

Lindy cut her eyes toward him, picking up on the innuendo. "So I hear," she snorted.

Dean stiffened and nodded, the smile disappearing. Normally, her snarky comments wouldn't have bothered him. Normally, he didn't take what she said to heart, but she'd thrown his reputation in his face last year during their argument. It was the reason he hadn't spoken to her until now. He didn't appreciate the reminder any more than the insinuation. Damn, judgmental harpy, he thought.

Lindy sighed as Dean picked up the pace toward town. She and Dean had always had friction. They'd been arguing since the day Seth had first brought him home to play. They'd just been little boys, and Dean had nearly white-blonde hair then that stuck up in every direction. They'd aggravated the then pre-teen Lindy to distraction. Since then, arguing was just this thing they did. She had to admit, to herself at any rate, that she'd been in the wrong the last time they'd argued. It didn't sit well with her to be wrong in the first place, but she wasn't usually so judgmental. She lengthened her own stride to catch up with him.

"Hey, I'm sorry. That was out of line." Lindy reached out and rested her hand on his arm briefly until he looked at her.

"It's fine." Dean said quietly, shooting her a brief glance.

"It's really not, and I am sorry, Dean." Lindy admitted with a sigh.

"Just forget it." He told her. An apology from Lindy was rare enough, particularly a sincere one. "Want some coffee?" He offered his thermos to her in a gesture of peace.

"No. Thanks though. I filled up at mom's. Plus, I had some when I first got up at 4. I think I'm over-caffeinated already." Lindy commented wryly. She thought about how she would handle the switch to decaf. She was about to find out. Now that she'd begun taking the prenatal vitamins and had appointments lined up to speak to the fertility specialist about potential treatments, she was cutting out the caffeine. She wasn't pregnant yet, but if she had her way she would be soon. She wanted to be ready.

"Yeah, same." Dean admitted. "Late shift followed by an early one."

"I didn't think you did that." Lindy said curiously.

"Well, you don't know everything, Lindy Carver." Dean replied with a wolfish grin.

"Hmm.." she replied noncommittally. "I've got to head into work. See you." Lindy said, turning toward her studio.

"Later." Dean said with a wave, watching her walk away. Those long strides sure did eat up the pavement. She always seemed to be in a hurry, but that was just Lindy. All that energy in that willow slim package. He sighed. He remembered watching her as a teenager, his first serious crush. It had embarrassed the hell out of Seth, but Dean had grown out of it. Well, at least they were back on speaking terms. That was something. He headed toward the fire station when he saw Naomi waiting outside. He rolled his eyes and then headed that way, dreading the confrontation. He put on his smoothest smile and walked toward her,

"Well, hey, Naomi! Don't you look pretty as a picture today?" he began.

About The Author

Crystal Jackson is a former therapist turned full-time writer. Her work has been featured on Medium, Elephant Journal, Elite Daily, The Good Men Project, Your Tango, The Urban Howl, and Sivana East. She lives in Madison, Georgia, with her two children. *Left on Main* is her first novel.